By Gary Shteyngart

OUR COUNTRY
FRIENDS

OUR COUNTRY FRIENDS

A NOVEL

Gary Shteyngart

RANDOM HOUSE

NEW YORK

Published in the United States by Random House, an imprint and division of Penguin Random House LLC, New York.

RANDOM HOUSE and the HOUSE colophon are registered trademarks of Penguin Random House LLC.

LIBRARY OF CONGRESS CATALOGING-IN-PUBLICATION DATA
Names: Shteyngart, Gary, author.
Title: Our country friends : a novel / Gary Shteyngart.
Description: New York : Random House, [2021]
Identifiers: LCCN 2021007132 (print) | LCCN 2021007133 (ebook) |
ISBN 9780593446348 (hardcover ; acid-free paper) |
ISBN 9781984855138 (ebook)
Classification: LCC PS3619.H79 O97 2021 (print) | LCC PS3619.H79
(ebook) | DDC 813/.6—dc23
LC record available at https://lccn.loc.gov/2021007132
LC ebook record available at https://lccn.loc.gov/2021007133

International edition ISBN 9780593448175

Printed in the United States of America on acid-free paper

randomhousebooks.com

2 4 6 8 9 7 5 3 1

FIRST BARNES & NOBLE SPECIAL EDITION

Book design by Simon M. Sullivan

To E.W.

Dramatis Personae

ALEXANDER (SASHA) SENDEROVSKY—*A writer and landowner.*

MASHA LEVIN-SENDEROVSKY—*His wife, a psychiatric doctor.*

NATASHA (NAT) LEVIN-SENDEROVSKY—*Their child.*

KAREN CHO—*Inventor of popular phone dating application and a high-school friend of Senderovsky's.*

VINOD MEHTA—*A former adjunct professor and short-order cook, also Senderovsky's and Karen Cho's high-school friend.*

ED KIM—*A gentleman.*

DEE CAMERON—*A writer and former student of Senderovsky's.*

THE ACTOR—*Described by the* Neue Zürcher Zeitung *as the world's greatest thespian.*

Various AMERICAN VILLAGERS.

ACT ONE

The Colony

I

The House on the Hill was in a tizzy.

Workmen's trucks streamed up the long gravel driveway. Two sets of plumbers from both sides of the river had been summoned to dewinterize the five bungalows behind the main house, and they did not care for one another. A broken set of windows in one bungalow had to be replaced posthaste, and a family of field mice had chewed through the electrical cable powering another. The handyman, who did not live on the property, was so overwhelmed by the state of affairs, he retreated to the extensive covered porch to eat a cheese sandwich in long deliberative bites. The mistress of the house, Masha, had lowered the shades in her first-floor office to escape the cacophony of modern tools and loud country cursing. At times, she would peek out to note the surfaces that would have to be wiped down after the workmen left. Natasha (who liked to go by Nat), her eight-year-old daughter, was upstairs, illuminated by a screen in the darkness of her room, in a lonely public world of her own.

The only happy member of the household was Alexander Borisovich Senderovsky, known as Sasha to his friends. "Happy," we should say, with an asterisk. He was agitated as well as excited. A windstorm had brought down the heavy branches of two dead trees flanking the driveway, scattering the vast front lawn with their dead white rot. Senderovsky liked to expound at length upon the "entropic" nature of his estate, the way all manner of growth was allowed to go its own way, sumacs elbowing out more well-heeled plants, ivy poisoning the perimeter, groundhogs bringing destruction upon the gardens. But the scattering of dead tree limbs made the House on the Hill look apocalyptic, the very thing Senderovsky's guests were coming up to escape. The handyman claimed a bad back and was not handy enough to remove all the tree limbs on his own, and the so-called tree guy had gone missing. Senderovsky, in his athletic pants and wildly colored dressing gown, had tried to move one of these prehistoric-looking branches himself, but the very first heave made him fear a hernia.

"Ah, the hell with it," he said, and got into his car. A word about the car. Well, not so much about the car, as the way in which it was driven. Senderovsky had only learned to drive three years ago, at the milestone age of forty-five, and only within the limits of a country setting. The highway on the other side of the river unsettled him. He was a fiercely awful driver. The half-empty local roads inspired him to "gun" the engine of his sturdy but inflexible Swedish automobile, and he saw the yellow stripes bisecting the roads as suggestions meant for "less experienced drivers," whoever that might be. Because he did not believe in road marks or certain aspects of relativity, the concept of a blind curve continued to elude him. (His wife no longer allowed him to drive with their child onboard.) What was worse, he had somewhere picked up the phrase "tooling around."

And now Senderovsky raced to his errands, mindful only of the speed traps, set with boring predictability on the frayed edges of towns or the school zones, where the fines could be doubled. First, he visited his butchers, two former catalog models from the city, now a husband and wife, who plied their trade out of a barn so red it verged on the patriotic. The two magnificent twenty-five-year-olds, all teeth and coveralls, presented him with a wrapped parcel of sweet and Italian sausages, glistening hamburger patties, and his secret weapon: lamb steaks that clung to the bone, so fresh they could only have been rivaled by a restaurant Senderovsky admired in Rome's abattoir district. The very sight of meat for tomorrow's cookout inspired in him a joy that in a younger man could be called love. Not because of the meat itself, but because of the conversations that would flow around it as it was marinated, grilled, and served, despite the growing restrictions on such closeness. By noon tomorrow, his best friends, the ones who had been so hard to bring together during previous summers, would finally unite, brought together by the kernels of a growing tragedy to be sure, but brought together nonetheless, in his favorite place on earth, the House on the Hill.

Of course, someone else was coming, too. Someone who was not a friend. Someone who made Senderovsky, already a drinker, drink more.

With that in mind, he sped to the liquor store in the richest village in the district, which occupied the premises of a former church. He bought two cases of Austrian Riesling at the south transept, another of rosé at the north, along with a fourth case of Beaujolais, wildly out of season, but a nostalgic wine for him and his high-school friends, Vinod and Karen. Ed, as always, would be the hardest to accommodate. Deep in the sacristy, Senderovsky picked out an eighteen-year-old bottle of something beyond his means, two bottles each of cognac and rye, and, to show his frivolous side, schnapps and a strange single malt from the Tyrol. The proprietor, a shaggy Anglo with a rosacea nose peeking out from his loosely worn mask, looked very pleased as he rang up the many purchases, his fingers clad in black disposable gloves.

"Just got a call from the state," he said to Senderovsky. "They might shut me down any day now as nonessential." Senderovsky sighed and bought an extra case of the Riesling and two bottles of an artisanal gin he had never heard of. He could picture Ed pursing his lips around a glass and pronouncing it "drinkable." When the final bill, adding up to just over four digits, meandered out of the machine in many long spurts, Senderovsky's hand could barely slalom through his signature. A special occasion, he consoled himself.

With his trunk now filled with bottles as well as meats, he gunned his car toward yet another village, this one fifteen miles north, to do some more marketing, after which he was due to drop off the meat and pick up Ed from the train station. At the exit for the bridge crossing the river, he ran into a line of cars. Nothing irritated Senderovsky more than the local version of a traffic jam. He brought a city impatience to the rural life. Around here it was considered impolite to honk, but Senderovsky honked. He rolled down his window, thrust out his long bony face, and honked some more with the palm of his hand, the way he had seen men do in films. The car in front of him was not moving. It sat low to the ground, a rusted wheelbarrow jammed into its trunk, a national flag fluttering from the driver's window, and a partly peeled sticker on the bumper that read I STAND BY MY PRES . . . Senderovsky realized that at this pace there was no way he could go to the store and drop off the meat before Ed's train arrived. Ignoring the very clear markings on the road warning against just such a maneuver, he whipsawed his car around, and within minutes was charging up his long driveway, once again cursing the fallen tree branches that ruined the approach to the House on the Hill. As he noisily threw the meat into the industrial-sized freezer in the vast white kitchen (the house had once belonged to a chef), he dialed the boy from across the river who came round to do the lawn mowing, begging him to get rid of the branches. But the boy had other things to do. "What things?" Senderovsky challenged, threatening to pay double. Out on the covered porch he confronted the handyman who was listening to old music on a handsome red radio, but all he got was "The missus told me I wasn't to move anything heavy on account of the back."

Senderovsky's own missus now stepped onto the porch in her kaftan, arms akimbo, her fingers pressed into the softness of her abdomen. "I can't work with all this noise," Masha said in Russian to her husband, mindful of the handyman. "It's a workday for me. My patients can barely hear me and they're agitated as it is."

"What noise?"

"There's drilling by the bungalows, and you're throwing meat in the freezer and yelling at the lawn boy."

"Darling," Senderovsky answered, using an inflated diminutive of the term: *dorogushka*. He had known his wife since they were children. Russian was a language built around the exhalation of warmth and pain, but lately Senderovsky had found his declarations of love for his wife stilted, as if he were reading them from a play. "The workers will knock off at three, as they always do," he said. "And I've only to pick up Ed and get the groceries."

The handyman stared at them for the aliens they were. When he had started working for them three years ago, they were of approximate size, two smallish figures, college professors most likely (a tiny but very active college was within striking range of Senderovsky's car), annoying in their requests and frugal in their outlays, but speaking with one slightly accented city voice. Now the woman had become larger, more local-looking around the waist and arms, while the man had done the opposite, had shrunk and emaciated himself and lost most of his hair, his only salient points a sharp nose and the brick of a forehead, to the point that the handyman suspected he was ill. In another reversal, the husband seemed happier today, despite the seeping sibilants of the language they spoke, while she had taken on his former briskness. Whatever this weekend would bring, the handyman thought, it would not be good. Also, he had heard that the Senderovskys' appliance repairman from across the river had not been paid in months even as the refrigerator in the main house continued to break down in interesting new ways.

The conversation continued, rising in pitch, until the woman turned to the handyman and said, "Would you mind trimming the hedges by the pool? Everyone else is busy."

"That type of work I'm not really cut out for," the handyman said. Despite the cold March weather, he was wearing denim shorts of an antiquated sky blue, and one of his legs was covered in iconography neither of the Senderovskys could understand, eagles, snakes, and cryptic symbols, which they hoped was not a sign of a violent affiliation. The first year they had bought the House on the Hill, after they had set out their nondenominational New Year's tree, the handyman had said to the husband, "I didn't figure you for Christmas-tree people." He had smiled as he said it, but they both had lain awake that night, wondering what he meant.

"The trimmers are in the garage," the wife said to the handyman. "We would really appreciate it." That was another change the handyman had noticed over the last few years: while the husband dithered, the wife now spoke with finality, a rubber band snapped against the fingers.

Senderovsky kissed his wife awkwardly on the brow and ran for his car. He tore down the driveway at forty miles an hour, rearranging the gravel behind him into a series of bald spots, and swung onto the road without checking for oncoming vehicles. As he picked up still more speed by the neighboring sheep farm, there was a rattling in the back, and he realized he had forgotten to clear out the cartons of alcohol. He wondered what would happen if he were to transfer a bottle of whiskey to the front of the car. On previous visits, he and Ed would swig while driving home, impatient to resume their friendship. Today, made happy by the arrival of his friends, and anxious by the arrival of his nemesis, Senderovsky wanted to flood his mouth with liquor, to stupefy himself in the manner of his ancestors.

The lot in front of the station was filled with European cars awaiting passengers. Senderovsky waved to a professor of Calabrese studies at the local college and to the owner of a surprisingly thriving café and bookstore anchoring the fashionable neighborhood of the little city right across the river. Seeing these friendly faces cheered Senderovsky. He was a respected figure in these parts. "You have a lovely family and a lovely home," his Los Angeles agent had told him during a visit several years ago, after another television project had collapsed.

The train was twenty minutes late, but finally its ancient gray form drew flush with the similarly gray line of the river. City folk clambered up the stairs from the platform to the station, breathless with age. Senderovsky spotted his first guest, relatively young and limber. Ed Kim toted a leather Gladstone bag, wore aviator sunglasses, and kept his hair dark. From the moment he had met him when they were both in their twenties, Ed reminded Senderovsky of a film he had seen about China's last emperor, specifically the dissolute stage when the hero wore a tuxedo and was the puppet ruler of Manchuria.

Senderovsky jumped out of the car. He was still wearing his dressing gown, a gift Ed had bought him at a Hong Kong shop called The Armoury. The two men regarded each other by the curb, Senderovsky playing the dog to Ed's cat. Usually, he would surround his friend in a skinny-armed embrace while Ed tapped his back with one hand as if burping him. "Ah, what are we supposed to do now?" Senderovsky cried.

"I'm over this elbow-bump business," Ed said. "Let me get a look at you." He lowered his sunglasses, the way some uncles do when they greet their young nieces. The creases around his eyes looked like they had been there since birth, while his expression was both distant and amused. Senderovsky's friend Karen, who was slightly related to Ed through a dissipated ancestor back in Seoul, also sometimes wore that expression, but she had only been able to pull it off after her recent success.

Ed managed to light a cigarette with one hand while simultaneously popping open the trunk and depositing his vintage bag. "So Masha told me to tell everyone," Senderovsky said, "no smoking in the car. In fact, no smoking on the property either. She says it can make the virus worse if you get it.

"But," he added, "I left an ashtray in your bungalow under the sink."

"Just let me get three drags in," Ed said. Sasha watched as he drew three cartoonish inhales and expelled the smoke into the slate air. As a younger man, Sasha had dreamed of becoming Ed. He still fantasized about spending a year traveling around the world with him just as soon as his daughter graduated from the very expensive city school for sensitive and complicated children.

"Also," Senderovsky continued, "she told me that no one should sit in the front seat. For distancing purposes."

"Oh, the hell with that," Ed said, opening the front passenger door. "People are really going overboard with this thing. I'll crouch down when we get to the house." The car filled with the aroma of fresh tobacco, which made Senderovsky wistful for a smoke. Ed placed a hand on the glove compartment, bracing himself for the landowner's torque. "What happened there?" He pointed at the dangling side mirror.

"The garage bays are too narrow," Senderovsky said. Seconds had passed, but the train station was already far behind them, and they were racing, swerving, past the skeleton of what, in three months' time, would become a farm stand. "I ought to have them widened."

"What's that Russian saying about incompetent people trying to pass the blame?"

Senderovsky laughed. " 'A bad dancer is bothered by his balls.' "

"Mmmm."

"Would you mind if we get some groceries? All I have is the meat and booze."

"I'm in no hurry," Ed said, and Senderovsky immediately thought of a fitting epitaph for his friend: HERE LIES EDWARD SUNGJOON KIM, HE WAS IN NO HURRY. He accelerated the car farther north along a tight state road that allowed for a view of the purple mountains across the river, each given a sophomoric American name. Peekamoose was his daughter's favorite. Meanwhile, as Senderovsky pattered on about the weather, the political news, speculation about the virus, the merits of sweet sausage versus hot Italian, Ed espied a great frontal system of boredom on the horizon, of endless upper-middle-class chatter, badly made country Negronis, cigarettes snuck. What could he do? His friend had begged him to come up, and the now-muted city would be more depressing still.

"So who else is coming?" Ed asked. "Besides the Exalted One." He was referring to the famous actor who was coming up for a few days to work on a screenplay with Senderovsky, the source of his friend's anxiety. "Karen, you said."

"Vinod, too."

"Haven't seen him in ages. Is he still in love with Karen?"

"He lost a lung to cancer a few years ago. Then he lost his job at City College."

"That's a lot of loss."

"Masha wanted him to come up, because his immune system might be compromised."

"I wish I was tragic enough for your wife to like me."

"Keep working on it."

"Who else?"

"An old student of mine. She published an essay collection last year. *The Grand Book of Self-Compromise and Surrender.* It made a splash."

"Well, at least she'll be young. Maybe I'll learn a thing or two. How's your kid, by the way?"

"Flourishing," Senderovsky said.

They skidded into a town that wasn't. The selection at Rudolph's Market, its sole business, contained goods that neither Ed (born Seoul, 1975) nor his host (Leningrad, 1972) had enjoyed in their early non-American years, candy that tasted like violets, bread that was so enriched you could use it for insulation. Alongside these outrageously marked-up nostalgic items were international ones even dearer, which Ed carelessly piled into a basket. There were fresh whole sardines that could be grilled before the meats, dirigible-shaped Greek olives from ancient islands, cheeses so filled with aromatic herbs they inspired (on Senderovsky's part) memories that had never happened, ingredients for a simple *vitello tonnato* that somehow came to over eighty dollars, excluding the veal. "I think we have enough," Senderovsky said with alarm. "I don't want anything to spoil."

They were standing in a long line of second-home owners. When the shocking amount due appeared on a touch screen, they both looked away, until the old woman behind the counter coughed, informatively, into her gloved fist. Senderovsky sighed and reached for his card.

Soon, they were raising gravel up the long driveway. It was only 2:00 P.M., but the workers had already left, along with their powerful trucks stenciled with old local names. "I'm sorry about all these dead branches," Senderovsky said. "I've been trying to get them cleaned up."

"What branches?" Ed was looking absently at his new home, at the bungalows rising up behind the main house like a half circle of orbiting moons. The sky was the color of an old-fashioned projector screen pulled down to the edges of the distant hills, splotched here and there by the hand of an inky boy.

Meanwhile, in her office, Masha had lifted up a heavy beaded curtain. She saw Ed clambering out of her husband's car with the languor that came so easily for him. Naturally, he had not sat in the back, like she had asked. She made a snort she instantly recognized as her grandmother's, a labor camp survivor. *Well, there it is,* her grandmother would say. The first of the children was here. More children for Masha to take care of, in addition to the one watching Asian boy-band videos upstairs, mouth open, eyes bleary, pacified. Soon the property would be filled with them, grown children without children. All of her friends were married, unlike her husband's (and none was crazy enough to visit someone else's house at a time like this). Masha shut off her screen, thought about changing out of her kaftan for Ed, but then went into the driveway exactly as she was.

Ed was walking with the leather Gladstone creaking behind him. Masha had partly grown up in New Jersey and had seen powerful men carry golf bags in a similar way. "How was the train up?" she shouted, her tone a little too needy, she thought.

"Charming," Ed said. "I got a seat with river views." He knew he had to get some preliminaries out of the way: "Thank you so much for hosting me during this time. It's much appreciated." He forced himself to take an exaggerated breath of damp air. "Mmm," he said. "Just what the surgeon general ordered. You both look wonderful. Sasha's really lost some weight."

The weight comment, he quickly realized, could be misinterpreted by Masha, who was beautiful but now reminded him of a noblewoman's portrait he had seen last year at the Tretyakov Gallery. The kaftan certainly didn't help. The two men walked silently up the cedar steps of the vast covered porch, which was connected to the main house and overlooked the bungalows, the centerpiece of the property and also its jewel, a screened-in world within a world.

"If you don't mind, I'm going to be a little doctorly," Masha said, "if that's even a word."

"Not at all," Ed said. Not at all he didn't mind, or "doctorly" was not at all a word? Masha had to think about it, which maybe was the point.

"I've made some rules," she said. "Since you've taken the train up, maybe you could change into fresh clothes before you sit down anywhere. But before that I'd like to wipe down some of the surfaces, which the workers touched in your bungalow. There's a lot we still don't know about this virus."

"Safety first."

She did not like his tone. Senderovsky stood beside them in a hunched-over position. He had had to serve as diplomat between two feuding parents for many decades. "Also in public areas like the porch and the dining room," Masha continued, "I'm going to try to space everyone out and also to give everyone a designated seat. I'm sorry if I sound like a killjoy."

"There's no right or wrong here," Ed said. "We all have to be ourselves during this crisis."

Actually, there was a right and a wrong here. Ed reminded her of her husband's parents. Talking with them was like dealing with a smiling adversary who kept a handful of poisoned toothpicks in his pocket. Every time you let your guard down, there would be a sharp prick at your haunches.

"Here's another question I have to ask. And this is really a compliment, because you're always going somewhere. Can you tell me where you've traveled since, let's say, December of last year?"

"Since December? Hmmm." Ed looked up at the stucco-clad main house, a neutral gray like the sky. People of a certain class, immigrants in particular, did not like to rock the boat. A second-floor landing and an adjoining window were yellow-lit at an odd angle, like a Mondrian painting—the top quadrant being the daughter's room, most likely. Ed had forgotten her name.

"Well, I went to Addis for the jazz thing," he said. "Then I went to AD to visit Jimmy who's teaching there." Ed drew a line in the air from (presumably) Addis Ababa to (presumably) Abu Dhabi. "I went back to Seoul for Christmas. No, wait." The line across the Arabian Sea stopped abruptly, and Ed's finger circled, dumping fuel. "I saw Suketu in Bombay, just for the weekend, then I continued on to Seoul." Sasha followed the line in the air with great interest, imagining it were he and not Ed doing the travel, a business-class whiskey in hand. A long time ago, after his childhood relationship with Masha had ended, but before his adult relationship with her would begin, he had worked as a contributing editor to a travel magazine, humping around both hemispheres with nothing but a notepad and some vocabulary. That interval contained some of the best years of his life, the expense accounts, the sweat of tropical cities, the drunken camaraderie of the Eds of the world.

"When did you leave Seoul?" Masha was asking.

"Oh, I see what you're getting at. I left right after Christmas, before things got bad there. And from there"—Ed's index finger was ready for a significant jump—"I went to the Big Island."

"In honor of our bungalow!" Sasha said, brightly. The bungalow reserved for Ed mimicked the one he and Masha had enjoyed during their honeymoon on Hawaii's Big Island, and it came with a feature no other house did—an outdoor shower, its walls rendered in seashells.

"Yes," Ed said. "My friend Wei got a bungalow at the Mauna Kea. Call me a bungalow hopper."

"Wei Li?" Senderovsky asked.

"Wei Ko. He's in biotech. I guess this is his moment to shine."

"And then you came back to the city," Masha said.

"Well, actually, no. My brother bought a vineyard in Hungary." Senderovsky remembered the Austrian Riesling and assorted alcohol still rattling around in his trunk, and prayed nothing had broken during his many trips, especially the eighteen-year-old bottle he had bought for Ed and the Actor to share. "I was over by Lake Balaton," Ed continued. "Did your families ever go there back in the day? Soviet vacations? The wine was plonk, but I ate a great veal liver soaked in butter and paprika, would love to know how they made it. And then London."

"Any reason for London?" Masha asked. Sasha thought that she sounded like a Heathrow immigration officer inspecting a visitor from a developing country.

"No, it was just—London," Ed said.

"Last question, I promise. Any trips to China or Northern Italy?"

"Nope," Ed said. He set down his Gladstone bag with a thud of frustration. "Wait, actually, I transferred through Linate once."

"That's Milan," Sasha said.

Both men noted the way Masha looked at her husband just then. But it wasn't her husband's suggestion that she wasn't worldly that irked her. They force me to be someone I'm not, Masha thought. They mistake my caring for authoritarianism, and then I have no choice but to become Stalin in an apron. But what option do I have if I'm to keep these cretins from getting sick?

"It was a very brief transfer," Ed said of his time in Northern Italy. "I'm sure I don't have it." When Ed Kim became nervous during conversation, he cupped his right hand behind his right ear, as if trying to make a conch shell out of it. It was a nervous tic everyone noticed, and he himself was well aware of, but he couldn't stop his ear cupping during times of social anxiety.

"I'm sure you don't," Masha said. "I really hate to go through all this. It's because of Natasha." Right, that was the daughter's name. Sasha, Masha, Natasha. They didn't even try, these Russians. "You can't be too careful," she added. "Any special requests for dinner?"

"Don't even think about it," Ed said. "I'm going to cook tonight. You just rest up. I've heard parents have it extra hard these days. And I'm sure Sasha's no help at all."

"We bought some amazing things," Senderovsky said. "We know how much you love fresh sardines." Masha smiled. Even if it wasn't true that they had thought of her, the lie was nice. She would settle for the lie. Ed thought he had caught a glimpse of her youth when she smiled. The new plushness of her chin reminded him of a Greek girl he had fallen in love with, almost a decade ago to the day, one of the last times he had ever loved somebody, had allowed forgotten parts of himself, the underside of his ankles, his eyelashes, to tingle for no reason. Senderovsky placed both hands in the fertile valley between his breasts and his throat, happy that his friend and his wife were getting along. There was complete stillness now, except for the sound of an overexcited tree frog and the handyman loudly clipping the hedges by the covered pool, as if protesting his lot.

A pebbled path ran between the bungalows, in a way that Senderovsky had hoped would create the feel of a tidy European village, the kind that would have never welcomed his ancestors. The bungalows formed a crescent around the main house, some overlooking a classical meadow, others a minor forest overrun by noisy animals. They were cozy in winter, as all small dwellings should be, and utilitarian in summer, but they lacked the visual flair of smoking chimneys or sliding porch doors. The luxuries were supposed to be communal: the fine food and even-finer conversation. There had been a dearth of laughter and clever ideas in Senderovsky's early homelife, and even though nowadays he went out to restaurants and the occasional literary party in the city, nothing pleased him more than being the ringleader of his country menagerie. Not to mention the stealth surprise of walking across acres of private Senderovsky land on a continent that had signed his adoption papers.

Alone, Ed unpacked his bag, laptop (he remembered now that there was no reception in the bungalow), chargers, fresh packets of balled-up Korean underwear presented by his mother's maid, polo shirts, a linen jacket (would he really have to stay into summer?), two ties, and a pocket square. He sat down on the soft, comfortable, Art Deco–adjacent bed and had what must have been a panic attack, his breaths coming in quick short bursts as if he was sucking air out of a balloon at gunpoint.

The sole window disclosed an ever-deepening gray, an artificial intelligence's idea of days passing on earth. He was so close yet so far from the city's fast-moving harbor skies. Were there ever contrails above the peaked cedar roof? Planes following the river down to the airports? He heard a purser's strict, pinched voice from what already seemed like another era: *Meine Damen und Herren, wir begeben uns jetzt auf den Abstieg nach Berlin-Tegel.* How many of his similarly situated friends around the world were looking out of a double-insulated window or up at a pitched cedar ceiling trying to calm themselves with similar incantations?

Above the headboard there was a lush photograph of lava from the Big Island's Kīlauea volcano boiling into the Pacific. Ed thought the composition was obvious but beautiful, interplanetary even, yet he scrambled up on the bed and moved the frame to make it about twenty degrees off kilter. He messed up the bed's careful sheets as if two lovers had just enjoyed a tussle on it. He spotted two carved wooden statues of pineapples on the modernist desk (noting that significant pineapple production had only ever taken place on Maui and Oahu, never on the Big Island) and knocked over one of them, adding some asymmetry to the deathly hospital order around him.

What would his mother say from her immovable Gangnam cocoon, her throat tingling with hot barley tea? Advice she would never follow herself. Be strong for your friends.

A woman—Masha, it would have to be—was screaming from the direction of the long covered porch. It sounded to Ed like "Gnat! Gnat! Gnat!" She was living in the country and afraid of a gnat? Ed leaned back on the bed, liberated a Gauloise from a crumpled pack, and stared down the blinking light of the smoke detector above him. Be strong for his friends? Velocity was his friend. Disappearing landscapes were his friends. He remembered that Sasha had left an ashtray for him under the bathroom sink. The rebellious cigarette quickly lightened Ed's mood. There was still some time before dinner, wasn't there? He had forgotten his earplugs but managed to fall asleep anyway.

2

KAREN CHO BOWED her rental car into the many dips and blind turns of the familiar country road, her driving skills only marginally more restrained than Senderovsky's. She had tuned in a satellite channel blasting songs from her youth and was trying to take it seriously, the way Ed always did, giving even the stupidest song his karaoke best. And this was not a stupid song.

Christine, the strawberry girl.
Christine, banana split lady.

She had missed driving since moving back from the West Coast, but, unlike Senderovsky, she could never identify the frisson it gave her, the sense of being slightly more American in the very act of piloting a many-ton behemoth down a road with excess speed, stuffing a hatchback with a family-sized pack of absorbent towels, clicking on the hypnotic metronome of a turning signal. Driving matched her new sense of power, which, if she were honest with herself, she still did not fully understand. "What does it feel like?" Senderovsky kept asking her after she had sold her so-called company, really just an idea, a software developer (her friend and former bandmate) and two intellectual property lawyers on retainer. She told him that she could now lash out at a white man in an expensive hoodie, safe in the knowledge that she would still get to keep her money when she was done yelling at him.

Now she's in purple, now she's the turtle.
Disintegrating.

Karen slammed on the brakes. "Whoa," she said. Since the divorce, she had started speaking to herself. A perfectly rolling green hill conjured up a dinosaur's back. The back was covered with woolly little ticks. She remembered now that a part of Sasha's property abutted a sheep farm, and so she pulled over and got out of the humming, beeping car. The sheep were lined up in rows as if practicing the very distancing prescribed for their owners. They had recently been sheared and now carried themselves like gangly teenagers. Some had their mouths stuffed with grass, but most were watching something beyond the fence separating their farm from Senderovsky Land. Karen wanted to take out her phone to snap a picture, but stopped herself. Recently, she had sworn to stop uploading photographs to the very social media that had made her rich, to enjoy moments instead of imprisoning them.

Karen walked toward the fence, along mounds of recently cut grass. On the other side of the road, next to an imposing new house, she spotted horses wearing sweaters. Horses in sweaters, what a life. It seemed almost impossible that the owners of the broken houses she had seen up the road, "shitbox Federals," as Ed had once described them in his Ed way, could breathe in the same rich country air as Sasha and some of his neighbors. She was surprised the nation's very atmosphere hadn't yet been tagged by an algorithm and parceled out according to its content. Some of her confederates back in the Valley were probably working on it. She stole a great big lungful of a budding forsythia, and then another, a city girl suddenly grateful. Easter would be coming soon, but her mother was still dead.

A sheepdog was pacing up and down the perimeter, yapping her head off about something, the sheep arrayed behind her watching the commotion patiently, assured by their leader's presence. Karen could make out a lone, tiny figure moving about in the incumbent dusk on the Senderovsky side of the fence and began to walk toward it, entranced. Why had she come here? The official version was to see her friends, whom she felt she had neglected since her success. Though the last time she had spoken to Vinod it was hard to contain her sadness. And her anger. Even after he had lost part of his lung to cancer, he was still working in his uncle's greasy kitchen. It was as if he was taunting her with how his life had turned out. She came close to actually offering him money or a make-work job—in other words, to breaking his heart. Well, better his heart than his remaining lung. His heart had proved quite resilient over the years despite everything Karen had done to it. So, again, why had she come here?

The version she told herself, the unofficial one, was that she wanted to see the Actor. It was true that in her new life she got to see a lot of famous people, but she had loved him since that first movie back in the late nineties, the one where he danced naked in that stupid hat, instantly her generation's darling. The idea of mixing in the Actor with the desperate charm of Sasha's bungalow colony had moved her to rent a car and leave the canceled city. Even during the drive up on the empty scenic highway, she had found herself placing one hand on the inside of her thigh, her breath unexpectedly warm, her upper lip scented like spring.

So there was an official reason for her visit and the unofficial one. But, former adjunct professor and current kitchen boy Vinod would ask, which one was true?

Now the prancing figure became clear: It was a boy, and he seemed to be—what? Her eyesight was getting worse now, especially in the dark. She was a year older than both Sasha and Vinod, which meant her fifties would be upon her in a matter of months not years. But no, as clear as a fading country day, the boy was prancing, dancing, clapping his hands, punching the air martial-arts style, while singing in a sweet girlish voice as the dog yapped her unheeded warnings and her charges watched raptly, too startled to *baa*.

When she heard the lyrics, Karen laughed out loud, much in the same way she had when her now ex-husband Leon had served her with divorce papers or when her lawyer presented her with an initial offer for her company. Her childhood had passed with almost no surprises, an endlessly swinging pendulum of parental insults and popular culture, being yelled at downstairs, self-soothing upstairs. (At least, her parents would have pointed out, there had *been* stairs, unlike her poorer relations in their cramped Elmhurst apartments.) The words the boy was singing were unmistakably in her mother's tongue, followed by the English chorus: *I'm so sick of this fake-ah love, fake-ah love, fake-ah love.* It was a boy-band pop hit from maybe two summers ago. She remembered hearing it on repeat while shopping for her deadbeat relatives at Lotte World, back when she had gone to Seoul to receive a week's worth of adulating press coverage for being a prized sample of her people, a daughter of Daehan Minguk made good.

The proto-Korean boy was wearing a cute white V-neck cardigan, tan slacks, and what looked like an adult tie that reached down to his thighs. A Korean school uniform gone off the rails. Karen was surprised but also not. Everything that happened within Senderovsky's orbit was always a little strange.

"Hi!" Karen shouted to the boy. There was no answer. Did he not speak English (beyond "fake-ah love")? *"Annyonghaseo!"* Karen shouted. The child looked up, waved, then went back to his prancing and singing. The sheepdog now registering two enemies, one of them larger than herself, began to growl, fury turning to menace, and the sheep started to bleat in response, even though some continued to chew mouthfuls of grass through their panic. And then Karen recognized something in the boy, the oval of the face, the elongated but stocky legs, the flare of the nose, this exact child who'd sat on Senderovsky's lap several years ago on the covered porch as he tried to explain—in a borderline racist way—how his daughter bore all the trademarks of the region around Harbin by the Chinese-Russian border, from whence she had been adopted.

"Natasha?" Karen said. The child kept dancing. The sheepdog and her charges now formed an angry dialogue, both with their perceived enemies and with one another, a shaken neoliberal confronting a steadfast one. "Natasha!"

"I go by Nat now," the child said, in between verses, thrusting out her chest, chastely pumping her hips, her moves too practiced to be real. Unbidden, Karen remembered the theme song to a television show improbably titled *Happy Days,* and how much it had meant to dance to it in her bedroom almost half a century ago, belly full with her mother's *ramyeon. Saturday, what a day, groovin' all week with you.*

"Nat, where's your mommy?" Karen asked. "And daddy?" she added.

The child waved in the direction of the House on the Hill. "I like your new bob," Karen said. No answer. "Let's go home and get something to eat. I just drove up from the city and I'm starving."

"No, thanks." The child sounded out of breath, but spoke firmly. She might have been going for hours.

"Your parents might be worried," Karen said. She took a step and grabbed one little hand. "I insist," she said. The child looked up, mouth pursed in anger. "Hey, I'm your aunt Karen," she said. "We played with my phone on the porch last time I was here. You remember me?"

"We're related?" It was such an adult question. But Karen could see where it came from.

"Sure," she said. "In a sense."

"My daddy said Uncle Ed was coming, but he doesn't like to play with children."

"No, he doesn't."

"But I don't remember you at all."

"Let me drive you up in my car."

"Mommy said I should never get into a stranger's car."

"Mommy's supersmart about that. But I'm not a stranger."

"That's what a stranger would say." The logic on her.

"True. But I really think they might be worried about you. It's going to be dark any second."

"Okay, but I have to say goodbye to the sheep and the sheepdog."

"Cool. I'd like to see that."

The child went up to the fence separating her from the barking, braying animals. "Goodbye, sheep. Goodbye, Luna," she said. And then bowed rigidly, like a boy-band member accepting an award. The animals seemed to calm down instantly, as if they had seen this routine before. Luna, her growl now hoarse and simmering, followed them to the brightly lit car with its clever Mancunian voices on the satellite radio.

"I don't really know how to buckle in a child," Karen admitted to herself as much as to Nat. "Also, I realize you and I shouldn't be too close."

"Because of the virus," Nat said.

"Yeah, until this is over. Which will be really soon."

"Or not," said the girl. Smart like her mother, Karen thought, and just as optimistic. She buckled her into the back realizing she had never smelled a child's sweat before and that everything they said about it was true. "Thanks, Aunt Karen," the child said politely. The last time she had seen Senderovsky he had complained at length about his daughter's difficulties and the fifty-nine-thousand-dollar tuition at a school that not only tolerated differences but, according to its card-stock brochure, celebrated them, to the point where Karen turned on her friend and with an eye roll that was a standard part of her vocabulary said, "Gee, maybe you should send her back to China."

She drove slowly up the long driveway, checking on her passenger in the rearview mirror. Even in the dusk, she could spot the white branches littering the front lawn like an arboreal Gettysburg. All these years and Senderovsky still couldn't take care of himself. That thought made her grin. Same, same Sasha. Her headlights caught an unfamiliar figure running toward them from the house, screaming very distinctly, "Nat! Nat! Nat!," and Karen's passenger announced, "That's my mommy." Karen squinted. She had always held the image of Masha from the early days when they were all worried that she didn't eat enough. Masha, in her motherly haste, almost ran headlong into the car, so that Karen had to pull over into the grass, a giant white oak branch crunching beneath a wheel.

Masha opened the back door and began to unbuckle her daughter, fingers fumbling, as she half shouted, half cried, "Where were you? Where were you? *Where were you?*"

"She was singing to the sheep," Karen said, quietly, having learned how to deal with unhappy parents in her formative stage, though that wasn't fair to Masha. "It was cute." They had all exited the car now, and Masha was on her knees on the gravel, bits of it stinging her feet, holding the child by the shoulders.

"You don't do that!" she shouted. She grabbed the long tie, one of Sasha's, most likely, and began to unwind it with fumbling fingers.

"No!" Nat cried. "Mommy, leave it on!"

"You'll choke yourself," Masha said as she ripped off the tie and shoved it into the pocket of her kaftan. The girl started crying loudly. Karen could now see Sasha descending from the house in what she refused to believe was a dressing gown. She did not understand Masha's fear. Had she really thought her daughter had run away from them? Where would she go?

"I probably should park the car," she said.

"Ah! Ah! Ah!" Senderovsky shouted. "Karen! Nat!" He looked disheveled and emaciated, and had carried himself like a fifty-year-old since he was eighteen. "You found her!" he said to Karen. "Oh, thank you. We thought she had run away. We almost woke up Ed to help with the search."

"Ed can't even find himself," Karen said. "And he's looked literally everywhere."

Senderovsky laughed. "So good to see you," he said. "If only we could hug."

Karen blew him a kiss. They looked at his wife and his daughter on the gravel, Masha whispering to her in Russian, words that only Senderovsky could understand, a calming mantra she deployed only in the most dire of circumstances: "I have a wonderful family and wonderful friends. I can do anything if I work hard and am kind to other people."

The mantra must have worked. The girl leaned over and kissed her mother several times on the brow and had her kisses returned. Senderovsky, with a creaking Russian *oy*, bent down and did the same, his dressing gown now draped in mud. "We do that to make sure we're the right prairie dogs," the girl explained to Karen.

"I'm sorry?"

"Prairie dogs have to kiss each other to make sure they're related because there's so many of them," Senderovsky said.

"May I kiss Aunt Karen then?" the child asked. "I think we're related."

Karen found herself stepping forward, expectantly, but Masha raised her hand. "Aunt Karen just came from the city, so we'll have to give her a little time," she said. And then to Karen: "Thank you so much for finding this crazy girl. I thought I was going to lose my mind."

"How old is she now?" Karen asked.

"I'm eight!" the child shouted. "Look at the birthday bracelet my mommy gave me with eight merino wool beads for each year. The beads spell out N-A-T-A-S-H-A, and an exclamation mark. Natasha! But I really go by Nat. Also 'she' and 'her' are my pronouns, though I reserve the right to change them later."

"She's eight going on eighty," Senderovsky said to Karen. "Anyway, sorry for the drama of our opening act. I promise it's going to be country peace and quiet from this point forward. Masha can help you get settled; I have to pick up Vinod from the bus station."

"You're not going to help calm your daughter?" Masha said, in, she realized, the wrong language. "What's wrong with you?" she added in Russian.

"I can't leave Vinod at the station. Not with his health. And she's okay now. She's had her prairie dog kiss."

Karen drove the rest of the driveway up to the garage while Senderovsky walked alongside her like an obedient liege. The futuristic car guided itself into a spare bay with verve. Senderovsky was saddened by the tumult that had accompanied his friend's arrival, while Karen was gladdened by her promotion to "aunt." She knew she would soon be bathed in her friends' many problems. Unlike her younger sister, and her mother, when she was still alive, at least these two would listen to her.

3

O NCE AGAIN SENDEROVSKY'S car attacked the innocent mailbox on a bend in the road leading to the bridge, further crumpling the naïve art on its side, an ageless Easter bunny delighted by a field of clover. Once again Senderovsky pictured a crying child—"They hit Bunny!"—and a consoling parent, "Not on purpose. It was just a bad driver." And once again his car's proximity-alert gong sounded, but only as the carnage was already underway. Senderovsky sped on. Someday, he would buy the property owner a new mailbox with a rabbit drawn by an artist from the city, something bound to appreciate in value if weatherproofed properly, but today he offered a silent apology in the form of a self-justified mumble: "So many things on my mind."

The twenty minutes of Nat's absence had been brutal, Masha's full-throated panicked voice (nothing more frightening to Senderovsky than a psychiatrist panicking)—"Natashen'ka!"—and his uncertain, unauthoritative one—"Nat?"—ringing around the property. Even though neither of them had been assigned to guard Nat, who, Senderovsky had presumed, had still been upstairs with her videos, he knew Masha would make him stand trial for her having gone missing. "She's already dysregulated from having school moved online, and now you're bringing five people to run around and make noise and do hell knows what." "It's good for her to be social." "With her peers, not these people." "*These* people. They're my best friends." "Oh, I know. *How* I know." "They can be parental figures, too. You love Vinod." "Vinod needs rest, not to take over the fatherly duties you've abdicated." "So you're saying she ran away because people are coming?" "She's worried about new faces. It's not like you're a stranger to generalized anxiety disorder." "If only I had conquered my social deficits as a child. I'd be doing a lot better than I am right now, that's for sure." "I remember you back at that bungalow colony when you were eight. You were pretty damn friendly. [Switching to Russian] We couldn't shut you up." "Exactly right. And this is Nat's bungalow colony." "Minus a peer group. While she's having [switching to English] identity issues." "While she's figuring out who she is." "And Ed Kim's going to help her with that journey?" "He helped me with mine." Just to be sure, this conversation never happened. But it could have, down to the very last therapeutic turn of phrase. How Senderovsky envied writers who had taken marriage as their subject.

Even worse, he had lost face in front of Karen. Since Karen's contributions to civilization had eclipsed his own, Senderovsky had felt even more in need of her approbation. Having a "*lovely family* and a lovely home," to quote his Los Angeles agent, would be proof that unlike his divorced, childless friend, he "had it all." And now Karen had seen his daughter run away, sing to sheep. (Although maybe she had taken it as proof of the child's imagination and independence. The younger Karen would have.) A few more incidents like that might segue into diagnostic talk, which would lead to still more mention of her schooling which was filled with the most perceptive teachers ever to wield chalk and where, despite their many interventions, Nat still did not have any friends.

And, while he was searching for Nat around the property, he had gotten a vague message from the Actor about being late, or maybe not coming tonight, or maybe not coming ever, which, if true, would mean there would be no progress on the script, which, in turn, would evaporate Senderovsky's half of Nat's fifty-nine-thousand-dollar tuition. Not to mention the costs of feeding his guests indefinitely and heating and cooling their bungalows. On the other hand, Senderovsky knew that once the Actor arrived, the atmosphere would change from a Visit to Sasha's Deluxe Bungalow Colony to an Evening with the Actor in Some Country Setting. He would either struggle to make himself heard above the Actor's beautiful silence or try to provide a laugh track, which in the end would mean the same thing.

Three cars had gathered at the intersection of two major state roads. Senderovsky had forgotten the rules on which vehicle should take precedence during such an event, assumed it was his own, and stepped on the gas. Similarly, half a mile later, he drove past a yield sign, but refused to yield. On the approach to the bridge, slowing down because of a likely police car waiting ahead (his side mirror was still dangling), he slammed on the brakes and heard a great reshuffle in his trunk ending with the unmistakable symphony of shattered glass. *Devil take it.* Once again, he had forgotten to remove the cartons of alcohol. He pulled over to the side of the road to the Kiss & Ride parking lot. Senderovsky, who had never lived by a far-flung train station, could never figure out why the lot was so named—an incitement to prostitution? He opened his trunk, which immediately reeked of spilled alcohol. He sighed. Could it be the eighteen-year-old bottle he had bought to impress Ed and the Actor (who, he had forgotten, didn't really drink)? He rummaged through the cartons until he sliced his finger, mildly, on a run of broken glass. He sucked on his finger for a while. Finally, he dared to look down. The expensive bottle was safe, but two bottles of country rye had crashed into each other and bled out into the carton. Senderovsky brought the carton up to his lips, tipped it over slightly, and drank, his tongue screening out little bits of glass. Now he was in his natural state, moderately drunk in his dressing gown, his wife and child a world away. If state law or federal law or intergalactic law would allow it, he would have spent the next hour at the Kiss & Ride drinking himself into tragicomedy before hurtling his car toward his friend. He dumped the remains of the bottles into a waiting trash bin, then stood by the side of the road, watching cars swoosh mindlessly onto the bridge, their drivers bathed in the electronics of their cockpits, looking small, indistinct, unprepared for this moment in history.

The city across the river had recently become fashionable, but was still studied by urban planning graduates as a cautionary tale. Highways meant for far-larger metropolises had been built to separate its neighborhoods by race, and like a not-especially-clever clinical mouse Senderovsky often entrapped himself in cloverleafs and roundabouts. The bus station, catering to an obscure statewide bus company, somehow ended up in the trendy, formerly Black part of town, by the thriving new café and bookstore and a score of restaurants with dim interiors and urbane prices.

Senderovsky found Vinod standing alone by the shabby building, two plastic suitcases at his feet, looking like a slightly updated version of his father the moment he had emigrated from India, too late in his life to succeed in the New World as the owner of a computer store. Masha had insisted on upgrading his fundless friend from a bus to a train ticket, believing it was safer healthwise, but Vinod had refused her aid with the same obstinate politeness he had refused Karen's.

Senderovsky braked within inches of his friend's suitcases and leaped out of his car. The men stared at each other. For a second, both were fifteen, back at their freshman orientation at the high school for bright beaten foreign youngsters. Vinod had a full head of graying hair haloing down to his shoulders, peppery whiskers commencing to a salty beard, and somewhere amid all those outgrowths were once-frantic eyes that had recently, politely, extinguished themselves.

"*Bhai,*" Vinod said, the word leaving his mouth like a short, pretty explosion.

"*Bhai,*" Senderovsky replied. The word meant "brother" in Hindi. During their college years and beyond, the two had lived together for a decade in an up-and-coming neighborhood just like the one where they now stood (until the neighborhood finally came, and they were asked to leave), and through all those years Vinod referred to Senderovsky either as a *bhai* or a *bhenchod,* which was a man who enjoyed relations with his sister. (Although *bhenchod* was also used in an almost ambient way to label anyone or anything unfortunate, in the same way Russians use *blyad,* or "whore," to describe the unforgiving world around them—"When will this *whorish* snowstorm end already?")

Senderovsky spread out his arms. "Can't hug," he said. "And, just to warn you, Masha's gone all epidemiological."

"She *is* a doctor," Vinod said.

"Psychiatrist." Senderovsky could air his grievances to Vinod with just one word, in a way he couldn't to his more prosperous and competitive friends.

"I'll get in the back seat," Vinod said as Senderovsky arranged his shiny luggage amid the cartons of alcohol.

"Are you sure? You don't have to. I'm very healthy. Though I have lost some weight."

"This way I can pretend I'm in a cab and you're my driver."

They quickly made a joke out of it, jousting in the accents of their parents, or, in Vinod's case, an accent he had never really outgrown. "Zis taim of day, I vood take Belt Parkvey," Senderovsky spoke in his gruffest Leningrad.

"Sir, do you vish to rob me?" Vinod protested. Senderovsky had failed to notice that, unlike most of his passengers, Vinod did not brace himself against the seat in front of him as he sped off, had not offered a prayer to any god, nor made use of his grab handle as Senderovsky swerved onto the bridge barely pausing to have his toll collected. He did register a very loud yawn, the kind he had never heard before his friend was diagnosed with cancer a decade ago. Before his illness, he could stay up all night, reinforced by a carton of Marlboros and a friendliness that rivaled Senderovsky's, but sprang from the same lonely fount.

"We'll be home in ten minutes," said his driver, but Vinod knew their exact point in the journey, the car suspended above the river, leaving the continent proper in the rearview. He looked behind him to catch the very last light of the day. It was like putting on a new pair of glasses. Green grass, gray sky turning deep blue around the horizon, a screen of unblemished purple mountains. If this was all a computer simulation, then it was a very good one. Someone, some*thing,* in some interstellar version of Bangalore, had really poured its all into this construct.

Vinod had memorized the Declaration of Independence in third grade to prove to the nativist school bullies how much he belonged here. In the last two weeks, as people started to die in earnest, as he understood the gravity of what was about to happen to him and to others, and *when in the course of human events it became necessary for one person to dissolve,* Vinod thought he could be that person. He accepted his friend's invitation to visit the countryside as a chance at dissolution, not so much into the usual alcohol and mild drugs, but into the stories he shared with the others. And if it came to it, he had papers at the bottom of his luggage, notarized papers, which would prepare him for any eventuality.

Now, despite Senderovsky's jerky driving, he fell asleep, dreaming of his father's Buick and all the places it had tried to go. Senderovsky watched Vinod sleeping in the back seat, his face pressed deep into the tinted Swedish glass, and he could not escape the strength of his own feelings, the untinted brightness of his love. Uncharacteristically, he slowed down to let the moment take.

4

V INOD STOOD BY the garage while Sasha rolled out his suitcases.
A city boy from birth (Ahmedabad, 1972), Vinod did not know
which components made the air sweet, didn't know what a passing
storm could do to the senses. "I'm sorry about all those dead
branches," Senderovsky said. "I'm trying to muster a posse to clean
them up."

Vinod had no idea what he was talking about. He looked up at the
main house, at the lit kitchen, and saw two figures moving about, one
auburn haired, the other dark. It must have been her. He laughed to
himself. All those novels he had read, and the one he had written, and
still there was no way to summarize the eternal feelings of unrequited
love. "You really are a *bhenchod*," Senderovsky had told him on a
grisly, condom-strewn pier back in the city, back in 1991, when he had
first confessed his love for their sisterly mutual friend. But now the
need for phantom caresses (and worse) had passed. He just wanted to
talk to her, to ask her how she was at this late hour.

They skirted around the kitchen, past the covered porch, but
Vinod did not run inside to greet her, even as he heard her nasally
voice (something about the virtues of Napa cabbage versus the kind
Russians liked), was touched by its workaday lack of melody or magic.
He wanted to savor his aloneness just a bit longer. He was staying at
his usual place, the Lullaby Cottage, its walls decorated by the lullabies Senderovsky's friends recounted from their childhoods, as rendered in bright cursive by a notable (and notably cruel) British artist
who had since fallen from favor. Senderovsky had written the intro-
duction of a catalog for an exhibition the artist had made out of cork

and dismembered ants, and the artist had painted the Lullaby Cottage in return.

Vinod looked to his own Gujarati contribution written directly above the headboard in saffron Devanagari script.

He wanders around and then I go searching for him.
Somebody saw him go into the flower-bushes.
Now let us trim the bushes and bring him back home.

Sleep, my baby, sleep.
My baby loves to swing in his crib.

"I think you can catch a snooze before dinner," Senderovsky said, snapping open a luggage rack and hoisting the luggage over its woven ribs, beads of sweat on his forehead, winded by the small task. "You've missed our hotel's turndown service, I'm afraid."

"If only you were capable of turning me down."

"Sorry?"

Vinod smiled with the yellowed stubs of his former smoker's teeth. "I just wanted to thank you for this stay. I'll thank Masha later."

"I'm just sad we didn't have you over last summer."

"I'm not keeping score. And I'm honored to be among the anointed at a time like this."

"Everyone's over the moon that you're here."

"Everyone? I had a bit of a run-in with our brilliant friend."

Senderovsky noticed Vinod looking away as he spoke. His love for Karen brought to the landowner's mind an old Soviet saying, apropos of the Great Patriotic War against the Fritzes, as the advancing Germans were called: *No one is forgotten, nothing is forgotten.*

"So she got angry at one of us on the phone," Senderovsky said. "What else is new? I think I spent all of the nineties being yelled at by her. At least once she got her nights and weekends plan."

"It was my fault. I should have just accepted her help."

"I think being rich is hard for her," Senderovsky said. "If I had that kind of money, I'd probably just get gout and die the next day."

"I was expecting you to say, 'She's worried about you.' "

"Should she be?"

Vinod looked at him with his politely extinguished eyes. "No."

Senderovsky was satisfied by the finality of the reply. "Good," he said.

"Okay, *bhai*, let me wash up and we'll go say hi to the ladies."

Senderovsky bowed to him like a majordomo after his master's return from the capital.

"One tiny thing," Vinod said. "I feel scared to even ask."

"I am your faithful slave, as they said in the old days."

"It's embarrassing."

"There's no such thing as 'embarrassing' around here. Skinny-dipping begins on May twentieth, speaking of. That's when we open up the pool. No excuses."

Unlike Senderovsky, and despite being swaddled in hair so thick it would give a mare pause, Vinod had never been shy about his body.

"Remember the novel I gave you a million years ago?" he said. "The one that you saved me from sending in to an agent? For which I'm eternally grateful."

Senderovsky was looking out the bungalow's single glazed window. Despite its soundproofing he imagined he could hear the resident woodpecker starting up a rare nighttime shift, perhaps confused by all the lights blazing around the property. "I think I remember something," he said.

"Well, that makes one of us," Vinod said. "I can't even think of the title now. I'm sure it was heavy-handed as hell. But I kind of wanted to take a look at it. Not to show it to anyone, but just to remember my state of mind when I wrote it. Now that we're all here."

"That sounds kind of valedictory," Senderovsky said. "You do know you're going to outlive us all."

"So, is there any chance you saved the copy I gave you?"

There was more than a chance. Roughly fifty yards from where the friends were speaking, in the extreme northwest corner of the main house's attic between two other shoeboxes containing yellowed international love letters women had posted Senderovsky during the wild period after the publication of his first book, sat a Teva active sandals shoebox. It contained the two hundred eighty-seven closely typed pages of Vinod's manuscript, complete with a rigid blue floppy disk, one of the last of its kind.

"I'm not sure," Senderovsky said. "I think it might be in storage down in the city."

"Oh." Vinod sighed. "Well, that makes sense. I'm just surprised you didn't throw it out."

"I would never throw out any Vinod Mehta memorabilia. I'll try to think of where it might be. Now go, go wash up!"

MASHA AND KAREN were both wearing masks at Masha's request, one at the stove, the other at the farm sink. Vinod did not expect his first sighting of Karen to take in only half her face, but the deep mottled hazel of her eyes and the concentrated sharpness of her gleaming forehead could still do the trick. He let himself float in the happiness, especially as she yelled out "Vinod!" through the muffle of the mask. "Oh, God," she said, "I want to hug you so bad."

"The doctor won't allow it," Senderovsky mumbled, mostly to himself. He was still lost in thought about that Teva active sandals box, the blue rigid floppy disk with all of Vinod's careful words.

"The bus ride was pretty safe," he heard Vinod saying. "Everyone had their own row. There was one person sneezing in the back, but she said she had allergies."

"We're going to pamper the shit out of you," Karen said.

"That's right," Masha said. "Vinod gets the best of everything while he's here."

"I'm super-duper fine," Vinod said. "I'll get through this like a champion. Fuss about me too much, and I might get cross."

Karen was a visual person, not a great noticer of language. But she remembered now the great sonorous delights of Vinod's verbiage and accent: Ahmedabad and Bombay filtered through Corona, Queens. The *w* was a *v*. The *d* as a double *t*. The poetic way he subbed "true" for "through." "I'll get *true* this like a champion." "Champion," not the American "champ," by the way. Denied suburbia, he had spent his childhood among too many aunties and uncles all shouting in tandem about the price of milk and the price of silk. And even to this day, she noticed, his voice still cracked in places where the cement had never been put in and allowed to harden.

Senderovsky realized something. "What the hell is going on?" he said. "Ed and I should be doing all the cooking, the sardines and the *vitello tonnato* and the sausages and lamb steaks."

"Ed must be tired after the ninety-minute ride from the city," Karen said. "You know, the change in time zones."

Vinod laughed. She was so brutal. Senderovsky smiled at his laughter. Masha commanded herself to feel good about the natural friendship between the three others in the kitchen. Karen had been so kind with Nat, and Vinod was always a darling. And, as her own therapist would bring up, her husband had chosen to spend his life with *her*. "I'll go wake Master Kim," Senderovsky said.

"Don't bother, we're almost done with the pasta," Masha said. "And we have the *jamón* and olives as a starter. And cheese for dessert."

"So when is our special guest getting here?" Karen asked.

"There's a chance he might not be coming tonight," Senderovsky announced.

The two bemasked women looked at each other from their respective stations. Few knew that Masha subscribed to the worst of the celebrity magazines and kept their tabs open on her computer, even during her online therapy sessions. This was something Senderovsky loved about her, found oddly sexual, even. All the fights they had had about bringing people up from the infected city had ended with Senderovsky flicking out his trump card from the bottom of the deck. "If the great thespian can come, why not others?"

There was a flutter of activity as Nat, still dressed in her Korean school outfit, but minus the tie, made a beeline through the kitchen, hollering about some "form-ah" of love, or so it sounded to Vinod, as she played an only child's version of hide-and-go-seek with herself.

"Hi, Natasha!" Vinod shouted after her.

"She goes by Nat now," Senderovsky said.

"Six feet from the guests, sweetheart!" Masha shouted after her. And in Russian, and in metrics: *"Dva metra."*

"I'm going to set the table," Vinod said.

"Gloves, please," Masha said. She had owned a carton of them, even before the calamity happened. The men snapped on their gloves without comment and started ferrying boxes of recyclable cutlery to the great covered porch. "What's it like to be reunited with the boys?" she asked Karen, who was stirring a prized batch of *pasta nel sacco* the Levin-Senderovskys had secured in Urbino during a rare family vacation abroad.

"I think they both need to eat more," Karen said.

That kind of comment set Masha off. It was too familial. She couldn't imagine herself saying as much to others, even of her own husband. The usual thought came to her mind in relation to the old Gang of Three and their crappy childhoods and screaming, needling mothers and fist-happy fathers: Was it Masha's own fault her parents had been so kind to her, so undemanding? Also, Masha realized, since her own sister had died from the same illness that had spared Vinod (though Inna had been a *non*smoker, not that the universe gave a damn), she had been irked by Karen playing the faux older sister to her husband and his friend. Every November, for example, Senderovsky forgot to congratulate Vinod on his birthday, and every November Karen reminded him.

"I think he still loves you," she said to Karen carelessly.

"Loves me?" Karen said. "I don't think Vinod is that predictable." But she thought it would be fine if he did. And sad if he did not. The last consistent flame in her life extinguished.

VINOD SET OUT eight place mats, each a Masha-prescribed distance apart, around the two outdoor dining tables, seven bearing copyrighted images from the American Folk Art Museum and one depicting seven Asian boys dressed for a prom in eternity. He set a child's neon spoon and fork on top of that one.

A covered gallery ran from the main house to the covered porch, but it was essentially set into the forestscape behind the main house and abutting the half circle of bungalows. Animals scampering about the forest would sometimes look in, stunned by the sudden appearance of the great glowing structure, a lit stove circulating embers in its northwest corner, its cedar and latticework camouflaged by sumac and vine. Many of the vast local properties teemed with hunters, but absent that danger, the hundred or so acres of Senderovsky's property served as a finishing school for the area's younger animals. Coyotes perfected their maniacal howls here, vultures learned to research prey from great capitalist heights, groundhogs taught their children to eat the roots of the expensive Christmas trees which removed the sheep farm from Senderovsky's sight lines as he drank dry fino sherry on his rocking chair. In turn, the porch overlooked a great noisy natural amphitheater. Vinod could hear what must have been wild turkeys gobbling somewhere, though it was hard to say where because of the acoustics, tree frogs and vagabond geese making an apocalyptic symphony, and, from the adjoining property, a sheepish farewell to the day, each deep, old-man bleat a note of protest at a nursing home. (Vinod thought of the sad news from Washington State he had read on the bus.)

"You know what," Senderovsky said to Vinod as he carried in a carton of liquor, finally emptying his trunk. "Apropos of your novel, I think one of the storage units got cleaned out by accident. And your novel may have been in it. I'm so sorry, *bhai.*"

"They can do that?" Vinod asked. "Just clear it out? Did you forget to pay?"

The sadness of his voice was unmistakable. "Probably a bureaucratic error," Senderovsky said. "This country's going to hell. I'll call down first thing in the morning."

"It's really not a priority," Vinod said, but he was hurt nonetheless. He had heard of a technology they were working on in Karen's neck of the woods which would allow you to freeze your entire state of being so that later you could upload your younger self and resume life where you had left off. It sounded no less impossible than anything else that was going on these days. Whatever that novel contained, Vinod thought it just might let him perform a similar operation, maybe even tear through some roadblock in his soul.

The porch door swung open, and the two friends turned to face Ed. He was wearing the same blue cotton jacket in which he had disembarked, chinos, and brogues, as well as a rested look. "Greetings, Vinny," he said. "Karen arrived? Leave it to the Asians to get here on time."

Vinod waved to Ed. The two men were curious friends, the way two dogs set off leash can sometimes run parallel to each other for infinite distances without sharing a glance.

"Where the hell were you?" Senderovsky said to Ed. "We didn't make the *vitello* or Masha's favorite sardines or the sausages or lamb steaks."

"Oh, crap," Ed said. He rubbed his eyes. "Is it too late? What will our Magnificent Amberson eat when he gets here?"

"He might not make it tonight," Vinod said.

"Leaving Senderovsky as the most famous person at the table," Ed said. "How convenient."

"Masha's been saving a *pasta nel sacco* for a special occasion," Senderovsky said. "And Karen is way more famous than I am these days."

"Ah, white truffles." Ed smiled at a glossy memory from Le Marche. "Well, I guess I'll go make Gibsons."

"You'll have to wear a mask in the kitchen," Senderovsky shouted after him.

"Do you remember when he ran me over with a golf cart?" Vinod said after Ed had forgotten to close the porch door behind him, a somersaulting moth making straight for the candlelight.

"I hope you've never forgiven him."

"You know my forgiving ways," Vinod said. "Look." He was pointing to what he thought was a convocation of fireflies on the front lawn, flaring their airplane warning lights low above the grass as if signaling to an advanced intelligence above. But Vinod had terrible vision, and firefly season was still months away. Beyond the vast front lawn and the imagined fireflies lay the curve of the road, its winter-cracked tarmac raked by a pair of approaching high beams.

5

Dᴇᴇ Cᴀᴍᴇʀᴏɴ ᴅʀᴏᴠᴇ like a daughter of the Carolinas, the highways and byways a natural extension of her sandal-clad feet. She sped past Northeast suburbs as if they were forests of short-leaf pine; she could sense the police presence up the road and wore a white-toothed backup smile just in case.

At the mouth of the road leading to Senderovsky's bungalow colony, she had spotted some true bungalows clustered about in peeling primary colors, the propane tanks unceremoniously placed by the front doors, the rows of mailboxes filled with garbage circulars and marked APARTMENT 1 and so on, as if they belonged to city folk and not the rural poor. Flags with obscure patterns of stripes and debatable numbers of stars abounded, some seemingly denying statehood to Alaska or Hawaii, or even Arizona. POSITIVELY NO ENTRY! a sign would scream in handwritten anger. TURN AROUND NOW! And Dee would be reminded of the fierce protection of meager property she had grown up with in a bungalow just like the one she was passing, amid the white poverty that had rightly served as the baseboard of the career she had recently built, the great rolling abusive monotony of it. Senderovsky's own immigrant memoir had had some of that flavor (albeit with jet travel and more hysterical men), which is why she had signed up for his class in the first place back when she was a graduate student down in the city, back when Senderovsky still taught.

"In three hundred feet, turn left. You will have arrived at your final destination," her car announced a bit grandiloquently. But had she?

Other than the Actor, who she guessed would prove to be a goof, she didn't know who was coming, or what to expect. No, wait, the woman who had designed the Tröö Emotions app was supposed to show up, a high-school friend of Senderovsky's, apparently.

She might have to put on an aggressive front, demonstrate her strength. Her essays were the equivalent of a new prisoner coming up to the toughest inmate in the can and slugging them right in the face. She wrote with a disdain for weak-bellied sentiment, mixed in with tough-love observations about the social class that had recently welcomed her into their messy brownstones. Sometimes her prose devolved into regional drawl and what one review called "Y'all-ism." As a corollary, she owned a beautiful pair of 1970s cowgirl boots of a deep red color with rainbow stitching flaring out in sunburst patterns (not that any of her kin had ever worn anything of the sort). Because she was tall and her face angular, her eyes a repository for a deep alien blue, she knew the boots and something simple like a peasant blouse would bring out a host of Pavlovian reactions in a wide cross section of educated East Coast men. All she had to do was open her mouth and confuse the situation. She had always been politically nebulous and often mentioned the fact that when Joan Didion was her age— Didion was Dee's stylistic godmother minus the regionalism—she had been a Nixon supporter in the early sixties. "My animus toward you runs on its own special fuel," she warned the reader at the start of her collection of essays, "so y'all best mind your preconceptions. This pigeon will not be holed."

And yet she was lonely. The virus was just starting to make a dead zone of her section of Brooklyn, leaving nothing but ambulance wails and possibly suicidal trips to the bodega. Her predicament was starting to feel personal. She had friends, but they seemed more interested in reaching out to one another than to her at this difficult time. Perhaps they had never thought of her as trustworthy.

At best, this sojourn would turn out to be an extension of Senderovsky's drunken car wreck of a writing workshop. When she studied under him, or rather next to him, he had been at the height of his powers and popularity. But he had never been intimidating, not to her, at least. Anytime a serious question was asked of a student's work, he would wear an expression that seemed to ask: *What am I doing here? At this fine institution? Me, Senderovsky?*

Also, she had tried Tröö Emotions on a first date with someone whose company she thought she liked, a bearded journalist covering the luxury-watch market, and it had not worked out for either of them. So, most likely, her teacher's friend was another Palo Alto fraud.

"Turn left," her car reminded her, its personality that of a fidgety beagle. It was not an expensive car, but it was hers, no payments, and it symbolized the ability to own a car in the city, to cough up the occasional parking fee. She turned the wheel with her right hand from midnight to seven o'clock. In the glare of her high beams, the tall grass of the front lawn fluttered up and down in the wind like her neighborhood's Jews at prayer. The gravel up the driveway was deeply uneven, and gigantic tree limbs were scattered about, outtakes in a documentary about bleached coral reefs. Was all this—the uncut grass, the dead tree branches—supposed to evoke the devil-may-care attitude of wealthy urban aristocrats who studiously rejected appearances? She had to get this right, to figure out who these people were in case she had to attack them.

The sight of the main house and the bungalows flanking it was more bewildering than intimidating. She had seen a photo of it in the newspaper's real estate section, Senderovsky having been given a chance to call his property his "folly," but the main house looked small and ordinary, and the only thing interesting about these structures— each not that much bigger than their impoverished counterparts down the road—was their unusual number. She could spy several people on the half-lit porch (candles?), which alone provided poetry. Her car beams rummaged through disheveled grass, insects dancing in the light, everything a little mythic and primordially Southern. Dee thought of a kiss in her high school's back lot, rough chapped hands at her bra, the dangerous mouth of an eighteen-year-old alcoholic, a torn windblown banner cheering on the team whose standing-room-only games she had ignored, SHOOOO, DOGGIES!

Senderovsky ran down the cedar stairs to greet her. He was wearing some kind of dress. So that's who he was going to be at this juncture. He had lost a great deal of weight and hair since she had seen him last at a literary party so rich and stuffy that they had both been tapped to provide diversity. She opened her car door and dug a sandal into the gravel. "Hey, Proffy," Dee sang, hugging herself to show how she would have hugged him if this was happening only a few weeks ago.

"Dee Cameron! Hot dog!" Senderovsky sang back, hugging himself, too. "You made it. Yay! And I'm a proffy no more. Just another civilian. They broke my sword, Dreyfus-style."

Dee had two very fine degrees, but she missed out on some of the cultural references of which the older generations were fond. That did not bother her. Even in class, Senderovsky would babble on, nervously, drunkenly—at times, she had to add a third adverb, charmingly—while the students pawed their phones beneath the giant conference table. "I brought an Armagnac," she said.

"Ooh la la!"

"I remember how you quaffed that shit down in class."

He grabbed her bags and put them down right away. His next hernia was just around the corner.

"Sorry, I overpacked," she said. "Girls' stuff. Let me help."

"No, no, no." Senderovsky grunted away. "Now what was that girls' school called? Miss Porter's. Well, call me *Mister* Porter." Again, Dee knew not what he was talking about, European or mid-Atlantic stuff most likely, but again she laughed as they circled the great yellow porch, the people within still indistinct, but two sets of male eyes clearly following her.

"THAT IS A surprisingly good-looking woman," Ed said.

"I can't see well in the dark," Vinod said.

SHE HAD BEEN placed in what the newspaper article had described as "the Writer's Cottage." The ordinariness of Senderovsky's projection of the "writing life" broke her heart. There were, she counted, seven antique typewriters and possibly one more in the bathroom. She could picture her former teacher piling the last Underwood on the blond-wood shelf next to the poster of a young Joan Didion—he was, to his credit, the first instructor who had given her a copy of Didion's *White Album*—and thinking, There. Everything's in its place now.

"This is the smallest cottage, but it's also the coziest," Senderovsky was saying.

"It's like a garret in the woods," Dee said, remembering a word he had repeated often in class.

"Exactly!" Senderovsky cried. That minor detonation inspired both of them to step apart. Senderovsky thought he could smell perfume, but maybe it was a floral shampoo. It had been almost two decades since he had pursued anyone, and during the official wooing of Masha he had never really cataloged his future wife's smells. She smelled, from the start, like home (a tragic beginning, he now realized).

"I'll let you freshen up, and then we'll go meet the gang," Senderovsky said.

"I'll walk up with you," Dee said. "Just gonna pee."

Senderovsky sat on the tiny bed—in his recounting, none of his guests had ever made love on it, those monkish writers—and listened to the sound of a muffled but hearty stream coming from the bathroom. He was excited by the day's many chapters, but already growing tired before the main event of dinner and the uncertainty of the Actor's arrival, and, hence, of everything else in his life. *Student peeing,* he thought to himself, not lasciviously, but filing it away for some possible future reference.

Dee wondered if she should wash her hands before wiping *and* after, but decided to be incautious and washed only when she was done. Senderovsky heard the sound of a young woman flushing a toilet and remembered that this had once had its significance. Dee read the framed quote next to the rusted antique mirror husband and wife had bought for nothing in the town across the river.

LOVE TAKES OFF MASKS THAT WE FEAR WE CANNOT LIVE WITH-OUT AND KNOW WE CANNOT LIVE WITHIN.—JAMES BALDWIN

"Hey," she shouted to Senderovsky over the sound of hands being washed, "did you just have that Baldwin quote framed in the last couple of weeks?"

"No!" Senderovsky called out. "We've had it forever. A happy coincidence!"

WHEN THEY GOT up to the porch, everyone was seated in their jackets and sweaters at a healthy remove from one another, as if they were organized criminals or dignitaries at the League of Nations. Senderovsky and his wife and daughter were clustered together, Masha cutting a slice of Spanish ham for a fidgety Nat on her lap. Dee counted four Asians among seven people, an instant outnumbering. The Asian woman was the important one, the East Asian man importantly dressed. No one was particularly ugly or attractive. She didn't mean anything by this census, Dee told herself, she was just processing.

That morning, she had run through their social accounts. The Actor's page was like a temple built by the sweat and labor of his fans. Karen didn't have one, which, given her controversial standing in the world of technology, was surprising. Sasha's social accounts she already followed; they usually constituted a drunk nightly cry for help and a sober morning plea for relevancy. His wife didn't have one as far as she could tell. She had never heard of Vinod.

Senderovsky was introducing her as his favorite student and a great success. Everyone was waving at her from across a distance, even Vinod, who was pouring out glasses of inky red wine with the prophylactic aid of an oven mitt. When her former teacher's soliloquy was over, no one knew what to say to the newcomer. "Y'all look so cozy in the candlelight," Dee said, leaning into her usual Southern repertoire. Ed smiled at her. Or, rather, intensified his smile, his right hand hovering in the vicinity of his ear.

"Vinod is going to get cold," Masha said. "Someone should start a fire."

"I'm fine," Vinod said. "And you can't catch a cold from the cold."

"Yes, that's an old wives' tale," Senderovsky said. "Can one still say that?"

"One can," Dee said.

"Vin, I can see your goosebumps from here," Karen said.

" 'Goosebumps' is a funny word!" Nat shouted.

"It is, honey, but let's say it quietly," Masha said. "Seriously, some-one should light the stove. Maybe a manly man?"

"I'll do it," Ed found himself saying, his eyes still on the newcomer in her skinny jeans and fleece. He rushed over to the stove and began to fuss with it. He had done this so many times before, on so many different porches, during so many different twilights, but this time was different. His fingers were like lead bars. He had abandoned a tray of Gibsons, which it turned out nobody wanted and which he would likely have to drink himself. "Help yourself to a Gibson, Dee," he shouted to the young essayist, the syllables thick and courtly in his mouth.

He wondered what was wrong with him.

"Thanks," Dee said, letting the vermouth flood her mouth, along with the tiny pop of the tipsy cocktail onion. "They're excellent!"

"What was Sasha like as a teacher?" Karen asked.

"We called it 'The Sasha Senderovsky Show.' I nearly peed in my pants every time."

"She said *'peed'*!" Nat shouted, spitting out little pieces of ham.

"Cover your mouth," her mother said.

"That *is* funny, sweet pea," Dee said to her. And to Masha: "Are we allowed to use that word?" The mother nodded unconvincingly.

"My daughter's very spirited," Senderovsky said. "But she's actu-ally pretty well behaved tonight, because it's fun to have guests, right?"

Nat didn't say anything, just giggled to herself, mouth full of ham. Precocity notwithstanding, she loved the bathroom humor her par-ents found unserious. *Peed.*

Vinod noticed Karen looking at the little girl, ignoring the rest of the table. Karen was thinking that Masha had put her in the larger two-room family bungalow as a way to highlight the fact that she had no children and now most likely never would. (As Leon had put it ever so dramatically during their penultimate fight on a private jet headed from nowhere to nowhere: "Thank God for small mercies.

You as a mother . . .") Or perhaps Senderovsky had put her there because she was now more important and deserved more space. The last time, she had been placed in a small strange room with a bunch of creepy lullabies scribbled over the walls. Now, six feet away from her, Nat was whispering the word "peed" over and over in a concentrated monotone as she built a poor man's A-frame house out of chunks of baguette. Karen wanted the girl to sit on her lap, wanted to run her hands through the bobbed black hair of memory. She had been estranged from her younger sister even before Tröö Emotions had "scaled," and did not even know where Evelyn was at this time or whether she was safe.

She remembered now that Masha had lost her younger sister. To cancer, was it? She looked across the porch meaningfully but without modulation, a look Masha misinterpreted as anger instead of sorrow. What does *she* have to be angry about, Masha thought.

"How's it going with that fire?" Masha shouted to Ed.

"No luck yet. The kindling's gotten wet." Ed glanced at Dee, who was sucking on an oblong Greek olive.

"A bad dancer is bothered by his balls," Senderovsky shouted to Ed.

"Let's go help him," Vinod said to Senderovsky.

"You, sit!" Karen said, but Vinod rebelled.

All the men fussed over the woodstove now, Ed and Sasha ignoring the distancing rules, but none of them really knew how to light it, not even the landowner himself.

Finally, Masha sighed and got up. "Please move over," she said, taking the poker from her husband. When the fire had been lit (a draft had to be opened to ensure success), Senderovsky realized Masha had given Vinod his exact place at the table so he could be closer to the warmth of the fire, his sallow face lit by a biblical glow.

"Masha's awesome," Ed said to Dee after he had retaken his place behind his Gibson.

"You probably laid the groundwork," Dee said.

There was a term Ed and Senderovsky came up with a long time ago in the city, after a drunken May Day spent on a Fifth Avenue rooftop: sundress weather. The air was still brutally cold, but, to Ed, tall, slender Dee was the essence of sundress weather. He wondered how many inches she had on him, even in flats.

"This is not *jamón serrano,*" Senderovsky was saying after his second glass of wine at the other end of the table, "this is *jamón* Montaño."

"What makes it different, Proffy?" Dee asked. She was hardly one for diminutives, but Russians seemed to appreciate them.

"For one thing, it's a thicker cut," Ed explained. He had failed to notice his right hand cupping his right ear as he spoke to her, but the rest of his friends did.

"Do you travel a lot?" Dee asked him, speaking louder, because his ear cupping seemed to indicate he had trouble hearing her.

"Oh, here and there."

"Once this is over, I'm going to hit the road myself."

Ed pictured something very specific: a cheap, rumpled room in Chania, on Crete, the sole window filled by a large many-domed mosque jutting out of the harbor, its optical white peeled clean by the sea, placed like a squid egg alongside a colorful devil-may-care row of Christian tavernas. And at the desk (because the single room of their minimal lodgings would still have a desk), this woman, Dee, was putting on a silver necklace he had bought her back in Athens, at the airport's satellite terminal, it must be confessed, because even though he tried to talk her out of it—"If you don't find anything better on the island, which, I swear, you will, we'll get it on the way back"—her mind was made up, and now the silver of the pendant glowed against the sunburn of her skin. "I'm going to put some aloe on you," the phantom Ed said to make-believe Dee. He had thought of every eventuality.

Ear-cupped Ed was about to launch into a dense and heartfelt soliloquy on the subject of journeys, when Senderovsky noisily pulled back his rustic chair and stood before the diners with his dressing gown and his glass of red.

"Oh, no," Karen said. "He's going to speak."

"Daddy used to be a teacher before I was born!" Nat said.

"That's right, and I was his student," Dee said.

"I think a really dumb person could learn a lot from Daddy!" Nat said.

Everyone laughed, Senderovsky wondering if the remark colored his daughter as too strange or too clever. "Even though we're technically outside, we use our inside voice," Masha instructed Nat. "And we think before we speak"—in Russian—"so that we don't hurt people's feelings."

Sasha surveyed his guests. Ed was studiously not looking at Dee. Dee was looking at Senderovsky as if her grade depended on it. Masha was breathing along with the girl on her lap, hoping, as ever, to meld her mind with her daughter's. Karen was sticking out her tongue at Senderovsky, which made Nat laugh, which made Karen laugh more.

Karen only ever dressed like she had just gotten out of a time machine, today a Salvation Army bateau shirt and thin-wale corduroys. (She had taken off her Bundeswehr army jacket because of the stove's warmth, or maybe Vinod's.) She looked better when she left the city, calmer. They all did.

"My dear ones," he said. "Welcome to the House of People's Friendship, as we used to call it back in the Union of Soviets. This is a scary time." Masha pointed to Nat and pressed a finger to her lips. He had forgotten his daughter's generalized anxiety disorder, though she was now mostly busy playing marbles with her olive pits and not really listening to him. "A scary time, but also a *fun* time," Senderovsky amended. "We have abandoned our city for each other's company, and we may feel guilty for leaving people behind who may get very sick." Again, Masha pointed to their daughter and her behavioral profile. "But not *too* guilty and not *too* sick, because we're all good people and we're here to keep each other *safe*. Now, I've known each of you . . ."

Senderovsky may have uttered some still-more-passionate sentences here and he may have felt tears building along his lower eyelids as he did so, but no one heard his words or felt stirred by the hot liquid sluicing gently from his orbs.

A tiny red car was crunching up the gravel. It stopped at the toppled branches, as if examining them, critically, and then continued along. Senderovsky thought it looked like the little vehicles that had been given out to invalids of the Great Patriotic War. Ed correctly surmised it was a Lancia.

"It's him," Masha said.

"Who?" Nat asked.

But no one answered.

6

THE ACTOR STEPPED out of the car. He was immediately aware of an audience readying their lorgnettes. He was in no mood. The scenic drive had been endless, and most of it had been spent arguing with his girlfriend on the phone. She had been unusually Glaswegian, so it was hard to tell exactly what she was saying, but the fight appeared to be about the timing of the Actor's visit to the countryside, and now it had lodged itself firmly in a space usually reserved for nasal headaches. Senderovsky was rushing toward him in what looked like Hasidic dress, his lips wine purple, the remaining tufts of his untrimmed hair leaning oddly to the side like a stegosaurus at rest. "You're here!" he said to the last of his guests. "I was so worried you wouldn't come. Because of your many messages." The Actor tilted his head and looked far away as if to say: Messages? There were messages? "I was just delivering a toast, but now I'll start all over again. But first, we go to your bungalow, no?"

"You tell me." Senderovsky's smile melted in the heat of his guest's indifference.

"Is that all your luggage?" the landowner asked. The Actor had slung a duffel bag inscribed with the name of a California winery and resort Ed despised.

"Only here for a few days."

"Of course, of course." They went up the path past the silent porch with its many eyes. Masha could hear Senderovsky's obedient blather and it made her sad. "The idea behind this whole property, the mad idea, I should say, was to create the bungalows on an even plane with the main house. The bungalows are between five hundred and eight hundred square feet each, the largest one meant to accommodate a small family, and the main house has bedroom quarters of about the same space meant for three people, myself, my wife, and my daughter. You'll get to meet them in a second, my wife is a huge fan. In addition, there's a kitchen, dining room, and living room with a grand piano that all residents can share. (I believe I've heard you play onstage.) While we're here there are no social ranks. Everything's a bit communitarian. Add to the number of people staying at any one time one other entity, which is our little society as a whole. When I was a child my happiest memories were of a bungalow colony on the other side of the river catering to Russian immigrants, cheap but tidy lodgings, wonderful people, such warmth! And here we are."

They were standing at the entrance of a bungalow, adorned by the same gray stucco as the main house. A motion sensor that always ignored Senderovsky snapped to attention immediately as the Actor neared, a halogen light spotlighting him and only him. "Although I must confess," Senderovsky continued, "that while all bungalows were created equal, this one may be my favorite. And my wife's, too. You'll see why in a minute."

He opened the door and turned on a light. The Actor could not see why. Maybe it had not been a minute. The walls were covered by rough-edged, handyman-made bookshelves, which were filled with volumes, some of them old and foreign. There were framed, fussy drawings and photographs of a city he did not recognize (Copenhagen, could it be?), a massive drawbridge accepting a carnivalesque cruise ship, an array of homunculi in baseball caps waving from its deck, an orange castle framed by two frozen canals and groaning under a blanket of snow no one had asked for, a map of a subway system written in an unfamiliar alphabet, the intersection of its green, red, blue, and purple branches forming the occasional parallelogram or backward 4.

"This is the Petersburg Bungalow," Senderovsky announced. "The city where my wife and I were born!"

"Huh," the Actor said. "Is one of these books *Crime and Punishment*?"

"That one!" Senderovsky said, stabbing a Cyrillic spine with his forefinger. "And a translation is right here, next to your bed. You are, of course, welcome to read anything you like. Make a little picnic if you wish and sit in the meadow, reading. I can think of nothing better."

The Actor smiled with his eyes. He was about to tell Senderovsky some unhappy news, and suddenly felt a syringe's worth of compassion for the man whose book he had been adapting for the last half-dozen years. Senderovsky—or "Return to Sender," as he and Elspeth had nicknamed him after they had rejected so many of his drafts—sounded different than he did back in the city or in Los Angeles. The Actor did not realize that the bilingual nature of time spent with his wife and daughter inspired in him a different soundtrack.

Meanwhile, Senderovsky enjoyed the Actor's smile and the way his presence inhabited the five hundred square feet of the Petersburg Bungalow. Back in elementary school, a dreadful place for the likes of short, awkward Senderovsky, students collected glossy informational cards with pictures of animals on them. The most desired card featured a puma resting its head atop its paws, white-furred mouth and yellow eyes conveying the height of animal thought and repose. If you flipped the card over, the puma could be seen licking its lips after a successful kill, its tongue reaching up as far as its nose, next to a series of statistics that demonstrated how fast the puma was, how sentient, how beautiful and feared. Time spent with the Actor, with those thoughtful eyes and white mouth, always brought that glossy puma card to mind.

The vineyard duffel bag fell on the floor with a surprising thud. "Listen," the Actor said, "there's something I have to tell you. I read the latest script. I don't want to waste any more of your time. I think it's best if we scrap what we have and start fresh."

"From the beginning?" Senderovsky could feel his dressing gown come open, the breast modestly covering his heart open for the Actor to see, especially its small pink capsule of a nipple. "But I thought you said we almost had it this time."

"I've finally diagnosed it," the Actor said. "I took it apart at the joints. The tone is all wrong for a pilot. We can't lead with humor. We have to build to it over the course of the first three seasons."

"But the network expects—"

"I'm not interested in the network. They work for us. They answer to us."

This, Senderovsky thought, was a profound misunderstanding of the situation.

"I'm going to take a whiz," the Actor said. For the second time that night, Senderovsky heard loud urination, a deep country toilet bowl supplying the acoustics of a cathedral. He looked at the framed metro map of a city once called Leningrad. He had not known Masha during the first seven years of his life spent in that city, nor did she know him through her eleven, but they were connected by the all-important blue line, officially known as M2. Senderovsky's metro station, Elektrosila, literally "Electric Power," was found deep in the charmless and tough-nosed southern part of the city (one of its neighborhoods would give the country its current president for life), while Masha's station was Petrogradskaya in the city's Art Nouveau north, the kind of place which might lead to someone saying, "There goes a real Petrogradsky intellectual in his slippers and dressing gown."

Needless to say, she grew up with the parents Senderovsky could only dream of, the kind that did not watch the state television of their adopted land with its screaming chyrons and grim blond hosts and unimaginative, murderous lies. Masha loved her parents, loved the language of her parents, and wanted Natasha to know the "gift" of her country's culture. But Senderovsky, despite his Petrogradsky affectations, was still the man from Elektrosila. He knew that he had been born in a sick country, a country now intent on spreading its disease to others through the social media channels and under the cover of night—its true gift of the moment. He knew that no matter Masha's intentions, Nat, the wild Harbin child living under their roof, would have no room for fermented kvass and red caviar and butter sandwiches and the poetics of Joseph Brodsky and bungalows such as this one.

And he knew now that the pilot script would never get done. And a check in Los Angeles would never get written. And months later, a year at most, the Sasha Senderovsky Bungalow Colony would close its doors, much like the scores of Russian bungalow colonies across the river, much like the one where he had met his beloved during Masha's first year in this country, fresh off the blue line of the Leningrad metro, her auburn hair still tied back as if by a white school uniform *bant*.

What could he do? How could he please the Actor? How could he keep his strange dream alive?

On the porch, they had been talking loudly about his films, his girlfriend of the moment and girlfriends past, the radiance of his eyes, the cut of his suits, his presence at the award shows (Masha even knew which Italian firm had supplied his shoes for the last one), and then they had quieted abruptly as he climbed the steps to the porch, his Russian Sancho Panza at his side. "Hi," the Actor said, and waved his hand as if from a departing *Queen Mary*.

Introductions were made. Time started to move slower for everyone but Nat. Having sensed a change in mood, the importance of the new guest, she scrambled off her mother's lap and started to run around the porch screaming, "She said she nearly peed in her pants! She said she nearly peed in her pants!"

"You have such a cute kid," the Actor said to Karen and Ed.

"Oh, snap!" Dee said.

The porch was hushed. Nat had stopped running. "No, *these* are my parents," she said, pointing out her non-Asian mother and father. "They're called Sasha and Masha."

"D'oh," the Actor said. He planted his face deep into his palm so loudly it must have hurt. Everyone laughed. "Please don't report me," he said.

Vinod mimed typing into his phone: "Updating feed . . . now!"

"Anyway," he said to Masha, "you have a lovely son."

"Actually," Masha began, but Sasha moved over and put his arms over her shoulders.

"Thank you for coming," he said. "Most of us are old friends here, but through your body of work we feel like we already know you. And even if you are not ready to be our friend, we will be yours."

The Actor nodded: that sounded accurate enough. He placed himself at the end of one of the tables, with Dee at one side and Ed farther along. He was offered a glass of red by Vinod, but he said he did not partake. "Drinking messes up my sleep." His presence, on the other hand, made everyone else drink with nervous abandon. Ed fiddled with the handsome red radio until it began spouting sophisticated Ethiopian jazz. The mood was tense and heroic at once.

Sheep started bleating from one property over. "I'm not a nature boy," the Actor said, "but shouldn't they be asleep?"

"We've woken them up with our loud music," Nat shouted.

"And maybe your shouting," Masha said.

"Did you know they're Border Leicester sheep?" Nat said to the Actor, coming much closer than was allowed. He didn't flinch, but her mother ran over and pulled her back. "Their wool is merino like my birthday bracelet"—she held the bracelet up for the Actor to inspect—"but it's longer and broad-crimped, so it's usually spun into yarn."

"You're such a smart kid," Karen said to her. "You should have heard her singing Korean pop songs to the sheep earlier."

"I love BTS!" Nat shouted. The Actor assumed that was the name of a band, and also that maybe the boy was not entirely a boy, at least not yet. "I'm part of the BTS ARMY. That stands for Adorable Representative MC for Youth."

"Maybe she can play us something later on the piano," Masha said. "She's learning the Suzuki Method."

"The Suzuki?" Ed said. "I never even learned the Hyundai Sonata."

The immigrants laughed. "Oh, Ed," Karen said.

Dee summoned a smile. She was missing more references than usual. White ignorant folk like me, she thought, we're the immigrants today. She looked at the Actor, who also shrugged.

"So," Masha said to the Actor, "I understand you're half Irish but also a quarter Turkish?"

"This missing quarter must be Gujarati," Vinod said. "How else does one become so handsome?"

"You know a lot about me," the Actor said to Masha.

"It's just that we have some salted Turkish air-cured beef in the pantry," Masha said. "*Basturma*. We eat it in Russia, too, because of the sizable Armenian population." She had spent half an hour trying to pick out what to wear for the Actor's arrival, an amount of time she had not spent with clothes since her twenties, finally settling on a white sail of a dress that she thought negated her as best as it could.

The Actor admired her eyes. How many decades had she spent with Senderovsky? He tried to imagine what that would cost in beauty. "I think I remember something like that from my grandma. And a kind of flatbread."

"*Lahmacun.*"

He snapped his fingers. "Bingo." Everyone laughed.

"I thought we were an international table," Ed said, "but our latest guest contains multitudes. Suck it, Walt Whitman."

"Suck it, suck it, suck it!" Nat yelled, her affect too aggressively boyish to Masha's ears. The girl had wanted to be Nate at first, but Masha convinced her that Nat, a shortening of her given name, was cooler. Already Ada Horowitz in her class had declared themselves nonbinary, but their father was the second-richest private equity manager in the city. And Ada was a class sweetheart, perfectly social in every way, unburdened by Nat's vocabulary and anxiety, anxiety that Masha's professional experience taught her would one day segue into depression. Masha knew how difficult childhood had been for her husband. Sometimes she would look at her daughter, lost in a BTS monologue or an unbidden discussion of Leicester sheep, and, with her own anxieties and Soviet residue at full pitch, simply think: Will anybody love my child as much as I do?

"I guess I'm the only real cracker here," Dee was saying. The Actor noticed her for the first time. She reminded him of a personal assistant he had had way back when, a lanky Texan who always spoke out of turn and didn't last long in the industry. Senderovsky gave a long-winded explanation of why Dee was important, mentioning a prestigious award she had just been given, the Young Literary Lion. (I have a lion and a puma at my table, Senderovsky thought.)

"I'll have to check it out," the Actor said. "I'm always looking for interesting things to adapt. At least once I'm done with Sasha's book. By which point I might be doing ads for the AARP."

Laughter proved trickier now, but it was still granted, with Senderovsky himself cackling at length, a fist curled under the table for his own personal consumption. The Actor was fond of humor at the expense of others. Senderovsky found this a shortcoming. He had only seen a few films starring his master. (He was not an avid film-goer; slow novelistic television was his favorite medium.) The Actor could emulate flawed creatures, his gifts were inestimable, he could cry at will at a version of himself that only partly existed, but he could never quite understand his own flaws. He was, in a sense, profoundly without Jesus. Like a small damaged atomic reactor he could generate his own array of "feelings," which he released into the air as background gamma. Everyone at the table except Senderovsky, everyone on the planet, in fact, wanted a dose.

Senderovsky checked back into the conversation. "There have been studies done about the friendships that form at the elementary and high-school level between four groups in particular," Vinod was saying in his best former adjunct professor voice. "Koreans, Gujaratis, West Africans, and Soviet Jews. Adolescents from these groups tend to form an unusual bond, although we don't know precisely why."

"A cool Nigerian girl would have been nice for our gang," Karen said. "Or guy."

"They came a little after our generation," Vinod said.

"So the three of you met in high school?" the Actor asked.

"Freshman year," Vinod said.

"I have almost no white friends," Senderovsky said. And, he wanted to proudly add, my daughter is probably gender fluid.

"Thank you, Non Sequitur Man," Ed said.

Masha had started bringing out the *pasta nel sacco* in her blue disposable gloves. The pasta was gummy, Senderovsky thought, certainly not al dente, and the white truffles, though tasty, made a bit of a mush. The landowner himself barely knew how to boil water.

"You should have seen these two when I met them," Karen was saying apropos of Senderovsky and Vinod. "The *things* they wore. I would lecture them all the time. 'When you guys dress the way you want to dress and you go to parties, people just think you're weird. When you dress like *I* tell you to dress, people think you're charming. Yeah, I know, it's a freaking shallow town!'"

"How did they dress?" Dee asked, between mouthfuls of pasta she thought delicious. "Give us some highlights."

"Yeah, how did they dress?" Nat sang out.

"Well, your *daddy* here wore puka shells!"

Everyone laughed, including Nat, who did not know what puka shells were. Masha checked this off as appropriate social behavior—the need to fit in.

"I can picture it all too well," the Actor said.

"And Vinny here was super into Teva active sandals."

"Oh," Masha said. "I actually saw a box of those up in the attic. Maybe they're yours."

Senderovsky and Vinod glanced at each other. "I thought that box was in storage," Senderovsky said. He nearly looked down at his own feet to hide his expression, thought that would be too damning, and instead turned to a tree between the bungalows in which a mysterious bird wearing yellow shoulder pads slumbered.

"What storage?" Masha asked.

"I rented a storage space down in the city."

Senderovsky was not a good liar, but his wife still wanted to believe him. Vinod, despite being brought up by his parents to be an apprehensive immigrant, was not suspicious by nature.

"Why would you do that?" Masha asked. "We have so much room up here."

"We should look through all that old stuff," Karen said. "I just found some pictures of us in my old Crown Heights place that are hi-*lar*-ious."

"Karen is our archivist," Vinod said. "Which is crazy when you think about it, given her schedule."

"What do you do?" the Actor asked Karen. He was being friendly. Participating. No one could call him disinterested. He swept back some of his hair just in case.

"She works in tech!" Nat shouted. "Her company has a licensing deal with BTS. Instead of 'Fake Love' they sing 'Real Love.' I just looked it up."

"Is that right?" the Actor said, perking up.

"She came up with the number one app of last year," Vinod said, as boastfully as if he was talking of his parent or his child. "Have you tried Tröö Emotions?"

"That's huge!" The Actor looked at Karen across the table with a kind of faux-bewildered "What are *we* two doing in this place?" smile. "My girlfriend wanted me to do that with her. I had to shoot her down."

"Too scared?" Karen asked.

"How much more in love can we be?" the Actor said.

"Aww," Masha said, misinterpreting his tone.

"I'm not even sure how it works," the Actor said.

"It doesn't always work," Karen said. "We're being sued by a lot of unhappy campers. Even though the download is free." She had failed to mention the spouses who lost their partners to the app and were now part of another class action suit.

"You take a photo looking into someone else's eyes?" the Actor asked.

"And *blam*!" Ed said. "You're both in love."

"Sometimes," Karen said.

"How does someone even come up with that?" the Actor wondered, throwing up his hands.

"Karen was just tooling around on her computer," Senderovsky said.

"Please never say 'tooling around,'" Karen said.

"She was just tooling around and she came up with it."

The Actor was still amazed by his dining companion. "But what's the *impetus* for even *envisioning* something like that?" he asked. "Were you cast as Puck in a high-school version of *A Midsummer Night's Dream*?"

"Let's just say that somebody didn't get any love as a child," Ed said. He paused dramatically. "And that boy was me."

Dee laughed. Ed noted the outsize form of her incisors. He had dated a girl with teeth like that in Italy, almost a foot taller than he was. She would bundle him up in her arms and carry an inert Ed around the streets of Bologna as part of a performance art piece she called *La Pietà Mobile*. This was almost thirty years ago. *A generation ago,* thought Ed. Most of the weirdness and wildness of the world had been snuffed out, even before the virus. Maybe some of it could come back now.

"You should try it," Dee said to the Actor.

"Me? With who? Or is it 'with whom'?" He looked to Senderovsky, who shrugged. Grammar was not his specialty. He only knew English by sight, like a pilot flying without the aid of instruments.

"You two should try it," Vinod said of Dee and the Actor. "It'll be cute."

"Can't we have one dinner without whipping out our phones?" Ed said.

Karen noticed the tone of his voice and looked at him and Dee and then back again, surprised. Ed never had feelings. "Or you guys can try it," she said, pointing to Dee and Ed. "You're sitting next to each other already."

"I don't think we can perform this experiment given the distancing rules," Masha said.

"That much is Tröö," Ed said.

"You must get so sick of that," Dee said to Karen.

"Although if Dee's game, I'm willing to take the chance," Ed said.

"Masha has a point re distancing," Karen said. "It's actually getting us into trouble now that things are locking down. We're offering a disclaimer: for domestic use only."

"I'm seriously game to try it," the Actor said. He looked around. "I mean everything is so goddamn boring these days. And we've got the creator right here with us. Dee, what do you say? What's the worst that can happen?"

"Fine with me," Dee said. "I don't fall in love, one way or another."

"That's accurate," Senderovsky said. "Everyone in the writing program was completely taken with Dee, but she just led them on."

Dee handed her phone to Karen, then got up and walked over to the Actor; for some reason it couldn't have been the other way around. "They're only doing this once and only for a second," Masha said to Nat. "Otherwise they'll keep their distance."

"Not if the app works," Ed said.

The Actor was about a head taller than Dee. He was wearing a denim jacket that seemed off-brand but was not. With her sporty fleece and deep-set blue eyes, Senderovsky thought, the two of them looked like a going concern, her sturdy Anglo features, his many ethnicities, one genuinely awkward smile and one a careful projection of awkwardness. "So what do we do?" the Actor said.

"Don't breathe on each other," Masha cautioned.

"Turn your heads about thirty degrees," Karen said from her director's chair. "And then just look into each other's eyes."

"Like we're in love?" Dee asked.

"That's the algorithm's job."

Dee looked up at the handsome man next to her. They could have been meeting at their favorite bar on Canal Street, which, like the porch, was also candlelit and bathed in Ethiopian jazz. He could have been just another especially lovely stranger straggling through a lifetime of lovely strangers. "Hi," she said.

"Hello," the Actor said. He could smell the heaviness of butter and parmesan on her breath and wondered if that meant they were too close, too viral. He pictured his own voluminous death notices. His expression filled out with sorrow that Dee mistook for desire.

"Say 'cheese'!" Nat shouted while Karen took the photo of them.

"What's happening now?" the Actor asked.

"It's formatting," Karen said. "Give it a sec."

"Remember that movie *Weird Science*?" Senderovsky said to his wife, who was seated next to him, Nat straddling her chair, perched on it like a footman (inability to sit and keep still, Masha noted). "We saw it on a projector back in the old bungalow colony." He added softly in Russian: *Do you remember?* But Masha was staring at Dee's phone along with everyone else. The entire porch was now frozen in oils, a rendering by Goya of a summerhouse outside Madrid full of courtiers and attendants, the expression of each betraying their true nature: flustered, frustrated, imperious, hopeful, desirous, desired.

"There," Karen said. She handed the phone back to Dee.

Dee looked at the enhanced photo. They did look happy in the candlelight, happy like old friends who hadn't seen each other in a while, happy like the trio of Senderovsky, Karen, and the Indian guy. The Actor was goofy, as she suspected, a beautiful goofy mop top of a man. But the photo seemed like nothing more than a prized social media artifact. She breathed out in relief, feeling safe. Nothing would stray her from the steady lonely course of her life.

"Tröö love?" Ed asked, his hand firmly around the soft lobe of his ear.

"I'm going to need a little more time to process it," Dee said.

"It's not instantaneous," Karen said.

"Uh-oh. I'm calling the Better Business Bureau," the Actor said.

"Maybe she was in love with you already," Senderovsky said. Masha looked at him and shook her head, sadly. *This is my livelihood,* he wanted to tell her. Dee went around the table, keeping her distance but thrusting the phone into her companions' vision. A polite consensus was forming. They were very cute together. They looked like a couple. They looked like they *could* be in love. This is what relative youth looked like. (The Actor was ten years older than Dee, but still younger than Senderovsky and his compatriots.) *Aww.*

"Here goes," Dee said as she held the phone out in front of the Actor.

"Should I be getting the prenup ready?" the Actor said. Masha groaned inwardly.

"Look at the eyes," Karen said. The Actor took that to mean Dee's eyes and he spent a few seconds examining them. Her eyes were flirty, mischievous, perhaps trying to conceal a kind of spite. She was trying to hold back, the Actor thought, trying to maintain a distance from his charms, which was in itself a compliment. He was ready to say something polite.

But then he looked at his own eyes. At the other end of the table Karen watched his expression change. His eyes in the enhanced photo were not his. They were not his photogenic eyes. They were not his bedroom eyes. They did not belong to Getty Images. They did not belong to his unimagined self. Maybe it was Senderovsky's earlier remark, but he thought of the movies of the 1980s, he thought of an extraterrestrial's elucidating touch, the flood of light and comprehension. This smiling man in front of him was who he needed to be, the final version, the finished version, and this woman, holding the phone in front of him, with her defiant strawberry cowlick and her unplucked brows, was who allowed him to ascend to that stage. He focused on his eyes the way he would focus on his lines. The Method was a site plan, but nobody knew how or why a role came together the way it did.

Karen now recalled that her pitch deck for Tröö Emotions had started with a photo of the Actor and the Norse royal he was dating at the time. Although he had never been a brand ambassador, he had always epitomized the broad strokes of the algorithm.

"Well?" someone was saying.

"Nice, very nice," the Actor said, and laughed. Others laughed with him. Dee laughed. But Karen knew that tone.

"Ruh-roh," she said quietly, her distance from others allowing the words to pass unheard, though Ed read her lips anyway.

Dee walked back to her seat once more. "It's a fun app," she said to Karen. "Whether it works or not, it makes you think about what people want from each other."

"That's right," the Actor said, still in his fugue. He looked over to Dee at the other end of the table, her body a blot of green and orange heat amid the blackness of his night vision. "If you don't mind," he said to her, "could you send me that photo?"

7

ALCOHOL IS THE gift of any narration, and any writer thrills to the *thwop* of a corkscrew being pulled. Now the protagonists will reveal themselves. Now there will be unchecked laughter and love. Now the principals will flirt and be cruelly rebuffed, and the loveless will sigh into their cups and try to remember what it was like to be wanted.

An hour later, every adult but the Actor and Masha properly drunk, Senderovsky found another bottle of *primitivo* between his legs as he struggled to get it open. "That can't possibly be safe!" drunk Vinod was shouting.

"My thighs don't have the virus!" Senderovsky shouted back.

"Doctor?" Vinod asked Masha. "Your professional opinion?"

"That would be a difficult route of transmission. Though we don't know yet what's possible." She noticed the stove sputtering in the corner, ready for a strong hand, which would have to be her own.

"I saw this on the platform of your train station," Ed was saying, holding up his phone for others to lean in and look, one at a time. It was a photograph of a sticker in red, white, and blue featuring some kind of extraterrestrial iconography, a deconstructed swastika entrapping the segments of a hissing snake and the words PATRIOTIC DE-FENSE LEAGUE. SLEGS BLANKES.

Senderovsky and Masha both thought of the many tattoos gracing the ankles of their handyman. "I've seen stuff like that around here and it's frightening," Masha said. "Down by the main road, someone has a flag of an eagle sitting on top of a globe. And the globe has an anchor running through it."

"I have three uncles in that organization," Dee said.

"The Patriotic Defense League?" Masha asked. "How scary!"

"No, the US Marines."

"Oh," Masha said.

"You go, girl," drunk Ed said to Dee. "You tell 'em! Down with the ruling elites!"

"Just so you know," Karen said, "Ed is the scion of a chaebol family."

"Chaebol light," Ed said. "And I'm the black sheep of the family. They got me on a tight leash these days."

"When using a foreign word it might be cool to explain what it is, or some of us might look stupid," Dee said.

"That's right," the Actor said. He looked at Dee in a blaze of heterosexuality.

The definition of "chaebol" was patiently explained to Dee by the two Koreans. "But my family doesn't own Samsung or anything," Ed cautioned. He was drunk now; his hand off his ear. A part of him did want Dee to understand that he had means at his disposal. Enough for a decent life, enough for Chania.

Masha was still thinking of the fascist sticker on the platform of the train station, and her unlit Sabbath candles (it was Friday), and her Asian daughter. "What does *slegs blankes* mean?" she asked.

" 'Whites only.' " Ed said. "It's Afrikaans."

"Great," Masha said. "Just great."

"More wine, Proffy!" Dee demanded.

"I'm going to cut you off," Senderovsky said, though he gave her a full pour, while looking at the Actor corner-eyed. He had noticed the way the Actor was staring at Dee and wanted to see where this was going.

Dee bolted down the thick fruity vintage. Ed was quietly selling her his vision of what constituted a memorable journey to Crete, but she seemed to have something else on her mind. She turned to Senderovsky. "You know, instead of building all these cottages or whatever you call them and inviting your friends up, you could just get to know some of the locals instead. I mean they're people, too, right? Ex-Marines and all."

"Right," Ed and the Actor said.

"Well, aren't you a firecracker," Masha said.

"Sasha doesn't really know how to make new friends," Karen said. She gestured at the convivial gathering. "This is all a ruse."

"You should make an app for *him*," Dee said. "Help a brotha out."

"Daaamn," Ed said.

"She was always like this in class," Senderovsky said, "especially after a couple of drinks."

"I hung out with some actual Nazis when we were researching *München am Hudson*," the Actor said.

"That movie was chilling," Masha said.

"'I think they got cum in 'em,'" Dee rapped into her wineglass, "''cause they nuthin' but dicks.'"

Senderovsky and his friends immediately recognized the rap song Dee was appropriating and smiled nostalgically. It had been a staple at the parties Senderovsky and Vinod used to throw in their tight but chaste studio after they graduated from a city college. The Actor had first heard it in high school. Dee must have been, what, seven when it was released? The Actor considered that fact. Her behavior, who she was, came at him like the tides. She was standing up against her former teacher, against the boredom of his kind, the timidity and lack of adventurousness. (Exactly the problems with his endless volleys of revised scripts.) *Look at me!* the Actor yelled in his mind, so loudly the surrounding sounds disappeared, the rustle of naked tree branches, the yip of coyotes catching wind of the awakened fear-pheromone-generating neighborhood sheep. *Why won't you look at me?* If you query, I will answer. If you inquire, I will enlighten. If you want the stroke of my fingers, the pinch of my stubble, the torque of my tongue, I will provide. *But first you must look at me the way I am looking at you!*

Masha had put her hands over Nat's ears. "Okay," she said, "I think it's time someone went to bed."

"I'm sorry, Nat," Dee said. "I shouldn't have used bad language. 'Dicks' is a bad word."

And she knows when to be contrite, the Actor thought. She's in control even when she's hammered.

"That's okay," Senderovsky said. "She'll have to learn about male anatomy sometime, why not tonight? But off to bed you go, *slad-kaya*." Sweet one.

The strength of the howl was unexpected. "No!" Nat yelled, quieting even the coyotes casing the sheep farm's perimeter. "I don't want to go to sleep!" She was running around the porch, getting dangerously close to others. The world was a whirlwind of nice things and unfair things; her head wanted to butt into Mommy's tummy, to ruffle through the beginnings of Daddy's new beard, to pass lightly along Karen's thin-wale corduroys, which she imagined as soft as blah blah blah *Llama Llama Red Pajama,* and why was she too old to read that book anymore? And what happened to their little apartment in the city, and what happened to Dennis the Doorman and the rumpled back of his suit, and what happened to her overlit classroom and the worlds her classmates constructed among themselves, worlds to which she wasn't invited but observed and cataloged from the Elba of her Quiet Mat, and what happened, what happened, what happened? Senderovsky watched his child running, howling, out of control. He did not know her thoughts, but he was registering attention deficit hyperactivity disorder, the borderlands of autism, loss of executive function, pragmatic speech deficits—all the therapists and specialized schools wanted a piece of her, all of them had a novel idea about what was wrong, but the only diagnosis that ever stuck was his and Masha's Ashkenazi one, generalized anxiety disorder. On an impossible order of magnitude. The one dream he had for his child: that she would not suffer an immigrant's humiliations. But even though she did not share in their incestuous gene pool, he could not deliver her from that particular pain.

Masha had caught up to her screaming daughter and now held her in her arms. She spoke authoritatively. "You don't want to go to sleep, do you, Nat?" The therapeutic voice. "This must be very frustrating for you."

"It is!" Nat burbled through her tears. "It's very frustrating."

"What can make you feel better?"

"BTS!"

"No screens right before bedtime. How about a prairie dog kiss?"

Karen watched the scene wistfully. She could feel the child's dry lips on her own forehead. "That's how they know they're the right ones," she said out loud. Vinod wanted to reach across the table and take Karen's hand. He had cried when he found out she was getting divorced, though he didn't know for whom.

"What does that mean?" Dee slurred. "Whatsa prairie dog kiss?" But Karen would not explain it to her. She kept it to herself.

After Nat and Masha had said their goodbyes, Dee got up and said, "Well, I better be a good girl and call it a night."

"No nightcap?" Ed asked.

"What's your email address so I can send you the photo?" Dee asked the Actor. He wrote it down on a paper napkin, steadying one hand with the other.

They watched her descend the cedar steps, listened to the clap of her sandals. (Wasn't it too cold for sandals, the Actor thought.) There was no reception in the bungalows, so she went into the living room to send the Actor the Tröö Emotions photo. It was a featureless room except for a Steinway and the heritage chestnut trim of its windowsills, the identities of its inhabitants broadcast outward toward the bungalows. There was one silver-framed photo of Senderovsky and Masha as twelve-year-old kids in the Russian colony across the river. They looked like they were sitting on a haystack, and their skinny innocence dwarfed Dee's at that age. Senderovsky had enough crooked teeth to fill half a smile. His eyes were on Masha, much as the Actor's had been on Dee. And Masha herself was a slim beauty with a pinch of something not quite European about her, which could have been explained by a heavy Russian tome on a bookshelf by the piano outlining the effects of the Mongol conquest of the Kievan Rus'. Dee walked outside, past the porch (once more, two sets of male eyes upon her, though different eyes than before), and toward her bungalow, which sat on its wooden haunches, bathed in a frosty glow.

"I should turn in as well," the Actor said after the door of Dee's bungalow was shut, the little house lit in amber. He got up and hugged himself as if pressing his heart back into place, one chamber at a time.

"But there's still a cheese course," Senderovsky said.

"We got a lot of work tomorrow," the Actor said to Senderovsky in a voice that he hoped conveyed his rank and authority but which, given his new affliction, failed to convince anyone.

8

" 'YOU SMOKE,' " Karen sang, passing an imaginary microphone to Vinod.

" 'I smoke,' " Vinod sang back, passing the microphone back.

" 'I drink,' " Karen sang.

" 'Me too,' " Vinod sang.

" 'Well good,' " Karen sang, " 'Cuz we gon' get high tonight.' "

Senderovsky and Ed sat on one of the porch's nautical-looking moisture-resistant couches (they had been designed with a beach house in mind), watching their friends dance to the music in the candlelight. "The first time we heard this song," house historian Senderovsky said to Ed, "was the night you and I met. It was 2001, a famous year, in that Fort Greene brownstone Suj and I used to live in. Remember my ex-girlfriend Suj? I wonder what happened to her." Ed shrugged. "Some guy was running around with a suit of armor, and one of the deputy mayors or commissioner of something or other was snorting cocaine in the third-floor bathroom with you! That's how we met, right? When I walked in on you and the vice mayor."

"Wasn't that the party where you met up with Masha again?" Ed said. He had finished a bottle of wine and the four Gibsons Dee had failed to drink.

"A lot happened during that party," Senderovsky said. "It was seminal."

Karen and Vinod fell in tandem onto the couch opposite, the one with the perfect view of the sheep farm beyond and its many rustic structures, a bungalow colony for quadrupeds. They were slicked in sweat and laughing, hands reaching toward each other, hungry for touch. Vinod was lost in the *cluck-cluck-cluck* of her dorky middle-aged laughter, the glint of her cheekbones. Karen felt the years falling away. When she reached for her glass on a side table she could have been reaching for a carafe of cheap Beaujolais at their favorite restaurant back in the day, a brasserie named Florent, the chrome-edged fortress of their origin story. Now she was scared of time's compression, scared of the innocence Vinod invoked. They kept telling her that now, and only now, her life finally attained "limitless possibilities." But all of these possibilities seemed quite limited and asterisked besides, born of unexercised stock options but not the understanding of others. The trajectory was clear: every passing year would mean being more alone, until even the bathroom mirror of her loft on White Street would figure out a way to reject her, would show her the face of another.

"You two are adorable!" Senderovsky cried. "Vinod, do you remember that party in Fort Greene, when we first met Ed? And when I met up with Masha again after twenty years?"

Vinod's smile faded. He found himself crossing his legs. "Yes," he said without affect. "Quite the party." He did not want to time travel at the moment, particularly not to that particular soiree. He thought once more of his Teva box and the novel within.

"Noona," Ed said to Karen through half-closed eyes. "Can you make me a cheese plate? Pretty please. I can't walk."

Karen sighed and went over to the table, where many sharp local cheddars and custardy Époisses and oozy, bacony Greenswards congregated around a field of grapes. She examined her distant relative, his opened shirt revealing a triangle of chest hair, his pocket square, his brogues. Maybe he thought he was suave, but he reminded her of a midlevel salaryman stumbling into Seoul's Apgujeongrodeo station just before the last train departed, headed toward his unforgiving mortgage and his unforgiving wife.

"Noona," Ed said once the cheese was placed in front of him. "You must have tried the app yourself, right? Does it ever work for you? Did you and Leon try it before you split up?"

"That's a bit personal, *bhai*," Vinod said.

"What personal, we're all best friends, right?"

"I'm glad you still have the capacity to fall for someone after all these years," Karen said, "but Dee is not the right woman for you."

"Oh, fuck you, *noona*," Ed said. The sentence made him laugh. He liked referring to her as his "older sister." Senderovsky was glad he hadn't brought out the expensive eighteen-year-old bottle, which Ed would have quaffed in a minute and forgotten the next day. "I'm supposed to hold out for a nice stable Korean Masha, right? Well, that's not all that's cut out to be either. No offense, Sasha."

"Eddie." Senderovsky extended his hand, even though that was against Masha's distancing rules. "Let's get you out of that pocket square and into some pajamas, what do you say?"

Ed snorted and looked around. "Faces look ugly when you're alone," he said.

"Up you go, Jim Morrison." As they hobbled off the porch Karen took something out of her pocket which Vinod's bad eyesight strained to identify. Could it be?

"Okay, this might be a totally bad idea," she said. "But I say we light this mother. Just like in the song."

"You mean, between us?" Vinod asked. "What would Masha say? We can't pass around a joint."

THEY WERE PASSING around a joint. Masha was in the spacious upstairs bathroom looking down at the porch. As secretive as a Marrano during the Inquisition, she had whispered *"Lehadlik ner shel Shabbat"* over her candles so as not to wake Nat in her adjoining bedroom, had extinguished them with one practiced exhale, and was now watching a man with one lung *smoking a joint that had just touched another's lips.* What was more, her husband was dragging Ed toward the Big Island Bungalow, the latter's arm draped around her husband's shoulder, alcoholic flop sweat glistening off the both of them.

These goddamn idiots.

After disposing of Ed, her husband returned to the porch where the joint was passed to *him.* The music on the porch was loud, thankfully Nat's window faced out the other side of the house, but now it was bested by their goddamn idiot laughter, their karaoke of the damned.

Half an hour later, Senderovsky clambered up the stairs and entered their bedroom, his mood cheerful, his eyes red. He finally slunk off his ridiculous dressing gown and stood before her in his athletic pants and white socks. "Wash your hands!" Masha seethed at him.

"Of course, of course," Senderovsky said. "Here, you can watch me." She stood over him in her bathrobe as he washed his hands for twenty seconds, the stench of marijuana overtaking the bathroom like a dirty hamper.

"So," she said, "how many of us have to die for your personal re-enactment of *The Big Chill*?"

"Please," Senderovsky said. "It's been a tough couple of years with the television scripts and all. Did you hear how your beloved actor made fun of me at dinner? I'm the only one he treats that way. He can smell weakness. Just let me enjoy a happy minute or two with my friends. Come on, Masha. I need this."

"Does Vinod need this? And you as an asthmatic. I heard you coughing in your sleep last night."

"Acid reflux."

"You're a doctor like our president now?"

"Vinod's been in remission for three years now. It was only stage two."

Masha started to cry. The drama of crying was anathema to her, a memento of distant childhood, and even back then it was her departed sister, Inna, who was prone to the attention-getting tears of a younger sibling. But it was the only way she could present herself to her husband as someone wounded, someone other than "Stalin in an apron."

"Masha," Senderovsky said. All of his emotions were peaking. He had asked Karen about the prognosis for the Actor vis-à-vis Dee and she had told him that he might be in a pliant state now, confused, disorganized, searching for direction. All this might prove valuable, might put the Actor in a vulnerable place when it came to the pilot script. Was this why he had invited Dee and Karen all along?

He followed his crying wife into the bedroom. "Mashen'ka," he said.

"Don't touch me. You might give it to me."

"But we sleep in the same bed," he said in Russian.

"I'm not even sure that's a good idea," she answered in English. It was rare for her to use the nonmelodious language of their adopted land this close to midnight. Senderovsky knew he was in trouble. In bed, he curled up to one side, facing away from her, blood pumping through the brick of his forehead with the force of Elektrosila. People of his class were both too rich and too poor to divorce. Some had even given up on fighting just as a precaution.

"You don't love me," she said.

"I do, *sladkaya*."

"You don't love anyone, really."

He did not answer. "What's in that Teva sandals box?" she asked. "What are you hiding from your so-called friend? What have you done this time?"

Senderovsky did not answer.

9

VINOD LAY BENEATH the Gujarati lullaby in his T-shirt and jeans. He knew the moment he shut his eyes, he would dream of the tube. Waking up with the tube deep in his throat, trying to pull it out with his hands, choking on it. He had read about a much younger and healthier man in New Orleans who had been felled by the virus and woke up trying to scream, trying to get it out, eyes wide with fear, more helpless than Vinod had been when he was told that the massive heartburn he thought had been the result of a pepper haunting one of his uncle's outrageously spicy *shaaks* was actually lung cancer. Unless this was all a dream and he was already intubated. The dancing with Karen, that lipstick-smudged joint passed directly from her lips, the care and concern of Masha and his friends, the unblemished purple mountains behind him as he floated across the river, the spectral presence of *the* Actor? How was any of this not a dream? Any moment now he would wake up to the horror.

Karen was showering. She knew the hot water always ran out in the daytime, Senderovsky's bungalow colony not having shed all of its Soviet pedigree. She felt her right hand between her legs. Not touching herself after sitting across the table from the Actor was like visiting a Swedish furniture emporium without indulging in the cheap comforting meatballs. Still, it took a long time, the rhythm of the water along her back carrying her across the finish line, her forehead pressed against the shower stall's linoleum, her entire being feeling guilty and small. She squeezed some more liquid soap into her hand. She pictured Vinod laughing like an adorable nerd out of an eighties movie, high out of his mind. Even his laugher had an accent.

She heard a radiator wheezing against the baseboards as if issuing a complaint against her. Of all the guests, she had two rooms. Two rooms for one person. A thought struck her. She ran into her bedroom and grabbed her phone, thinking for some reason that her sister had left her a message. But there was no reception in the bungalows, and without connectivity the phone was but a dark obelisk, its display a liquid retina of false stars.

Dee also slipped a hand down the elastic of her underwear. Let's just do this, she thought. She hadn't fallen for him, but didn't a film of his make her cry? This was back in the day when she was trying to transition from quasi-suburban Southern shitbox to incense-reeking Bushwick studio and spent her days in a state of enhanced vulnerability. He was inspiring, wasn't he? How many young women like her did he help carry on his shoulders from the minor metros to the major ones? Hadn't she started writing so that she could one day meet someone like him? But it was work nonetheless, her breathing not cooperating, the anger that could reliably drive her forward this time holding her back. Portrait of a social class, she thought bitterly as she let out a final exhale, her pelvis rumbling quietly to a stop, the framed Joan Didion staring down with cool compassion. Afterward she felt giddy, as if she had won some small literary prize or an online flame war. "You're lucky," she heard herself say into the darkness of the tiny room. Why on earth had she said that? Because she had escaped the virus-ridden city? Because the Actor now seemingly loved her? Because she had entered a world where Spanish hams bore many guises and names? When she closed her eyes, Senderovsky's wine-stained immigrant teeth appeared before her, broken and fatherly. "Hot dog!" he said.

Masha didn't care if her husband heard her, which he did. She spread her legs, the bed flooded with her own scent, which, if only her husband remembered, was magnificent. She alone had a concrete fantasy of the Actor, him on top in the most obvious of ways (what she lacked in imagination, she made up in ardor), on this very bed, her hands pressing into his chest because she couldn't accept all of him at once. So much had been written about the softness of his hair and the color of his eyes that in order to claim a new part of him she focused on the enamel of his sclera. White is the color of infinity, Malevich had proclaimed. Afterward, she spent a good hour staring into darkness, until she could make out the entirety of the room, the chestnut trim of the windowsill, the cheap paper shades, the prosaic rectangle of the light switch. When was the last time she felt both this good and this scared? The airport hall reeking of terrible cinnamon buns, her nervous husband at her side, scanning the departure board for Beijing, anticipating the transfer to Harbin, the rush of a crowded new country, the first live glimpse of her daughter.

In his bungalow, Ed dreamed of Chania. Unfortunately, the scale of his drunkenness had erased all short-term memory, and Dee wasn't there to enliven his travelogue. The dream came to him in the form of an endless quest. He kept trying to get back to his hotel but was lost in the rotisserie of Greek summer streets. He had to deliver a beautifully hand-wrapped gift to his mother, waiting for him in the hotel lobby, but he did not know what was inside. All he needed to do was hand it to her, and then his mother's maid would hand him a packet of balled-up underwear in return. The gift was but a detail; the *underwear* was the point. As it were, Ed walked the dusty streets wearing nothing from the waist down.

BY THE TIME he heard his wife snoring, morning was almost upon them. Senderovsky softly creaked his way up to the attic and soon emerged with a Teva sandals box, trailing cobwebs behind him. As he walked out the front door leading to the front yard with its dead white tree branches, the sleepless Actor entered through the rear with his phone, looking to mate it with the main house's signal, the password written in Masha's elegant post-Cyrillic handwriting on the refrigerator's chalkboard. He downloaded the Tröö Emotions photograph along with everything else he could about Dee, including her *Grand Book of Self-Compromise and Surrender*. It had been reviewed no fewer than four hundred times by media outlets from Cleveland to Catalunya. Every time he saw the same stock photo of her, he pinched it bigger with his index finger and thumb. Her eyebrows were never plucked and her sober stare was more powerful than her tipsy one. Lately, there had been a minor scandal. She was associating with some miscreants from the questionable right: "Some of these people are very erudite and cannot be easily dismissed. They channel the mindset of poor folk who happen to be white and who we would like to believe have no minds at all." Her contradictions throttled him. He loaded up the most attractive photo of her, a simple one taken by phone at a reading, at a podium, spaghetti-strap dress and high-cut bangs, halogen light. Breathless, he ran back to his cottage, to the useless books and the map of the Leningrad metro and the firm new bed crying out for his body's delight.

SENDEROVSKY STOOD AMID the felled white branches, death all around him, Vinod's novel snug in its box as it had been for two decades. The garbage cans sat at the end of the driveway, covered in dew, waiting for pickup. If he carried out his plan, Vinod's words would be lost forever. Senderovsky ruminated over that fact. How he hated his dressing gown right now, and all that it represented, the sniveling, the posing. All of it was the very opposite of Vinod's novel, a portrait of his parents when they were university students in India, when they were still in love. That rare impossible thing: a young man's novel about a subject not himself.

Senderovsky stood before the gray March heavens as if waiting to be judged, a balding man in need of a haircut. No, he couldn't do it. But returning the manuscript to the attic was out of the question now that his wife knew about the box and suspected its contents. He looked around. The property was shared by many groundhogs, but its most irascible tenant had been dubbed "Steve" by his daughter. Steve had an overweight furry body mottled with orange highlights, and like a prosperous American with several condominiums, he had dug more than one cavernous hole for himself. He summered by the one near the pool, at times actually flopping himself out on the pool deck in a happy rodent stupor. During the leaner months, he lived by the Christmas trees flanking the west perimeter of the property from whose delicious sweet roots he would make winter meals. It was this hole Senderovsky approached now with the Teva sandals box under his arm.

A thought occurred to him: Would Steve eat literature? Weren't pages made of the same stuff as trees? This would have to be a temporary solution. As he stuffed Vinod's novel into the marmot's subterranean townhouse, Senderovsky saw a black pickup truck pass on the road, beams lit against the incomplete dawn. A corner of the Teva box still stuck out. Senderovsky scooped out a large mound of hard dirt with his genteel city hands and tried to mold it around the box like an impromptu sandcastle.

Once again, he heard the rumble of a motor. The black pickup had apparently circled around and was passing in the opposite direction. Now it had stopped completely by the edge of the driveway, flush with the main house. A window rolled down and a hand with a phone emerged. Sasha watched it snap a picture of his bungalow colony. The window rolled up. Sasha strained his eyes after the passing truck. Was there a sticker on the back? The deconstructed remains of a swastika? *Slegs blankes?*

Up in her room, Nat greeted the new day. She rubbed her eyes in the way we think little children do, even if her mind was racing at an adult speed. The green front lawn scattered before her, begging her to come out and stomp all over it. Her mental picture of the terrain was interrupted by an unexpected interloper. Her daddy was on his knees in his dress burying something in Steve's winter palace. As if he were Steve himself.

Life with Daddy was a perpetual encounter with a daisy. He loved her, he loved her not. But he was, and Mommy always agreed, very funny. The Sasha Senderovsky Show, as the nice new woman Dee had called it at dinner last night. Nat's mommy loved her all the time, but Nat could never be good enough for her. There was a Nat whose body she inhabited, but also another Nat (*Natasha* was her name), who lived in another country (*Rossiya* was its name), in another city (*Sankt-Peterburg*, they now called it), who probably looked like a young version of her mommy or Aunt Inna, who had gone to heaven (which, as a classmate whose family owned horses had informed them, did not exist).

But something had happened last night that made an impression on Nat, perhaps the greatest of her short life. Her mother was right in that Nat missed many social cues, but some facts were incontrovertible. Namely, the Actor was important. Jin- or J-Hope-level important. One of her classmates had an actor for a father, and the school turned into an entirely different institution when he deigned to appear during Family Sing-Along to perform a Calypso-inspired version of "Itsy Bitsy Spider." And last night the Actor had hinted what she had always known. That her parents weren't really her parents. Or they weren't entirely her parents. Just as she wasn't entirely the person her "mother" thought she was. And if she didn't belong to them, then maybe she belonged to no one.

Also, he had called her "lovely."

Nat went to the bathroom to brush her teeth with her imported BTS toothbrush (Jin's pouty smile a great way to start the day) and then to wake up her mother and tell her about the new funny thing Daddy was doing in the front yard. As she spit out the saccharine swirl of children's toothpaste, the very thought of her daddy on his knees in front of Steve's lair made her laugh. She looked at her reflection, multicolored toothpaste on her upper lip, surprised as always by the fact that the night had passed, but the Nat in the mirror remained.

ACT TWO

Entanglements

I

THE PROPERTY HAD not slept well. Tissues and other sundries now coursed through the channels of the septic system, despite the signs Masha had placed in the bathrooms of the bungalows asking guests to PARDON OUR COUNTRY PLUMBING. After two showers (Dee's and Ed's), the water supply was about to run dry for the day, with at least one disastrous consequence, as we will soon see. Various birds gathered in the thick forestscape behind the covered porch to hold a public conference on a great windstorm that was now approaching from Newfoundland. A groundhog peeking out from behind a dogwood watched his benefactor and enemy the landowner use his winter hole as a personal storage space and was unprepared for such a change in their relationship.

Meanwhile, the bungalow residents, minus sleeping Vinod, gathered on the slope of the hill to observe a rural ritual: a man with a buzz saw wearing safety goggles and a large cowhide strap around his waist was transforming the Jurassic bleached tree limbs covering the front lawn into mere logs, which would then be placed in a Pascal's triangle by the porch, ready for the stove's devouring.

"Now the fun really begins!" Senderovsky declared. "Now I can have the lawn properly mowed. And then you know what we'll do? We'll set up a badminton net! There are deadly ticks in the grass, but we can still play if we wear long socks. Has anyone ever heard of lawn hockey?" (No sport by that name existed.)

"Hey, Dee," Ed said. "You want to go for a walk? I can show you Sasha's street."

"We call it a road around here," Senderovsky said.

"Thank you, Farmer Sasha," Ed said.

"Sure," Dee said. "I mean what the hell else do I have to do?"

The Actor, unshaven with a few bits of sleep around his Ottoman eyes, was unhappy. He had wanted to do many things with Dee, ranging from the ecstatic to the mundane. Perhaps he could tag along? No, that would appear desperate. And there was more. Earlier, he and Karen, Ed and Dee, had given each other quick tours of their bungalows, and the Actor had found out some disturbing things. Karen's bungalow had two rooms decorated the color of a suburban dental office, but nonetheless double the number of rooms he had. Senderovsky had claimed that the Actor's bungalow was special, but either it was special only to him or this was an attempt to demote the Actor.

Nat had run out of the house and was bounding toward them. "Aunt Karen! Do you want to visit Steve the Groundhog's winter house with me?"

"Distance," Masha commanded. She had heard from Nat that her husband was storing things in the groundhog's hole, which seemed beyond the pale even for him. She wondered if it was time to put on her clinical hat.

"Sure, honey," Karen said.

The Actor turned to Senderovsky. "In my bungalow in twenty," he commanded the landowner.

THE TREE GUY silenced his saw to give Dee a full state inspection as she passed. She returned the favor. A nice face, shy smile revealing some broken teeth, perhaps a couple of roadhouse fistfights in his wilder days. But now she was applying his biography with a thick country brush, the very thing she detested in her urban readers. Maybe he had just fallen out of a series of trees and broken his teeth that way. Ed wanted to say something about the tree guy's saw, but he was at the moment confused by the difference between a buzz saw and a circular saw, and he wanted to get the terminology right. He was still aching over the fact that he had called the road a "street."

They passed through the driveway promenade of leafless oaks and elms and turned past the sheep farm. They walked on opposite sides of the road, maintaining distance, their voices raised over the tree frogs. Ed swept his hand across the sheep-filled hills and said to Dee, "To many people this evokes the English countryside." He realized he sounded as affected as Senderovsky.

"Never been," she said.

"Your book didn't come out in the UK?"

"Yes, but I only did a reading in London."

"Of course, of course." She was wearing snug sweatpants and the same fleece as yesterday, her sandals were now running shoes. Ed ruminated on all this, trying to keep all of his daydreams at bay, their ridiculous journey to Chania, the silver necklace around her sunburned neck. The weather was still cold, the clock had only recently sprung forward, but the sun pressed a warm hand against his collarbone. And against hers. A line of sheep in their naturally occurring black knee-high boots were jumping over a rill, flexing their hind legs like horses as they did so. A pair of horses on the other side of the road, clad in their woolly sweaters, watched them like the members of an Olympic jury.

"This is all very beautiful," Dee said, almost in the form of a concession.

"Was it like this where you grew up?"

"In parts," she said. "I think we'll get to those parts up the road."

"English countryside gives way to Appalachia," Ed said. He realized just how offensive that may have sounded, but Dee laughed.

"I feel like we're on a reality show," she said. "Like there's a truck with a camera following behind us."

"I'm obsessed with this Japanese one."

"I bet Sasha's house doesn't even have a television."

"You bet right."

"So where you from?" she asked. Now it was her turn to be embarrassed. The question could connote that he wasn't American, despite his perfect accent. This had happened to her at a reading in Minneapolis with a Laotian audience member (Laotian *American*, she had to remind herself, or maybe Hmong American), and she had felt shamed by her ignorance, by the way she represented herself and her kind. She had cried in her hotel room and afterward over an expense-paid meal of craft beer and chicken tenders, the guilty tears and the expense account both a first for her. But also the Laotian American woman, a student at an expensive local liberal arts college, could have been nicer to her, could have corrected instead of reprimanded. "I mean which part of the country?" Dee said.

"Now that's a really tough question," Ed said. "I went to college here, but truth be told I'm not a citizen."

"Your English is way better than mine," she said with an exaggerated drawl. They were passing by a small estate, the downward slope of its rolling aquamarine lawn fitted with a sign that read HATE HAS NO HOME HERE in many languages, including the three Ed had grown up with. "But last night you said you're Korean, right?"

"Not formally," Ed said. "I have Swiss, UK, and Canadian citizenship. I guess I have to nab me something in the EU after Brexit. Lots of folk becoming Maltese." So petrol princes and sunbaked Russian orangutans were now just *folk*. What was wrong with him?

"But you spend time here? In the city, I mean."

"Sure. Plenty. Home away from home."

"And you never felt like becoming an American?" She didn't know why she was pressing him on this one point.

"That's for people without options," Ed said. "Sorry, I mean . . ." He trailed off.

"No, I get it. Nation in free fall. Where did you go to college?"

"School of Foreign Service in DC. My mother wanted me to be a diplomat. But it just didn't take."

"Well, you're not super diplomatic," Dee said. He looked across the road at her. She was smiling. That memory again: Bologna, junior year abroad, that tall ridiculous girlfriend, being carried in her arms, *La Pietà*. "But I bet a lot of your friends are diplomats."

"The *children* of diplomats." He realized he needed some commonality with her at this point. "Senderovsky is one of the few self-made people I know. Him and his high-school friends."

The liberal estate continued to scroll before them. In a pond made by a careful human hand, a gently streaming duck, its head iridescent, was talking up itself to anyone who would listen. Rich people's chickens crossed the road, their heads held up high. The road sprinted upward, away from the ideal pasturelands and toward the state road. The sun disappeared behind a prayer shawl.

"Why does Sasha do this?" Dee asked. "Have all those cabins? It must cost a fortune to maintain."

"You mentioned that at dinner," Ed said. The gentle slope was winding him. He had to stop smoking. Yet how desperately he wanted to smoke. He took out his pack of Gauloises.

"I was drunk and rude last night," Dee said. "Not one of my proudest moments. Can I bum one?"

They met in the middle of the road, both with their arms extended. Ed passed her a lighter, then thought better of it, came up to her, dangerously close, and lit the cigarette hanging from her mouth. All the bungalows were outfitted with the same cheap floral shampoo, and while Ed hated the greasy clump it had made of his own hair (just this morning, he had sent away for a better shampoo), the scent of it on Dee made him feel as if they were fellow travelers who had met on the high road, pilgrims destined to find each other. She exhaled the smoke away from him, but he wanted to follow it, to draw it into his own nicotine-greased lungs. He needed to say something about Senderovsky that would build trust between him and Dee. He knew how curious she was about her former teacher, how curious we all are about our mentors.

"I don't think his finances are very sound," he heard himself say. "I think he's floundering."

This had the intended effect. Dee nodded as she smoked, her face pursed in thought. "Does his wife make a lot of money?" she asked.

There was a striver's innocence to that question. "She used to be in private practice," Ed said, "but now she works for a nonprofit for old Russians with mental problems. Her sister died a few years back."

"That's terrible."

"That's when she switched jobs."

"I think Sasha once called her 'the moral conscience of our family.'" They both laughed. "These cigarettes are strong."

"Sasha's been trying to make up the difference with TV work," Ed said, now fully enjoying the gossiping.

"Even though he doesn't own a TV."

"*Ding, ding, ding!* Maybe that's why his shows never get made."

"Poor Sasha."

"Not meant for these times," Ed said. They were both somehow cheered up by this conversation. "But he means well."

They were passing tract houses with green-gray rusted siding now, the properties uniformly square and evocative of the city's outer boroughs, but with a full acre to their names. A red sign on one lawn, its grass cut to within an inch of its life, read ALL LIVES MATTER.

A few houses down, a pregnant corgi ran down the lawn to yap at Ed and Dee. Its owner, a middle-aged woman in rollers, followed her down, shouting, "Bessie! Don't go in the road!"

"Go back to your mommy, honey," Dee drawled to the dog, which immediately stopped in her tracks, mesmerized, tail poised to wag.

The woman in rollers stared at Ed. "Get over here now!" she screamed, presumably to the dog, but her gaze still on the gentleman with three passports. As the dog turned around and waddled back, her stomach scraping the grass, her owner turned to Dee and said, "Sorry 'bout the bother."

"No worries at all," Dee said. "She's a cutie pie. Looks about ready to burst."

The owner's face looked burned by the morning's brief guest appearance by the sun, or maybe she was an alcoholic. She continued to glance back and forth between the members of the unlikely couple, perhaps trying to figure out what the man was wearing (a sleek black tailored piece known as the City Hunter jacket). "Well, if you want puppies," she said to Dee. Then she turned around and stomped off toward the house, the corgi lapping at her feet with love, unaware of the fact that her own children were just offered to a stranger.

"Conclusions?" Ed said as they walked away.

"She said 'Don't go *in* the road,' to the dog," Dee said. "Not '*on* the road.' The road is something you enter. Alien to your own property."

Ed nodded. "Your anthropology is sound," he said. "You should have seen the look she gave *me*."

"Your people aren't getting a lot of love from the state media these days."

"My people? I'm Anglo-Swiss-Canadian." They both laughed. Dee noticed an American flag done up in black, blue, and white, which also connoted a far-right disposition, fluttering from the back of a stationary black pickup truck. Maybe Masha wasn't entirely wrong about the content of this particular neighborhood, though these people, she reckoned, would never do her family harm. The calculus of a small northern town like this wouldn't allow it to happen, at least not to a nominally white couple. On the other hand, the state of the nation was changing rapidly.

"Let's maybe turn around," she said.

A towheaded child jumped on a trampoline and did a spectacular somersault as if he were on television. He smiled and waved at Dee upon completion. "Real nice!" she shouted his way. Ed tugged at the sleeves of his City Hunter jacket.

They walked back in silence until she asked him for another cigarette. "You're going to get me addicted again," she said, and Ed thought he heard honey in her voice. As the cigarette slipped between her lips, as her eyes narrowed to accept the hit of nicotine, as his vintage lighter bathed the cigarette's tip in flames, Ed put his other hand around her and pressed her bony shoulder in a way he assumed was friendly, once, twice. You could do this—in other words, light a cigarette for a person, and tap their shoulder while doing so. Almost as a way of steadying oneself while wielding the lighter. On the other hand, many years ago at a rural train station in Slovakia, a handsome man had propositioned Ed over a cigarette in a similar fashion—lighter, shoulder press, shoulder press—and, hungry for experience, he had given it some thought.

What the hell was he doing now? His emotions were a pregnant corgi escaping *into* the street. Maybe it was the tenor of the times. Single people were scared of dying alone. He remembered the anxiety of entering the Big Island Bungalow, of seeing just how little awaited him. Maybe there was nothing to lose anymore. (Although this morning, upon waking, upon thinking of her, he had righted the photograph of the Kīlauea volcano above his bed, in case Dee ever paid him an extended visit.) Two dogs were snarling at them from behind an electric fence. Only Ed flinched; Dee just kept smoking. Next time they saw something beautiful, he would ask her.

The sun returned as soon as they entered the liberal estates section of the road, where hate had "no home." They walked past a babbling brook that may have been spring asserting itself in full or a broken pipe up the road. Cattails ran along its length, bowing in the wind, shimmering like grain. The time seemed right now. "So I wanted to try that Tröö Emotions app with you," Ed said. She looked up, startled, and Ed thought she was about to say something polite, so he continued: "Just for scientific reasons to be sure. I'm exactly like you. I don't fall in love. Not for two decades, at least. And it clearly doesn't work on you either." He was babbling like the brook.

"So you just want to disprove it?" Dee asked.

"Maybe that's it. I feel like our lives are so much under the spell of technology these days."

"But I think it does work for some people," Dee said. Ed assumed she meant the Actor. Was she aware of his feelings for her? It seemed like everyone else was.

"Forget it," Ed said. "It was just a stupid thought. I guess I'm bored. It's just a parlor game in the end."

"I don't know," Dee said. "There's something offensive about it. 'Spell of technology,' like you said. We sign away our rights, and Karen makes a shitload of money. And for what? Many of us have worked so hard to channel our emotions away from easy love."

"Exactly right!" Ed said. They were so alike in some ways. But he felt dejected by the fact that she wouldn't try the application with him and that she wasn't looking for "easy love." They stood before a barn rotted away through the decades by a series of economic downturns, its gambrel roof see-through enough to permit a view of the mountains on the other side of the river. Clouds cast shadows over the mountains, like dark spots on an X-ray. They were less than six feet apart, and he wanted nothing in his life but the smell of her cheap floral shampoo. If he reached over and took her hand, he surmised that it would be hard, callused, not from the farmwork her ancestors knew but from the steady urban anxiety that was her life now, the constant rubbing of thumb against forefinger.

He watched her stare through the transparent barn, smoking, smoking. She was thinking that she had never met anyone like Ed. He was so outside the system he probably was the system. He reminded her a little of the luxury-watch journalist who had tried to date her, the one who chewed on the left side of his mustache until it curled. They were both *fussy*, with their clothes, their words and mannerisms, the way they stood both ramrod straight and internally slouched. Did a content person live inside those well-groomed shells? When he lit her cigarette, twice, he had broadcast both shyness and sex, which is why she had requested the second one. No algorithm at work, just a man shuffling through his card deck looking for a trump. Could she have sex with him, then cast him aside? It would be hard given the Japanese reality show format of the next few weeks or months on the Senderovsky estate.

And also, what was the deal with the hand always cupping the ear? Was he receiving instructions from his extraterrestrial masters?

But she was mostly preoccupied with other matters. Even before the virus, there had not been enough attacks on her book. Recently, she had had to take matters into her own hands, had tried to ignite controversy and get invited to a morning show, but the situation kept changing, and there was little room to maneuver. Should she please that Laotian American student at the expensive Minneapolis liberal arts college or incite her?

They walked back toward the house, both in thought.

As they passed the sheep farm, the driver of a black pickup truck with heavily tinted windows, charging down the road at double the speed limit, slammed on the brakes and cruised to within a few meters of them, the engine flexing under the hood, the crackling sound of coolant being displaced. A hazy, presumably male figure waved at Dee, then, not receiving a wave back, floored the gas, skirting right past Ed, enveloping him in the pickup's fumes.

He waved after it defiantly.

2

"I'VE BEEN REREADING Odysseus this morning," the Actor said.

Oh no, Senderovsky thought.

"I was thinking about my own commonalities with Odysseus. And with Misha." Misha was the name of the character the Actor was supposed to play in the adaptation of one of Senderovsky's early novels. He was the son of a wealthy Russian oligarch who tried to escape to the West in a long, roundabout journey that took him through a former Soviet republic riven by civil war. "Me, Misha, and Odysseus share a lot in common," the Actor was saying. "We have a worldliness, a cunning, we're tricksters. But we're constantly battling our hubris. And by hubris I mean self-entitlement, which is the same thing."

Is it, though? Senderovsky asked himself.

"Yes, I'm self-entitled," the Actor was saying, "but that's what drew me to this role to begin with. It's the most natural elucidation of who I am as a person circa right now. It's the rare role that lets me plunge feetfirst into myself."

"I see," Senderovsky said.

"Do you, though? Because—"

The em dash above may make the reader think there was a break in the Actor's speech, but it was only a break in Senderovsky's consciousness. His eyes were watching the Actor pace, puma-like, as he was known to do in his most excitable moments, up and down the short length of the bungalow, constantly removing the hair that cropped his eyes like an ancient veil. Ed had recommended a Japanese reality show to Senderovsky, and he was now reminded of the way the young women on that show also continually brushed their hair away from their pretty faces as a way of punctuating their dialogue. Senderovsky was also reminded of the classroom. Not the one he led in his decade as a professor, which could never have been tarnished with an epithet like "didactic." (One of his students had drunk so much Armagnac during a seminar he had to be transported to the university hospital.) He was thinking of his early years in the country, sitting in a classroom without English, trying to follow the ramblings of some unprepared, anxious educator, while his mind returned home to Leningrad, to the metro, to the whoosh of its rubber-clad tires, to the chess moves of a junior novel he was already plotting in his overstuffed mind. Did Nat have any memories of the Harbin orphanage, despite arriving in this country just shy of four? He planned to ask her at a much-later date, frightened of what she might reveal to him.

"*I'm* returning to Ithaca," the Actor was saying, "I'm readying my bow and arrow to slay Penelope's suitors, but those suitors are *me*. Or, rather, they are the parts of me that need to be slain."

Senderovsky thought he was catching on. "You want to slay your self-entitlement," he said.

"No!" the Actor shouted. "Have you been listening? Self-entitlement is my fuel. It's the bag of wind that what's-his-face gives to Odysseus. It lets me be the trickster that fools the Cyclops. Do you know what this script lacks, what all of your scripts lack? One word. Subtext."

"I taught a graduate seminar on subtext," Senderovsky said.

"That's your defense for a shitty script? Academia?"

The Actor launched into another soliloquy, this one more impassioned than the last, sometimes holding up a hand in front of his face and talking into its palm, as if for want of a skull. Senderovsky had seen him agitated, but never like this. *He's really in love with her,* Senderovsky thought. How could he use this to his own advantage? According to Karen he might be "confused, disorganized, searching for direction." What if he got Dee involved in doing a very minimal rewrite of the script? Could that be a sense of direction? Would that help get the script over to the network?

"Instead of starting on the image of Misha ripping into a crawfish with his bare hands while rapping about his wealth on top of an inflatable duck, we start with a dream sequence in which he envisions himself spinning a globe, over and over, Russia, Europe, the Atlantic, America, Russia, Europe, the Atlantic, America, Russia"—Yes, thought Senderovsky, *I get it*—"as a pair of eyes hovers in the distance, like the cover of *The Great Gatsby*. And only by episode eleven does the audience realize what it has known subconsciously all along. That those are Misha's dead mother's eyes."

"But that's ridiculous!" The outburst had left Senderovsky's mouth of its own accord. There was no way to invite it back in.

"What did you say?"

"I'm sorry," Senderovsky said. "I simply meant that this is still a comedy. That's what the network bought. Dreams of dead mothers are inherently not funny. Why can't we share a little laughter with the audience? Especially given the times in which we live. Wouldn't it be selfish of us to hold it back?"

"I can't work with you," the Actor said. He went to the bathroom and turned on the tap full blast. This gave Senderovsky time to weigh his options and gather his thoughts. Once they were gathered, he straightened his posture and puffed out his chest. When the Actor returned, he would be ready to say the following:

"If you don't like my scripts, you're free to leave anytime."

Senderovsky never imagined himself capable of uttering those words—most of his income now depended on the Actor and the script—but there they were. Why did he say them? Because he knew the Actor wouldn't leave the House on the Hill, his Tröö Emotions in tow? Senderovsky got up and walked to the door.

"Go to your house and think about what I've said," the Actor said. "Think about how your own emotions are sabotaging this project. And while you're at it, think about where you've placed me in relation to your other guests." Senderovsky thought he was being symbolic, but the Actor swept his arm to indicate his dwelling.

"Would you like me to displace one of my friends so that you may have a bungalow more to your liking?" Senderovsky said. "I could ask Dee. Her cottage is meant for writers. You might be inspired. Should I ask her to switch?" The Actor said nothing, but the puma eyes blazed.

3

KAREN WAS RUNNING down the hill, her arms windmilling around her. The child flew ahead of her, past the gray short shadows of the oaks and poplars and aspens, onto the parklike central stretch of the lawn, and toward a sentinel line of Christmas trees meant to block out the sheep farm and its inhabitants' daylong volley of bleats.

"There it is!" Nat shouted. "Aunt Karen, look!" She fell to her knees in front of a hole. She wore a long, featureless yellow skirt over a wide pair of boy's jeans held up by an ugly elastic band. As Nat fell to the ground, Karen pulled up the sides of the skirt to make sure she wouldn't get grass stains on it, feeling the phantom movements of her late mother in her arms.

"Look!" Nat said, after she had moved some dirt out of the way. "There's a box!"

Karen scrunched down next to her. It was impossible to maintain Masha's prescribed distance, not in any sense. The hole was dug beautifully, a perfect round enclosure that brought to mind the industrious flurry of an animal's paws. "Steve the Groundhog brought the box here?" Karen asked.

"No. Steve can't carry boxes. He plants sunflower seeds around the lawn."

"Steve gardens?"

"He puts sunflower seeds in his mouth and then he sprinkles them all over the lawn, so we're going to have plenty of sunflowers in case we have to stay up here for many years and never come down to the city."

Nat continued to rabbit on about Steve and apocalypse while Karen reached into the hole and carefully extracted a wrinkled and partly torn Teva active sandals box in the unfortunately combined colors of tan, yellow, and brown, the *v* in "Teva" presented as a pair of wings draped over the adjoining letters. Who came up with this typography? And didn't Masha and Senderovsky get into a discussion about this missing box last night?

"So wait," Karen said, "if Steve didn't bring the box down here, who did?"

Nat looked at Karen with worried eyes. Anxiety presented itself as a dry patch at the back of her palate. It made her want to burst out in nervous language, what she had overheard her mother call monologuing. The dilemma: Was it right to share a secret about her daddy with Aunt Karen? At dinner Aunt Karen said many things about her father, the kinds of things the teachers at Nat's Kindness Academy would consider "out of bounds" and which Nat often overheard with great interest from her square on the Quiet Mat. But Mommy had explained to her before the guests arrived that older people liked to "make fun," that was how they showed love for one another, by making jokes that sometimes sounded cruel—for example, that Daddy was a "bad dresser." Karen was very handy with such jokes, but Mommy explained she was a very loving person underneath. (Underneath what?)

And probably the Teva box was part of a game, a scavenger hunt for grown-ups. So it was okay to reveal the truth.

"Daddy put it in Steve's hole."

"What?"

"And he didn't even ask Steve's permission," Nat whispered.

"Well, that's very interesting," Karen said. She stood up, her joints creaking. "You know what we should do?" Nat shook her head, excited to be part of the game. "Let's take the secret box to my bungalow, make sure it's safe from Steve, and then figure out our next steps."

"Yay!" Nat shouted.

"Let's do it quietly and make sure no one sees us."

They ran up the hill like spies broaching an enemy compound, sneaking serious looks back and forth. Oh, my heart, thought Karen as she watched Nat run ahead of her, a singular mole at the nape of her neck, her arms engaged in jerky jogging motions she must have picked up from her father on the rare occasion he had to move quickly. Karen didn't know how to talk to a child. She wasn't like Masha with her "prairie dog kisses." And yet the child had sought her out first thing in the morning. Karen and her sister Evelyn also had their version of the Quiet Mat when they were Nat's age, when English was still as thick as oatmeal in Karen's mouth, although, unlike Nat, they also had each other.

Karen opened the door to her bungalow, and the breathless child scurried inside, jumping on a beanbag, which must have been Sasha's or Masha's attempt to channel the American idea of "families." There were also several framed Dr. Seuss posters, rough faux-Scandinavian wooden toys, and a board game called Love Is Letting Go of Fear—in other words, the waiting room of a child psychologist.

And so what? Karen thought. Was this not better than growing up in Elmhurst with her own parents, where every word and every gesture was a command, a note of displeasure, an infringement on childhood's sovereignty? Was this not progress? Who was she to criticize Nat's parents? At least one of them was trying.

They settled in front of each other on a Southwestern-style area rug with their legs crossed. Karen was about to open the box ceremoniously but thought better of it. "Let me just make sure it's nothing bad," she said to Nat.

"What do you mean by 'bad'?"

"Something for adults only." Nat opened her mouth with pleasure. Many things were converging in her mind: grown-ups "making fun," a groundhog's residence being conscripted for nefarious purposes, a box that was "for adults only." All this, too, seemed tied to the Actor's bestowal of approval last night, all these signs of new beginnings, alliances, and responsibilities. Nat wanted to grow up, but not entirely. Although she and college were separated by exactly one decade, Nat dreamed of attending the one in the neighboring village so that she could still be close to her mommy. She had heard that many graduates of her Kindness Academy ended up at that exact college. The collegians drove large hand-me-down cars into her village, where a burrito restaurant catered to them, and moved at a leisurely pace around the two main thoroughfares, sometimes pausing to point out something in a store window and laugh. Unlike Nat's young classmates, they never seemed to carry books around or read them, no *Llama Llama Red Pajama* for them, but they often gave Nat a hazy smile (they were stoned) that seemed to be an invitation to join them someday, to wear pointy glasses and drink tall *horchatas* from a single straw.

Karen opened the box a smidge and narrowed her eyes. "Oh," she said.

"Can I see?"

"It's just a bunch of papers."

Nat had leaned over and peeked in before Karen could close the box. "What does 'Hotel Solitaire' mean?" she asked. "Is that like when my mommy lights her Shabbat candles by herself?"

"No, honey, it's just the name of a book. I don't know what it's about."

" 'By Vinod Mehta,' " Nat had read off the cover sheet. "Does he sell a lot of books like Daddy used to?"

"I think this is a different kind of book. A private one."

Karen was the archivist of the trio of friends, as Vinod had mentioned the previous night, but this particular shard of memory had long slid out of her grasp. She remembered a damp dark bar in the Ukrainian part of town, her hand on Vinod's. He was crying, wasn't he? He never cried, even after she would present him with her latest boyfriend, usually a tall Irish guy on an H-1B visa. She remembered feeling her corduroy shorts sticking to a filthy seat, she heard herself telling him something in the bar's perpetual gloaming: "Fuck him. What does he know? He should send it to his agent to get an honest opinion."

Her memory hiccuped. Vinod's likeness was saying something to her out of the shadows of the bar, but it was hard to decipher. The place was mostly staffed by a pretty grad student in a tank top who always looked aggrieved, but treated Vinod, also a graduate student at the time, with collegial good humor. Karen tried to approximate the dialogue. "Let me read it, Vin." "I can't." "Why not?" "Because it's the biggest defeat of my life." "Sasha can be a dick about other people's work." "Are you kidding me? He blurbs every goddamn book they send him." "He can also be a bit of a weasel." "He's just trying to save me the embarrassment." "It's not like *my* career is going gangbusters." "This isn't a career. I thought I had something." "Maybe you're just not a writer." "I don't want to be a 'writer.' That's the last thing I want. I thought I had just one book in me that could mean something to someone. To a young person maybe." "You are a young person." "I'm thirty-one!" "I bet it just needs work. Let's sit down, the three of us, and talk this through." And on and on, her own heart breaking alongside his. At their lowest moments, they always overcame their parents' programming, always offered each other more than they had ever been given.

"So Daddy wanted Steve to read Vinod's book?"

Karen looked at the child, visualized the gears of her sweet mind turning.

"You know what," Karen said, "I think he wanted to keep this a secret, maybe as a surprise. And we should keep it a secret, too."

"Can *we* read Vinod's book?"

"I'm going to read it first, just to make sure there's nothing naughty in it. And then maybe I'll read some parts to you."

"I'm already at reading level Y," Nat said. "That's two grades ahead of where I should be."

"That doesn't surprise me." Nat's interest in the mysterious box satisfied, she played with the edge of her skirt, rolling it up and down. "What is it, honey?" Karen asked.

"Aunt Karen."

"Hm?"

"Do you know Korean?"

"Just a teensy bit. But not like your mom and dad can speak Russian. They're native speakers, especially your mom."

"Can I tell you a secret? But you have to promise you won't tell anyone."

"We've already got a few secrets going," Karen said, pointing to the Teva box. "This bungalow can be our secret clubhouse." She thought immediately of having her assistant send in "secret club-house" decorations, whatever in hell those might be.

"I don't really want to learn Russian," Nat said. "I mean I can speak it pretty well already. Probably on level Y. But I really want to learn Korean. I want to go to Korea and meet Jin, RM—that stands for Rap Monster—Jungkook, Suga, Jimin, J-Hope, and V. Do you watch their videos?"

"Sure," Karen lied.

"Really! Who's your favorite?"

"They're all so cute. Who do you like the most?"

"Jin?"

"Me too," Karen said.

"What were some Korean words your mommy used to tell you?" Nat asked. "Can you teach me?"

Karen thought of what it would be like to take Nat to visit her father in Florida, the only living member of her family she could still locate. But she's not your blood, he would say after a thorough examination. Or maybe he would accept an adopted granddaughter at this late hour. Broward County seemed to be opening new subtropical perspectives for her father; he now watched the liberal channel on TV, and an older white lady at his condominium complex was apparently closing in on him and his aviator sunglasses and his mini-fridge with its king's ransom of last Lunar New Year's *ddeok*.

Another thought occurred to Karen: Did the boy-band-obsessed Nat only like her for her Koreanness? Like certain men did?

A housefly was barnstorming through the living room of her bungalow, attaching the sticky pads of its feet to every mauve surface it could find, casually scanning for sustenance with its three eyes. It processed visual information at seven times the speed with which we do, thereby rendering a human's approach in slow motion. This particular fly had already outwitted Senderovsky's thwack at least three times in the past week and saw the out-of-breath handyman as a comical figure. And so nothing had prepared it for the cardboard form of Love Is Letting Go of Fear smashing it clean into the wall and swiftly robbing it of the sweet buzz of life.

"*Jo-ta!*" Karen screamed as she pulverized the insect. "That's what my mommy would say whenever she swatted a fly. It means something like 'nice job.'"

Nat grabbed Love Is Letting Go of Fear and swatted it against the wall for no good reason, leaving a secondary imprint next to the corpse of the fly. *"Jo-ta!"* she shouted.

"Very good," Karen said. "You have very good pronunciation."

"What else? What else? What else?"

Karen thought of the other words that left her mother's mouth on a daily basis. *Jo-ta* and the accompanying swoosh of a fly swatter may have well been the kindest of them. "There's *Nuh sook je hae!*"

"Nuh sook je hae!" the child shouted, her accent perfect. She stood with her arms extended in a martial arts pose. "What does it mean?"

"'Do your homework.' Your mommy probably tells you that in Russian when you haven't finished your work."

"No, I like doing homework. Tell me more!"

"Piano chyeo!"

"Piano chyeo!" Nat shouted, again perfectly.

"'Practice your piano,'" Karen explained. "Which I'm sure you already do."

"I can play all of *Swan Lake*."

"Tee-bee kkeoh!"

"Tee-bee kkeoh!" The breath left her lungs with a precision Karen could never quite master. It wasn't just mimicry; it was borderline spiritual. She must have listened to her K-pop with a fanatical ear. "What does it mean?"

"'Turn off the TV.'"

"We don't have a TV."

"Believe me, I know."

"Nuh sook je hae! Piano chyeo! Tee-bee kkeoh!" Nat started marching around the room, shouting out the parental commands, as if filming her own private Korean version of *The Sound of Music*. As she heard these words that could jolt her and Evelyn to the quick, Karen felt them deemphasized, neutered, turned into the playthings of the second generation. (Technically Nat had not been born in the country, but still.) Words that had tormented Karen were now the silly singsong march of an eight-year-old trying to communicate with the

members of a cool Korean boy band that had conquered half the world (imagine *that* happening back in Elmhurst, back in 1979).

Karen's reverie was interrupted by a male scream outside, or more accurately a human shriek mixed with a puma's growl, loud enough to send Karen running to the window.

She peeked through the screen, trying to identify the source of the commotion.

Oh my God.

She reached for her phone and pressed the camera button, then selected Video.

"Stay where you are, honey," she commanded Nat.

4

MASHA WAS TALKING to a patient when she heard the shrieking. The view on her screen was of a bedroom in a typical apartment in a Rego Park mini-tower, the morose and faded redbrick kind in which she had spent nine months out of the year as a child. (The other three were spent more happily with young Senderovsky and their friends in the bungalow colony up the river.) Instead of a closet, with which every American apartment is equipped at least three times over, the tenants had bought a high-gloss armoire, which also functioned as a wall-length mirror, and Masha could see her bespectacled afternoon face being reflected on its surface along with the usual schmear of menorahs and provincial lacquer boxes. The woman on the screen could have been a Senderovsky, perhaps her husband's aunt, one of those peroxide battle-hardened Russian women in their early seventies growling and sighing their way through a lifetime of dysthymia, if not full-on depression, now compounded by the obsessive-compulsive disorder which the virus had only trebled. Perhaps that is why this particular armoire glowed so brightly today; a bottle of glass cleaner could be spotted sitting beside the woman, awaiting her attention like a loyal pup.

The patient, Lara, spoke in the same breathless torrent of words Nat used when she was overstimulated, monologuing, as it were, about the day she had spent on her favorite social media platform. There Lara had learned, as several of Masha's patients had learned that morning, about the microchip that was inserted deep into the nasal passage during testing for the virus at the behest of the liberal Hungarian-born billionaire they referred to with maximal spite as

"Dzhordzh Tsoris." The virus, it was now conclusively proved, was engineered by the evil ex-Magyar in a lab as part of an attempt to take over the world through this snotty microchip and return it to the Marxist masters of their youth. Masha sometimes scrolled through her patients' feeds, a heady free-for-all of paid-for racism such as *An Honest History of Black People and the Democrat Party,* conspiracy mongering along the lines of "If you get headaches while wearing a mask check this video out," and Vladimir Horowitz in coattails playing Schubert at Carnegie Hall. That all three things could coexist in such proximity could be dubbed "the Soviet Ashkenazi Paradox," and any attempts to bring up the fact that the anti-Tsoris propaganda often focused on the detail that the billionaire was every bit as Jewish as most of her patients (some of the "articles" they posted had Tsoris styled in a yarmulke and *payes*) would have no effect. Her job, as she saw it, was to provide a comforting presence; her soft freckled face alone calmed these overexcited immigrants, along with a steady run of anti-anxiety medications and serotonin reuptake inhibitors, which she passed off as "sleeping aids" to her rabidly anti-psychiatric patients. The very fact that they would even talk to her—a *terapevt,* as she called herself to her patients, implying any kind of therapist, such as a physical one—under the auspices of a Jewish not-for-profit was testament to her skill. "I'm here to listen to *you,*" she would begin each session, using the formal pronoun.

As Masha watched Lara, an aquatic blue to her manic eyes, rage about Tsoris's plan to nasally control and bemask her, her own mind was elsewhere, on her daughter and her unwanted guests. There was a tub of homemade egg salad in the refrigerator and bread with high fiber content, but would they figure out how to make sandwiches from these two staples? Senderovsky claimed they would. And then there was the endless daily playlist of Nat's own therapists and virtual classes (well, not today, it was Saturday, though Masha continued to work) and voluminous yet easy homework focusing on interpersonal skills and the joy of loving everyone, which both bored her child and highlighted the underdeveloped range of her emotions. It was an odd delight to see Nat and Karen running up the hill at a full gallop—an adult friend still counted as a friend, no?—but she worried the child would exhaust Karen with her repetitive interests, chiefly the boy band, and her occasional flashes of temper and need for order and control.

"If you're still having trouble sleeping," Masha said to Lara, "sleeping" being a stand-in for "functioning," "I might increase your dosage to twenty milligrams. Many of my patients take that dosage with great results."

"I don't care if I live or I die," Lara said, which in Russian was equivalent to "I'm doing fine, thank you so much for asking."

"Although I know Tsoris would want me dead," she added.

"Well, that's one good reason to keep living," Masha said.

Lara smiled, her ceramic government-provided teeth glowing in the smudgy lens of her daughter's outmoded laptop, the daily conversation with Masha the highlight of her quarantined day. Lara lived alone, her husband first pickled and now fully dead, but Masha thought she saw a child's *tapka,* or household slipper, briefly reflected in the armoire, caught in the action of scampering past and slapping down the apartment's brief hallway on the way to the living room television set or the cabbage-stocked refrigerator or the precisely mowed central yard between the redbrick towers, where various ethnicities used to clump together like wet socks coming out of the washing machine. This was a mirage, of course; the child did not exist, only the framed picture of her sister next to the monitor forever receiving a law award she never particularly wanted, gray sullen Jewish eyes, her head bent tiredly toward her older sister, in the same way Russian bungalow colony Senderovsky would try to slot his head in the crook of her neck while they were sitting in their bathing suits by the colony's tiny aboveground pool, a torrent of feeling flowing one way between them.

Fuuuuuuuuuuuuuuuuuuuuuh!

She must have misheard the yowl in her reverie. But, no, there it was again. A resident bobcat (or was it "mountain lion")? A beast torn asunder by another? No. She heard words now. Ugly words. "One minute please, Lara Zacharovna," Masha addressed her patient using her patronymic. ("*Nu, nu,* do as you must," her patient replied, as if her entire existence was but an endless series of pushbacks and

rejections.) Masha ran through the living room with its silent Steinway and cheerless pastel sofas, through the kitchen with its beast of a
chef's stove, its farm sink and professional espresso maker, and out
onto the gallery connecting the main house to the porch, where—

Where she found the most perplexing sight of her life.

THE ACTOR WAS naked, his dark head lathered in an iridescent plume
of shampoo or conditioner, which flowed ceaselessly from his curls,
as if he were a vanilla fountain. "What the fucking fuck?" he shouted
through the slits of his soap-covered eyes. And then upon sensing
someone's approach, "Help me! Fucking help me already!"

"I'm here," Masha announced herself, her eyes already having
skimmed the trunk and twin ears of his genitalia, but not yet having
the time to process the shaved and styled fuzz of pubic hair above.
"Did the water cut out?"

"Yes, it fucking did! I can't live like this. This conditioner
contains"—some ingredient she had never heard of—"it needs to be
washed out immediately! There could be retinal damage."

"Here," Masha said, "I'm going to take your hand now, okay?"
She glanced around to make sure there was no one watching them
(from the vantage of her bungalow, Karen was recording everything
with her phone), and then grabbed his hand, the wet soapy warmth
of it pulsing with life. He squeezed it like a panicked child. She led
him inside, the conditioner still spilling off of him in great torrents
and coating the rustic wide-beamed floors in opalescent industrial-
grade suds. "I can't live like this!" the Actor moaned. After only eighteen hours at the Senderovsky estate his outlook was already fully
Russified. She led him into the bare-bones downstairs bathroom and,
even though he was being led, he announced, sadly and dramatically,
"I can't see," as if this was now his permanent condition.

She switched on the shower, but only a quick burst of water came
out with a country snarl. The sinuous W of his buttocks filled her
mind, knocking out Nat and Lara Zacharovna and the failed state
that was her husband. There was an incongruous tuft of hair right
atop them where the primordial tail would have found a home, al-

most a mirror image of the shaved outcropping above his twin ears and trunk, and she needed to stop looking below his waist. "I keep buckets of water around in case something like this happens," she told him.

"In case something like this happens?" he yelped blindly. "This has happened before?"

She gently pushed him into the shower, her hand between the sharp blue shoulder blades, and told him to bend down. "I'm sorry I'm short," she added.

He bent over for her slightly. She grabbed a bucket of water, hoisted it up, self-conscious about the size of her forearms, and began to pour the contents into the impossible thickness of his hair, massaging it with both hands, trying to get out the lather, which had already started to cement. He put a strong wet hand around her waist to steady himself, feeling no need to apologize for the severity of his touch. With his body forming a Russian г in front of her (thinking in alphabets calmed her), she could now see the contrast of the two hardened clumps of his breasts in free fall and compare them with the soft run of posterior, the slightly feminine hips, which lacked the usual indented lines of reasonably priced men's underwear. (Did he wear any at all, or were they as silky as a Mormon's garments?) The air filled with the strange musk of what must have been the special conditioner, bringing to mind the deer-hide rug her uncle Artyom "the adventurer" had brought home from far Yakutia or thereabouts. And all this was happening in a fly's slow-motion time, her eyes recording everything with as much fidelity as Karen's phone. "It might take a while before I get this out of your hair," she said, feeling sweat start to coat her armpits despite the bathroom's groaning fan above her.

"Not just the hair," he said through his teeth.

"What?"

"Not just the hair." His mind was feasting upon itself, the images carouseling about. He saw Dee, he saw his own eyes watching Dee in the enhanced photograph, but he smelled *this* woman, a twin pinch of morning dairy and sweat. Yes, he smelled this woman, the wife of the man who had just insulted his writing, his process, his substantial education, his love of the Greek classics. He stood before her hunched over, naked but powerful. Was he wrong in thinking that her hands caressed his scalp with more than a practiced mother's touch? That they were hungry for him? He prided himself on knowing several persons of imperfect physique, but he had never thought he would stand naked before one of them. Through the slits of his pained red eyes he saw her pendulous bosom, the rosy fluster of her thick arms, and the folds of her neck, and although he knew that in the current sociopolitical climate many things were not allowed, perhaps this was still his due.

"Not just the hair," he repeated, breathing heavily now. "Wash all of me. Get it all out." He thought of adding "if you'd like," or "if you can," which would soften things and maybe even indemnify him, but he held back, proudly, his penis starting to rise on its own accord.

She saw all this. Heard the excited tremor of his voice and felt her own lack of control at the edges of her fingernails, inside the warm pouch of her underwear. She wanted to speak now, to speak one sentence after the next, to monologue in the manner of Nat or Lara Zacharovna, or to call her late sister and tell her everything that happened in endless run-on English sentences, not caring if her accent returned or not. But no, this wasn't for anyone, not even for her dead sister. She thought of the final scene of her favorite movie, which happened to be set in East Germany, a former Stasi member buying a book about his life and being asked by the salesclerk if it was a gift. *"Das ist für mich,"* the aging former Stasi man had said, without affect, but with clear emotion. *This is for me.*

"Where do you need me to wash?" she whispered, the cartilage of his ear bending between her fingers, her cracked lips just 2.54 centimeters away. He reached up and took her other arm, at first unsure of where to place it. Again, he was aware of the tenor of the times, but somehow her age and profession calmed him. She was a medical doctor, she came from an era of different understandings. He put the hand against his chest, where he helped her make arcs around the hardness of it, and then reached down to massage the bellyfuls below. And now if she increased her arcs she would soon gather all of him. He wanted her to take her time, he wanted to be in control and also to be teased. At first, when the water had cut out in his bungalow, he imagined playing a recently blinded man in some extremely limited series on a new streaming network, using his panic, his loss of control, as propellant into a new dark (he had missed his own pun) place. But, as he had said to Senderovsky, all roles led to himself. And now she was caressing it, ostensibly to get the suds out, but with a practiced muscular motion. There was a word he wanted to say, a proper name, but it might not end well for him. Then again: a medical professional from an era of different understandings. He was sick of holding himself in check all the damn time.

"Dee," he said out loud, as close to a moan as he could. "Oh, Dee."

The woman stopped. She wouldn't look up to face him. "Don't stop," he said. "Keep going."

Masha recoiled, loosened her grip, but then there were the same words on endless loop: *Das ist für mich, Das ist für mich, Das ist für* fucking *mich!*

There was a lot of it and it mixed with the deer-skin-smelling suds circling the drain, until it was hard to distinguish what was his and what came from an expensive foreign bottle. She turned off the water, and he faced her now in complete silence, a tall Mediterranean body, the closed double brackets of his chest, the pre-sex of his belly, the stubbly well-shorn fuzz of a pornographer's dream, and the menagerie of bobbing animals below. His eyes were red as if he had cried, and in every movie he had ever made there would be a scene where his lucky tears flowed and slalomed down the woodwork of his face like the catharsis of a nation, like an ancient rite. All this had been hers. Was that the right way to look at it? In the possessive? "There's egg salad if you want for lunch," she said.

He snorted, but then reached up to touch her cheek. "Your husband ought to fix the plumbing system," he said. "But until he does, I want you to keep those buckets ready." He smiled "boyishly," he thought.

"We'll see," Masha said. She handed him a towel.

"You don't want to towel me off? Finish what you started?" There was a joke in there somewhere. Plus the insinuation: she had started it.

"I have a patient," she said, the sudden realization of her responsibilities to a person in (perpetual) distress entombing the birth of her own quick pleasure. She walked out, passed all the familiar sights, the big and little tokens of culture that cluttered her small home, holding her still-wet hands out in front of her like a proof of concept. The concept being that she was alive and strong and wanted, if not loved.

5

"'My name is Luka!'" Senderovsky happily sang along to the satellite radio as he bounced up the driveway at an obnoxious speed, scrutinizing a lawn now completely free of blanched tree branches. "'I live on the second floor!'" An undeniably male and colonial feeling seized him. He had stood up to the Actor and, with the aid of Tree Guy, he had stood up to the detritus of a windstorm and thus to nature herself! The rest of the day would pass with grace.

An instant fog had settled over the property, and he could see a stack of freshly laundered towels in the upstairs bathroom window that put him into a deep, familial calm. Once again, everything was in its place. "You have a lovely family and a lovely home," as his Los Angeles agent had said. He coughed into his hand for a good minute as he parked the car, his lungs seizing from the effort. It was the acid reflux, for sure. He should limit his alcohol intake and avoid chocolate and acidic foods.

Speaking of such foods, he had just driven to Rudolph's Market in the village due north at Ed's request to pick up a trunkful of items including a mysterious and expensive bottle of "Tunisian pimento & citrus confit." As he got out of his car, he saw the Actor walking out of the house with a towel wrapped around his waist, his hair a dark halo, his ankles tough but slim, like Karen's.

"Hello," Senderovsky shouted to the near-naked man. "Yoo-hoo!" A thought occurred to him. "Did the water cut out in the bungalows?"

"Just another day in paradise," the Actor said, pouting.

"Please go inside," Senderovsky said. "I'll have my handyman look at the pipes. You must be freezing."

"I'm perfectly fine," the Actor said. "I like the cold."

He turned around and left the landowner to what he imagined was a dark state of perplexity. On the way out of the house he had seen the overexposed photograph of the young Senderovsky and his wife-to-be, a charismatic-looking child with resplendent Eastern cheeks, atop a haystack. He remembered Senderovsky's howl at one of his authorial suggestions—"But that's ridiculous!"—and counterbalanced it with the feel of his wife's surprisingly deft hand upon him.

"Karen says it's better to take a shower at night!" Senderovsky shouted after him. "I should have announced it earlier."

"Fix it!" the Actor shouted back. Now he was playing a dictator atop a balcony, someone who did not need to use more than two words at a time. But back in the Petersburg Bungalow, he deflated. He sank into a hard modernist chair beside a hard modernist desk and slumped over like a schoolboy caught. First, there were the possible consequences. He scrolled through what had happened just minutes before. Had he crossed a line? Many of his Y-chromosome-bearing colleagues were now in the clink, metaphorically speaking, after decades of touching women and instructing women to touch them. The excuses about her generation and her professional standing seemed weak. If anything, she had the resources and wherewithal to eviscerate him. The best he could come up with now was that she was "European," and perhaps this was not the first time she had cheated on her sad-sack husband. Still, he should not have said Dee's name out loud as a final insult. That was as over the top as one of Senderovsky's scripts.

Which brought him to Dee, of course. *She was responsible for this!* No, it wasn't Dee. It was Karen and her algorithm. She was no better than the social media platform guy, the little orange snot at the congressional hearings. They were all scoundrels, out to destroy him, out to destroy the country. And now, thanks to Karen, his heart was not his own. And neither were his eyes.

His eyes. His eyes in the photograph. His eyes beholding her. Her being beheld by his eyes. That was the moment of climax in the shower, Masha no more than a handmaid (was that another joke?), all of it unspooling from himself, the want and desire and *need*. He had needs. He had a past. If he were smart about pursuing Dee, he would set aside a few months and write a memoir. Maybe now was the time to do it. Then he could present it to Dee and say, "It's all in here. There's no need to exalt me. No need to guess about who I am. I'm just like everyone else." Except he wasn't. He did not ask for his level of self-entitlement; it was bundled upon him like a curse along with his talent and the twin dolmas of his eyebrows. Of course he had suffered! You didn't just fall into his level of range without suffering. But the particulars of how he had suffered, the "throughline" of his pain, yes, that's what needed to be explored in the memoir. "Here is who I am, Dee." A writer could say that even more accurately than an actor. "I wrote this for you, Dee." He knew exactly whose name would go on the dedication page.

He took out his tablet. It would be funny if he used the same style as hers for his own memoir. "I wrote this *like* you, Dee." An homage. *The Grand Book of Self-Compromise and Surrender* by Dee Cameron. Now that was a good title. He clicked past the copyright page, gray light slanting through the window poetically, which brought his hand to his hair and a reminder that given his contretemps with the conditioner he had to run a brush through it sooner rather than later. His phone buzzed—sometimes the reception would get through for a second or two in the bungalows, the invisible probing hand of a cellular tower in the hills above—but he wouldn't pick it up, and later he would tell his Glaswegian Elspeth that the reception was, to use a word from her language, "wonky."

What if Dee's book was devastatingly good? Could he get through it then? Would he despise her talent or learn to accept it? I have to stop being competitive, he told himself. He could handle the woman he wanted to be with forever having a minor kind of fame, instead of a failed kind like Elspeth's. (She was a retired model-activist.) There was a knock on the door. What if it was Dee? He hopped on one leg while sliding on a convenient dirty pair of underwear and a T-shirt. "Just a minute!" Jeans were slid into and a bushel of hair eased to the side. He opened the door.

It was the Indian guy holding what looked like a rough-hewn

blanket under his arm (it was actually a handcrafted area rug Senderovsky picked up in Paraty, Brazil, during a raucous literary festival), and clothed for the weather in a very pragmatic spring jacket handed down from a rich cousin. "Excuse me, Mr. ——," the peaceful intruder said, invoking the Actor's beautiful last name. "Would you mind if I get a book out of your bungalow?"

The Actor nodded, resigned to being friendly. "I'm sorry, I'm awful with names, you are—"

"Vinod. I'm looking for a copy of *Uncle Vanya*. It's right over there." The man with the soft extinguished eyes knew exactly where Vanya sulked amid the colorful mass of bookshelves. Why wasn't *he* given this bungalow? Perhaps the Actor could ask for a trade.

"I believe I saw you in a very avant-garde version of *The Cherry Orchard* in Berlin once," Vinod said.

"Yes," the Actor said. "When I was much younger. I played the actual orchard, if I remember correctly. Or the personification of it."

"A very tough role, but you carried it off with aplomb."

The Actor smiled and waved away the compliment. "I'm just a vessel. Chekhov was the genius?" He hadn't meant it as a question.

"It must be exciting to collaborate with Sasha," Vinod continued.

" 'Exciting' is not the first word that comes to mind."

"He's a great writer. I've been lucky to see him grow over the years. I even tried my own hand at writing a novel once, and he was kind enough to read it and give advice. He's a teacher at heart." The Actor was touched by the earnestness of Vinod's friendship. He rarely saw the same affection among men in his own circles. "You would make a terrific Uncle Vanya, by the way," Vinod said.

The compliments felt soothing to the Actor because they seemed to come from a place of real noncompetitiveness. Unlike Senderovsky, his friend had compliments to spare, and no need to constantly prove himself. He watched Vinod glide over to a bookshelf by the map of the Leningrad metro and pluck out the mentioned volume.

"Actually," the Actor said, "I always wanted to play the self-entitled professor who comes to visit Vanya and his family. The one who owns the estate. Can't remember the name offhand."

"Serebrakoff."

"Yes! My stay with Senderovsky might really ground me in that character." He felt very erudite to be having this conversation.

Vinod said nothing, merely shook his head and smiled. The Actor admired the five hundred eyelashes which staffed Vinod's tired eyes almost as lushly as did his own. "Are you reading anything interesting these days?" Vinod asked, his arm circling the rows of books imprisoning them.

"I just downloaded Dee's book of essays."

"I read it last year," Vinod said.

"Oh. What did you think?"

"I think she's trying."

"Trying what?"

"She's trying to figure it out."

"Aren't we all?"

"No, I don't think so."

The Actor couldn't understand if Vinod was complimenting Dee's book or not. For some reason, he felt the need to try to sway him away from Senderovsky and toward himself, to form what network press copy would call "an enduring but unlikely friendship."

"Sasha tells me you lost a lung," he said.

"Just part of a lung," Vinod said.

"He exaggerates everything, doesn't he?" the Actor exclaimed. But Vinod did not reply, only nodded noncommittally and bowed slightly. The Actor thought he detected a coldness. When Vinod had left the bungalow, the Actor suffered a sudden burst of loneliness, which was redirected as anger. "What do they all want from me?" he said loudly, unsure of whom he was speaking but using one of his hands to make the point. He knew he would find his own company unbearable until dinner, until he put on his finest shirt and saw her again.

And then what?

VINOD AND HIS area rug walked down the steep green path to the meadow, the same meadow Senderovsky had recommended to the

Actor as a place for quiet reading. ("I can think of nothing better.") The grass was tall, unmowed, and Vinod tamped it down with his hands, some atavistic memory of the Oval Maidan, straw-colored, anemic grass beneath his feet, the crack of a cricket bat, men and boys yelling to one another, excitement not meant for his sharing. Maybe there had been a picnic basket, a pretty aunt with a mole containing one whisker, oily *pakoras* and *dhoklas* warm to the touch. Lately these pushy self-proclaiming memories were asserting themselves without end, but how to tell which were real? The mind at his age resembled the watery stew the Parsis used to make out of goat brain at the Cafe Military down in Churchgate, the overhead fans spreading the aromas of the musky nonveg food, whipping through the memory of the first beer ever to have touched his lips, fat pubescent cousin Gautama cheering him on to two decades of heavy drinking.

He made a little area for himself and beheld his surroundings. The meadow ran a good ten meters beneath the rest of the property, and the strange midday mist was settling in along with Vinod. When he glanced up, the great cedar porch, the stucco main house (so close to the stucco of his second youth in Jackson Heights), the stationary satellites of the bungalows, all this reared itself up before him as if it had just appeared out of nowhere, summoned by a madman out of Gogol or Cervantes. And now Vinod marveled at the scope of Senderovsky's project, the great happy waste of it all, an undertaking so vast it couldn't help but summon the words "bankruptcy court." Unlike his friends, Senderovsky did not have siblings or a traditional immigrant nuclear family; each bungalow served as a correction to his parents' and forebearers' panda-like lack of ardor.

The mist seeped into Vinod's lungs (plural), and then it ran in great lazy torrents against the housing project above, shrouding and unshrouding the great Californian expanse of the cedar porch (the place mats had already been washed and set out for dinner) and the bungalows with their slightly pitched roofs, so that, in the words of American magicians, "Now you see it, now you don't."

The tree frogs had started up once more with a greater urgency than ever, but no one other than a party of starlings sheltering in place within a dead elm could pinpoint the source of their agitation, a storm on its way from Canada. Alone in the mist, Vinod tried to read the Russian play as he saw lights spring on and falter off in the houses above, like a code, the rooster on the weather vane over Karen's double-sized bungalow spinning about manically, but finally pointing his beak away from Newfoundland. Vinod would be lying to himself right now if he said that he did not want her caress here amid the cold and the damp. He still loved all of her, even the grace-lessness of her hungry, perennially dissatisfied immigrant soul, even the cruelty of her turns of phrase and the foulness of her triple-espresso breath. But he had to think like a character in a Chekhov play, forever taunted by desires but trapped in a life much too small to accommodate the entirety of a human being. That was why Che-khov was eternally beloved. There were no dashing personages in his works galloping toward an end point like the Actor's renown or Karen's algorithm, only vanishing horizons, only overgrown mead-ows from which one could look above and try to discern misted land-scapes.

He opened the book, but was overtaken by fear. None of this could be real. Again, he remembered the bridge crossing the river just yesterday, the rest of the continent behind him, the purple moun-tains a little too perfect for their own good. And just now he had had a delightful conversation with the Actor, one of the most admired cultural workers on the planet. And the next however many weeks or months would be spent a stone's throw away from Karen, whom he had not properly seen in at least as many years, certainly not since Tröö Emotions was sold to the pudgy-faced chairman of a happy-go-lucky Japanese bank.

So what was *really* happening to him?

A drowning death was how he had heard it described. Young peo-ple drowning in their hospital beds. Drowning in their lung fluids, drowning in themselves. He touched his mouth and his throat, feel-ing for the ventilator tube, but all he came up with was his own dry lips and Adam's apple, hard and hanging. (But what if his hands were restrained?) He jumped up wearily and boxed at the mist. Mist! It was almost too easy a metaphor for the drugs probably coursing

through his body, keeping him soft and docile and successfully intubated.

Or back to the simulation hypothesis. He thought again of the
programmers at the Interstellar Bangalore, the ones responsible for
this whole universe. "Lord," he said to whichever one had been assigned the string of code known as Vinod Mehta. But that word was
too religious, too "Lord Rama," for its own good. "Sir!" Too colonial, too deferential, too in need of an exclamation point at the end.
"Entity," he said, finally, which felt right, if bureaucratic.

"Entity responsible for this," he said, "I hope and pray, if that's
how you like to be approached, prayerfully, that you are not a sadist.
That you will deliver me from this in due time. That you will allow
me to reach the end point and exit from whatever you have created."
He stopped and looked around. The mist was billowing now as if he
had indeed caught the attention of a vast malevolent entity, or at least
its production department. But how beautiful it looked, this soupy
violence of the swirling damp. How well it outlined the stark nakedness of the trees, every one now a Russian birch in Vinod's *Uncle
Vanya*–influenced imagination (and in his imagination only). And
not all were naked either. The Japanese maples were starting to come
in red. An extended branch hung over Vinod, and he could make out
a baby woodpecker in his tiny crimson cap trying unsuccessfully to
learn his parents' craft. But with each peck, the bird overturned and
fell off the branch, then fluttered up to try again. And all this routine
activity was happening as the mist convulsed around them, as if the
bird's code ran independently of the mist's code, as if they had been
programmed separately.

He thought of walking up toward the hill, toward whatever safety
his Lullaby Cottage promised him, the safety of the notarized documents at the bottom of his luggage. (Was the "Lullaby" another hint
at the drugs keeping him under?) Another light, muted and modern,
flickered on in Karen's bungalow, in what Vinod did not know was
her bathroom. It calmed him like the sight of a lighthouse in the
storm, and now the mist felt gentle and caressing, a wet sponge
pressed against a child's forehead to keep the fever down. He could

not explain the sudden change in his mood, the absence of fear. He did not know that she was sitting down on the toilet with a copy of the novel he had written almost two decades ago, her eyesight straining at the ten-point font, the complicated sentences running into one another, but slowly, buoyantly, replicating the circularity of its author's mind, which she knew and loved.

The baby woodpecker had finally claimed his birthright, and the sound of his tiny drill echoed through the meadow. Vinod sat down on his Brazilian area rug and opened *Uncle Vanya* again. He read: *"A country house on a terrace. In front of it a garden. In an avenue of trees, under an old poplar . . . It is three o'clock in the afternoon of a cloudy day."*

It was so, precisely.

6

Ed used a slow-burning charcoal briquette, which kept things moist, a must for the tender sardines he was about to grill. Since the walk with Dee, he had spent the day preparing for dinner. He would make up for his laziness the day before. He would give them (fine, her) the best meal they had ever had in a rural setting. The recipe for a spicy and unusual variant of tired old mayonnaise-heavy *vitello tonnato* came from one of the finest chefs in Turin, and right now Ed did not care that it was a summertime dish as the fickle weather kept playing with his hopes and dreams.

The mist was finally lifting, just in time for an early dinner. He had sent Senderovsky on several culinary errands, and now he spotted the Russian on the front lawn, down on his knees, poking at what must have been a hole in the ground. Was he fussing with the well? The shower situation was even worse than usual; Ed had barely gotten a trickle of lukewarm, sulfur-scented water after his walk. He watched Senderovsky croak up the hill, his face blanched, his hair agitated. "Have you seen anyone on the lawn today?" the landowner asked.

"Not since you threatened to put up the badminton net," Ed said.

"Strange, very strange," Senderovsky muttered. His heart was aflutter, Vinod's novel was missing from Steve's winter palace. And just when he had found the perfect place for it in a disused compost bin in the garage.

"I'm going to need you and Vinod soon to help out with dinner," Ed said.

"Aye-aye," Senderovsky said, giving a crisp salute. "Is that a Negroni?"

"I found a bottle of vintage 1960s Campari in the larder," Ed said. "Do you mind? It looked pretty rare."

"I *have* such a thing?" Senderovsky asked, as if he was speaking of a dolphin caught living in his basement. "Help yourself, then. I'm going to lie down for a minute." He coughed loudly into his hand, tasting metal.

Ed had promised himself he wouldn't drink, that the evening would pass with him as a battleship launching bons mots across the bow of the USS *Dee*. But tumblers of Negronis kept finding their way into his hand, and his tongue kept seeking out the cubed cool of the ice tinkling within. How did Senderovsky not drink himself into a stupor the half of the year he spent up here? Ed vaguely remembered slumping over his friend's shoulder on the way to his bungalow last night after saying some unkind things, but he could never be ashamed in front of Senderovsky, who, he now realized, was more of a brother than the real article back in Seoul.

He prepped over the next hour, the vintage sixties Campari growing low in its bottle. He had blanched the sugar snap peas, one of the secret ingredients to his *tonnato,* and was now carefully charring them on the grill. The anchovies and tuna had been pureed and introduced into the mayonnaise, capers, lime juice, and, another secret ingredient, three quartered habanero chilis, then blended into a silky smoothness and strafed with kosher salt. The cold veal was then covered with cilantro leaves and pumpkin seeds, a dash of the pimento and citrus confit, and finally the creamy avalanche of the *tonnato* itself. By the time he was finished, his fingers burned with habanero heat, and he wondered if the dish wouldn't offend the more timid palates. Cilantro was always a controversial ingredient, and he wished he had surveyed Dee's feelings on it.

Senderovsky and Vinod appeared before him looking glum and dazed, respectively, like two conscripted privates in an Austro-Hungarian army about to be vanquished. He quickly set them to task, ferrying things between the kitchen and the covered porch, checking on the grill while he relieved himself, and, most important, keeping him company, making him less nervous and thus moderating his alcohol intake (or that was the idea).

"Nice look," Karen said as she hobbled over, face still distended from recent sleep. Ed was wearing his mask low under his chin (in other words, pointlessly) and had a cigarette hermetically sealed into his mouth. For once he wished Karen wasn't being sarcastic. "Look at you go," she added as he gently raked the coals. She had never seen him be this industrious. He's completely in love with her, she thought.

He had stuck the sardines in a bowl and coated them in olive oil. The rest of the guests were now starting to filter onto the screened porch from their respective houses, and Dee passed him wordlessly, dressed in a collegiate parka and wearing a sly toothy smile. He nodded to her like a professional. Showtime, he thought to himself, a half glass of Campari sloshing around his mouth. The *vitello tonnato* was on the porch. The lamb steaks had been defrosted. He threw the sardines on the grill and watched the little fish sizzle, his eyes tight in a deep meditative stare, his apron and City Hunter jacket coated by a new layer of fish and char. The key was flipping them without losing too much of the delicious skin, and this required a surgeon's grace. When the sardines were plated atop a bed of arugula, the latter would wilt from the heat—a sign that everything was in order.

Just then, a ghostly Senderovsky appeared through the remains of the fog, coughing into his fist but holding a strategically necessary plate of quartered lemons, which Ed immediately squeezed onto the fish, the lemon juice stinging his habanero-scorched hands. "Bring these up immediately," he commanded the landowner as he ran to his bathroom to wash the grime off and to anoint himself with a quick spritz of nonoffensive cologne.

By the time he got up to the porch, the guests gave him a standing ovation. He glanced quickly at Dee, straining to separate the sound of her hands from the others. "You haven't even tasted anything yet," he said to them.

"You're blushing!" Senderovsky said.

"Just look at the presentation," Dee said. "It's like something from a cooking show."

He stopped himself from bowing to her. "Eat, eat," he said, reminding Karen of something her mother used to say to her over breakfast: "Eat, eat, why you so fat?" Vinod was thinking of the Florent dinners he had shared with Karen and Senderovsky, three broke, starving students dipping fries into a big white pool of aioli sauce, carving out flaky little disks of goat cheese from the great big cylinder of the stuff, snapping back mussel shells and pulling out the meat with their teeth, the one time they could gorge at will without adhering to Karen's codes of cool.

A similar hunger had settled upon the diners. Conversation ceased as the adults tore into the food, their chewing loud and uncouth (Senderovsky was reminded of his mother invoking the Russian prohibition against making the *chavk* sound with an open mouth, *Sashen'ka, ne chavkai!*), plastic knives sawing at *tonnato*-soaked sheets of veal or carefully peeling sardine flesh from its spine. "Oh my God," Dee cried, her eyes full of tears. "It's so hot!"

"Too hot?" Ed was worried.

"No, perfectly hot. And these snow peas, they just go so well with the veal and the sauce."

"Textures," Senderovsky said, resuming his unasked-for role as Dee's teacher. "The softness against the crunch."

"This is flipping amazing," Karen said. "When you put your mind to something, Ed."

"Oh, these sardines," Masha said, filleting a glossy section for Nat. "They couldn't be more perfectly grilled. It's like I can inhale their essence." It was unusual for her to be so lyrical, Senderovsky thought. Was she the one to have extricated Vinod's novel? She sometimes took walks down the front lawn between patient calls and Nat's classes and speech-therapy appointments.

"I made them just for you," Ed said to Masha, turning to Dee with a wink to signal that it wasn't true, that everything was for her.

"You should write a cookbook," Vinod said.

"The world needs another Mediterranean cookbook like I need another ulcer," Ed said.

Only the Actor remained silent, and while normally they would try to suss out his opinion, the guests remained too enthralled by the food to notice its absence. He felt their lack of interest morbidly.

"Where did you learn to cook like this?" Dee asked.

"I lived in Italy for a while," Ed said. "When I was younger."

"Remember when you and that countess started a bilingual magazine about the rivers of the world?" Karen said. "What was it called?"

"Wasn't it just called *Rivers* slash *Fiumi*?" Senderovsky said, his mouth making the *chavk* sound with impunity now, his quarantined mother too far away in Forest Hills to hear.

"Let's not go there right now," Ed said, and Karen raised her hands in surrender. Ed reached for a bottle of Riesling (the newspaper would soon declare it the most underrated grape of this particular summer) and poured himself a glass to the brim, realizing he should have first asked Dee if she needed a refill. To bring up *Rivers/Fiumi* right now, after his victory with the *tonnato* and the sardines? He would never forgive Karen for that. So he had wasted his youth on silly indolent things fueled by ancestral money. So what? Were the eight hundred readers of *Rivers* ruined forever by his attempt at twentysomething romanticism, inspired by a combination of his love of Huck Finn's journey down the Mississippi and the only family trip on which his father had been too drunkenly passed out to humiliate him, a luxury steamer belching its way down the wide contours of the Nile? By contrast, Karen's invention was actively destroying people's lives, the Actor's included.

Quiet returned to the table. This communal meal would be different from the first. Every diner except for Senderovsky had learned something new about another, and the secrets were as piquant as the habanero-laced *tonnato* they were now shoveling down without regard for the country plumbing. Karen stared at Senderovsky, knowing that he had tried to entomb Vinod's novel inside a groundhog's hole. Nat stared at Karen knowing that she would teach her Korean and then one day she would be ready to meet Jin and J-Hope and Rap Monster in Seoul. Dee and Ed glanced at each other, companions after their long walk, she aware of his desire, he trying to gauge his chances. The Actor glanced sideward at Masha, knowing the consistency, the *texture,* to quote her husband, of her touch. And Masha stared at her plate knowing the heat of the Actor's sideways stare, which she feared contained both pity and derision.

"Okay," Ed said, "who wants lamb steaks?" They all raised their hand except for Vinod and Nat, both moralists when it came to lambs. "They're coming in bloody unless you say otherwise."

Soon the rosy little strips of meat attached to the bone were heaped onto plates, and the flimsy recyclable knives proved useless. The six lamb eaters brought their defenseless quarry up to their mouths with their hands and tore at the flesh like lunatics. The meat, succulent but tough, required a dedicated carnivore's persistence, and each eater concluded their mastication with a lick of first the index finger, then the thumb. Senderovsky was particularly taken with this dish, an emblem of his bungalow colony at its finest. "Before I'm buried I want my body drizzled in olive oil and salt," he said.

"Daddy's not going to die for a long time," Masha told Nat. "He was just being silly."

"I might die before him!" Nat sang out.

"Now why would you say that?"

"Yeah, why?" Karen said.

"Because of climate change."

Ed, pleased by his food's reception, had just finished an extra sidecar of artisanal gin and felt his tongue loosened accordingly. "I call Nat's generation Generation L," he pronounced. "As in 'last.'"

"Ed, what the hell is wrong with you?" Karen said.

"All I'm saying is that it's irresponsible to bring a new person into this world," Ed said.

"Which they didn't!" Karen said. "No one here brought anyone into this world."

"I'm still totally fertile," Dee said as a sidebar, "but I'm with Ed. No more children."

Oh, the Actor thought.

"Yeah, I'm adopted," Nat declared to Ed.

The Actor perked up, sensing his rival was about to be taken to task. A silence overtook them, filled by the mad chirping of birds sensing the first tranche of wind descending down the Berkshires. Senderovsky realized that he had not put any music on the handsome red radio.

"'Adopted' means Mommy and Daddy are not my biological parents," Nat explained. "It means I didn't come out of Mommy's stomach."

"Oh, I know, honey," Ed said. "I didn't mean anything. You have great parents. You're going to live a long time." He had never used the word "honey" before, either to a child or a grown-up, and its disbursal from his mouth made him feel even more guilty of some unspecified crime.

"Not sure about that, but thanks," Nat said. Dee and the Actor laughed. Her mother cringed. An adult could say that sentence, but not a child. Just the other day she had said, "I don't miss the city *entirely*," and that last word saddened Masha. Was Nat even experiencing a childhood? Not entirely.

"Hey," Nat said, "I learned the words to 'Alouette' in English, do you want to hear them?"

"Not right now, Nat," Masha said.

" 'Lark, nice lark!' " Nat sang, her pitch perfect. " 'Lark, I will pluck you. I will pluck your head! I will pluck your head! I will pluck your beak! I will pluck your eyes!' "

"Okay, enough please," Masha said. "That's not a nice song."

"It *is* a nice song!" Nat shouted. "It's French Canadian!"

"Natasha Levin-Senderovsky! Do you want a time-out?"

"For saying it's French Canadian?"

"Let's all just relax," Senderovsky said. The whole dinner was slipping away from him. And after all the money he had spent on the lamb and veal and the mayonnaise hand-whipped by a family across the river.

"You just ate a lamb," Nat said. "Okay? It had its eyes and head plucked, too. Someone killed it. It was Generation L, too. But you didn't care, did you?"

"You see what you did?" Karen said to Ed.

"Did what?" Ed said. "You ate the lamb, too!"

"I'm not talking about that," Karen said. "You upset her with what you said."

The Actor thought it was time to provide moral context and gravitas. "The bottom line," he said, "is that Nat is really exceptional. Like that Swedish girl with the Asperger's."

"Excuse me?" Masha said.

"Alouette, gentille alouette!" Nat shouted. *"Alouette, je te plumerai!"*

"Nat, you were told to stop," Masha said.

"I was singing in French," Nat said. "That way you won't have to hear the bad words."

Karen could see the child's entire life before her, the rebelliousness, the combativeness, the drug use, the affairs with tall Irishmen with H-1B visas looking for "something different," the fleeing from parents who had no business overseeing her life. What if she, Karen, stepped in right now and tried to make her adolescence easier? What if she offered herself not as a parental substitute but as a much-older sister? And this time she wouldn't fail.

"Let's go upstairs so you can watch BTS in your room," Masha said. "You're done eating anyway."

"No! I want to stay with the grown-ups!"

"I'll go up with you," Karen said. "You said you wanted to show me how you play piano."

"Piano chyeo!" Nat shouted. "That's in Korean. *Tee-bee kkeoh!* Not that we have a *tee-bee.*"

Ed looked at Karen, surprised, as did Masha. In addition to the hold she had on her husband (and Vinod, of course), Karen was now teaching her daughter another language. There was nothing inherently wrong with that, except maybe she could have consulted her. "If you two want to go play the piano before bedtime, that's fine," Masha said, the starkness of her voice matched by the gathering wind. She wanted Karen out of her sight. "But just one song and then off to bed."

"Yay!" her daughter cried as she and Karen adjourned to the living room.

"Wow, I'm sorry," Ed said to Masha and Senderovsky. "I'm just not used to being around children. Although she's almost too smart to be a child."

"But she *is*," Masha said. "A child."

"I do that, too," Dee said. "I forget how to talk to them. I have nieces, but they're nowhere in Nat's range of intelligence."

Yes, thought Masha, talk some more about how my daughter is different from others.

"Sasha always taught us that having a child is expensive, but great for material," Dee continued.

Ed laughed. "Oh, that is prime Senderovsky."

"Is that what you told your class?" Masha said. "Is that why you agreed to adopt?"

"Well," Senderovsky began.

"He also said to marry 'a professional,'" Dee said. "That was the only way to survive as an artist."

"I'm glad he followed his own advice," Masha said.

"Sasha's a survivor," Dee said.

They all chewed silently while passing around the Riesling bottles, their green contents gleaming and sloshing in the candlelight, until Karen came back onto the porch, looking, Vinod noticed, radiant and dimpled. "Done with *Swan Lake*?" Masha asked. "I'll go put her to bed."

"She's already in her pj's," Karen said. "She was really tired and just needed to be tucked in."

"She'll need a glass of water next to her bed and her little towel."

"The one with Llama Llama Red Pajama on it?" Karen asked. "I put it under her pillow along with a photo of Jin."

The most tender part of her relationship with her daughter, the bedtime rituals during which Nat regressed to someone even younger than her age, was so easily appropriated by another. She was less mother, Masha thought, than caretaker, lesson planner, and unwanted therapist-at-large. One day her daughter would share with Karen the prairie dog kiss, if she hadn't already, and then Masha might as well move to the attic.

The Actor meanwhile was slowly moving his chair toward hers. "So," he said to Masha, one eyebrow raised, "you went to New Haven, too?"

"How did you know?" She looked at her husband, who was sucking on a lamb bone with his shoulders hunched and his eyes dimmed. "Have you been talking about me?"

"Not at all," Senderovsky said.

He must have looked me up, Masha thought. He went through the trouble. "Well, I graduated many moons before you," Masha said. Her shyness throttled Senderovsky. He had expected his wife to have a crush on the Actor, but this took him back to the Russian bungalow colony, back when eleven-year-old Masha was in love with a tall dumb ox named Oleg who had been mostly in love with himself and something called a LeBaron.

The Actor sat back in his chair and surveyed the audience and the discomfort he was sowing among its members. He was wearing a shrunken tan gabardine shirt of faux-military appearance that would have looked affected on anyone but him—a statement of intent in its own right and a riposte to Ed's studied rakishness. He could wear anything, do anything, do anyone.

"So, Vinod," he said, speaking as if to an old friend, "have you ever been in love?"

There was a rustling among the three original friends who, proud graduates of city colleges all, had already been put on edge by flagrant mention of New Haven. But the Actor liked to ask uncomfortable questions. He felt he deserved that privilege after baring himself in front of his audiences.

"Who hasn't been in love?" Karen said, preemptively.

"I'm asking Vinod," the Actor said.

Masha felt it now—his cruelty—and she chastised herself for not being turned off by it. So he was the type to survey a group and attack its most vulnerable. "What was your major again?" she loudly asked the Actor. "Theater?"

"I've been in love with Karen most of my life," Vinod said. As he said it, he was looking into his plate and its three perfectly gnawed sardine skeletons, at the economy all that careful gnawing represented. Senderovsky wanted to run across the table and hug him.

"And you've been aware of that love, I assume," the Actor said to Karen. "I ask all this from a place of caring."

"We have a friendship that's stronger than any physical love," Karen said.

"That sounds pro forma," the Actor said.

Vinod straightened up and directed his gaze at the Actor. "My love for Karen," he said, "has been the most fulfilling part of my life. And, yes, I've loved others, been with others. Not too many, but still. Karen and I are friends, but we're just too different."

"How do you mean?" The Actor was now playing the part of a dogged television interviewer. He would soon reveal a greater truth for the benefit of all.

"I've had ambition, but unlike hers I could not fulfill mine. But my disappointments have remained my own. My grief is private, and that's how I've always liked it." Ed sighed in affirmation. "The older I get, the more I delight in people who orbit parallel to me but remain always out of reach. My friends, the writers I admire, and, especially, my one love." He lifted his glass to Karen, then set it down without drinking, as if to illustrate the point of what he had just said.

The first five pages of Vinod's novel ran through Karen's mind. She still did not know what to make of it, but she knew she would only read five pages a day so as to ration it. His pronouncement came as a gift, the kindest offered to her in years. There was only one way in which she knew how to pay it back. "Excuse me," she said and left the table.

The diners glared at the Actor. It reminded him of the rare occasion during which he played the bad guy and not the dark and unknowable young man fighting his own history. But this did not trouble him. Being hated was something he could work with. "Comp lit," he said to Masha. "And thanks for giving me a hand earlier." His gaze skimmed Masha's figure. "My water cut out," he announced to the others. "Not to worry though! The mistress of the house is on top of it." Now he was speaking in the landowner's cadences, occupying his space.

Senderovsky began coughing into his fist. "I'm sorry," he said, his eyes watering. "I don't have it. The virus. It's acid reflux." He continued to cough, loudly enough so that the Actor moved away from him and once more toward Masha. The Actor thought brashly of reaching out and touching her hand, which sat like a pale dumpling on her lap. He felt one leg reaching out toward hers under the table. She felt its proximity and did not know what to do. *Inna, help me,* she thought in Russian. *Inna, I've lost my strength.*

"Maybe I'm old-fashioned," the Actor said, "but I think people should have affairs."

"Apropos of what?" Dee said. So, he had caught her attention, finally.

"Sorry," he said. "Apropos of nothing. The country life is getting to me already. I'm just"—he smiled—"rambling." Senderovsky continued to cough as punctually and rhythmically as the guitar strums of the Caetano Veloso he had forgotten to put on the radio. Whenever he looked at the Actor and his wife, he couldn't think of the many roles he had played onstage and onscreen, while Senderovsky himself had played only one, the clown. Though it had been a most lucrative venture for a while, and he was once even offered tenure at an important university in the city (which he had foolishly rejected to pursue TV work).

"Maybe you should go to bed," Masha said to her husband. Ed and Dee were both wondering if the emaciated man was running a fever and tried to reconstruct their interactions with him. His cough certainly sounded dry, a telltale sign. Vinod got up to bring him a glass of water.

"I can't lie down," Senderovsky said. "It'll make the reflux worse. I need to stay erect." Dee remembered some of his word choices during their class, which she would gleefully dissect afterward at a sawdust-floor bar with her fellow students. Someone had even made a document of "Sasha Sayings" which was stapled to the cork bulletin board of the graduate student lounge and, for all she knew, remained there still, swinging crookedly off a thumbtack.

"Damn, I ate a lot," Ed said to Dee, rubbing his belly, trying to remind her of his cooking. "We have to go on more walks or I'll get all tubby." He weighed, at present, one hundred and twenty-seven pounds.

"'Your body dysmorphia brings all the girls to the yard,'" Dee sang, a tune from Ed and Senderovsky's early thirties both had forgotten. She wasn't as drunk as yesterday, but was tipsy enough to register as a comfort the strengthening wind beating against the screens. "Hey, do you have that Japanese reality show you were talking about?" she asked Ed.

"Yes, I've downloaded most of it," Ed said. He reached for his jigger of gin and drank it in one go. "We could stop by my bungalow if you'd like and watch it." He paused for a second, propriety getting the best of him. "Everyone's welcome," he said.

"I think I'll go and work on the script," the Actor said. "Someone's got to." Masha watched him spring up, his movements sore and static, then felt the absence of his knee next to hers. He was angry at Dee, she thought. She remembered the little fishes her father had used to bait the sea bass of Long Island Sound, the way they used to thrash on the hook, unsuitable for anything but dying between the teeth of a more important animal.

They heard Karen stomp inelegantly up the steps. She did not say anything, but walked over to Vinod. She held a small receptacle in her hand brimming with a peach-colored substance. "You have to put this under your eyes," she said. "We've all been having sleepless nights, but you, honey, need to show off those beautiful peepers."

She popped open the container, scalloped a bit of cream with her forefinger, and began to paint the half-moons beneath Vinod's eyes. He smiled until his dry lips split along the seams. "You don't have to," he said. "Whom do I have to impress? Other than you."

The diners watched the ritual take place, only Senderovsky recognizing it as such, because she had done the same for him and for Vinod many times during the younger days of their friendship, applying creams and balms and so-called product, smoothing them out for the old age of which she had been so frightened, her mother's only prescriptions for life: good looks, good homework, good college, good marriage, good sons, good death. As she worked on his eyes, they all noticed the care with which she labored, as if Vinod was a sacred object, a talisman, as if nothing mattered more than to send him into the world slightly less blemished. Ridiculous, Masha thought. She's leading him on in the same way the Actor is leading me on.

"Well," the Actor said, surveying the scene. "My job here is done. Good night."

"Sleep well," Ed said, victory in his voice. "Just knock on the door if you want to watch the Japanese reality show with us." The "knock on the door" implied that he and Dee might be half naked at the least.

"Oh, I've been dying to see that show," Karen said. "Vin, you want to come?"

Ed sighed.

7

E D SET UP his laptop on the desk between the pineapple sculptures, and Dee (as well as Vinod and Karen, the interlopers) slumped down next to the edge of the bed, their drinks in hand, giddy at the prospect of low entertainment. "Okay," Karen said. "I have to show this to someone, or else I'll freaking die."

"What is it?" Dee shouted. She wondered what it would be like to be Karen's friend, this important woman who could so easily act like a child (and befriend an actual one), the opposite of all the serious people she knew back in the city.

"But you have to, like, sign a mental NDA," Karen said. She took out her phone. "Seriously, this stays between us." Vinod made the gesture of zipping his lips. He was happy that she was happy. She used to start every night out by asking them, "Okay, what's the gossip?" and he and Senderovsky would compete to make her laugh and gasp like two city-college Scheherazades.

"So," Karen said, "I was playing with Nat in my bungalow, and I heard this scream. And. Okay. Just watch this."

They leaned in as far as the virus allowed. At least three of them had seen the Actor naked in films, and one of them had seen the side profile of his penis before on the London stage. But here his nakedness was without positioning or affectation, his rage, his screaming ("Get it out!" "It's like fucking fire in my eyes!") were honest, he was his brutal naked self, and he had no control over his life or even what he could see out of his eyes wide shut. The drama of his real self exceeded that of his screen self; it was both sadder and funnier to watch. (Perhaps, thought Ed uncharitably, he was not such a great actor, after all.) But he's beautiful, Dee thought. Oh my God, how beautiful, this man just two bungalows over. It was as if he had captured not just himself through his helpless yelping, but her as well, a pretty animal always managing to get lost amid an alien tundra. And every part of his body, including the hidden ones, was exposed as if just for her, beckoning with their imperfections. Yes, he shaved down his pubis like an idiot, but a matching trail of hair descended from the tailbone to the heavy moons of his testicles, and, short of having an assistant or a girlfriend take care of it, there was nothing he could do about it. But now she knew. And now she wanted to help him through the algorithm that had ensnared him. Or did she? Ed sat no more than two feet away from her, breathing dangerously, his face looking cross. It was so wonderful to have him by her side at dinner, to walk with him through virgin landscapes, to listen to someone half a lifetime older who had already given up on reproduction and entanglements and so much more. His lips would taste fine, like lamb and veal and gin and quartered lemons, like her own.

Ed could smell her alcoholic breath. "Enjoying the view?" he asked, hoping he sounded droll. His hands still burned from the heat of the habaneros and he wanted to be alone with her, to embrace her closely, to let her feel the tingle of his eyelashes and the strength of his arms. She had seen the Actor naked now, but he also had a body, and it too was trim and cared for.

"Oh my God," Vinod said. "No!" Masha was now on the deck, and her stare was affixed most prominently where by Abrahamic law and custom it should not have been (though who could fault her?). To further the contrast with the naked man, she was dressed in a mid-income blazer for her video calls, though her feet were bare. And then she took his hand. She turned him around carefully like a tugboat guiding an oil tanker into port.

"Didn't you hear those two tonight?" Karen said. "My assistant went to New Haven. Asking what your major was is how those people flirt. I bet he's sampled the goods already."

Vinod laughed at her outer-borough mercantile phrasing.

"Maybe you shouldn't have taken that video," Ed said. "You know, privacy." Karen shrugged. Ed understood that to Karen and her ilk from the Valley anything that involved pixels and a thumb was always permissible.

"Should we tell Sasha?" Vinod asked. "I'm sure she just took him to the bathroom and—"

"And helped him wash off!" Karen shouted. Dee laughed.

"Well," Ed said. "Thanks for that. Are you guys sure you still want to watch this show? It'll seem dull by comparison. No horny Russian shrinks or nude stars of stage and screen. You have been warned."

The show began and they watched it as it was intended, as background entertainment, as a soft soothing noise. In accordance with the rules of Russian novels, each thought about another. "Night, Karen-*emo*," Nat had said to her, the child's hands folded before her warm face in the default position of Christian prayer, a pretty Korean boy and a truculent llama beneath her pillow, the world guarded and impeccably safe from viruses and men.

She should take her somewhere, Karen thought. Somewhere far away. Two sisters making a life together. The plan built in her mind like a storm. And Vinod? Could she love a man she pitied? But what if she no longer pitied him?

THE WIND PRESSED against the Actor's window, thumping it back and forth, making sleep impossible. He had to get out of here. What would the next weeks look like? Getting handjobs from Senderovsky's wife while Dee ignored him at dinner? He had peers who craved humiliation more than anything, so-called action heroes who liked to be flagellated and "pegged," but he did not count among their number. He would get in the Lancia and be back in the city by early morning. He would live dangerously among its emptiness. He would make a statement of brotherhood, or sisterhood, with the cashiers and grocers who remained. But he couldn't! He wanted to run out and serenade her bungalow with his impeccable singing voice. But what if the window opened and it was him? He pictured a pocket square tucked into polka-dot pajamas, a victorious smile, her rustling in the bed behind him. Or maybe, despite the storm, despite the cold, they were taking an outdoor shower together, the very outdoor shower that had been denied him in the Petersburg Bungalow. He put on a robe from the California vineyard Ed despised and took his tablet to the main house. Outside, the battering wind leaned into him, misjudging his strength as they all did. In the quiet of the kitchen, the lights of the espresso machine blinking semaphore, he clicked through her oeuvre some more, impatiently settling on her social accounts. And there, posted just an hour ago, was the enhanced photo of the two of them. Elspeth would see it and leave a message of garbled intensity. His publicist would say something both worldly and worried. His fans—ah, but who cared about them. They would adjust. She posted their photograph together. She wanted the world to see. He put the pad down on the counter and smelled the fish and rotting meat in the garbage, the windows working fast in their panes. *Come to me,* he said to the wind. *I am the trickster Odysseus. You will fill my sails.*

SENDEROVSKY SAT UP for the prescribed hour before going to sleep, hoping to ease the acid reflux out of him. But he still coughed. Dryly. "Let me just take your temperature," Masha said.

"Oh, look how kind she is now," Senderovsky said in Russian. "Maybe you can help me take a shower, too."

"I don't know what you think happened," she said in English, "other than me once again having to clean up your mess."

"I used to think your accent was so sweet when you spoke in English," he said. "Just because you came at a later age. I wanted to guide you. I wanted to help you adapt."

"Keep talking in the past tense," she said. "Who can blame you given the way our future looks."

"Shifting the blame," he said, "how au courant."

"And now you're talking to me like you're on social media," she said. "Oh, Sashen'ka. Don't stop being clever and pithy. It turns me on so much." She shut off the light and he could hear her turning away from him, the bed grunting in its own practiced language.

WHEN THE SOUND of his cough woke him up, the wind was ripping through the trees, hungry for leaves but settling for the branches, which it cracked with a horrific groan, one by one, like a torturer in the Lubyanka.

Goddamnit, the wind *does* sound like a freight train, Senderovsky thought. He was the sworn enemy of clichés; the one time he had raised his voice at Dee in class was when she used "robin's-egg blue" to describe the shade of a nursery that had never existed in her particular reality. He got up and slid open one of the blinds. The moon was absent, but two ghostly beams ran down half the length of the driveway, attached, most likely, to a black pickup truck with SLEGS BLANKES on its rear bumper. He had had enough of this. He would call the police. No, he would go down himself, come what may. He put on his athletic pants and dressing gown, converting their ridiculousness to armor, and grabbed a woolen hat off a peg in the mudroom.

Outside, the wind threatened to lift him off his feet and carry him, gown flapping, to a graveyard of English nannies and broken umbrellas. But Senderovsky persisted. He sloshed through the mist coating the special glasses he wore at night. (His night vision was also fading with age.) As he entered the high beams' long field of vision, he saw what the wind had already wrought no more than halfway through the night, the lawn now covered by an even-grander assortment of blanched tree branches, the embodiment of a universe without thought or care, rife with heartbreak, sprinkled liberally with disease, its inhabitants walking lamb steaks.

"Fuck!" he shouted, uncharacteristically.

Even as he strode toward the beamed interloper at the end of his driveway, Senderovsky took the wind personally. He had just given the tree guy eight hundred dollars in cash he did not have. And for what? Nothing changed. The dead trees kept falling. He could not win.

"Who are you?" he shouted toward the solitary figure behind the wheel of the pickup. He could not see a gloved hand tapping upon it, the call letters of a terrestrial pop music station coming in green over the dashboard. He tried a kinder tack as he approached. "Are you lost?" he shouted. And then in his best American, "Mister, are you lost?"

A crack popped past him. A gunshot? And then another crack. He covered his face with his opened gown and fell to the ground, gravel against his stomach. The cracking sound returned, but this time it wouldn't stop; an object was groaning under the wind's unremitting torture, its pleas ignored, until a chunk of elm, an antler of wood, began to separate from the tall bare yellow trunk right above Senderovsky.

Ny vsyo, he thought in Russian. *Well, I'm done for.* But as he closed his eyes, he found himself being rolled off the driveway and into the soft ditch of the lawn, the beneficiary of an unseen providence. A terrible crash curled him fetally. Moments later, when he opened his eyes, the utmost extremity of the immense sundered branch was tapping him on the forehead with an insistent finger, the way Nat sometimes did to wake him up at an early hour. The wind kept at it, but now country rain that put his wife to sleep without fail had started sluicing against the Rushmore of his forehead. The freshly sundered tree limb gave off the gamy odor of young summer skin. It was dead black now. The power had failed all across town, much as it was failing across the country. The truck down the driveway was gone.

ACT THREE

Out Like a Lamb

I

"THERE ARE BEAUTIFUL cattails on the side of the road," Nat informed Senderovsky over breakfast two weeks after we had last seen them. Per her therapists, her eye-contact skills were poor, but now she was looking into his eyes directly, as if trying to befriend him with her innocence. How did Karen merge with her so well? How could he not acknowledge that he was the father of a remarkable child, who noticed everything, processed it differently than those with fewer anxieties, those with quieter minds, and spoke with utmost honesty? It was still not too late to be a complete parent to her if he could find the solvent that might decalcify his love. His beloved espresso trembled in his hand and he crunched at the high-fiber cereal in his mouth. "Look at them if you go for a walk today, okay, Daddy?" Nat said.

"Okay," Senderovsky said. But, to paraphrase a last line of a famous author, he did not move. Instead of the soft brown beams of his daughter's eyes, he saw the truck's lights at the end of the driveway, bathing him in their malevolent illumination.

PEOPLE WERE DYING in the city. Some more than others. The virus had roamed the earth but had chosen to settle down there, just as the parents of Masha, Senderovsky, Karen, and Vinod had chosen it four decades ago as a place to escape the nighttime reverberations of Stalin and Hitler, of partition and Partition, of the pain that radiated not in distant memory but cracked outright from their own fathers' hands.

Catching a signal in the main house, the bungalow colonists learned of what was happening a hundred and twenty miles down the river, and they felt many things, but mostly they felt guilt. It was so unconscionably lovely where they were. The weather remained fickle, but even its fickleness was something to behold. A fine layer of snow after a heatstroke day. ("You're gonna be okay, flowers," Nat sang anxiously to the daffodils she and Karen had planted by the main house, in full view of Masha's office.) A heatstroke day interrupted by a new sprinkling of snow, which rested like bits of wet sugar on Nat's tongue. Even the nightly windstorms, which continued trashing Senderovsky's lawn with comical consistency, were in their own way breathtaking, the trees—now sprouting their first leaves—swaying in long measures like midnight dancers.

Guilt. Because they were safe here in their own community, and after two weeks of Masha-imposed semi-quarantine they no longer needed to maintain distance from one another, with the exception of Senderovsky, whose cough only worsened by the day. "I don't have it," he would announce every night at dinner, their one communal meal, after suffering a consumptive fit, his eyes wet with tears. "Acid reflux," he would add as the Actor made a show of moving away from him and toward Masha, whose knee now received him, warm and ready beneath the table.

Guilt because there was sumptuous food (everyone but Senderovsky put on weight, even Vinod), educated and intriguing company, and, for some, the first tendrils of love. No one was more affected by the stark difference between town and country than Vinod. There were, he realized, a series of refrigerated trucks parked behind his local hospital in Queens, collecting the forklifted bodies of the dead. He wrote, guiltily, to his fellow workers at his uncle's restaurant. Whenever they would write back, he would be happy they responded. But upon reading their messages he would put down his phone and look out the window and watch the ricks of hay being prepared in the adjacent meadows while the mating monarchs migrated north feasting on milkweed in a sweep of black and orange. Why was he here and why were his co-workers there? Because his parents had documents? Because educated Indians were in the grand order of things prioritized over uneducated Mexicans? Even as he had objectively failed by the standards of his family, first as an adjunct in the merry field of "writing and rhetoric" and then as a common worker, he found himself here, at the estate of a fellow classmate at an elite high school, sheltering in place, sheltering in space.

He had come here to dissolve—his words, not ours—but it was the city that was dissolving behind him. If she wasn't here, if she didn't make him happy every day with her predictable banter and nosiness, with her unexpected love for Senderovsky's little girl, he told himself he would leave for Elmhurst at once.

But he stayed. They all did. Even as the indolence of the country life made them slower, softer, wobblier on their feet. The only exception, yet again, was Senderovsky, whose anxiety gurgled in the same acidic bath as his reflux. He couldn't sleep and not just because his cough kept him awake. (Masha wore earplugs now.) He considered summoning a police car to investigate the black pickup truck, but he worried the arrival of the state troopers would scare Masha and the colonists. He kept his fear to himself, along with the memory of the oversize elm branch that might have killed him that night and the kindly force that rolled him to safety. For how much longer would he stay lucky? When he tried to breathe after coughing, he could hear the grind of his lungs and esophagus like the gears of a rusted superannuated clock. Each morning he smelled his own armpits, because the virus was said to affect one's sense of smell. The familiar barnyard odors were there, but when he looked into the mirror he could not locate the gaze of his eyes, only their hollows. Who was sitting behind the wheel of the truck ready to assault his colony? Who had taken Vinod's novel? Who had figured out the truth?

2

THE JAPANESE REALITY show was the steady *taiko* drumbeat of their isolated lives. The pace was nineteenth century, at best, and sometimes Vinod or the Actor would put down the Russian play or novel they were reading and wonder if they were still watching the show instead. The setup was traditional to the genre, three Japanese women and three men in their twenties were given a fancy house in Tokyo or in Hawaii or elsewhere in Japan. But unlike the Western equivalents, the Japanese roommates rarely betrayed one another or erupted in profanity or succumbed to onscreen lust. They probed their friendships and dalliances and extended romances so shyly, with such a lack of surety, that Ed and Senderovsky and Masha and especially Vinod thought they were watching a parallel universe in which they were reborn as young and good-looking middle-class Japanese just starting out as retail workers and chefs and online personalities.

There were to date about a half-thousand episodes, and Ed knew them all by heart. How could this man without entanglements be so taken by a show where an entire thirty minutes could be spent discussing a slight rebuff over a bowl of soba noodles? How could Ed run to the bathroom in tears every time a spunky, naïve half-Indonesian wrestler got rejected by her crush, a laconic self-involved basketball player?

Senderovsky also found the show heartbreaking. The failures of the onscreen young people brought to mind his own. They reminded him of his loveless early years, before he had sold his first book. Just as then, his finances were in free fall. The bill for removing the dead trees exceeded four thousand dollars, and he had had to take out an additional credit card from a usurious last-ditch lender. And now it was imperative for his marriage to fix the water situation in the bungalows and the main house. Yes, Senderovsky had heard that his wife and the Actor were involved in some kind of intricate cleansing ritual. He would sometimes press his ear to the door of the first-floor bathroom where he knew Masha kept emergency daytime water buckets, though he never heard anything. Also, there were rumors of Karen having taken a video of something untoward. When Senderovsky thought of his wife sexually, he returned to the wild Fort Greene party during which they had reunited in 2001, the smooth tanned skin, the way the light shone off the twin pivots of her bare shoulders, her youthful flirting and exaggerated med-school-student toughness. Had she any of that vitality left? And if so why would the Actor deserve those long-stored-away final dregs of life?

The handyman had come to look things over but could not pinpoint the problem even after folding himself painfully under several washbasins. "Well," he said, "looks like it's time to call in the general." By which he meant the general contractor who had built the cottages. Normally, Senderovsky would laugh at this joke, file it under "country wisdom," but today he grew impatient and cross. "What do we pay you for?" he bellowed.

The handyman stood at his full rural height, his features pink and childlike, his true age impossible to pinpoint, but all of him huffing with displeasure, fogging the cheap lenses of his glasses. (What if *he* was the driver of the black pickup? Perhaps his antagonist stood right before him, ready to crack him open as the elm branch should have done on the night of the storm.) "Thing is," the handyman said, "you haven't paid me in two weeks. And I don't work for free. Missus got"—he mentioned the scientific as well as Christian name of a disease and some of its ghastly features. "We got bills, too. Only for us it's a matter of life and death."

Senderovsky watched his truck, gray not black in color, race down the fairway of his lawn and disappear with an angry rightward swerve. The general contractor was summoned, a skinny college-educated man who spoke in vexing, incomplete sentences and charged in increments of ten thousand dollars. He drove a black pickup, which he kept in country-authentic condition, spring mud still coating its flaps. Had this been Senderovsky's tormentor, owner of the gloved hand tapping the wheel at the end of his driveway? No, it wasn't possible. Senderovsky had always paid his bills to the contractor on time. Plumbers and electricians and tree guys came and went, but one never stiffed one's contractor in the country.

"I'm going to have to sonar the pump, looks like," the general said.

"What does that even mean?" Senderovsky cried, his Russian accent returning. "We are not on a submarine." But the sonar would soon reveal a crack in the pump, which meant the entire mechanism had to be replaced at a cost of ten thousand dollars, excluding labor.

"I understand you've been having trouble paying some of your service providers on time," the general said, pressing on the bridge of his urbane glasses and looking around philosophically.

"Some income streams have dried up," Senderovsky said. "Because of the virus," he lied.

"Be that as it may," the contractor said.

Senderovsky began coughing into his fist now, the same dry, monstrous heaves that rocked him at the dinner table. The contractor stepped away and pulled up his mask. They were wearing them in the wealthy villages now. Just the other day, Senderovsky had seen an old man in a blue surgical mask walking behind a little masked girl on the main street of a gingerbread town, and the scene struck him as the beginning of the end of the world.

"I'll always have money for you," Senderovsky said. "Please, just start the work. It's imperative."

AROUND THIS TIME of financial troubles, his Los Angeles agent called, her voice smooth and deceptively creamy like a chilled chia-seed parfait. "How's my favorite Russian novelist-cum-screenwriter?" she breathed into the phone.

The virus had stopped production, but now that the middle classes were in bed in their underwear for the foreseeable future, the need for "content" was greater than ever. According to his agent, another series had failed to be renewed at the network, a medical drama about people dying of contagious diseases, and now they were scrambling to replace it with something funny and far removed from the dystopia of the present day. Senderovsky's script had again found favor with the network's mercurial head.

"I'm ready to go, but he won't sign off," Senderovsky said of the Actor. "He doesn't want it to be funny. He wants *The Odyssey*."

"Screw him," the agent said. "Tell him we have a slotski at the networkski."

"He's an executive producer."

"So is my cat at this point. Or I should say my *koshka*."

The agent had been a Russian minor in college.

"You know how he is. He lashes out at me. He's competitive. He's flirting with my wife."

"What are you, the Commissar of Hurt Feelings? Don't act like a child, Peter Panovich. We got a series to make."

"Can I ask for an advance against my back end?"

"Ha ha ha! You still got it, humor-wise. And I know exactly who should direct the pilot." She mentioned the name of an Indian woman, whom Senderovsky recognized from a science fiction series he had tried to enjoy. "I visited her vacay house in Kerala," the agent said. "She has a lovely family and a lovely home."

Senderovsky now recalled that the agent had said the same thing about his house and his wife and child upon visiting a few years prior. Like a fool, he had carried those words in the little purse he had sewn beneath his heart as a child, a repository of all the American words his parents would never utter. He had once again forgotten a cardinal rule: that a person living beneath an eternally blue sky could find comfort in the gray landscapes of others. As long as there was wheatgrass and yoga *somewhere* in the world, everything and everyone was "lovely."

Still, a slot! And talk of actual directors and actual pilots. Now he had a clear mission and an even clearer obstacle. His entire life hinged on his ability to move it out of the way.

DEE AND SENDEROVSKY were on the porch's weatherproof sofas overlooking the meadow and the sheep farm beyond. The carpets of grass and the far horizon still soothed Dee, but not to the same extent as when she had first arrived. She, too, was starting to wonder, although without any of Vinod's philosophical gambits, if any of this was real, if she had been trapped and mounted like one of Nabokov's helpless butterflies for the amusement of Senderovsky or some much-higher power.

"I have here," Senderovsky announced, presenting a sheaf of papers to Dee, "the pilot to our series. I'm dying for you to read it."

"Sure thang," Dee said. "I love everything you do. It's always funny."

A Fokker D from the nearby aerodrome for antique planes made a stuttering pass around the bungalows and was now heading back to the mowed stretch of grass that served as its landing strip. Senderovsky thought he could make out an iron cross on the side of the old biplane. More *slegs blankes*? Was he being watched from the air as well?

"And there's a tiny favor I'd like to ask," he said. "If you read it and like it, maybe you can spend some time with our thespian friend and tell him so. I think it would be so helpful for him to hear a perspective from someone he really respects."

Dee laughed. Her mouth was graceful, Senderovsky acknowledged, in the same way he found the mane of the palomino down the road graceful. "I feel sorry for him," Dee said. "That algorithm is so dicked up."

"My bet would be," Senderovsky said, "that even if you take away the algorithm, he would still be in love with you."

"Bullshit, Proffy," Dee said. "He barely looked at me before we took that photo."

"He falls in love with artists and thinkers."

"He hasn't even read my book."

The door to the main house creaked open, and Masha emerged carrying a heavy pail of water, wearing a sundress still a few weeks out of season. She was headed for the Petersburg Bungalow. She saw Dee and her husband, wondered how she should compose herself, *if* she could compose herself, and decided that no composition was necessary in the end. She smiled, waved with her free hand, and continued on her way to the Actor's cabin, the water sloshing loudly in her pail, her gait veering to the left (her right leg had gone numb during the night), and her dress sticking to her posterior, until, with a trembling hand, she straightened it. They watched her leave the pail at the Actor's door, knock twice, then quickly turn around and head back, her eyes minding the fur of her slippers.

The Actor opened the door wearing nothing but a demonstrative pair of European underwear, looked down at the pail, and called out, "Masha!" When she wouldn't respond, he shouted as if to an errant dog, "What's wrong with you? Come back!" Then he glanced at the porch, saw Senderovsky, and especially saw Dee, and managed to both open his mouth and shut his door at the same time.

Masha's brazenness affected Dee more than it did Senderovsky. She thought of what the pail of water, its very sloshing, represented. She thought of its uses and of Masha's pale dumpling hand. She considered herself uncritically, saw her many advantages, and decided to also grow bold. "I'll read your script and talk to him," she said. "Maybe you can lay the groundwork. Make it look like it was your idea. Hello? Are you listening?"

Senderovsky watched his wife in the sundress return to her patients and her child's lesson plans and thought of the raft of mystery that floats between two partners, even contented ones, as they turn in for the night. He wished he could fall in love with someone as his wife evidently had done. He had chased after beauty for such a long part of his life, until he had caught up with it and found it, like everything else, worthy of no more than a chapter or two of heightened prose.

Now all that mattered was the property and its salvation. The dewy land and the rustle of dying trees and the companionship of friends disembarking at the station and the sound of grilled meat being turned over, once, twice—all of it must remain his until the day he coughed his last.

3

"IF YOU ARE interested in my wife, I could look the other way." Senderovsky was holding the pail of water in front of him, surprised by just how heavy it was and yet how easily his wife had carried it.

"You can put that down," the Actor said. "And I'm not interested in Masha." He had just been taking a turn at himself beneath the sheets only to be interrupted by the arrival of the wrong Senderovsky.

"I am telling you this as a gentleman," Senderovsky said. "I am not bound by old constraints."

"What a weasel of a man you are." The Actor wiped his hand on his European underwear.

"Look at it my way," Senderovsky said. "I did not grow up with the advantages you had. Advantages physical, financial, emotional. And yet here I stand before you. Offering a bucket of water my wife brought to you. I assume you have your own sponge. All I want is for us to move forward and for you to be happy."

The Actor sneered. He wondered if he could continue his daily soapings with Masha now that her husband knew and the excitement of the transgression would be gone. In the end, Senderovsky ruined everything.

"You think you're better than me, don't you?" the Actor said.

"Not at all," Senderovsky said. "It's not a competition."

The Actor slung on a T-shirt that barely covered his navel. He did not want to talk about Masha, but he did want to talk.

"Maybe you're right about advantages," he said. "Some of us are light on our feet. We can pivot. We're not afraid of learning new things instead of living in the past. I did not just study 'acting.' I am not just an 'actor.' I studied dancing, music, literature, history, theology, physics both practical and theoretical."

He gestured to the bungalow redolent of books and mouse droppings. "And in the end, I am better than you. I'm a better driver than you, a better sous-chef, a better flight mechanic, a better commercial fisherman, a better private investigator, a better and certainly more courageous astronaut, and, if I took the time to really learn the craft, a better writer. I also know how to communicate with people, how to elicit their frankest emotions. And I know how to make them come. So that's the difference between us."

"I think I get it," Senderovsky said.

"I'm not sure you do. I don't do this for the money. I don't do this to be loved. I don't want people to laugh or cry with me. If there's applause, fine. Silence is dandy also. I don't need cute articles written about my apartment or my favorite soap. I have respect for the work that I do. From the moment I saw the stage, I was awed by it. What awes you about the work you do? How does it humble you?"

"Although," Senderovsky said, "permit me a lame defense. Even those of us without your natural advantages must still make do in the world. There's a Russian term: *krutista*, meaning 'to spin around.' To spin around from one thing to another trying to make ends meet. That's the human condition for most of us. We spin and spin like a dreidel in December. We go, as they used to say, 'in service' to others. Aren't we all in service to you?"

"Tell your wife she can come and finish what she started," the Actor said. "Because, yes, she started it, if you must know. She put her hands on me first. How little she thinks of you."

"But what about her?" Senderovsky said.

"What about who?"

"The one you really love. Dee."

"Fuck you," the Actor said. "It's not me, it's the algorithm. She sees me as a robot because of what your friend did to me."

"What if I could do something about that?" Senderovsky said. "What if I could bring you together naturally? She's a writer, you're a writer."

"I never said that I'm a writer. Only that I would be if I applied myself. I might start a memoir, actually."

"She wants to go on a walk with you," Senderovsky said.

"She said that?" The Actor met the landowner's gaze. His face was red, but his chakras were pulsing blue. Senderovsky was taken by his vulnerability. "What about her walks with Ed?"

"I think she's capable of walking with more than one person," Senderovsky said, his voice now cold and authoritative. "Maybe you can talk about the script. I printed out a version for her."

Ah, the Actor thought. It has something to do with the script. He's enlisted her. That was the angle from the start. "No, this is not a quid pro quo at all," Senderovsky said, anticipating the Actor's objections. "I just want you two to have something to talk about."

He turned around to leave.

"When?" the Actor shouted.

"When what?"

"When can I go for a walk with her?" So now he was asking permission. Like a supplicant. Like a man "in service."

"I'll let you know," Senderovsky said. "But it shouldn't be long now."

THE DAY PASSED between cold and warmth, but he dressed in a way he hadn't since the virus arrived, skinny jeans and a white tee, all designed to showcase his elemental attractiveness, even at the cost of continuous shivering and preternaturally erect nipples. He also wore a cap with the logo of a defunct baseball team low with sunglasses so that it would be harder for passing motorists to identify him.

At the foot of the driveway, per Senderovsky's instructions, she awaited him in her usual sweatpants and fleece, and the fact that she didn't care to change her daily outfit for him depressed the Actor. "Hey, thanks for agreeing to take a walk with me," he said. Already he sounded ridiculous: hoping for favor instead of disbursing it. He had to act like the man he was. On a busy shooting set, among hundreds of concerns circulating about, each crew member had two others: *What is the Actor's mood? What can I do to please him?*

"Ed and I always walk in this direction," she said. "Should we try going the opposite way?"

"Yes," he said. "So mysterious. In this direction. To go walking." What did that even mean?

It was the late afternoon, the day's glare turning soft around them. "I hear it's finally going to stay warm next week," the Actor said. "God, listen to me small talk."

"Love me some small talk," Dee drawled. "The smaller the better. Yessir." He laughed. He was, like most of the important Actors, far shorter than one imagined, of very average height, really. Practically, this meant that her non-nose was about even with his full chin, now dappled in soft wiry fur and cleansed with milled Danish soap that he had ordered for this very occasion. He wasn't of that ethnicity, but he reminded her of some of the older Jewish boys in her neighborhood fresh from the local cheder, their eyes still glossy with scripture now bedeviled by the sharp light of the Christian outdoors. How those yeshiva boys looked at her, or rather looked away from her, all of them aflame with the worst and most common kind of want, the want that is unarticulated, shriveled purple, and forever stuck in the chest. His want wasn't so different from theirs, was it? Karen's algorithm had that feel of fundamentalist religion to it. She herself couldn't fall in love, Dee thought of the Tröö Emotions inventor; she did not have the courage to accept Vinod's love, and now millions around the world had an unnecessary cross to bear, were suffering from the very desire she herself refused to countenance.

They should just get it over with. Let him pump away for five minutes with those soft, unexercised forearms gathering her up in some dense unmowed glade and then maybe they could take a selfie together and move on. Just this morning she had asked Masha for tweezers to pluck her eyebrows into shape, and before she left her bungalow had carefully checked her teeth in the mirror. Still, she wouldn't dress up for him. Let him eat fleece.

Animals began to present themselves as they walked. A golden ruffed hawk floated directly above them, surrendering to an updraft. "That must be nice," Dee said. "To just coast."

"I glided once," the Actor mumbled, but he wasn't even sure if that was the right verb to describe what he had done once over a patch of the Mojave Desert, the sun like fire on his back.

They passed another sheep meadow, this one a much more ramshackle version of the one near Senderovsky's estate. A black sheep was sunbathing on its haunches away from its comrades. That was me as a child, the Actor wanted to lie to her, but restrained himself. He had been sleepless and working through his own biography all of the previous night in preparation. They passed a rabbit who stopped in fear as they approached and craned his thin, breakable neck, his cottontail shaking miserably. Perhaps that too was me at some point, the Actor thought. But at which point? A deer on the road stopped, looked at them, then very slowly and elegantly lifted up one leg as if he was about to play the piano.

"A deer," the Actor said. Great. He was identifying common animals now. "Beautiful," he added to qualify it.

They passed a man petting a horse over a fence with great tenderness. "Hey, Echo," the man was saying, looking deep into the saucers that showcased the vastness of the animal's soul. (On the way back, they would see the horse, alone, looking them over expectantly and licking his sensitive, prehensile lips.) "You have a real pretty pony there," Dee said to the besotted man, who waved friendly to them.

They passed a country family, their faces glum and consumptive, the kids wearing oatmeal-colored sweatshirts with the names of local public schools. The adults glared at them hatefully, assuming they were from the city, until Dee said, "Hi, y'all. They say it's gonna get warmer any minute now." And then there followed an exchange of waves and minor humanity. "Ed loves it when I engage like that," Dee said to the Actor.

"I bet you keep him safe on your walks," the Actor said.

"We passed a pickup with a Confederate flag that read HERITAGE NOT HATE. Hoo-boy, those folks looked about ready to murder Ed, until they saw me." They both laughed.

"What would we eat if they murdered our chef?" the Actor said. "Oh, look at that. A box turtle."

"She's a snapper," Dee said, bending down to the creature beginning her long and dangerous journey across the road. "Wonder what she's up to. It's too early for her to be traveling to lay eggs."

"Poor thing's going to get run over," the Actor said. He decided to grab the prehistoric animal by the shell and carry her over to the other side of the road where a pond the consistency of split pea soup awaited her.

"Hold up, Ranger Rick," Dee said. "Don't just grab her like that. We had them alligator ones that could really take a finger off." The Actor sighed. He wished he had had that level of engagement with nature growing up and the vocabulary to articulate it. Senderovsky's little girl had said something strange the other day (among the many strange things she would say), "You can always trust nature." He didn't know if it was true, but he envied the little girl her youth in the country. He usually avoided roles that were set in the vast amphitheaters of the West because the silence of nonhumans mystified him. But Dee was now talking to the turtle.

"Here you go, honey," she said. "Now I'm just taking you by the back of the shell, not going to touch your tail, sweet pea. Don't want to hurt your spinal column. And now I'm turning you around just so I can drag you better. So you're looking backward, but you're going forward." The Actor watched the animal's Jurassic legs scramble against the tarmac as her shell left a wet trail across the road. She snapped her jowls behind her once, but soon succumbed to Dee's measured motion.

A black pickup truck slowed down and would not pass until the operation was concluded. It sat there in the middle of the road, its engine growling with expectation. The animal's eyeballs turned continuously within their scaly enclosures, showing all black or all white, and the Actor wondered if she was scared. He wanted to comfort the creature, but did not know how. To pet it? The shell was an obvious impediment, and nothing about "snapping turtle" suggested an easy exchange of warmth. One could only do what Dee was doing.

Once she had dragged the turtle to the scummy pond across the road, Dee spun it around by the back of the shell so that it would face in the right direction, so that it wouldn't be confused. That last gesture caught the Actor unaware, and he felt himself slackening with the onslaught of unexplained but often useful sadness that he used as a placeholder for love. He did not know that in addition to being funny and combative and Southern, Dee could also be kind. If there were Truer Emotions beyond those he saw in the enhanced photo, he did not want to find himself falling through their depths.

The owner of the black pickup honked twice, perhaps to acknowledge Dee's good work. The Actor strained to see its occupant through the tinted windows, but he could only see himself.

A TICKLE OF rain fell upon them, and Dee wanted to know if the Actor was cold in his tee and if he wanted to turn back. He had never been more vehemently against an idea. If they kept walking longer, he felt, they would find each other, broaden their connection beyond their encounter with the turtle, even as they stayed mostly silent, her reflection in his sunglasses pleasant and assured.

The road ran out of pavement and they trampled through the wet dirt beneath a cool shady scrim of pines. Once the pines ended, they came upon a clearing filled with clumsy structures that brought to mind an apocalyptic version of Senderovsky's estate. There were little clapboard bungalows surrounding a stucco House on the Hill with its own attached covered porch (though the screens had long been torn into metallic sheets that now flapped in the wind ominously). On every abandoned building one could see the chalked scribbling of adolescent and teenaged children worldlier than one might expect in the countryside: "Ömercan Güldal was here. Turkey rulz!" "Hello from NBA Future Superstar João Sousa." "Gianni Fusco, Bunk 12, making boo-boo in your ass. *Forza Italia!*"

"I think this was like an international children's camp or something," the Actor said.

"I believe you are correct," Dee said, pointing to a roadside sign half hidden by creeping sumac that read CAMP INTERNATIONALE. It was festooned with children's drawings of the flags of their many countries. "Why don't we get you out of the rain." She took his hand and led him to an outdoor theater space smelling of moss and rotting wood. A giant globe had been painted above the stage in the same sloppy adolescent manner as the rest of the signage, along with the legend ACTORS SHOW US THE TRUE FACE OF THE WORLD.

"Well," he said, "I can't argue with that sentiment, can I?" His hand was still in hers and she had pressed her thumb into his palm in a way that he thought bespoke intent.

"That is exceptionally poorly phrased," she said of the sign.

"I think English got abused a lot around these parts," he said. "Along with the victims of Gianni Fusco. You have a pretty laugh, by the way. Could this be the first time I made you laugh? Intentionally, I mean."

Now was not the time to kiss him. They sat down on the stage, and she leaned her back against his shoulder so that they faced away from each other. His tee was wet and he shivered profoundly and she thought of the little rabbit they had scared along the way. An empty box of condoms sat next to her; the orange price sticker told her that they were half as expensive here as in the city. The rain was getting louder against the roof of the outdoor theater, but somehow it did not leak and they both felt safe for the moment. She thought she might have to change that.

"I'm sorry," Dee said, "about what Karen did to you."

"If there's an antidote, I don't want it," he said. "Although she did offer me first dibs for free."

"Why wouldn't you want it?"

"It's no different than falling in love without it, in the end."

"What do you mean?"

"You fall in love with yourself first. With who you want to be when interacting with the person you think you're in love with. Sorry, my English not so good. I hope you can understand NBA Future Super-star."

She didn't laugh. "Go on," she said.

"Then maybe, if you loosen up a little, you fall in love with what the other person really is, but primarily you still love them because of how they enhance you. Now you just have all these backup reasons to love them." He was speaking very fast. He was once again onstage, in his manic state, which would win him plaudits with anyone but her. "Like when I saw you help that turtle. I thought, Oh, that's who *she* is. But the project remains the same. Self-fulfillment. Ed doesn't love you as much as he loves the closed circuit that you make out of him."

"There are two conjectures here. One, that I am ultimately not lovable, except maybe when animals with thicker shells than your own are involved. And two, that everyone is as self-obsessed as you are. That no one else can appreciate another person on their own merits."

"That's three conjectures. And you're lovable enough. And I'm not going to lie and say I'm not self-obsessed. And it didn't used to be that way when I was unknown. That's been foisted upon me by society."

"So society got to you before Karen's algorithm did?"

"See, we're in this trap where we think that people who are fortunate, often through their own hard work, aren't allowed to be unhappy."

"Most of literature is about privileged people being unhappy. *Anna Karenina* much? Like, what the fuck does Uchi the hairdresser have to be upset about?" Uchi was a roommate on the Japanese reality show whose wooden box of prized beef, a gift from a grateful client, had been eaten by his girlfriend and other roommates without permission.

"They ate his meat! They stole a part of his identity."

"And Karen's algorithm stole your identity?"

"No, this *is* my identity."

" 'My identity by itself causes violence.' "

"Huh?"

"It's from a song. N.W.A."

"Why do you know so much old rap?"

"Because I'm white. How is pursuing me your identity?"

"Because I've fallen in love—"

"Stop saying 'in love' so easily. It makes you sound even more programmed."

The Actor sighed. "There's no way I can make you look at me as something other than a cripple."

"We're going to fuck soon," Dee said. "So I want you to start being more seductive or it's going to be very lame."

"Goddamnit it," he said. "Why do you have to be like this? You're so bellicose." Dee thought of her mother, the angry way she flirted with policemen and magistrates and bill collectors. Bellicose. But it was too late for her to change the basic formula. Someone like Ed made sense for her. He cooked well; he spoke nicely; he would, as they used to say without irony, take good care of her. So why, besides "being central to the culture," as Senderovsky had once described him, was she here with this man?

"I'm helping you," she said. "I'm chipping away at the algorithm. I'm making you feel less special about yourself for being quote-unquote in love with me. Because Karen or no Karen, there's nothing special about your feelings. The world is burning up, if you haven't noticed. We're all Generation L now."

"Go ahead, quote your boyfriend. The only reason you like him is that you're not intimidated by him."

"Who wants to be intimidated?"

"People should be intimidated. Love should be a scary thing. We should tremble in its presence. Or else you end up like Sasha and his wife."

"You mean *your* girlfriend."

"Please. We're all just trying to pass the time."

"Unbelievable."

"You know what I overheard him say once to his agent? He called me 'the honey-eyed man with the rotten soul.' This was before I touched his wife."

"And you let that get to you? Sasha's career peaked so long ago I can hardly remember what all the hullabaloo was about. Russia something-something."

"Like you haven't read his pilot script. Like that's not why you're here."

"No, I'm not a spaniel who does as told. Though if I were you, I would just do this fucking show with him and get it over with. Not like your career's going anyplace special these days either. I looked up the reviews for *München am Hudson* and *Terabyte*. Jesus."

"Great. Thanks for that. And now you just want to fuck to get *this* over with, too, don't you?"

"That's life. It moves forward. To its logical conclusion."

"You're going to fuck me without any pleasure."

"That's entirely up to you."

He grabbed her by the shoulders and spun her around. "No," she said. "Don't even try it like that."

"I wasn't trying—" He let go of her shoulders. "You know what?" he said. "I'm supposed to be the Actor, but I'm the only one of you who's not acting all the time. I'm the only one who's not just copying or imitating. Because that's now what my craft calls for. Look at you bunch. The Russian writer. The soulful Brahmin. Asian *Brideshead Revisited*. And you. The drunk Southern fireball."

"Take off that filthy wet T-shirt," she said. "How stupid to dress like that on a cold day. While there's a virus floating around. You want to impress me? You think I don't know what your body looks like? We all know what your body looks like. Hooray for having a nice body."

He started to take his T-shirt off, but managed to rip it under the armpits in the process. "People can see us," he said, nodding at the road curving before the theater space.

"And that bothers you?" she said. "The whole world's a stage."

"'Actors show us the true face of the world,'" he said.

"What?"

He pointed to the sign above them.

"Off with the jeans," she said.

"No."

"No?" She avoided his little boy's gaze, the trembling of his eyes. "Fine," she said. She unbuttoned his jeans, one by one by one. With his underwear halfway down around his ankles, he looked trapped in the moment. But he was also erect, and the triangle of his pubis had grown in especially dark. If she ignored the look on his face, she could be with a man.

After she had taken off her fleece, he noticed the perfection of her body, skin still taut and young, along with a gloomy pink bra that seemed a size too large. The sweatpants came off like a sheath. The underwear was different from the bra, filigreed, and now he wanted her warmth more than anything. What could he take and what had to be given away? "I go down on you?" he asked. "Or?"

She rolled to her side, looking away from him. He spooned her, hands on her bra, awkwardly massaging her breasts. This was the best part, she thought. Skin to skin. She did not look into his eyes or try to understand the smell of his hair, the awful conditioner he used on his Samsonian locks. There was a delicious loneliness to the hands on her bra not daring to go beneath the straps but also the warm, panting bulk of a man behind her, his breath professionally sweet against her earlobe. She tucked aside her panties—*Panties,* he thought to himself, registering the miracle of them and the miracle of their absence—then guided him inside and he smiled when he heard the familiar sound of entry.

She hadn't realized how hard the wooden planks of the pollen-covered floor would feel against her hip (for sure, there would be a bruise, a memento to be examined in the shower, if there was any water left tonight), and now her eyes settled on an old Nerf football, long abandoned by the likes of Ömercan Güldal and João Sousa, the teeth marks of a local possum still visible against its tender skin. And the graffiti everywhere, these kids proclaiming themselves for the next generation of campers, a generation that would never come. This was all part of the moment that she was inhabiting, alongside the billions of moments that constituted the daily madness of the planet. She pushed harder against him, felt her buttocks against his soft hairless flanks, wanting to give him something extra of herself, maybe even to prove that love was still possible. Her breath was fog in the pregnant air.

Her thrusts made him lose his rhythm. Now he was suspended inside her, nothing less. Everyone uses me, he thought. Like a natural resource. Elspeth, Masha, this woman. And I let them. I enjoy it. Why can't I be the rabbit on the road? The sheep apart from his brethren, sitting on his haunches, alone? Why do I have to work so hard to be vulnerable? Who made me the hawk forever stuck in the updraft?

When a pickup truck's wet tires crunched against the dirt road, when its high beams ran slowly, very slowly, across the single shape they had made of their bodies in a burst of yellow extraterrestrial light, he hid his face but came straightaway.

"I don't want you to hang around that old woman anymore," Dee said, when they were dressing.

"I won't," he said. He hoped she wouldn't see his grin in the growing darkness. She wanted him all to herself now! Strange, under any other circumstance, he would have lost interest in her right at this moment. And then an old instinct took over, and he had to ask like an idiot: "Are you on birth control?"

"With extreme prejudice," she said.

On the walk back, both lost in thought, they passed half a dozen examples of roadkill scattered across the wet tarmac. The Actor recoiled at each animal, but Dee understood a dead possum as well as anything. Still, it was strange that each creature was bleeding above the eye, as if shot by a marksman with a .22. What kind of people lived on this road? At least the snapping turtle was safe within her split-pea pond.

She looked at the darkened figure of the Actor, the optical white of his tee ripped at the armpits, his hands spread before him as he remembered grasping her buttocks on the cold empty stage.

4

"THE GEH GOES *meong-meong, meong-meong*!" Nat barked.

Karen clapped her hands and reached out to tickle her under her tough skinny little arms. Children really squealed when you tickled them—that was a fact. Would Nat remember these pleasures when she was older? Karen did not remember her own. It was all a mess of stolen television hours, cassette tapes clasped into Walkmen, computer programming classes her father made her take at the local Y (who but him knew they would pay off so handsomely?), and the private "Mongoose" language she had invented with Evelyn, snorts and grunts and clicks of the tongue their parents could not understand, its logics as intuitive to her as BASIC or C++. But had anyone ever tickled her? She crossed her arms and tried to tickle herself under the armpits. Maybe it only worked when someone else did it to you.

The child woke up earlier than her parents, so they got in a Korean lesson before Masha hauled her off to the joyless pursuit of Russian and third-grade math and the steady flow of practical therapies. ("Mommy, how long is today's session with Dr. Sandra?") For an entire hour Nat and Karen lived in a world where piggies did a properly piggy *ggul-ggul-ggul*, because on what planet could a fat pink-eared *dwaegi* possibly produce a mannered sound like *oink*? They focused on animals at first, since they were surrounded by them. A *geh* was both a dog and a crab. A *neoguri* was a raccoon dog, a curious citizen of East Asia, more akin to a fox. Steve, on the other hand, was clearly a *mamo*. (Every language should have almost as many vowels as consonants, ten to sixteen in the Hangul alphabet.)

She was in no way qualified to teach Korean, Karen knew, having herself been brought up in that embarrassing immigrant mix of being spoken to by her parents in the true language and replying in the shameful adopted one. Only Vinod and Senderovsky had held on to their respective tongues with flair, although Karen always thought it had made it harder for them to blend in, to accept that they were fully here and not there (witness Vinod's persistent accent and Senderovsky's bungalow madness).

But Karen loved hearing the sound of her own half-English, half-Korean garble, and it was hard to keep Nat from repeating it at the dinner table, where they could both see Masha's hurt and surprise. "Many great writers spoke Russian," Karen once told her over Ed's scorching cod *livornese*, "like your dad." But there was no Russian analogue to BTS, no J-Hope with his weird "acorn" pouch and perfect *aegyo* (performative cuteness), and certainly no sweet lovable Jin with his corny jokes and thick sculpted lips. It fascinated Karen how her original homeland was now open to the world, while Senderovsky's did nothing but try to undermine the few good things about it. No wonder the child wanted one and not the other.

The walls of her bungalow were now transformed. She was on the phone daily with her assistant, shepherding an endless parade of trucks up the gravel driveway, Masha watching the parcels being unloaded at the driveway's terminus and carried off to Karen's bungalow. In Masha's mind the words "I'm losing her" fought hand to hand, syllable to syllable, with "But she's so happy." During bath time Masha had tried cooing Russian songs about accordion-playing crocodiles as she tried to tickle her daughter, to make her squeal, but the child moved without affect between her hands, the warmth of the day and its attendant joys still on her skin. At least her screen time was down, replaced by imaginative play. Her speech was less rigid, more pragmatic. Isn't this exactly what they wanted out of the Kindness Academy? A friend? Karen was close to fifty but, in Masha's estimation, stunted in all the right places.

Karen's living room was covered with Hangul on the walls and little homemade flash cards of all the consonants and vowels. Nat would put together combinations of each, the diphthongs undulat-

ing throughout the simple room, while the other room was covered
with BTS posters from the *Love Yourself* tour and a scratchy suppos-
edly microfiber BTS bedding set which Karen would change as soon
as she came home from watching the Japanese reality show in Ed's
bungalow or dancing with Vinod on the covered porch. In Nat's
imagination, the members of BTS all secretly lived in Karen's bungalow when they weren't touring, and they had become her friends. She
and Karen watched videos about which food they liked to eat, J-Hope
predictably choosing good old *haembeogeo* (diphthongs, assemble!)
and kimchi fried rice, while Jin skewed more delicate with his love of
lobster and cold summer buckwheat noodles with brisket and apple
cider vinegar. "Come on, Ed," Karen said, "make *naengmyeon* for
Nat. She's dying to try it. Take a break from the Mediterranean shit.
All that *chee-juh* is giving me gas. Don't be so self-hating."

They were setting out dishes on the porch, the golden hour giving
way to the gloaming, Vinod already reading on his area rug in the
newly mowed meadow below them, leaning back on one elbow, his
legs too stiff to be crossed.

"I don't do Korean," Ed said. "It's a whole different skill set. And
it's still too cold for *naengmyeon*. And our family's not from the
North, anyhow."

"At least do kimchi fried rice. I'd make it, but I burn everything. I
have no patience. The last thing my mom said before she died was
that I was always destined for a short marriage."

Ed tugged on his cigarette and exhaled a tight, ungenerous stream.
"What's happened to you, *noona*?" he said. "I'm worried."

"About what?"

"About the kid. This virus will be over someday, and then you'll
have to say goodbye to her. She's not your daughter, you know."

"Thanks, Ed," Karen said. "What would I do without your blister-
ing honesty?"

"You want to be Korean all of a sudden, then talk like one."

"Why do you hate me?" she said.

"Why do you think I hate you?"

"Because of Dee."

"I'd have a chance with her if it wasn't for your fucking product. And don't tell me she's not good for me like you're an expert on what's good."

She looked at him. He still had most of his hair, and his jawline remained strong, but age was creeping up around his eyes. She thought of tomorrow's lesson with Nat. How did you say "spider-web"? A spider was a *geomi,* so . . .

"And another thing," Ed said, using his lit Gauloise as a teaching tool, "don't pretend like Nat doesn't have issues. I've heard her screaming her head off over nothing."

"She's barely eight."

"And repeating things over and over, not making any sense. Masha's a therapist. She can help her."

"Masha's a fucking mess, if you haven't noticed."

"Why not stick to what you know," Ed said. "Why not stick to manipulating people into despair."

"Oh, Ed," she said. "What do you want me to say to you? I never wanted to hurt you."

He didn't say anything. The smoke continued to issue forth in the tight blue notes that formed the bulk of her father's vocabulary. It was so hard for her to think of Ed as a romantic when he had already seemed like a fifty-year-old *ajeoshi* as far back as college, exhaling smoke out of one corner of his mouth, inhaling liquor into the other, the mannered expensive dress, the sunglasses.

"*Joesong hamnida,*" Karen said. Just yesterday, she and Nat had practiced apologizing formally in Korean, in case Nat ever accidentally stepped on J-Hope's foot or shoved an elder on Seoul's metro when the two of them would finally be able to visit.

"Your accent," Ed said, "is atrocious."

THE DAYS PASSED, and soon *naengmyeon* weather would be upon them, even if Ed refused to make the icy summer dish. The air smelled moist and dank, and at midday the neighboring lawns glistened and the poorer denizens of the road washed their cars. The apple blossoms had come out and Senderovsky parked his nose on a low branch.

Aaah! The gullies by the road ran dry and the visiting geese learned to do with less. Steve the Groundhog turned up by the pool deck, rushing about sun dazed and boisterous like a London taxi driver taking his two weeks on the Costa del Sol. Bees and carpenter ants, the unionized workers of the animal kingdom, began to carry out their parallel construction projects. Peony, rhododendron, and dog-wood seasons came in turn, bombarding the property with their pollen, and only Ed in his sunglasses refused to sneeze, brushing at his nose with his wrist when the urge to do so struck him. In the Lullaby Cottage, Vinod donned kurta pajamas and looked more elegant and natural in the new heat than his fellow colonists. Among the fairer residents, raw, wind-chapped hands became soft and pink. And just when the unisex seventies rugby shirts Karen ordered for Nat finally arrived, it was too hot to wear them (though she did, anyway, because Karen-*emo* got ones to match).

The pool was ready to be opened and dewinterized as soon as Senderovsky found the funds to satisfy an outstanding debt to the company that serviced it. In the meantime, the promised badminton net was set up on the front lawn, and they learned that Vinod, dressed in T-shirt and dhoti, and even with his pulmonary capacities reduced, played hard and dirty, pretending to scramble clumsily for the shuttlecock to deliver a light serve at best, then spiking it across the net with glee. He even developed an uncharacteristic evil laugh to match, an approximation of the mustachioed demon on the bottle of Hawaban, the powerful laxative known all over India, who says, "I am hungry," after shitting copiously. Vinod and his brothers would try to imitate his supposed laugh as they squished and elbowed one another on the pleather couch left over from the previous renters—which could alone have served as the crest and coat of arms of the county of Queens—shouting, "I am hungry!"

"Ow, Vin!" Karen would shout when the spiked shuttlecock smacked her in the forehead. "What the fudge?"

"Fifteen to eight, Vinod," Nat would announce solemnly, her scorekeeping duties a sacred rite.

In Vinod's victorious smile, Karen would sometimes espy an element she had not encountered since his illness a decade ago: the wiggly little cornichon of want, the added heat of his smile, and the embarrassed way he clutched his arms to his sides after a victorious serve, to hide the rivulets of sweat pouring down over his wrists. To hide them from her.

IT WAS THE book that changed her mind. She had read Vinod's essays and short stories here and there—some of them had been well received and had earned her friend the sad status of a floating adjunct in several suburban university systems. She and Senderovsky would often groan privately about Vinod's lack of wolfish ambition. When they had been younger and battling for their reputations, they would find Vinod's softness a necessary antidote to their own ferocity. "What's up with our boy?" Senderovsky would ask into his little Finnish cellphone of the era. "He didn't submit his dossier in time," Karen would say, "so he's out of the running for the tenure-track job." "Can you please try to smack sense into him?" "Me?" "Yes, he loves you. I'm just his brother from a freckled mother." "Well, it's too late now."

It was always too late. Though it had taken time for Karen's own career to spark. Despite her geeky C++ childhood and the immigrant-ridden math high school she had attended with Vinod and Senderovsky, she had gone to the city's fashion institute and only crossed over from fashion (with its impossible margins) to technology in her midthirties. ("In some ways, it's the same shit," she had told her first interviewer, a bit too truthfully, after Tröö Emotions had scaled. "You're trying to get a mass of people to mistake themselves for someone else.") At first, she was dismissed by the all-male start-up ensembles where she worked as the resident hipster, the cool Asian girl who played ukulele at a bar in Bushwick no larger than a subway car and designed mind-bending logos, but Karen was taking notes all along, slowly assimilating information as she had her whole life. Her secret weapon: she had no one to impress, not the office cast of code-crunching megalomaniac Aspergerians, many graduates of her specialized math high school, not even her mother or father, both of whom had no idea who she was or what she did, and wanted simply for her to produce two brilliant children, at least one of them male.

During the rough years before her success, however, Vinod's meandering lack of progress felt like a balm. "I'm going to turn into Vin," she'd tell Senderovsky after a setback. "I'm not sure how that's possible," he'd snort. "No, we're going to move in together. I've always wanted to live above a bodega." "Think of the convenience!"

But now there was the book. Karen still read a decent amount, but she certainly never saw herself as a committed reader like her two friends. There was a Japanese writer she loved because his clear sparse prose always put her in a settled mood. (The reality show she watched at Ed's bungalow sometimes gave her a similarly peaceful and satiated feeling.) Vinod's book came at her from a different direction.

If he had set it in Queens—her borough, their borough—the signposts would have been there for her, and she would have sailed through the pages laughing at the familiarities between her immigrant upbringing and his, in the same way she did with Senderovsky's novels. But this book was set in India, at a university in a large city that she presumed was not Bombay. (For one thing, it was inland, and there were many allusions to its provinciality.) She would read five pages a day to herself and then quote some of it to Nat just to hear his language leave her mouth. And then they would sneak into the main house to look up terms they did not understand, Nat happy to be in on a secret project with Karen-*emo*.

The Congress Party. Partition. Sikhism. Jammu and Kashmir. Pukka sahibs. Indo-Saracenic. Lakhs and crores. An *aarti*. The text was dense with the lifeblood of a country, with arguments and counterarguments, with political shenanigans and the postcolonial habits of a Westernized elite. She still didn't understand all of it, didn't know which bits were comedy and which were not (Senderovsky would liberally supply exclamation marks to guide his readers), but the density of the text made her feel that the author was trying to mimeograph the past that had made him into Vinod Mehta, and if there was beauty or laughter amid the ten-point font, fine, and if not, then no one could accuse him of cleverness or lying.

But, more important, it was also a love story between two people and a society that would rather see them apart. This was conventional to be sure, especially for a story set in India, with its frequent allusion to family status and fairness of skin and the brutal constraints of caste. But the protagonists were familiar to her. They were his mother and his father, their love treated almost as a sacred object, Vinod's only birthright. This was his parents' passage out of innocence, the jerky years between a decent middle-class upbringing in a poor country before the travails of immigration to a wealthy one.

Here, the young man who was Vinod's father did not strike him across the temple, did not disburse a daily cry of *bhenchod* over the strum of his own impotence, and the young woman who was his mother did not belittle him, did not compare him with his two older brothers whose many-toothed smiles and simple mercantile greed were an engraved invite to American success. Because this was a "love marriage," rare for its time and place, the protagonists had to fall in love. And because they had to fall in love, Vinod had to plumb the best his parents had to offer each other during their youth, ignoring the dross of their later lives, the inevitable disappointments of Queens, the stark hatred of their respective families.

And finally, the book was about them. About Karen and Vinod. About a man making a case for himself to a woman, even though it was clear that he was not yet up to the rigors of adulthood or the tasks of being a father.

A thought: If they had started a relationship when they were young and later had a child, would Vinod have become a version of his father? It was impossible to think so now, but had she thought so then? That beneath the gentleness lurked a raised open palm? Was that one of the reasons she had rejected him? When they were still in high school, in the very first year of their friendship, all three had sworn to one another never to have children, and only Senderovsky had broken that pact despite once being its most adamant proponent.

WHEN SHE WAS halfway through the book, she wondered if she should tell him that she was reading it. They had gone to his Lullaby

Cottage one night after smoking a pungent new strain of marijuana her assistant had sent up from the city—it elicited a kind of gentle paralysis so that everything seemed to happen a minute later than it did—and she could see herself running back to her bungalow, reaching under the bed, and taking out the Teva active sandals box. "Why?" she would ask him, holding the box aloft. "Why didn't you give this to me before? Why didn't you have the strength to stand up to Sasha? You could have had a different life."

She took her time applying the eye cream to his dark pouches, massaging the deep circles of ancient memory, and in the country quiet they could both hear the rising and crashing waves of each other's breaths. Look how old we are, they were both thinking. They had spent so much of their lives boarding buses and watching the figure of the other recede in the dust.

If it were to happen, he would have to take the first step. He had told himself that he was sheltering at Senderovsky's for another reason, closing out the books. But *No one is forgotten, nothing is forgotten.* What if he were not a Chekhovian character trapped in a life much too small to accommodate the entirety of a human being? What if he—

What if he reached into the small jar and dipped his finger into goo the color of cheap coffee ice cream? It was cold to the touch, but his finger would warm it. And then seemingly a minute later—because of the lag induced by the marijuana—he had brought his index finger up to her eye, to the opposite eye she was touching with her own finger, and smeared "just a tiny bit," as she would always say, across the slight dark ridge under her eye.

"What are you doing?" she said, laughing.

"You've been taking care of us for so long, I thought I'd reciprocate," he said.

"I can put it on myself," she said, immediately stung by her own pride. *I can do it myself!* The daily mantra of her childhood and beyond, spoken to anyone who would listen.

"But you shouldn't have to," he said.

He moved her hand aside, bent over, and kissed her on the lips. The shock of it kept her eyes open, even as his closed with religious feeling. She moved her own lips faintly against his, watching his ardor. How did it feel? It felt like Vinod was kissing her, the soft pelt of his mustache scented with turmeric. That was always the problem: that she would know how every second of their romance would transpire, that this was the most expected moment of her life, and yet, if she breathed instead of hyperventilating, she could enjoy the work of those unsurprising lips.

Her eyes remained open, and they saw "a handsome older gentleman," as her dead mother might have said in English, parroting a line from radio or TV. Their noses touched, always a comical interlude, but then she felt the sex of his hand massaging her nape. When it came to physical encounters, of which there were plenty in her youth, she normally had no problems moving straight to bed—that's what it was for, after all—but now she caught herself.

"Oh, for God's sake," she said. Within the green walls of her high, trapped within the primary colors of the Lullaby Cottage, she now fully registered where they were and who they were. The bungalow felt like the dorm of an artsy college, the kind neither of them had attended, though Vinod had been accepted everywhere he had applied, New Haven included. "What are we doing?" she said. She planted a palm on his chest. Was it to hold him back? For a moment, neither of them knew, but it felt so nice to touch his chest, to feel its wholeness after all he had suffered.

"I was about to say I'm sorry," Vinod finally said. "Sorry for kissing you. But I'm so tired of all of my apologies."

"Good," she said. "Fuck your apologies." They looked at each other in the glow of the collegiate lamp on his desk. "Can you do something for me now?" she asked.

"What would you like me to do?"

She lifted up her arms. There were tiny rolls of fat beneath them now, which he found endearing. "Can you tickle me?"

"Seriously?"

"Uh-huh."

He reached under, feeling her warm sweat and then the crinkly barrage of new underarm hairs. "Ha," she said, tentatively, wishing she could surrender to Nat's wild bouts of laughter. "Ha!" she said again. And then she started laughing, great jags of squealing joy. *Ggul-ggul-ggul*. Was this what she had wanted all along? How hard was it to be happy in this fucking country?

"Do you want me to stop?" Vinod asked.

"Nooooo!" She was breathless now, panting, and the lullabies written all over the walls were singing to her in their distant alphabets. "Okay," she said, her eyes wet, her nose snotty. "Okay, stop." He took his fingers away, fell silent for a moment, then lifted up the sleeves of her bateau T-shirt and caressed her shoulders. "I've never been tickled before," she said, sighing at how good his hands felt, wondering if the calluses on his fingers were the result of his last job in the kitchen of his uncle's restaurant. No, they were always there, weren't they? He had been born callused. "God, I am so stoned," she said.

"You are a crazy, crazy girl," he whispered, enjoying how those simple words sounded in his mouth. She wrapped her arms around him and found herself kissing his hair, which, though leavened with gray, was still absurdly plentiful. He pressed her to him and kissed her neck, even softer than he had imagined. "What are we doing?" she kept whispering as her lips descended to the neck hair which crawled up his nape like a worsted turtleneck, hair she had always urged him to shave, but which now felt fine, or, more to the point, in need of kissing. "Oh, Vin."

Hearing his own name, or an American fraction of it, made him sad, and he did not know why. It was as if he had forgotten who he was for a moment. As if he had entered the body of another Vinod and that was the body she had needed all along. He stopped kissing her neck, though it pained him to stop. The wheezing of his battered lung returned and he remembered that he had come to Senderovsky's bungalow colony to dissolve, and he was now doing the opposite, taking on more presence and solidity, challenging the engineers in the interstellar Bangalore to constantly come up with new code. What if he couldn't keep up with her love? Or his own?

He felt her heave against him in a series of spasms and, within the fog of his high, finally understood that she was crying. "It's okay, baby," he said, taking the American "baby" out for a spin, a word he'd never used with his one serious girlfriend, a tall, also Korean fellow adjunct almost perplexing in her sadness. He kissed the sparse hairs at the crown of her head and felt his high dissolving. "It's okay," he repeated. What had he done? He shouldn't have kissed her. They moved apart and he took her face into memory—the contrast of her doughy nose with the cheekbones that were only getting sharper with age—as if he would never see her again.

"I'm sorry," she said. "I'm sorry for what he's done to you."

"What do you mean? Who did what?"

She took him by the hand and led him outside. Despite his fading high, this arrangement felt familiar. Back when the world was Kodachrome, she had led him and Senderovsky by the hand to all the places in the city where a velvet rope needed to be lifted, places where they felt like impostors in Teva sandals and puka shells. "Look," he said, "in the meadow, fireflies. I think they're finally here!"

"No, honey," she said. "It's still too early. It has to be June."

"It's almost June."

"Late June."

"Just pretend they're here and kiss me."

"Where everyone can see us?"

"Where everyone can see us."

From the darkened porch Ed and Senderovsky watched the kiss unfold in real time, each leaning forward as if they were observing from a theater balcony. ("Oh, God," Ed said. "What the fuck is happening now?") She took him to her bungalow. The light flipped halogen against the dark. A blind was drawn so that the landowner and the gentleman could see nothing further.

Karen bent down and reached under the bed, feeling the nylon coarseness of the BTS *Love Yourself* sheets against her forehead. He stood behind her, ramrod straight, as if the role of lover required army precision. She noticed that and found it sweet. Would it be right to do this to him now, right after their first kiss? When they were stoned?

She stood up, kicked the Teva box farther under the bed, turned around, and placed her palms around his stubby cheeks. "Let me guess," she said, "you shaved just this morning?" It was something from the past, her making fun of his hirsuteness.

He noticed just how thoroughly she had swept the floors—she couldn't help herself, even in the country. "Remember," he said, "back in Queens, how we used to watch *The Simpsons* together and talk on the phone? We'd talk about the show while we were watching it. My parents still had a rotary phone."

She put her hands on his buttocks and squeezed. "You were in Elmhurst and I was in Jackson Heights," he said, bathed in memory, unable to stop talking, even as he brought his hands up to her chest, passing through some mental tollbooth, into a world where he was finally allowed to touch her like that. He pictured her coming out of Senderovsky's pool as he watched the fullness of her body. When they would go to bed together, he would still be able to smell the chlorine on her neck, like an olfactory afterimage.

"I was just a Metallica song away," she said.

"That's right, that's right," he said. "You were into metal for some reason. I'm so glad that only lasted through sophomore year."

She let herself fall backward on the bed, bringing him down with her. He weighed so little (too little, the old version of her said). The erection she felt against her thigh was no longer sacrilegious. They were not family, no matter what she had told herself, no matter how much she had needed a family.

A shot rang out in the distance. Karen wondered briefly if it was hunting season as Vinod pulled the bateau T-shirt off, grasping like a schoolboy at the clasp of her bra.

Senderovsky and Ed heard the shot three meadows over. The stove had gone cold for the season and only a solitary candle still cast the two friends in funereal shadows. Senderovsky listened to the retort echo against the far hills to the east where the whiteness of the partial moon slumbered amid a sky of black and blue, forming the flag of a small Baltic country. Hunting season was not until the fall. What did it mean that they were shooting guns already? And here they were, showcased within the cedar jewel box of the porch above the meadows, two talkative targets bathed in candlelight.

"It was because she was half Indonesian," Ed was saying. Finally, he had found the proper use for his pocket square, blowing his nose with abandon, the sound of it dull and elephantine. He was shocked by his own tears, though it felt surprisingly fine to cry in front of the emotional Russian. "The fans posted racist stuff all the time. They called her a monkey."

His favorite housemate on the Japanese reality show, a twenty-two-year-old budding female wrestler, had killed herself after being taunted online. The show had stopped filming because of the virus, and now there was a chance it would never return. "She was the nicest of all of them," Ed said, wiping his eyes. "When she fell in love with the basketball player, she was so shy and so honest about it. And when he turned her down, it's not like the hope went out of her. She just wanted someone to love her. And because she was a wrestler, and a *hāfu,* and because she was both girlie and a tomboy, because she didn't tick all the boxes they need her to tick in a conformist society, they bullied her to death."

Senderovsky thought of Nat. Masha checked for signs of bullying after every school day the way they checked for ticks in the countryside, but all they could elicit out of Nat was that she was safe on her Quiet Mat spinning out her own fantasy world, sometimes talking to herself in a half whisper through the entirety of a lesson, which to Masha's chagrin her teachers did not discourage or "redirect" because they wanted to "honor that part of her profile." The only time she had cried was when she tried to get the whole class to dress up like members of BTS, and the kids thought she was being authoritarian, even though all she had wanted to do was to share the one thing she loved.

They drank quietly, listening to the radio, trying to decide if they both still liked Brian Eno. Senderovsky thought it might be time to steer the topic to the real matter at hand. "I don't think you should leave," he said to Ed, who had already packed his Gladstone. "Dee doesn't love him. She's just toying with him."

"I heard the great showman finally okayed your script," Ed said. "Good for you."

"He's no longer doing his assisted showering with Masha either," Senderovsky said. "Now that he's got what he wanted."

"He asked me the other day if I could teach him how to grill a lamb shoulder," Ed said. "I bet he was cheating off the Asian kid in high school, too."

Ed lit a cigarette and Senderovsky quickly supplied an ashtray stolen from a middling Bogotá hotel during his traveling years. "Karen says they're close to the antidote," he said, noticing that Ed had the rare ability to smoke and weep at once (a skill learned at his mother's knee). "Then you can have another shot at Dee. Speaking of shot." He poured Ed another glass of the outrageously expensive liquor he had finally brought out for this occasion and gave himself a little taste. (It was against his nature to drink something so dear.) After the liquor hit all the sensitive parts of his esophagus like a pinball igniting the pleasure centers of its machine, he began to cough loudly.

"Where am I supposed to go anyway?" Ed said. "London? Seoul? My brother's Hungarian vineyard? What would I even do there? So many parts of me are closed off for repairs right now. I might as well see her in person than in some angry memory."

"I personally envy you that you can feel something for someone," Senderovsky said. "When I stopped falling in love, my art died. I don't even remember what love is like."

"It's like having a stuffed nose all the time."

"Hmm."

"It's like pouring a jeroboam of champagne down your throat and then forgetting how to swallow."

"Okay."

"It's like lighting a Romeo y Julieta with your own thumb."

"I got you."

The lights had gone off in Karen's bungalow, and both men knew what that meant. "I hope Vinod remembers how to work his thing," Senderovsky finally said.

"They say it's like riding a unicycle."

"Imagine wanting someone all your life, and then you go to bed with them and you discover that it's just like doing it with anyone else. Or that it's worse. Maybe you don't like something trivial about them. I once broke up with a woman because saliva pooled in the corner of her mouth. What an idiot I was."

"It's the little things I'll miss about that show," Ed said. (Often the two were happy talking past each other.) "The way at the end of the season, they'd all get together to clean the house. Imagine that happening anywhere but Japan."

"When Vinod and I were roommates living in that fifth-floor walk-up on Washington Street, we always fought over who would take down the garbage. After a while, we just kept it in the fridge so that it wouldn't attract water bugs. That's how Karen would introduce us to her beaux sometimes. The guys who kept garbage in their fridge."

Ed yawned.

"Here's the thing," Senderovsky said, "you know I never ask you for anything. Would it be possible to borrow a small sum of money for a month or two, just to pay off the pool company and restock the alcohol? There's a huge tranche of money coming from the network now that things are rolling."

"I don't understand why you didn't ask me earlier," Ed said. "You've basically been feeding and boozing five extra people for the last two months."

"I come from one of those proto-Arabic cultures where the guest is sacred. Also, you never offered."

"My mom's new lawyers keep me on a tight leash. But I'll scrounge something up. Will ten thousand help?"

Senderovsky nodded. His sense of pride was aching.

The lights came on in Karen's bungalow again. "What was that, fifteen minutes?" Ed said. "Not bad for someone Vinny's age." He had stopped crying and seemed suddenly in a good mood. Senderovsky wondered if it was because he had asked him for money.

Now they heard shouting, not just Karen's piercing soprano, but Vinod's deep, unused bass. For most of his life he had spoken so quietly, so worried of being scorned for his accent, that teachers had often asked him to repeat himself. "Sounds like love," Senderovsky said, but he was worried about any potential discord between his best friends. *Just when I got the money to open the pool,* he thought.

Karen's door clanged open and a series of automatic lights flicked on to showcase a breathless Vinod running toward the covered porch dressed only in his pajama bottoms, his skin sallow in the artificial light. An object that registered as colored cardboard flapped in one hand and he ran with an anger that made his steps too long, like a drunk man who thinks he can overtake the horizon. Karen emerged behind him, pulling a T-shirt over the gloss of her naked belly. "Vin," she shouted. "Come back!"

"Something tells me we'll be untangling this mess for weeks to come," Ed said.

Vinod did not respond to Karen's shouted directions. That in itself was frightening. As he flung open the door to the porch, nearly removing the flimsy portal from its hinges, both Ed and Senderovsky saw the lit fury of his eyes.

"Whoa," Ed said.

And now Senderovsky could positively identify the object in Vinod's hand and he felt himself rise to defend himself, even as he heard Karen drawing nearer to the porch, shouting words that were not part of their common language.

Vinod was upon Senderovsky, a small man towering over an even-smaller one, one fist curled at his side as if he were his own father entering their Jackson Heights kitchen–cum–boxing ring.

"Did you lie to me?" he shouted to Senderovsky.

"Okay, okay," Ed said, thrusting one meaningless hand between the two antagonists. "Calm down. This is not like you."

"Was it good?" Vinod shouted. "Was it? And then you lied to me? Because, you're—you're—a fucking—" He was not sure he could break the rules of their relationship, the three-decades-old established order of things: Karen at the top, Senderovsky by her side, Vinod orbiting whosever gravitational pull was stronger at any given time.

"A fucking fraud!" he finally shouted.

As Senderovsky looked into his friend's eye from the corner of his own, he thought: *My God, he's an adult now.*

And: *This is the end of our family.*

"I'm sorry," Senderovsky said, just as Karen flip-flopped onto the poorly lit stage of the porch, just as Vinod, using the hand that was not holding the remains of the Teva box, slapped Senderovsky with precisely felt fury across the left cheek.

The drunk and unsteady landowner received this familiar childhood insult just as it was intended. His neck and jaw cracked audibly, his ankles connected with the coffee table upon which the expensive bottle of liquor was perched, and his weight toppled both off their axes, glass and wood and flesh mingling for a second, then each succumbing to gravity in his own unhappy way, the shouts of the two bystanders drowning out the noise of the shattering.

5

Two days after Vinod had slapped Senderovsky on the porch, a news item began to trickle out of the Midwest and to assume ever-larger importance. Every adult was horrified to a greater or lesser degree, and among themselves they took positions ranging from "This is a new low for our country" to "What did you expect?" Some were frightened by the marches and the sprinkling of broken glass in the city ("They're not riots, they're uprisings," Senderovsky publicly corrected his wife), while others wished they were running through the streets themselves, illuminated by the fire of burning trash cans, the way the city used to be in its heyday.

In any case, everything they saw and heard when they downloaded the day's news to their tablets reinforced that they were residents of a semicircle of houses surrounding a so-called House on the Hill, flanking a covered porch and a pool that was being brought to life by a trio of chlorine-bearing technicians in uniform. They were as far away from the uprisings as they could be. They were watching a double disaster through glasses pressed to binoculars pressed in turn to a telescope.

The news affected Senderovsky more than it did the others. He watched the video footage of the Midwestern murder-by-cop over and over while he was on the toilet locked in the upstairs bathroom. He memorized the scene. The ugly institutional shoes, the ugly institutional pants, the baton and flashlight and walkie-talkie, the up-turned sunglasses worn high over the buzz cut, and beneath all that brute institutional force, a dying man crying out the last word that was likely also his first, those two repeating syllables, *Ma* and *Ma*.

And then he was a man no more, but a lifeless slab hoisted on an institutional gurney, and there was static and instructions and dispatch codes. All of it perfectly commonplace, like an order for Gruyère cheese placed at the local market for curbside pickup.

During the ascending phase of his career a speaking service had dispatched Senderovsky to give rousing lectures about coming from a failing country and transforming himself from a bullied immigrant to a successful landowner with nearly a hectare to his name. He had by then published a memoir describing the difficult relationship he had had with Mother and Father Senderovsky, but he would end his mostly comic lectures on a serious note by thanking his parents for doing one thing right in their lives, for subjecting themselves to refugee humiliation in order to bring him here to this clime and soil, away from the oppression of their disintegrating homeland.

But what if it had all been a mistake? Was it a coincidence that the two countries that seemed the most interested in sheltering and then putting to work the Soviet-fleeing Senderovskys with their magnetized Soviet chessboards and lacquered folk-spoon collection were apartheid-era South Africa and *this* country?

All these years, Senderovsky saw, but he also did not see, or pretended not to see. (Or refused to see.) When he decorated his Petersburg Bungalow, when he spoke to his wife and daughter in upper-caste Russian, when he wrote comically about the world he had escaped from, of fat oligarchs run amok, when he put on the metaphorical *shapka* and epaulets for his Los Angeles agent, he distanced his gaze from the country he inhabited. In the end, he had fled from all the land that was not in his possession. He had made of himself a protectorate. (And who would protect him in the end but the local sheriffs?)

He had been a refugee to this country and now the countryside provided an added refuge. From a childhood based on kasha and blows, he had risen to the kind of stature that will allow him and his friends, his chosen ones, to outwit the virus and whatever else a collapsing ecology had in store. File that, along with three proofs of privilege and the appropriate fee, at the local county registry for the American Dream.

As an immigrant his mission had been simple. He was brought here by his parents to make money off what an important Jewish author had once termed "the American berserk." You came, they laughed at your accent on an urban playground, and then you were given your degrees and guided into battle. By which point, you were just a scab sent in to reinforce the established order. In the video, as the white policeman was draining the air from his Black victim's lungs with his knee, another cop, a Hmong immigrant, stood in front of him in a wide-open stance, daring anyone to come to the dying man's aid. He could have been a Russian, a Korean, a Gujarati. All of us, Senderovsky thought, are in service to an order that has long pre-dated us. All of us have come to feast on this land of bondage. And all of us are useful and expendable in turn.

At the mouth of the state highway, away from the liberal estates, they were putting up blue flags supporting the police. Senderovsky saw them on a walk and shuddered at the way the flags flew, stiff and new, as if unsure of themselves and their capacity to instill fear. In case the point of the flags wasn't subtle enough, muscular dogs ran down one property's minor hill to growl at passersby. (Karen and Nat avoided the house on their walks because the unchained dogs fright-ened them.) Imagine what it would take for Senderovsky, the owner of the largest (by area) estate on the road, to ring that doorbell (after evading the dogs) and demand (beg?) for the flag to be taken down? What would he say? "Sir, it offends me"? "Sir, I'm scared." The whole point was to offend him. The whole point was to make him scared.

He wanted to leave. To get on a plane. To flee them all. But where would he go? Across the ocean the ground swelled with the blood of *his* dog-bitten ancestors. Isn't that where one belonged? Because oth-erwise, wasn't he, as Vinod had finally called him, after thirty-three years of observation, after an entire Jesus of a lifetime, *a fucking fraud*?

"WHY DIDN'T YOU show the manuscript to others?" Senderovsky said. He and Vinod were standing by the espresso machine, watching it perform its morning ablutions before preparing the first cup. Days had passed since Vinod had hit his friend. "You knew people in publishing. Why did you count on my opinion alone?"

"You told me not to send it out," Vinod said. "You told me it would destroy my career before it even got started. You said to work on something else. A funny novel about growing up in Queens."

"Why did you trust me?"

"Because you're family."

"Who the hell trusts family? Would you trust your brothers to do right by you?"

"I'm going to borrow money from Karen," Vinod said, "and buy you another bottle of whiskey and fix the coffee table." The offer of money hurt Senderovsky even more. It implied that everything Vinod had lost because of his jealousy was beyond measure. I broke your liquor, you broke my life.

"There was a line in your book," Senderovsky said. "It's right after the first time your parents kiss in the Parimal Gardens. And the father is angry the next day. He's in love, but he's angry because"—Senderovsky closed his eyes to quote—" 'She had taken away what he thought would sustain him for life. The character of the lonely man, his aloneness bordering on the holy. Wherever they went, whichever rich country would give them a visa, whatever more she would give him of herself, just as she had a moment ago given him the moist creases of her lips, he would never forgive her.' "

Vinod was amazed at Senderovsky's recall, how he had even remembered the name of the unremarkable gardens where his parents courted back in Ahmedabad. Had he read the manuscript many times since? Is that why he still kept the Teva box? For inspiration?

"And there were more lines like that," Senderovsky said. "Plenty more lines on every page. You spoke the truth without being clever about it. You revealed your parents, while I hid mine in my shadow. All I had was cleverness. Cleverness paid well for a while."

"I want to leave here," Vinod said. He picked up the completed espresso cup, swirled the copper within, and swallowed the hot contents in one go. "All this is poisoned for me now. I feel more alone on the same estate with you than I would in my studio apartment."

"You're not going back to Elmhurst," Senderovsky said. "And with your permission, I'm sending *Hotel Solitaire* to my literary agent tomorrow."

"We've spent so many years of friendship together," Vinod said, "without ever saying a proper 'fuck you' to one another. So, let me be the first to say it. Fuck you, Sasha Borisovich Senderovsky. Fuck you and your stupid comic novels and your stupid comic life. I'll find my own agent."

As expected, he did not feel better using those words. He was merely borrowing them from someone else, someone native-born and entitled to use them without the trace of an accent.

"No," Senderovsky said. "You're not going. You're staying here with her. It's safe here. And it's easier to fall in love. And we can fix this, you and me. If it bothers you to see my face at the dinner table, you can eat in her bungalow or I'll eat alone in the kitchen."

Vinod washed his espresso cup in the sink, without saying a word.

But they continued to assemble for dinner, all of the eight residents, as if this was the only requirement of their stay: the daily climb up the cedar steps, the familiar placement along the table (Ed and the Actor had recently swapped places, so that the latter could sit next to Dee), the nodding of the heads in culinary appreciation as Ed made use of the latest local ingredients to appear at the local farm stand, cherries and squash. But, as mentioned, a new quiet reigned, a semaphore of love between Karen and Vinod and Dee and the Actor, but mostly brooding silence as the bungalow residents absorbed what their host had done against their most kindly member.

Only Nat talked and talked, about BTS and sunbathing groundhogs and the Korean-language cartoons she was watching with Karen (and now also Vinod), as if daring the others back into conversation. She was trying to defend her father's honor, to remind them all that there was nothing more he liked than hearing the voices of his beloved guests, even as his toasting hand remained on his napkin, his eyes skirting over the cherry sauce with which Ed had nimbly coated his pork chops.

"The *mal* told the *ori* 'you walk funny!' A *mal* is a horse and an *ori* is a duck. But *mal* also means 'bad language.' That's why the horse is always saying bad things. And that's when he told *hama* hippo 'you're so fat' and the *hama* started to cry.

"Well," Nat said when she realized no one was going to reward her for her language lesson. "It's not easy being a child in the time of the virus."

After dinner, when the Actor suggested to Masha and Senderovsky that he and Dee should move into the main house (he claimed to need the signal now that they were going into preproduction) and Senderovsky and Masha and Nat should move into the Petersburg Bungalow, Senderovsky could only grunt assent. "We have to keep him happy now," Senderovsky whispered to Masha in Russian. "We're almost there."

In her office, Masha's Russian patients rejoiced at the nightly clashes between the protestors and the police throughout the country. They had never really cared for this land, these elderly Soviet immigrants feasting off the full smorgasbord of government support. They had been sickened by its promiscuous diversity, all but destroyed by its first Black president, and now they were going to take it back at last.

Photographs appeared on their social media feeds of the mug shots of Black men sneering into cameras alongside ungrammatical broadsides in English: "This man . . . went into Windmere gated community to steal a car. He beat the home owner to death with a bat, then went into their home and beat their son to death with a bat. This is equivalent, to a knee on an innocent mans neck . . . Ask yourself . . . why are you afraid to share this!!!"

And everywhere they turned, a man named Beel Gates awaited them with his monstrously long vaccine needle. Under the guise of the fake virus spread by his friend Dzhordzh Tsoris, bespectacled Beel would bend them over and "vaccinate" them right in the *popka* turning them into Marxist zombies who would be content to live in a society without "STRONG MASCULINE MEN."

They reserved a special hatred for Chicago's mayor, a short gay Black woman married to a six-foot-tall white woman, these two socialist "freaks" who ran "the worst black-on-black murder city in

America." What would her patients think of her own family? Masha wondered. What would they think of Nat? Why was she helping them, healing them, listening to their twisted monologues, when she and her sister had never known such ugliness, when there had been no one in their own family to counsel or save?

On the day the Actor told her she should no longer wash him, confirming that Dee was now returning his affections, she heard a ringing in her ears. It was like church bells ringing in old Russia announcing the start of a snowstorm. On the previous days, she had shown some initiative in the shower, had opened her blouse and put one of his wet, soapy hands upon her breast, where he squeezed for a while, perhaps issuing a Morse code of distress to his publicist, and then she had placed another of his hands beneath her skirt, whereupon he recoiled and said, most stupidly, "But you're not wearing any underwear."

After that shower, as she was washing her own hands, he said, "I want to stop being in love. Can you recommend addiction therapy?" She said she had colleagues who could possibly help, although they were still doing studies on the effects of Tröö Emotions, figuring out which category of maladies the effects of the algorithm best fit. He had come up to her then, as she was at the sink, talking in her calm therapeutic voice, and pressed his naked bulk against her skirt, rubbing against her buttocks in great circular motions, as if he still had more to give. "Thank you, Mashen'ka," he said. She had taught him the diminutive of her name. "You're the only one who gives a damn about me." And when she went back to the main house, to her office and its monitor full of squeaking angry Russians, she sat down and felt the wetness of him on her skirt and thought she would cry out joyfully right in front of her Lyubas and Laras if only to show them what it was like to still feel something other than hate.

And then it was all over. Her husband was involved, obviously, had spurred Dee to reciprocate the Actor's interest so that his pilot script would advance, knowing what it would do to his wife and, come to think of it, to one of his best friends, Ed. Was he any kinder, in the end, than the Laras on her screen, any better disposed to empathizing with the grief of others?

The Actor had rejected her on a Friday; this she remembered, because during her secret Marrano ritual that night in the spacious upstairs bathroom she had brought her palm down on both candles during her *lehadlik ner shel Shabbat*—her Actor-washing palm, to be sure—and was angry at the flames for extinguishing themselves so quickly, for neither cleansing her nor refusing to let her feel hurt anywhere but within the four chambers of her most problematic muscle. *So we used each other,* the Russian voice in her kept saying in a nontherapeutic, pragmatic, Lara-like way. We used each other, and then it had to end. Two people had needs, the needs were met. What else had she fantasized? That they would run away together? That she would mean everything to him? That they would have a bedside hotel breakfast in Los Angeles when this was all over? Every relationship was transactional, and no one ever gave more than they had to.

And now her husband was found out as his best friend's jealous betrayer. "Why did Daddy want to hide Vinod's manuscript in Steve's winter palace when everyone says it's so good?" "Not everyone, honey. I haven't read it, for one." "But Karen-*emo* says—" "That's enough. Daddy's not perfect, but he's not *that* bad." (Great, now she was defending him.)

So now she and her husband were both abandoned and scorned, the insulted and the injured, sentenced to a five-hundred-square-foot cabin on their own property, alone amid the field-mouse droppings and the coyote howls and the nearby guns going off off-season, the subdued *pop-pop-pop!* of their retorts getting closer every day, until someone would finally reclaim their bravery and aim straight for the two salt-and-pepper heads gathered over the samovar. Yes, the revolution was coming for them, too. How many revolutions would they have to live through during the never-ending historicity of their goddamned lives?

But the world of the colonists was about to change irrevocably. And, this time, it would have nothing to do with the Russians.

6

I T HAPPENED THREE weeks later. Dee woke up in Masha and Senderovsky's bed, listening to the prodigious rustle of trees that were close enough to touch from the main house's second floor. Directly below her, the Actor was adjusting the futuristic knobs of the espresso maker to his satisfaction. The main house was a treat, especially with its strong signal for her laptop, but there were things Dee missed about their love affair when each still had their own bungalow. He had been giddy and manic then, coming up with strange new ways for them to express their love. He had suggested that they exchange their dirty underwear and keep it on their desks while they worked. The handyman, finally paid in full by Senderovsky and excited to see his foreign employers reduced to living in a cabin, happily hoisted the desks from Dee's and the Actor's respective bungalows and set up snug new offices in the house's now-empty bedrooms. ("What a beautiful couple *you* two make!" he had said.) She told the Actor his underwear-exchange idea was disgusting—"But you're just so Dee-licious!" he had shouted—but then they fought through his proposition with great charm, and eventually a silky, musky thing found its way onto her desk, draping one of the Underwoods from her old bungalow.

What was it like to be involved with the Actor? It was all-consuming, like watching him from the front row of a movie theater, the volume of his musical voice blaring, his face up close, constantly puzzling through new things with unbridled enthusiasm, lighting up with pleasures he had surely experienced before but which he now repurposed as new and exclusively theirs. ("This is the first time I've ever really encountered an apricot.")

"I love you," he would say first thing in the morning.

"I respect that," she would answer. Fine, he would think. Respect was but a signpost on the road to love. All he needed to be was more lovable.

NOW THAT SHE had plenty of signal around her, each morning Dee indulged in the privilege Senderovsky used to enjoy, the ability to tune in to social media before even brushing one's teeth. She found herself surprised by how much she liked the vitriol directed against her by the Actor's fans, some of whom posted side-by-side photographs of Dee and her predecessor, Elspeth of Glasgow, to highlight the deficiencies of the former. The photo they used of Dee was usually the least attractive they could find, her eyes squinting at the flashbulb of some literary festival red carpet, her face betraying unfamiliarity with even this minor form of fame.

What did it matter? They were now crowned as the first couple in the age of the virus. Her book was enjoying a very modest uptick in sales, and her publicist had called to congratulate her on her new relationship. On this particular morning there had been great response to the photo of her and the Actor holding a baby squash together on his feed, her head curled into his shoulder with an impish smile, both of them with their bushels of long, tangled virus hair, under which he had written "We're learning to make babies!" as if they had grown the squash themselves and not picked it up at a farm stand. Also, this implied they might soon become a family, which was just the kind of outrageous statement the Actor could get away with.

She was lying atop a stack of pillows, their cases only recently denuded of the starchy scent of their former owners. They had forgotten to have sex that morning, an omission she could live with (it would be imprudent to get too used to any routine), and the bough of a scraggly elm kept elbowing the window as Dee scrolled through her many mentions, until she thought to herself: Damn, we ought to get the tree guy to trim these trees. Just the other day, after they *did* have sex right upon waking, and as his body lay next to hers looking a tiny bit deflated and suburbanized on the faux-rustic Craftsman-style bed, he had lifted up his head full of dense black curls, looked around, and said, "You know, I'm not in love with this house. There's nothing special about it."

"The chestnut trim of the windowsills is supposed to be extinct or something," Dee said.

"I wish it was open plan," the Actor said. "Then it would better fit in with the nature around it, like the porch does."

"Maybe we can ask permission to remodel," she had said.

And he just laughed and said: "Permission granted."

Dee and the Actor did not know it, but this furniture—and indeed the house itself—had been picked by Masha and Senderovsky be-cause it was happy and light, the opposite of their parents' dark ar-moires and heavy Eastern European curtains.

But lying on the bed now, alone, eyes still blinking in the austere early morning sunlight, Dee's long, wide mouth ("Just horsey enough for my tastes"—The Actor), began to open and slacken, her breath-ing became irregular, panicked ("I love to hear you pant, baby"), and her hands curled with great, almost tensile strength around the in-nocent shell of her laptop ("I can tell you used to work out before all this").

What the hell was happening?

A different line of attack was presenting itself across the blue-and-white landscape of her favorite social media channel, and it wasn't the sexist blather about her appearance versus Elspeth's. No, these com-ments, multiplying in real time, were about an essay Dee had written about the seminal American racist film *Gone with the Wind,* which was having a moment after a new streaming network decided to remove it from its offerings after the recent uprisings.

The essay had been written just as the initial burst of enthusiasm for *The Grand Book of Self-Compromise and Surrender* had begun to die down among the country's small but ever-bored readership and as another book about growing up poor and white began to overtake it on the lists.

Dee had decided to skew provocative at that point, while still functioning within the safety of the left. The essay—not her finest, she would be the first to admit—centered on a childhood obsession with *Gone with the Wind,* which had started with a trip to Atlanta with her mother and her abusive boyfriend of the moment—he had recently learned that the key to his broken Datsun could better serve as a weapon—a trip which proved to be a great financial and psychological expense for her family (they had stayed at a crumbly motel on the outskirts of the Georgian capital and had run out of gas money on the way back), but which also became a life-changing trip, as it inspired young Dee to buy the novel upon which the movie was based, which then led her to keep her first journal, written on the backs of a ream of Agway customer service forms that had fallen off a truck (perhaps this had happened, perhaps not, but this was how she chose to tell the story), which culminated, two decades later, in a graduate classroom with the drunken Senderovsky and then all the rest of it.

On the face of it, the essay was hardly a lit match thrown into a gassy oven. It started out by first laying out all the obvious things wrong with the movie, beginning with the servile portrayals of its Black characters. But then the essay pivoted to the poverty of its viewers (the Cameron family included) and a longing for a fabled, romantic past these Scots-Irish folk had been forced to live off after everything else (the jobs, the hope) had been taken away.

The essay danced along these lines, gently herding the reader in one direction and then surprising her with a shunt in the opposite. Throughout, one could find Dee's patented bare-knuckle tone directed toward the moneyed reader of leisure. How dare this reader not consider the sources of Dee's poverty and her own complicity within the scope of rent-seeking capital? How dare she condescend to young Dee for her love of the only narrative in her life that wasn't disposable trash bought at the "Facial Care" aisle of the Piggly Wiggly?

At several junctures, Dee referred to her impoverished compatriots as "my people," including at one point a long descriptive list of her kinfolk. (As Senderovsky used to say in his graduate-school class, "When you run out of ideas, just write down a list. Readers love lists.")

Dee's list included ". . . Part-time coyote skinners, drummed-out

Fort Bragg PFCs, psoriasis-covered Bible-school lunch ladies, social security disability regs thumpers, racist cops just itching for the right motorist to pull off the tarmac . . ." Concluding with the line: "As much as you might hate them, as much as you would loathe sharing the aisles of a big-box store with them (you're more into small, well-scented shops in formerly Black neighborhoods, anyway) and their screaming, undereducated children (my nieces and nephews), *these are all my people.*"

A screenshot of that passage appeared in mention after mention now colonizing her feed, the words "racist cops" highlighted next to the rubric "mypeople."

To make matters worse, in *The Grand Book of Self-Compromise and Surrender,* she had twice featured a racial epithet issuing from an uncle's mouth ("I wanted it to explode across the page," she had said in a previous interview), which now too was part of a screenshot next to "mypeople" and "ShitDeeSays."

And then there were the photos of her next to miscreants from the questionable right during her provocative "I'll defend to the death your right to say it" phase. And then quotes from those khaki-and-cropped-hair far-right types commenting in the most obviously disgusting ways about what was happening on the streets of the country after the recent murders and the uprisings, followed by the words "another Dee Cameron approved quotation" and, of course, "mypeople, mypeople, mypeople."

THE AIR HAD gone out of her, and when it returned she smelled morning breath and sweat. She felt disassociated from her body, one leg cold as roadkill against the other. She sat there, with the laptop jammed against her crotch, both her right eye, a frequent victim of eyestrain, and the cursor on the screen blinking away.

Again, what the hell was happening?

She had been found out, exposed. But for what? All of this had been allowed just weeks before. Everything she had written came with just the right amount of nuance. It had been lab tested and publicist approved.

It was like the time the Laotian American had corrected her during her book tour, but that was a private moment. This was on social media, which meant it had been imprinted on the face of God.

Some of the new missives had attached the name of *his* three-million-followers-plus account. "Have you been following your girl-friend lately?" "Not a good look for you, babes." "Maybe you can do GlenRacist Glen Ross next." "Stick that baby squash up your GF's ass." She continued to sit there, paralyzed. Soon his footsteps would echo up the stairs, and they would commence another day of farm-stand hopping and posing for pictures. Would he laugh it off? Would he claim that nothing could happen to the First Couple of Quarantine? That they were too cute to fail?

But there was no such thing anymore. She had been thrust beyond the cordon sanitaire and now interred on the wrong side of history.

No, it could not be!

She would not allow it!

She did not know how she had gotten there, how her legs had gained the agency, but she was now standing naked in front of the bathroom mirror, brushing her teeth. She opened the door to the medicine cabinet so that she wouldn't have to look at her face, at the white toothpaste frothing at the corner of her mouth like the final effects of a hemlock intake. Senderovsky had cleared out most of his voluminous medicine, but there was still a shelf stocked with a stool softener and a stool hardener named ExitPro and Carpathium Plus, respectively. If she swallowed all of those pills at once, might she implode?

She rinsed and flossed, everything by the book. Now she would get in the shower and clean, clean, clean, the steaming hot water of the newly fixed shower making her skin rosy and dappled, anything but white. She did not hear him enter and only registered his presence after he had slipped his arms around her waist, his breath full of caffeine and the nonpareil sesame bagels his agency had sent him from Montreal. "Get away from me!" she screamed.

"What?" He had put on his hurt, bewildered baby face.

"I'm sorry," she said. "I need to shower first. I'm gross."

"When has that ever stopped us?" he said, leaning in for a kiss, which was rejected. Then, quietly, cutely, like a boy who's done wrong but wants his parents to love him again: "But, Deeeee . . . I like you stinky."

"Great," she said. "Just give me a moment. Okay? O-*kay*?"

"Okay," he said, hands in front of him, surrendering, eyes glossed in innocence.

She tried to compose herself, but instead she fell to the floor, sobbing, and he stood there, with a look of horror on his face, which quickly gave way to instinct and the instinct guided him as it always had in the past. He fell to the ground next to her, cradled his head into her lap, and began to weep alongside her, his tears, shudders, and hiccups gradually supplanting hers, until they had become far more genuine than her own, until she stopped her weeping entirely and lay there as if in a trance, listening to the sounds of his unsubstantiated grief.

7

THAT DAY, AS Dee Cameron was presented to the world in a
newly unwelcome public light, Karen and Nat had gone on one
of their morning walks, both of them singing "Fake Love," "Boy in
Luv," "War of Hormone," and other BTS hits, as well as songs from
an educational cartoon about a silly Korean tiger who wants his
mother to acknowledge him as a *hyo-ja,* or good son. They usually
walked as far as the house where the pro-police flag fluttered black
and blue and where the dogs ran up to the edge of the property in
full bark. The pollen season for the devil grass, rye, and oat that had
coated the Northeastern lawns like the hide of a well-cared-for terrier
inspired a heightened allergy in Nat, and to temper her sneezes Karen
put a high-end filtration mask on the child and a matching one on
herself.

They were now walking past the sheep farm, the morning sun too
weak to add bronze to their skin, as Nat hopped on one leg, or
skipped on both, or ran in her dorky helter-skelter way down the
tarmac, or turned around and did "the bull," which meant plowing
at full speed into Karen's stomach, knocking the wind out of her a
little, but all in this cheerful childish way, and Karen would shout her
late mother's happiest refrains, *"Ohmama-ohmama-ohmama!"*

Just then, a pickup truck (its color would remain a subject of contention) rounded the bend of Senderovsky's property, and as it approached Karen and the child it appeared to pick up speed and tilt its
snout toward them.

It happened within half a second. Usually, Nat liked to wave to
passing cars (and what loveless creature would fail to return a child's

wave?), but this time Karen barely had time to grab Nat and pull her out of the way.

According to Karen, the truck passed within half a foot of the child, at most, the wind swooshing past both of them like an added insult. "Fuck!" Karen yelled. She put her hand on her mouth as Nat looked up at her. "Sorry, honey, sorry."

"What happened, Karen-*emo*?"

"That truck, it came so close to us. But it's okay."

"My daddy's a bad driver, too," Nat said. "Mommy took the booster seat out of his car so I can't even ride with him to the store."

Nat quickly plunged into her usual "anxiety talk," and now the sheep were bleating as if they had seen the near accident (or was "accident" the wrong term?), and two white horses on the other side of the road—a father and a son—nodded to them as they passed. A biplane from the nearby aerodrome flew directly above them, trimming the low clouds like an aerial lawn mower, and Karen looked up at its black iron cross on its bottom wing with suspicion. Nothing felt safe anymore.

She moved Nat to the grassy banks of the road and walked alongside her, keeping an arm out in front of her as if that alone would protect her from whatever came next round the bend.

That was her first thought: I had failed to protect the child.

Her second thought: Protect her from whom? It occurred to her now what the driver of the pickup had seen, an Asian woman walking with an Asian child, both of them wearing masks, at a time when people who put up black-and-blue flags honoring the police were inclined to despise such people.

So, as Asian mask wearers, she and Nat now constituted a double threat in the eyes of the homicidal motorist. And now she tried to backtrack and remember what she had seen beneath the glare that coated the truck's windshield. Neatly trimmed, military-grade hair, it seemed like, a faint mustache and chin beard, sunglasses, a smirk? She couldn't be sure, though. In fact, she may well have been thinking of the videos she had seen of the Midwestern policeman stepping on the innocent man's neck. Maybe there really only was *one* singular white man staring down at the world from his official boots and his official vehicle and his official sunglasses hanging high over his official smirk. And the end result of all that officialdom? A one-ton truck passing within half a foot of an eight-year-old child.

Karen dropped off Nat with Vinod, who was staying in her bungalow, and knocked on the door of the Petersburg Bungalow. The landowner emerged in a cheerful caffeinated mood, printouts from the show's second episode fluttering in his hands (INT. OLIGARCH'S SWISS HAREM—NIGHT). After his recent disgrace with Vinod, he was happy to receive any and all visitors. "Let's smoke some morning pot like we used to!" he cried.

She told him of the incident with the truck and his daughter, her voice verging on the critical, as if this was somehow his fault, as if he had chosen this dangerous locale for his dacha on purpose.

Senderovsky thought of the high beams at the end of his driveway, the falling elm branch nearly cutting short his time on earth. "What color was the truck?"

"What? Why would that matter?"

He ran out the door to find the best reception and, an hour later, a large Ford was raising gravel beneath its boatlike frame, and from the top of the hill Karen and Senderovsky could already make out the tan felt Stetson perching on the head of its driver.

STATE TROOPER BURNS wore a blue surgical mask that did nothing to conceal the squareness of his jaw. Given everything that had happened in the recent history of policing in the country, Karen found his good looks annoying. "One second while I get a mask," Karen said.

"No need to, ma'am," the trooper said, friendly. He had been kind enough to take off his sunglasses, or maybe that was pro forma. His eyes were blue to the point of caricature.

They ran through the nature of the incident. "And you're sure he was trying to hit you?" Trooper Burns said. "You say he was trying to make a curve."

"He was trying to *scare* us. Isn't that a crime? We're two Asians wearing masks."

"I don't quite see."

"You don't quite *see*?"

Senderovsky touched her arm. "She's talking from a political standpoint," he said.

Karen shook off his hand. "I'm saying it could be a bias crime," she said. She did not like the meekness of her own voice. If she could shout at white men in hoodies back in the Valley, why couldn't she stand her ground with a policeman on the East Coast?

The trooper made some notations. The arrival of his cruiser at the top of the hill began to rouse the colonists from their usual afternoon torpor. Vinod had come out of the bungalow and Masha was coming down the cedar steps from her office in the main house. (Only Dee and the Actor remained upstairs lost in her new travails.) They gathered around, trying to catch small bits of detail. A rogue pickup truck had tried to kill Karen and Nat? Masha immediately ran into Karen's bungalow, where Nat had been deposited, to see if her daughter was okay, finding her adrift in a usual midday monologue (Vinod her patient listener), but no more anxious than usual.

"And what color was the truck?" Trooper Burns was asking as his gaze followed Vinod's skirtlike lungi, and Senderovsky's the single black stripe running down the trooper's trousers.

"Gray, I think," Karen said. "I'm not sure."

"Do you think we could ask your daughter?" the trooper asked.

"Again, she's not my daughter," Karen said.

"She's my daughter," Senderovsky said. "Vinod, would you mind getting her?"

Nat, Masha, and Vinod soon walked back up the flagstone path. "I'm the mother," Masha said, preemptively. "Nat, honey, when you were walking with Aunt Karen, a truck may have broken the rules of safe driving—"

"Just like Daddy does!" Nat shouted.

"In any case, he came too close," Masha said. "Do you remember any details about the truck, Nat?"

"No. It just came too fast."

"Do you remember the color?" the trooper asked.

"I think it was gray," Karen said.

"I think it was green," Nat said. "Like dark forest green."

"Are you sure it wasn't black?" Senderovsky asked. "Did it have strange decals on the back?"

"What?" Karen said. "No. It wasn't black. Where do you get black? You weren't even there. And what decals?"

Senderovsky looked around the assembled colonists and sighed. "Nat," he said, "could you go into Mommy's office and watch videos for just a tiny bit?"

"No, I want to stay out here!" Nat shouted. "This is exciting!"

"Honey," both Masha and Karen said at once, but Karen had already bent down on one knee, taken both of Nat's hands, and looked her in the eye.

"Okay." The child spoke so placidly, with such rare understanding and obedience, that Masha looked away from her and Karen and toward the squat bungalow she shared with her husband, toward a frontal mass of grayness that was drawing upon them, promising another summer storm, along with the expensive mess of more mauled tree limbs and possibly the delight of double rainbows after the fact.

"I haven't wanted to alarm anyone," Senderovsky said when his daughter had left, "but for a while now there have been some disturbances, which I thought maybe were accidental. But now I think they were not." The trooper took note of his speech and wondered if he was a foreigner or mentally ill or both.

And now Senderovsky spoke of the black pickup truck with the strange decals on the back passing by the front lawn with regularity and the way this same truck had parked itself at the end of the driveway with its high beams beaming daringly during the notable windstorm of months past. And then he spoke about the shots fired closer and closer to their property despite this being the season when hunters extended a truce to the bounding deer and newborn bobcats. (Masha confirmed the military exercises she had heard at night.)

The trooper wrote all this down, marveling about the role pickup trucks of many colors played in the urban imaginations of these people. But he had heard of an increase of disturbances in this area, of strange young people wandering aimlessly over clearly signposted private property, of trucks roaming without purpose, of people having even more sex than usual at the old abandoned international children's camp. "In times like these," he said to the bungalow colonists, "we all have to be careful. You're set back on the hill here. So if some bad guys decide to pay a visit, your neighbors might not see them. You'd be on your own."

The statement shocked the colonists. They were both isolated and exposed. They were on their own.

"But you said the truck you saw was black?" the trooper said to Senderovsky. "Not gray or green like the two young ladies said."

"Yes," Senderovsky confirmed. "No. I don't know."

"Anyone you think might plan to do you harm," the trooper asked. He looked around the many structures of the property. "Maybe someone that did work for you."

"Many people work on this property, but they are all handsomely paid," the landowner said. "No, I would have to agree with Karen. This sounds like a bias crime. Oh, also, some of our visitors are prominent." He mentioned the presence of the Actor and Karen's occupation. The trooper nodded and proffered Senderovsky a card with one of his gloved hands.

As the cruiser drove down the driveway, pops of gravel tickling its underbelly, Masha turned to her husband and said, "Well, thanks for letting us know that we've been stalked for the past three months." She walked back to her office, noticing the shouting of the new lovers upstairs and the fact that she didn't give a damn about their problems.

8

H E WAS LOCKED in the bathroom with his publicist, his agent, and his manager on the line. They were taking their turns with him. The electronic world had been churning all day, a new discovery popping up every minute, as tens of thousands of the Actor's underemployed fans began their own unpaid investigations. One social media sleuth had figured out that the Actor was staying on Senderovsky's peculiar estate and, using social media, also deduced the identities of the other bungalow colonists of note. The newspaper article about Senderovsky's bungalow colony (title: "A Dacha of His Own") was dug up, reposted, and ridiculed en masse. People were asking on social media: "Are you a Sasha, a Dee, or a Karen?" Dee's original Tröö Emotions–enhanced photo was somehow resurrected (she had erased it shortly after posting), and this led the agent, the manager, and the publicist to ask a new series of questions. Was the Actor in love with Dee under duress? Was this all Karen's fault? Was she holding him hostage with the app? Did the Actor need to be exfiltrated under cover of night? Because there was no way, they surmised, that he could have given up Elspeth for "someone like her."

"I know you like a brother," the manager was saying, "and there's not a racist bone in your body."

"There's not a racist bone in *her* body."

"I'd like to bring up your Turkish grandmother," the publicist said. "You come from a Muslim background. That's a fact."

"I don't want people to dig too deep into that," the Actor said.

"What do you mean? You've mentioned it in tons of interviews."

"Let's leave that alone for now," the Actor said, cryptically.

He had to call Elspeth right away, his agent said. (She now represented both the Actor and the activist-model.) The window was closing on her forgiveness. Given the Tröö Emotions of it all, given the fact that he had acted ("correct choice of words," said the manager) under duress, his former girlfriend was amenable to a face-to-face meeting. She was hurt and angry, there were words she would have to say which were not words he had heard in a long while from a human person, but this was the only way out for him now. They had to lean on "technology run amok" as an excuse for him falling in love with a racist. The agency owned fractional membership in a plane that was currently parked about an hour and twenty minutes south of the Actor. Because of the virus, the roads were nice and clear. All he had to do was get into his little red Lancia and drive a tiny bit.

"Or," said the manager, "let's try this on for size. You were never lovers, merely friends."

"You made a friend and she betrayed you," the publicist said.

Yes, they all agreed, that was good. He had made a bad friend under duress.

There was a knock on the bathroom door. "I have to go," the Actor said.

"One last thing," the agent said. She had been a dramaturge in a previous, less remunerated life and had remained a fan of spoken gravitas.

"What?" The Actor sighed.

"You have to remember that you're not just a man. You are not just a 'person.'" The agent paused for effect. "You are a responsibility onto this world."

As THEY SAT down to a dinner of swordfish and finocchio, the thunder, a known overactor, couldn't help itself and rang out in a succession of monstrous bursts, scaring sound-sensitive Nat and confusing the newly frightened diners who mistook some of the thunderous peals for gunshots. Karen and Vinod, whose chairs both faced the driveway, periodically checked for incoming pickup trucks.

After ten minutes of silent chewing had passed, Dee began to talk.

She put her hands beneath her chin in the manner of her author's photo and then spoke calmly and brightly the way one talks to the British.

"I was watching Nat and Karen set out the place mats today," she said, "and I just got to thinking. We pretend we're so diverse around here. As Sasha himself announced so proudly back when we had our first dinner, 'I have almost no white friends!' But, still. I have to ask: Where are the Black people at this table? Where are the gay people? The noncisgendered people?"

"Where are the Latinx people?" Nat said in the same tone as Dee, her hands also folded beneath her chin. They had recently had a Cinco de Mayo "module" at her school.

"And where are the poor people?" Dee said, ignoring the child, realizing how much she disliked precocity among the elites, and wondering whether she could bring that up as a way of castigating Nat's parents but not the child herself.

"One can always go right back to the city," Masha said to Dee. She had been following Dee's travails on social media like everyone else at the table. "The virus is ebbing there and also there's plenty of economic diversity if one knows where to look."

"I think Dee is having a tough day," Vinod said, "and we should try to help her in a nonconfrontational manner."

"Oh, I agree," Dee said. "Let's be nonconfrontational. And let's stop with the lying please." She pitched a quick knowing glance to Senderovsky, the known liar. "I say we do a little exercise. We go back to our rooms, take out our calculators, and come back with a full disclosure of our net worth. That way we know just where we are situated within the system. I would also itemize income taxed at an unfairly low rate, capital gains, for example, and underline inherited wealth. If you need to call your money managers, you can bring us the results at dinner tomorrow."

They heard a thunderclap and then sustained bleating from the sheep meadow, a reminder of the ovine world beyond. The colonists remained silent.

"Since I can see how scary this idea is to most of you," Dee said,

"I'll be happy to go first." She took out a piece of paper and unfolded it. "My total net worth is two hundred thirty-eight thousand three hundred forty-five dollars and twenty-three cents. About nine thousand dollars of that is my car after depreciation, and about twenty thousand is in a retirement account, i.e., invested in the market and taxed accordingly. I own no property."

No one spoke. There was but the clanging of cutlery against plates. "Wait a minute," Karen said, "is that supposed to be a little or a lot?"

"It is what it is," Dee said. "My goal is to be transparent."

The laughter they heard was Masha's. It was rich and theatrical (and historical) and suddenly reminded Senderovsky of why he once loved her. "I'm sorry," she said. "I think Dee is trying to say that she's poor in comparison to the rest of us. That she's suffered. That her actions need to be excused on that basis."

"That's not it at all!" Dee shouted.

"You're, what, thirty-one?" Masha said. "When I was your age, after college and med school, I was worth *negative* two hundred thousand dollars."

"When I was that age, I was addicted to horse tranquilizer," Senderovsky said. There was laughter around the table. Masha put her hands over Nat's ears.

"I have maybe three hundred dollars in the bank," Vinod said. "My father says he might will me his Buick."

"Honey," Karen said to Dee, "that's actually a lot of money for somebody in their early thirties." Her voice was lacking in malice. She feels sorry for her, Ed thought.

"Says Karen of *White* Street!" Dee said. The name Karen had recently become a pejorative for a certain class of white women.

"I'm not that kind of Karen," Karen said. "I'm the kind that nearly gets mowed down on the street because of how I look. And how do you know where I live? I bought my place with an LLC."

Dee smiled at her. She realized she had no allies among the women. How predictable. "You take no responsibility for what happened to us, do you?" she said.

"You fucked up," Karen said, Masha's hands again on her daughter's ears. "I have, too. Many times. This is a country full of successful fuckups. No one remembers anything. Just clear the deck and start again."

"Maybe *you* can hide behind your millions," Dee said.

"And you can hide behind your two hundred thirty-eight thousand."

Ed felt terrible for Dee. She was not an inherently bad or particularly racist person, he thought, but she had miscalculated terribly. "I'm proud that you've earned every single cent of that," he said to her. "In a way that I couldn't." Dee avoided eye contact with Ed, worried that if she saw his solicitude she might, against all of her being, start to cry.

After a few seconds of silence had elapsed, Vinod said to Dee, "I read your book."

She blinked in surprise. "You have?"

"Yes," Vinod said. "I guess I was too shy to talk about it with you, since I'm not a published author myself." Dee, Ed, and the Actor looked at Senderovsky, accusatorily. "It's very well written."

"Thank you."

"I think it's about this country's negotiation with white supremacy. You're trying to understand many contradictions, contradictions that came with your birthright."

"It wasn't much of a birthright," Dee said.

"But, ultimately." Vinod stopped for a second. The thunder tried to interject, but no one heard it. "Ultimately," he said, "it's hard to know which side you're on."

"I'm with the side of the people," Dee said. "Isn't that obvious?"

"On the side of your people," Vinod said. "Which is to say, on your own side."

Mypeople. The Actor saw what he hadn't before as he scrolled through her social media mentions. The hopelessness of her position. And of his own. She was trapped. He was trapped. What if he looked into her eyes and failed to see his unimagined self, the man he needed to be? This reality cut through him, eviscerated his Tröö Emotions, filled him with anxiety on a Nat scale.

What if loving her made it impossible to love himself?

She was seated next to the Actor on the western edge of the table so that, in normal circumstances, to look at the beauty of the setting sun was also to witness the beauty of them. But the sun was out of contention tonight, clouds shaped like countries swept in in its stead, the wind cleaving them of their Alsaces and East Timors. And the two lovers looked cleaved of each other as well.

Ed watched her. He could reach over and hold her hand. He could internalize the sordidness of her struggle, her helplessness, and he could walk her through to the other side. It had recently emerged that the housemates on the Japanese reality show had been coached all along. Just actors in a play. Playthings. And so was she, after all, with her tidy middle-class bank account and her grasping middle-class soul, although she had had the temerity to think she could write and talk her way into being someone original. Their gaze met for a second. She would not unwrinkle her lower face for him, the lower face that lived within the catalog of past slights and which counterbalanced the wit and sparkle of her eyes, but he would still take her as she was. If given the signal, he would sweep her into the folds of a long and complicated dilemma, into a mistake they could make together.

9

MASHA AND SENDEROVSKY lay in bed in the Petersburg Bungalow, listening to the sheets of rain steel-drumming the expensive new roof. Country rain. Dacha rain. It still meant something to
Masha. Instinctively, as if this was 1983, she reached her hand over and
took Senderovsky's. She used to hold hands with him in the Russian
bungalow colony across the river all the time, thinking it was platonic
for her, knowing it was not for him, but still doing it. Even back then
he was a source of entertainment for her, a "one-man clown posse,"
always ready with the stupid joke about babushkas and cabbage-soup
farts. And still she married him. And still she loved him.

"The first tranche from the network is going to be deposited this
week," Senderovsky said. "Though I do owe Ed ten thousand and
another twenty to the general and the workmen. Which won't leave
much."

"It must be scary for you," she said. "Running out of money."
They were speaking, therapeutically, in English.

"They've commissioned the next two episodes already, so we're in
good shape." What he left unsaid was the fact that if the Actor broke
up with Dee, if he began to once again cast a critical eye over the
scripts or if he were to drop out completely to distance himself from
Senderovsky and his Dacha of Doom, the money would stop at the
first tranche. She felt him squeeze her hand and knew he was worried.
There were more squeezes to follow, until he finally fell asleep,
coughing all the while.

She lay awake for another hour, until someone began to turn the
knob of the bungalow's front door. Masha jerked up. She had made

all the residents lock their doors at night after hearing the state trooper describe the defenselessness of their property. She thought of waking her coughing husband but instead ran to the door herself, peeking past the blinds.

It was Nat, beneath a colorful Wanna One umbrella (they were a rival boy band to BTS; Nat couldn't stand to get the umbrella with her real heroes wet), still wearing her polka-dot frock. Masha ushered her in. "What happened?" she whispered.

"I wanted to sleep next to you and Daddy," Nat whispered back. The back of her neck felt sticky to Masha's touch. Karen had probably failed to bathe her. Masha found herself worried that Karen might wake up in the middle of the night and discover the child was missing. Why was she so concerned with Karen's feelings all of a sudden? "I wrote Karen-*emo* a note," Nat whispered, reading her mother's mind.

She briskly climbed into bed and found a groove between her parents into which she curled, her arms around her knees. Masha buried her nose into Nat's dirty hair and began to breathe in all she could. Senderovsky blindly draped an arm around Nat, but without the moonlight streaming through one open window his wife and daughter could not see his dreamland smile. Eventually, Masha did see that his big hand had found her little one, and she begged herself to forget the fact that when the kids pared off at the Kindness Academy before proceeding to lunch or recess (there was a lot of recess), there would often be no one to hold Nat's hand but the teacher.

"You should get a health app to monitor Daddy's cough," Nat whispered. She had learned a lot about apps from Karen.

"Shhh," Masha whispered back. "Count backward from ten in any language you like and then you'll be asleep."

"*Desyat,*" Nat began. "*Devyat, vosem, sem, shest, pyat, chetyre, tri, dva, odin.*"

"*Tak derzhat,*" Senderovsky whispered in his sleep, his father's rarely tendered praise bright and sweet against his palate.

KAREN AND VINOD were snoring with abandon, their arms desperately tight around each other, as if the final smokestack of the *Titanic* was disappearing into the waves behind them. Ed had taken two sleeping pills, first one and then an hour later another, a left hook to the jaw and then a right hook, and was now knocked out on the edge of his bed. A flute was playing dimly in the subbasements of his consciousness, and he floated toward that excellent sound, disembodied.

Dee's face was buried deep in her pillow and she had to maneuver at times to draw a breath. The sex had helped calm her. He had given his all, and his all was wonderful. She had even bit his lip out of what she could only surmise was passion. They laughed when they realized she had drawn blood, but still kept going. He loves me, the idiot, she had thought. All the mentions on her favorite social channel were wrong. She was worth loving.

He couldn't sleep. There was the thunder and lightning and the (mostly ornamental) fan turning above him. *Apocalypse Now.* The second shot of the movie. Willard looking at the rotating fan in the Saigon hotel. They were in the middle of a war, he thought. The bombs were coming down like in that Graham Greene novel about life during the Blitz. He touched himself and brought his fingers up to his nose so that he could smell the both of them. Give me the strength, he thought. But the strength to do what?

He wanted to sing a song he remembered from watching *Sesame Street* as a kid. (A latchkey kid, he thought with soothing self-pity.) It was an adaptation of a British nursery song, sung as a round by a family of cartoon turtles. He had since heard it performed onstage as a round for four voice parts. He sat by the window and began to mouth the words, first in his natural bass, then mentally switching up to tenor, alto, soprano.

Come follow, follow, follow, follow, follow, follow me.
Whither shall I follow, follow, follow?
Whither shall I follow?
Follow thee! To the redwood, to the redwood, to the red-
   wood,
Redwood tree!

He opened the window, softly so as not to wake her, and leaned out into the rain to sing with his stiff but competent voice. *Wither shall I follow, follow, follow . . . ?* He leaned into the question mark with every verse, even the final one that deserved an exclamation instead. He felt himself getting hoarse as the rain pelted him, as the air congealed into mist. He wanted to be onstage, singing, crying, giving. It was what he was meant to do. *You are a responsibility onto this world.*

At four in the morning, he was still awake downstairs, staring at the photograph of Masha and Senderovsky sitting on a haystack, him with crooked teeth, her with her dimpled chin, as if announcing their future together. *To the redwood, to the redwood, to the redwood, / Redwood tree?* His phone beeped from within the pocket of his robe. His team on the West Coast was also awake. He read through messages full of desperate, capitalized letters. There was a video now, apparently. As in: YOU HAVE TO WATCH THE VIDEO! And: THIS ISN'T YOU, RIGHT? And: WE MAY HAVE TO PIVOT FROM "JUST FRIENDS" STRATEGY. But it was him. Him and her, on a run-down stage surrounded by grass. The footage was mostly dark and grainy, grass green with occasional flashes of violet and blue, but every once in a while the scene would be illuminated by high beams sweeping past the curve of the road so that one could catch the rhythm of him pushing into her from the side with pneumatic fervor. The videographer kept crawling closer and closer through the navel-high grass of the abandoned camp to the stage, capturing him and her in pixels. There was no audio.

Nat always woke up early and entertained herself until the adults were roused. From the window of the Petersburg Bungalow she saw a familiar figure carrying a duffel bag toward the garage. She couldn't find her sandals right away so she put on her mother's *tapki* and shuffled out in those great flapping enclosures. The little red Lancia was pulling out of its bay slowly and under cover of fog. "Wait!" Nat screamed. "Wait!" She tripped on a *tapka* and slid onto the gravel, skinning her knee. The little turtle of a car continued to roll slowly down the driveway past the tree stumps of violent storms past, then, with the pointless flare of a turn signal echoing down the gray empty street, made a left toward the state road.

Nat looked at her skinned knee, raw and bloody, more exposed and frightening than actually pulsing with pain, and before she could account for what had loosened inside her, began weeping quietly and without theatrics, tears gathering on her chin and then dropping with the heavy thud of monsoon rain pellets onto her polka-dot frock. When she was done crying, she sat in the gravel drained of the will to move, waiting for a grown-up to come and take her home.

ACT FOUR

The Death of
Alexander Borisovich

I

RAZGAR LETA. SENDEROVSKY'S two favorite Russian words. The height of summer. Or, to be literal, "the summer's burn." A perfect crop circle had been torched into the landowner's bald spot—he loved the sun so much he did not see why one needed to be "protected" from it—and Masha tended to it daily like a farmhand with a truculent animal. *"Nu, vot,"* she would say ("Well, now you've done it"), rubbing a combination of creams into his red scalp and sighing contentedly.

Nat looked at this newfound public intimacy between her parents with her usual anxious eyes. It wasn't just them. After the Actor had left, everyone behaved differently, more kindly, less self-consciously, as if this was just any other summer but with blue surgical masks and spent bottles of hand sanitizer littering the side of the road. But without the Actor, the uniqueness was gone, the initial feeling that her parents weren't really her parents, that she had been granted the permission to choose her own destiny, that this Jin-level famous personage had called her "lovely" and that maybe she was. While her ties to Karen-*emo* (and Uncle Vinod) remained, she was now unmistakably also part of that small unit of Levin-Senderovskys that blundered through the world with their strange diets and reminiscences. She loved them, too, even when what passed for their love felt like a tether around the sun-bronzed stalk of her neck. She felt it her duty to make them happier even if some of her own happiness was lost in the exchange.

As THE MERCURY reached for the tip of the thermometer, the nation celebrated its own birthday with an unrelenting sense of shock. The corpses were stacking up in other parts of the country. The refrigerated trucks were heading south and west. It was becoming apparent that the country's president might never willingly surrender his power, and Karen's assistant began proceedings for her to regain her Korean citizenship.

Stranded social novelists up and down the river dutifully photographed hard-to-identify flowers and took notes on the appearance of gathering storm fronts and menacing thunderheads. More than one could be found looking up at a slumbering owl or a sunburned meadow beseeching their higher power to *help me make something out of all this stillness.*

Meanwhile, the landowner's estate buzzed with animal and human-animal activity. Steve the Groundhog had decorated his poolside-adjacent hole with lilacs, or so it looked to Nat (actually Uncle Vinod had decorated the lair himself and convinced the child that it was the marmot's doing). Traveling birds—warblers?—would invade a tree, ravish it with their chirping, and then abandon it just as quickly and for no discernible reason, like bored American tourists at an ancient historical site. Karen and Vinod would sneak into Ed's outdoor shower and have monumental sex, their four hands pressed against the seashell-studded walls as they worked each other to completion, even as Vinod occasionally put a hand to his mouth to make sure that he wasn't intubated, that all this was really happening. He had transferred his luggage to Karen's bungalow and unpacked all but some emergency underwear and the notarized papers at the bottom of one suitcase. He wouldn't need them now. He was healthy and strong and in love. Karen was helping him prepare query letters to agents. He could at last abandon the character he had written for his father, "the lonely man, his aloneness bordering on the holy."

With the Actor gone, it was as if a factory owner had left and the workers strolled dazed past the silenced conveyor belts. How should they behave among one another? Was all this theirs now? What would they do without the boldface name above the front gates? Strangely enough, the seven remaining colonists became closer. They all had their faults and their past tussles (recall Dee's last outburst at the dinner table), but they all liked one another at heart, were by now as familiarized with each other's company as siblings or polar explorers. Now they had lunches as well as dinners together, gathering in the kitchen en masse at 12:30 P.M. promptly to throw Masha's egg salad onto peasant bread. And at 3:00 P.M. during weekdays, when Nat was on a call with her speech therapists, those forty or older ran to the pool for a quick skinny-dip, mixing their happy nudity with the pungency of Karen's marijuana.

And then there was Dee.

When a lover stalks off, we miss the heat of his touch first, the skin-to-skin contact babies crave and that Nat had never known. (A surviving photo from her orphanage shows her at the beginning of life, dark lashed, squirmy, with many tender folds to her wrists, but no one to clean them regularly or hold her through a night's cry.) And so Dee felt her abandonment on a dermal level. She tried to readjust, but every single square inch of Senderovian territory that she passed throughout the day called for a handsome man's touch, called for that skin to skin. *And I never even wanted to love him!* she would say to herself. But the skin told another story, and when the sun began to set she would touch the nape of her own neck, just to know that touch was still possible. In the future, she thought, the Karen Chos of the world will develop golems instantly conjured from roving atoms who will embrace us and hold us through the night only to dissolve by daybreak, and then there will be no need for any of this cruelty. (Or for humanity, really.) But until then? Until then, she was in pain.

Given that the colony now reminded her of the one failed relationship she had had in the last decade, given the traumatic footage of them having sex down the road, which had destroyed her privacy (her most private parts had been covered by his body in the video, but that didn't really help), her original impulse was to flee. But where would she go? She swore she would never look at his social media, but she did anyway, and it was clear that his handlers were positioning him as having rediscovered the ills of racism (without mentioning her, of course), and now he was throwing out one obvious initiative after the next, acting camps for Black children on a fifty-acre retreat in Central California (the anti-Senderovsky-bungalow-colony), which also introduced the participants to the complete farming experience (they were now selling produce at the original farmers' market in Los Angeles) and even a socially distanced re-creation of *Gone with the Wind*, but with the races of the characters reversed. (This would soon enough lead to a new series of problems for the Actor and his team.) She saw his doe-eyed appeals to donors and sponsors and couldn't help but think that the extra-winsome sadness he brought to these performances was not just his newfound understanding of structural racism but the fact that he still loved her and missed her.

Well, to hell with that! Her own situation was slowly improving. A group of earnest intellectual men in button-down shirts had written a letter on her behalf in a prominent magazine. The word "censorship" had been used. There were claims that she would be fired from an upcoming teaching appointment, claims which weren't true. At first, Dee considered writing an angry response, telling the world she did not need their help, that once again they were misunderstanding her, these rich, educated-man types. But in the end she welcomed the intervention, indeed any point of view affirming that she was not a bigoted monster. So now armed with the letter, she could go back to the city to get into new and better fights with the usual combatants, to surprise her accusers and redefine the terms of her banishment. She was about ready to get into her nine-thousand-dollar vehicle and shove off, but someone else kept her glued to the wide-plank floor of the Writer's Cottage (to whence she had been repatriated from the main house after the rightful owners had reclaimed possession). The reader is correct in assuming the identity of this individual.

She had never stopped going for walks with Ed, not during her three weeks of romancing with the Actor and not after. Remarkably, her affair with the thespian rarely came up as a subject of conversation between them and instead they talked about all the stupid things young (not that Ed was especially young) urban people of the moment talked about, the vagaries of social media, the flavorful *mee krops* and *tom kha gais* they had last slurped down in February, their path through the brambles of high society, along with gossip about other people being brought down, forced to recalibrate, rephrase, and recant.

After the dinner with the Actor and Vinod's hurtful words about her being on the side of her people, Ed began to talk about the members of his own family and their manifold awfulness. If you searched for them online in Korean, you would discover their role in the destruction of labor unions and the many monopolies they wielded since the times of the Japanese occupation. You would learn about scalding cups of tea thrown at subordinates and even the flogging of an elderly chauffeur, a decorated military man, after he had fragranced a company limousine with the wrong type of air freshener. Because rich people were excused from the suffering of the world, they had to invent their own more elaborate and personalized forms of suffering and then to inflict baroque versions of that stunted interiority onto others. And that was just the public stuff. There were arranged marriages to violent schizophrenics, corrupt divorce proceedings, stolen children, suicidal mothers, shamed children shunted off to Rhode Island and London art schools. No one, but *no one*, was happy, just shuffling through cosmetic surgery clinics and watch boutiques in a Valium haze.

"And yet," Ed said, "how can I claim to be entirely different from my relatives? How can I claim to be divorced from all those years of feudalism? I'm supposed to throw off the yoke of history all by myself? That's a nonsense American idea, that one can just"—a very loud snap of his fingers—"change. My skin is too thick to be shed. I can choose not to abuse a chauffeur, but I can't alter the manner of my gait as I tipsily saunter to the waiting car. My oppressiveness is priced in."

"I'd rather be considered bad," Dee said, "than to actually be false. Everything I write is a time stamp in history. Everything, no matter how horrible and self-indicting, is, I swear to God, honest. Can I be blamed that the portrait which emerges does not fit the requirements of the moment?"

This was, she had to admit, the button-down letter-writing men's prescription for art as well—that it had to be reflective, not revolutionary. The artist, according to them and in line with their experiences at New Haven, stood in the vicinity of history processing its raw nature through her own blemished experiences and typing the resulting observations into the Notes application of her phone. That was the job description. But what if this particular job had suddenly become irrelevant? And what if irrelevancy, not cultural tone deafness, was the real specter that haunted the bungalow colony, haunted her and Senderovsky and the Actor as well? The hour for chronicling the situation had passed; it was time to seize the telegraph station and detain the provisional government. Maybe that was what drew Dee to Ed in the first place: he had placed himself outside the game. He did not publicly render an opinion on anything, and no power could hold him accountable for his action or his speech. If society collapsed, he would put on an ascot and waltz over to the nearest still-functional one. (He had Canadian citizenship.) He did not even own a social media account.

A pickup truck passed and Ed waved to its sole occupant who dutifully waved back within the sunlit dome of his vehicle. Since the Actor had left the colony, there were no incidents with homicidal trucks (cause and effect?), but Ed now took it upon himself to wave to every car rumbling down Senderovsky's road. He had even acquired something of a reputation among the locals as the Waver of V—— Road. To not wave back at him had become a local faux pas, no matter the color of the flag swinging off one's porch. Dee thought she understood some of the reasoning for his fake cheer. Senderovsky once accounted for his own self-abusive Russian Jewish humor as a demographic imperative, the need to make fun of himself before the dominant group (Christian Slavs) could get a chance to do so, to self-slap before being punched down. There was something of that in Ed's happy wave, too, along with an overblown "model minority" smile that disappeared with the sound of the car's passing swoosh or became genuine when he turned and looked into Dee's face. This made her happy. There was a lot going on with Ed, but only she got to see the whole of it. The daily Ed walks gave her purpose and pleasure. They saved her from her fruitless encounters with social media, which meant they also saved her from herself.

THERE WAS A restaurant known for its hand sanitizer in a charming and progressive nearby town, once the center of the nineteenth-century riverside whale-processing industry. The restaurant was Southeast Asian in nature, a cuisine Ed claimed he could not success-fully replicate for lack of the right ingredients, and it proffered food and collected payment without any human contact at all, except for a sterilized nod at the counter once the credit card information had clicked into place. After picking up their tray, the diner adjourned to a table within a vast tented former parking lot where each table was separated from the next by at least three meters.

Ed and Dee drove down to the whale-processing town in a fit of excitement. They were sick of rural anthropology and desperate for new spice. It was almost dinnertime at the colony, and on this day the colonists would be deprived of their chef. (The fact that both he and Dee would be absent raised one of Senderovsky's considerable eyebrows as well as his wife's smaller woolly caterpillar.)

Ed marveled at the privileged, Senderovsky-like way Dee drove past the dappled fields in her unexceptional car, as if death was not an option for her even when the lane markers were clearly being violated and all of the cockpit instrumentation beeped and buzzed in protest. "I hope you won't flog me!" Dee joked after she had run a tractor off the road with her impudence. "I know how particular you Kims are about your chauffeurs."

He laughed behind his aviator sunglasses and wondered if they were on a date. In his beloved (and now debunked) Japanese reality show, a nerd had asked a beauty on a date and she had suggested they go to Costco with the rest of their roommates as a way of turning him down. It had become known as the Costco Incident. He did not think of himself as a nerd, yet had studiously avoided that type of incident his entire life and had many empty Moleskine diaries to show for it.

They waited for their food along a pathway lined with cute signs about mask wearing and distancing, which we don't need to reproduce here, then collected their trays and sat down at a table in the middle of the restaurant's buzzing big tent, where they were soon molested by a wasp. "He's harmless," Dee educated her date as he tried and failed to shoo away the large clumsy insect with his fluttering hands. "He's a cicada killer. They don't sting."

"Huh," Ed said. He rolled up the deadstock cotton sleeves of his banker-striped shirt and refastened its thick mother-of-pearl buttons around the biceps of his tanned arms. "You shouldn't dress up so much," Dee said, observing his ritual. "Just wear plainer things. You have such a nice body. Give us a peek."

He did not know how to respond. "Oh," he said inwardly while presenting her with a blush. He opened the cardboard containers of sweet potato curry, black pepper wings in Vietnamese fish sauce, and a "Romanesco" *larb* studded with little gem lettuces and pickled chilies, and began to distribute the food. She poured two cups from a refreshing bucket of mezcal and grapefruit liqueur. As they toasted silently, they looked deep into each other's eyes for a long, bashful beat. He drank down to the bottom and wiped his mouth with his naked hand. He didn't care anymore. If it didn't work out and he had to go to Chania alone, he would simply lock himself in a hotel room and drain the life from his body in one way or another.

"Dee," he said, "I love you."

"I know," she said, immediately.

And almost as immediately: "I think I love you, too."

He nodded thoughtfully, picked at his *larb* with mass-produced chopsticks, knowing he could no longer eat any more of it, delicious as it was. Even though the tables were far apart, his senses were now heightened enough that he could hear every conversation around them (mostly they were about local real estate), and his poor bladder was now consumed by that sweet, lovely panic that accompanies reciprocated love.

"Any more thoughts about what we just said to each other," Dee ventured. "Or should we just talk politics?"

A towheaded and poorly masked five-year-old boy wearing an I AM

A FEMINIST T-shirt had wandered very close to their table and was soon accompanied by his likewise-dressed twin. "Kent! Lorimer!" a freckled mama yelled from a nearby table. "Don't come close!"

"That's okay," Dee shouted back, even as she put on her own surgical mask to protect herself from the invaders. The feminist children retreated, kicking up gravel behind them. Ed had spent so much of his capital on his declaration of love that he no longer knew which other words were still in his possession. He decided to gamble and say something stupid.

"You look beautiful in your mask."

She laughed. "Are you saying my mouth and chin are ugly?"

"No, I just . . . The gauze matches the color of your eyes."

"Oh, God. Make this year go away."

There was so much brimming, and brewing, within Ed that he wondered how to keep it all within himself, how to stop it from coming out as a fountain of tears or a loud "Romanesco" belch or heavy black smoke steaming out of his ears. They were staring at each other again, hands mechanically reaching for the grapefruit mezcal, mouths anxiously swallowing. "Should I keep my mask on between sips?" she said. "Does that turn you on?"

"You know me better than that," he said. "You know everything I'm thinking. Always."

"I'm thinking right now you want to touch my knee with yours under the table."

"See! That's exactly right."

"And now," she said as he began to rub his knee against hers, "you're kicking yourself for not wearing shorts so you can feel how smooth my skin is. Correction, you're kicking yourself for not *owning* a pair of shorts. Which we will have to remedy right away."

"You see right through me," he said. "The writer's mind gives you an advantage."

"Fine, then what am *I* thinking?"

"I'd rather not say."

"Oh, come on! Not fair!" Her voice was high and unusually girlish. She more than knew the rudiments of flirting, he thought.

"You're thinking that you've never been kissed by an Asian man."

She brought her hand up to her mouth in shock, mimicking, inadvertently, all of the young women on the reality show. "Oh my God," she said. "You just racialized this."

"Was I wrong?"

"Well."

"Then you racialized it first."

"Okay, fine. Where should this kiss take place? Right here in front of everyone?" Both of them now realized that after Dee's recent public contretemps she might be recognized by some of the tent-restaurant's patrons, all of whom were heavy social media users, even Kent and Lorimer, the five-year-old twins. Dee did not want to lose any more of her privacy, even though publicly kissing an Asian man, as he had correctly limned her thoughts, could only help her at this point. (A famous neo-Nazi television personality was now dating a Black man, not that Dee would compare herself to her.) "Let's go somewhere else," she said.

The propriety of Ed's cotton shirt and the way he helped her up from her wooden bench meant they couldn't just rush to her car and drive at double the speed limit to the Big Island or Writer's Cottage. (Which would be better for a first tussle?) Instead, they had to do something date-like around town before giving in to their animal best. They walked over to the town's main street, which sloped from a considerable height toward a promenade overlooking the river. Perhaps there they would find a suitable space for their first unhurried kiss.

The town was full of distressed art galleries and outrageously priced antiques shops. All the goods now had signs against racism next to their price tags. Toward the river, a housing project sheltered many of the town's nonwhite citizens, and a small Bangladeshi community had set up residences and shops nearby. The easy pace reminded Ed of a recent visit to Trinidad, and indeed a storefront was cheerfully hawking island food to the locals. He made all of these observations to Dee at a rapid clip, and as she compared the Actor's blathering with his, she found them similar in some ways, but Ed's crooning was less intense, less self-conscious, the warble of an observer, not a participant. Again, she found it matched her own new outlook, a traveler just passing through a series of delightful hell-scapes on the way to oblivion, and the way he sweated in his over-done formal shirt lent him all the personality she could handle in a man.

As they walked through the white section of town, Dee caught a few stares from passersby, as she was clearly recognized for her recent misadventures. There was more surprise than disgust, the well-tuned minds quickly doing their social calculations: Why, yes, Senderovsky's "Dacha of His Own" was only fifteen miles due south, so why shouldn't she be here? And who was this new gent? Was he infamous, too?

In the Black and Bangladeshi sections, the stares faded away; she was not a seasonal celebrity here, merely a tourist. Upon crossing the street separating the races, Dee and Ed joined hands, as if making a very lame statement of their own. He was still talking about the Caribbean—about Cuba, evidently (frequent mentions of Raúl and Fidel and "state-run shops")—and the talk was as ambient as a sound machine or an air conditioner as they both floated in a haze of grape-fruited mezcal and the excitement of two hands constantly squeezing out signals that ran counterpoint to whatever he was saying. Who cares about the gayish nights he spent along the *malecón*? the squeezes said. Who cares about this whale town as one of the finest examples of nineteenth-century vernacular American architecture? This is all just class-based courtship. What we really are, maybe, is in love.

A green Parade Hill looked over the promontory at the wide expanse of the river, here forked over a large but uninhabited island, concealing the town on the other side (the ragtag namesake of a city of antiquity). Clouds hid then revealed biblical sunbursts and everything around them—the cute children talking in adult language and tossing back their braids, a distant Victorian lighthouse in the middle of the river recalling another empire lost, a crowd of Bangladeshis barbecuing goat by the train tracks against a backdrop of purple mountains fading blue, gray, gone—everything was lit up in professional cinematic ocher that meant they had the license, indeed the duty, to kiss each other. They did so quickly, then slowly, as if each had run a long exhausting high-altitude race and now had to breathe life back into the other. Their eyes were closed and she tried to think of nothing but him and he tried to think only of her, they tried to banish the *why* of what they were doing and concentrate only on the *how*, and for the most part they were successful, moaning kindly in appreciation of what the other had to offer, fingers caressing the undersides of each other's ears, his thick mane, her sweaty tendrils clinging to her neck, while the impudent little kids on the bench next to them kept making fun of their ardor, boys daring the girls to "mess" with them, too.

"What were you like at my age?" Dee asked when their tongues had decided to take a short break. This brought to Ed's mind their significant age difference. He worried that when he would speak of the past, he would sound and look old, as all ancient storytelling men did.

"It's funny that we're sitting by a river," he said, "because when I was exactly your age, I was still living in Italy and that was the year I had published that bilingual magazine, *Rivers/Fiumi*."

"The one about all the great rivers of the world."

He sighed. "Well, the idea was that we explored the complexities of societies by interrogating the rivers running through them. Maybe back then we didn't use the term 'interrogate.' "

As a child he had lived in fear of being scolded and maybe he feared it still. For thirty-one-year-old Ed, nothing had been worse than being told he was wrong. That's what *Fiumi* had taught him, how hurtful it was to try something and still remain inconsequential. But as he told his story to Dee, he managed to see just how funny all of it was. How steeped the world was in artistic failure, even as the artists (and sometimes the society around them) failed to recognize that failure as such. Gradually he began to do what Senderovsky always did when he spun a tale—he began to make fun of all the principals, chiefly himself. As soon as one acquired a liberal education, huge parts of life became an elaborate joke. Maybe that's what you paid for when your parents' check cleared with the bursar—the rights to the joke.

As the sun lowered itself into the mountains, they saw that there was no choice but to head home and escalate the situation. They passed two very young people sitting on the hood of an old domestic car. To say they were "necking" would be to indemnify the participants from the fire ignited within Dee and Ed. For starters, one of the young woman's breasts was fully out of her bra and was being held and caressed, "staged" in local real estate parlance, by two roving hands as she straddled the young man with her denim thighs, her buttocks flexing back and forth as she dry-mounted him. They were within full view of the town's only housing project, and they looked, to use a highly American descriptor, like movie stars. One also had to note that they were of different races, she white and he Black. Ed and Dee processed this fact through their own racial lenses.

"Wowee," Dee finally said. "Young love."

Ed was finding it hard to breathe. I may be old, he was thinking, but I can do this, too.

They were so lust-struck and dazed as they ran to Dee's car that they both failed to realize they were not wearing masks. An older woman shielded her child from their advance and castigated them with her eyes of pale blue. Once in her car, they attempted to kiss, and she tried to sneak one of his hands up her bra, but he said, "No, honey, please, just drive us home. Go as fast as you like. I can cover your speeding tickets."

She pulled out of town, and the cornfields and apple orchards took on a festive golden-hour glow, but each second felt painful and burning. She unbuttoned the top of her jeans. "Just squeeze your hand in there," she said.

He reached over the gear stick and tried to touch her as instructed. "Maybe shift your seat back a little," he said.

They swerved past an empty school bus. "Fuck you!" Dee yelled to the driver. "I'm trying to get laid here!" His tongue was inside her ear. "No, I don't like that, sorry. Kiss my neck!"

She was at eighty on the speedometer, and a voice that sounded like a chime that had just been taught to speak English announced: "Driver alert, please pull over and take a break!"

"Not tonight, Satan," Dee said, stepping on the gas some more.

She noticed Ed had slung back to his seat and, amid his heavy breathing, had put his hand on his crotch. "Oh my God, are you going to masturbate in front of me?"

"No!" he shouted. "It just hurts a little. I'm going to loosen things up a bit."

"Oh, please do," she said. "I'd love to see you jerk off."

"You're driving," he said weakly. "We're in a car."

She threw off her seat belt and raised herself up. The car's chiming voice was crazy with despair. With both hands off the wheel and one foot on the accelerator, she stripped her shorts and panties down to her ankles. "Give me your fucking hand," she said.

"What?" he said as he reached for the wheel and tried to keep the car steady. Dying right now would not be a problem for him. She brought his fingers inside her. "Oh," he said. "Dee."

"We can do it in that cornfield." She moaned, as the car hurtled madly from one side of the road to the other.

"They can see us," he whispered, two fingers suspended inside her. They passed a sign that read OUR PRAYERS HAVE COME TRUE. WELCOME BACK, PASTOR ED. "Everyone can see us."

"I don't give a fuck. Fuck everyone."

"Oh, God." He was massaging her now, circularly, while examining the willowy blond triangle above her sex with more scrutiny than he had deployed in his entire life. If only he had been as diligent at university, he might have graduated with honors (or just graduated).

THE CAR WAS bounding up the gravel driveway as Ed was trying to extricate his hand from within her warmth. (How desperately he now wanted to place each perfumed finger into his mouth.) She stepped on the brakes, and the car skidded, sideways, into an inopportune position blocking all the garage bays at once. They plopped out of the car as she pulled up her underthings and shorts with one hand and began to run toward the closest of the bungalows, which would be his. They heard Nat's voice ringing from the covered porch: "Dee! Ed! We still have some food left! My mommy made borscht."

"That's okay," Masha sang to the almost-lovers as they ran past the porch. "I'm sure they've eaten already."

Ed could hear Vinod and Karen and Senderovsky laughing, but he did not give a damn.

The Kīlauea volcano above Ed's bed was still donating a steady stream of lava to the Pacific. As soon as the door was shut they were upon each other, their handsome faces clanging ("Ouch") as they tried to get better purchase. "Sorry, but not sorry," Dee said as she ripped to shreds Ed's deadstock cotton banker-stripe shirt. "You should never wear that again," she hissed. "We should make beautiful rags out of it. Out of all your shit."

Ed's vision was flirting with darkness, the oxygenated blood in his body was flowing in one direction—he had to remind himself to breathe. She put all of him in her mouth, she licked him below, he explored both orifices with his tongue and fingers—they worked so hard at times they forgot the nature of their assignments and merely breathed hard into the other's genitals or listened to the textures of the other's moans. He wanted to ejaculate, but held back. "Can we do anything?" he asked. "Like maybe weird things?"

"Fuck you for even asking permission," she said.

"Put on your mask," he said.

"You really do hate my chin."

"Will not dignify with reply."

She put on her mask with shaking hands as he, just as shakily, positioned a hanging bathroom mirror against his stupid modernist desk so that she could see herself, then knocked the fucking Hawaiian pineapple statues off with one horny hand. There was a loud sound, his and hers, as he entered her from behind, all of her naked, sprawled against the desk, except for the familiar, by now totemic blue of the surgical mask around her face.

Oh, no, he thought. Could my asking her to put on a mask be interpreted as an attempt to muzzle her? Or an appropriation of Islamic face covering? What does it mean for me as a—

And just then, he came.

2

THE HEAD OF the network had called Senderovsky personally to tell him they were officially passing on his show. He expected as much after the Actor begged off. "It's not just that," the network head said. "It's the subject matter. Oligarchs, hookers, payoffs. A former Soviet republic won't seem that different from 2020 America to the viewer."

"Doesn't that make it pertinent?" Senderovsky asked.

"No, it makes it depressing."

After the call, which had taken place a week before Dee and Ed consummated their relationship, he paced the cool dark empty living room of the main house, grieving his loss. Yes, it was over now. Even his agent in Los Angeles had stopped calling him with her stale Russianisms and mentions of his lovely home and lovely family. The bank would take the bungalow colony. Well, fine! He would move to the city, to their tiny apartment, and do what? Write a novel? The very thought repulsed him. He could see the words and sentences accreting on the screen as mourning doves cooed their reviews on his windowsill. He could imagine himself cribbing the best lines from his past, regurgitating his youth, now that the future was but the slow dull tick of a metronome atop the Steinway. He had come so close to having his own television show, to being *someone*. Now he would have to angle for a teaching job, as some kind of adjunct at first, maybe hoping a full-time position opened up. He would become, essentially, Vinod. Except that Vinod had actually written something brilliant.

And so Senderovsky sulked amid his living room, bumping his hip against the Steinway, tripping over Nat's junk on the floor. (When had she come into possession of an archery set?) He had always said the right things on social media. He cried when they killed that man in Minneapolis. He was an ordoliberal. He believed in the role of the state in the social market economy and the redistribution of things. Reparations, if that's what it took. But now he would go further. He would renounce all his privileges. He would not write another novel so that others could be heard. If he were summoned to give a talk or reappear in Hollywood, he would fly in economy class. But if he followed through on his vow of poverty, who would pay for the basic necessities? Who would pay for Nat's Kindness Academy?

And here was the strangest part: as his career prospects dwindled, Senderovsky looked at the members of his minuscule family with fresh morning eyes. Karen, his most successful friend, wanted Nat for a daughter; the Actor had desired his wife as a "handmaiden." What kind of fool would he be if he didn't appreciate what he had? Now that they had moved back into the main house, Nat back into her tiny room (though she did have occasional sleepovers at Karen and Vinod's) and he and his wife into theirs, a familial charm had fallen over him, best exemplified by the contradictory smells of bacon in the mornings and Sabbath candles on Friday night. He rolled on top of Masha one night after she had *lehadlik*'d her *ner shel Shabbat* in the dining room and had lost his nose in the musk of her hair and she held his skinny, childhood-evoking shoulders with two candle-warm hands, tightly, as if he might fly away, then lightly, because she knew he wouldn't, and they thought of nothing but the glow of certain objects and the strangeness of marriage and the comforts of a home regained. For the duration of their slow coupling, he had even forgotten to cough.

Masha now found herself in the mood for her husband and for the life they hadn't shared in so long. She had decided to take a leave of absence from her work with the elderly Russians. This happened during a visit to her parents in a Jewish suburb of Boston. She had driven there with Nat, a red cooler full of cold borscht and baguettes for sustenance (she would not trust the hygiene of the road stops), which had reminded her of every childhood road trip undertaken since she and her *bant* had landed in America, thirty-seven years ago to the month.

They sat, bemasked, in a tiny backyard, she and Nat on one side, her parents on the other, two delightful gnomes talking at their granddaughter and engaging in the act of anxious mindless chatter (*boltovnya*, as it's called in Russian) at the rapid clip that Nat preferred. They loved her so much, even though she looked nothing like them, these descendants of a tiny sweaty tribe that had seen its share of *tsoris*, Dzhordzh and otherwise, and now, for academic reasons (her mother still taught introductory math at a large Catholic college) found themselves on the cusp of a historic American city, all eyes on a Harbin girl in a tunic as green as the cluster of elms that shaded their little garden of which they were so proprietarily proud. (*"Nu, ne chorosho zhe li u nas, pryamo kak v derevne"*—"Well, isn't it great here, just like in the country?")

"Your mother helps people like Grandpa Boris and Baba Galya feel less angry," Senderovsky would explain Masha's psychiatric job to Nat, referring to his own parents. But was she helping them, the Laras of her world, to help Senderovsky himself? Maybe that was the truth instead of the lie she had told herself—that she wanted to ease someone's sorrow in Inna's language. And now her parents, small and gray but still vital and funny, warbled before her and her daughter and she could hear in the nonaggression of their language just how minimally humiliated they had been by the immigrant experience. What a stroke of luck that had been for her. Luck she could own, instead of passing on the pain of others to her daughter. And now that her husband was out of work, how could she not return to private practice? Yes, sell the bungalow colony, retreat to the city, rent an office in a leafy part of town, and help wealthy white native-born Americans talk through their atomized lives and commune with their share of historical blame. Imagine counseling people who actually wanted the world made better instead of ethnically cleansed.

They lit the twenty-six-hour Yahrzeit candle (So many candles in my life, she thought) in the backyard, even though the anniversary of Inna's death was still a month away, but they were together now, and perhaps it wasn't a bad omen to have the ceremony early. The Levins argued over who should light the candle, and Masha said, "But the mother should, of course," and that predictably made her pretty mother cry (how Masha wanted to hug her, how she wished the virus would disappear so that mothers who lost their daughters could be properly comforted), which made Nat nervous, and so Masha pressed her close as the wick caught flame and the pale yellow light emerged among them like a clean new soul. "My God, Inna would have loved Nat," her mother said in Russian as she blew out one of the Wegmans matches. "I understood that!" Nat shouted, and Masha, being Masha, instead of celebrating her trilingual daughter had to think of the question Nat had posed to her during the long ride over: "Do you think I could be Korean? Maybe you adopted me from a Korean orphanage."

And she had answered, eyes on the road, heart in her hands, and in contravention of her training and deep reservoir of Petrograd common sense, "I think that's what happened, honey. I think that's where you're from."

THEY WERE GETTING ready for dinner. Ed had on his first pair of Bermuda shorts ever, a gift from his girlfriend. He had fermented his own Napa cabbage and was serving a BTS-themed dinner for Nat, which consisted of J-Hope's beloved kimchi fried rice and *haembeo-geo*.

And now we must talk about what Vinod and Senderovsky were wearing above the waist. They were wearing nothing. Both were now so comfortable among their friends that they chose to dine in the evening heat wearing only a pair of shorts for the landowner and a checkered lungi for his friend. Nat looked back and forth between her new uncle's sarong-like garment and the muscular surgery-scarred body above it (she had just watched breaststroking Vinod surface like a sea monster with a loud gurgle as he raced across the pool) and her father's heavy, womanlike bosom. Well, thought Masha, this is who we are. Without the Laras in the back of her mind, the sight of two near-naked friends whose sense of masculinity would disturb roughly half of the country relaxed her. Masha rolled back the sleeves of her own blouse to reveal the new bronze of her shoulders, felt the subtle wind graze beneath her arms. So much pleasure still to be had in this world. Karen, too, sat in her clingy swimsuit, a one-piece that made her look, in Vinod's eyes, unbearably young, as if they were about to grab their landlines, punch in those sonorous numbers, and spend the next half an hour discussing a live episode of *The Simpsons* while downstairs their parents raged against the machine and each other.

Nat was piling mounds of kimchi on her *haembeogeo*, her hands soaked chili red, her mild palate accepting the heat of her idol's favorite food. Karen and Masha knew that one of them would have to deal with her cranky stomach later, and both now selfishly hoped the other caregiver would soothe their child. Ed and Vinod were leaning toward each other, quietly discussing aspects of lovemaking with the ardor of senior collegians who had lost their virginity only as of late. Senderovsky, drunk on one of the forty-eight bottles of retsina Ed had just ordered to commemorate a public joy, was singing, to himself and his wife, a boisterous Russian song about a locomotive hurtling toward socialism. Karen was coaching Dee on the use of teleconferencing technology for her classes in the fall, perhaps trying to make up for all that her own technology had done to her, while Nat put her head on her *emo*'s naked, chlorinated shoulder and commenced a volley of perfectly timed kimchi farts. The mysterious bird wearing yellow shoulder pads had come out with her family for a makeshift worm picnic in the monumental forest just behind the porch. Two hatchlings, dazed by the sunlight, happy because they had not yet experienced the full cold of this continent, pecked at each other while their dad sat on a high branch singing about the journey that had brought all of them here; not a love song, exactly, but a rendering of his life and worth, as a beast of this earth, as a parent, as a lover, as a migrant, as a bird. And if we are to suspend our secular beliefs, even for half a paragraph, we can imagine the migrated souls of all the human ancestors presently at table, looking over their bloodline progeny gathered together over the familiarity of cabbage and fried rice and the unfamiliarity of a meat disk between two circular pieces of bread, happy as parents in a playground when all of the children assembled play together quietly and at peace, and no one's young feelings are hurt, and everyone will go home still innocent.

Of course, by the logic of fiction, we are at a high point now. This respite, this happy family, these four new lovers, this child slowly losing her shyness, all of this must be slated for destruction, no? Because if we were to simply leave them feasting and ecstatic, even as the less fortunate of the world fell deeper into despair, even as hundreds of thousands perished for lack of luck, lack of sympathy, lack of rupees, would we be just in our distribution of happiness? And so we sigh, cross ourselves, mumble the Kaddish, perform our *pujas* and *wudu,* all in preparation for the inevitable, which, in this case, comes with the crunch of gravel down the driveway.

3

THEY HEARD THE crunch of gravel down the driveway. It was Saturday, and they were not expecting workmen. Senderovsky had collected more household money from Ed and Karen (and a pittance from Dee), and now the elaborate machinery of the estate functioned perfectly and in tandem. Hot water flowed out of new noncopper pipes, hedges were trimmed by the now-cheerful handyman (he had used a state subsidy to help fund a new motorbike), and painful carpenter ants were slaughtered en masse by workers from a company across the river (motto: *We kill with skill*). Most important, the cable company sent a representative to install routers in the bungalows so that the colonists could resume their work lives. Senderovsky took that as a sign that they might stay indefinitely, the prospect of which gladdened him, though he knew he would run out of money before the first snow.

As the diners heard the crunch of gravel, those facing away from the driveway were loath to have to turn around and inspect the newcomer, to have their magnificent peace destroyed as it sometimes was by the orgiastic cry of the distant train lumbering up to the state's capital. What now, they thought. Company? Guests? And on such a pretty day? Well, who needs them! Or, in Senderovsky-speak, to the devil with them! Masha reached for her purse and its treasure trove of masks.

They fixed their fading visions on the vehicle graveling toward them, its noisy advance initially shaded by the ghost of a long-dead apple tree. Eagle-eyed Nat was the first to understand what was happening. "What the heck?" she shouted, the last word recently taking pride of place in her innocent vocabulary. Dee, a champion at the optometrist's chart, next recognized the car's familiar irregular shape and blanched. Senderovsky sprang up from his chair and covered his breasts, as ashamed as Adam after his first helping of pie. And Ed laughed so sadly Vinod had to reach over and slap his back in commiseration. The colonists looked to one another, as if for the last time.

"MAY I SPEAK to Dee?" The question was directed at Senderovsky, as if he was her father and this was a different century. The Actor stood at the door of the covered porch. It was clear to all that he was experiencing technical difficulties: His hair had been cut professionally, but it flamed above him like a torch at a failed Olympics, and his eyes had the dimmed luster of dead coral clothed in a mist of algae. Sweat slicked across his forehead as if it had been moved to and fro by a windshield wiper, and his car, whose engine he had forgotten to turn off, sputtered and whirred behind him like a stinkbug at the end of summer.

Dee sat with her back to him. "You shouldn't be seen here," she said, loudly. "It's not good for any of us."

"Yes, please leave," Ed said.

"I got this, sweets," Dee said.

"Then at least let me talk to you," the Actor said to Senderovsky. "I have some news."

"Keep your distance," Masha said to her husband, handing him a mask.

THEY WALKED INTO the Petersburg Bungalow, and Senderovsky closed the door behind them. He carried himself like a game warden caging a dangerous animal. He put on his mask and opened the windows. The Actor looked at his former abode, and every single memory touched him nostalgically, from the second he had set down his duffel bag on the night of his first arrival to the moment he triumphally hoisted the same bag to the main house to claim his rightful place with Dee. This was the dormitory of his humble romantic beginnings with her, his boarding school of love, and he stood in it now an older and properly ruined man.

"I talked to Bob Gilderdash," the Actor said to Senderovsky. This was the head of a small but prestigious network, a discreet rival to the one that had first commissioned the series based on the landowner's book. "I sent him your scripts. The funny ones. He's a huge fan of your work. He visited Moscow in 1979 or whatever, so naturally he was knocked the fuck out. He said putting this show on the air was a national imperative no matter who wins the election. Direct quote."

Senderovsky digested the news. The old hunger gnawed at him, the chance to be somebody again. And yet he was concerned. Amid the dead coral of the Actor's eyes there floated a strange new darkness. His gaze was fixed slightly above Senderovsky's shoulder even though the Actor was well known for his unshakable eye contact. Senderovsky decided, for the first time all summer, not to lie. He decided to be strong and faithful to his friends. "She's in love with Ed," he said. "I think she was from the start, though she had trouble admitting it to herself. Why not leave her alone?"

His words, he noticed, had no effect on the Actor, one way or another. Surely, he had seen happy photographs of Dee and Ed on her social channels. Surely, he had enough congruency with the human experience to know those smiles belonged to people who desired each other, who were smiling for each other even more than for their audience. "I can make it work," the Actor said. "If you help me, I'll help you."

"You should talk to Karen," Senderovsky said. "She said there's maybe a way to help you. Sit down with her. Go over the options. I never thought I'd say this, but you look just horrible."

"May I stay the weekend?" the Actor said. "I don't know where else to go. My team won't talk to me unless I stay away from her. I took the agency's plane in the middle of the night."

"I'll have to ask Masha," he said. "You should wear your mask at all times."

"I don't have it," the Actor said. "The virus, I mean." He slapped his hands together thrice in quick succession, as if at a flamenco show. "Listen," he said. "I have an idea. The three of us should run away together."

"Me, you, and Masha?"

"Me, you, and Dee. I can make you important. All this"—he swept his arm around the bungalow—"could be just a funny past, an asterisk on your bio page. You'll be a player. I'm about to start a production company. We'll call our own shots."

Senderovsky shook his head from side to side in the manner of Vinod's mother, that famous noncommittal Indian "yes-no."

Once his reluctant host was gone, the Actor sat down hard on the bed and wiped off a slick of sweat. His secret sharer had been with him for five days, possibly risen out of a bathroom aerosol plume in a Palm Desert gas station where he and Elspeth had stopped in the middle of a long knockout fight that ended with both pugilists crying inside the West Coast version of the Lancia, a topless old Alfa Romeo, but only one of them stricken. Or perhaps it wasn't the fecal plume, but the coughing elderly man who had stumbled out of the bathroom before the Actor took his place astride the toilet, the top of his own mask hanging ineffectively below his nose, holstering it. Or perhaps it was a parting gift from Elspeth herself, who, though asymptomatic, had just enjoyed a low-grade undocumented tryst with a daredevil Los Angeles influencer of variable hygiene. Even now, the secret sharer was probing every sector of the divided Berlin that was the Actor's body, looking for greater purchase, pulmonary union with this sleepless animal, the constant sour taste of extinction in his mouth.

The Actor stood up, felt Dee's presence nearby, told himself this was the time for fortitude and not desperation. He coughed once, twice, felt a now-familiar liquid rumble in his stomach and the heave of the snap-pea-and-blood-orange salad he had eaten on the plane rising high into his esophagus, and nearly made it to the bathroom before he threw up.

NEGOTIATIONS WERE AFOOT throughout the main house and the bungalows. Emergency councils were being held on the porch and in "breakout rooms." Voices that had been placid for weeks were suddenly being raised. Colonists wept. Or held back their tears. Only Nat was happy about his return, the fulfillment of her prophecy, the proximity to greatness. She had asked her mother to let him stay. She and Karen would sew a stylish new mask for him and then isolate him for weeks. She thought he was a wounded bird.

"I DON'T LOVE him and I don't want him," Dee said to Ed. "Stop talking about him like he's some kind of rival. Like I don't get to choose."

"There must be some ember here or there," Ed said. They were in her cabin, surrounded by typewriters, the presence of which inadvertently heightened their vocabulary.

"What ember?"

"Ember of desire. On your part. For him."

"Don't go all English as a second language on me now."

"Fuck you," Ed said, surprised he could still be hurt by her remark. "I'm just thinking about your career."

"How can you say that? I'm supposed to choose between two men for my career? Between a man I want and one I don't." Ed realized his blunder and was ashamed. She stormed out and he followed her into the warm lunar night.

"I love that you're a striver!" he shouted after her. "I love that about you!"

She ran down the driveway and into the beams of a truck idling at its terminus. She thought she saw what looked like a barely legal country boy in the driver's seat, seat belt off, his speckled chin still a work in progress, his eyes fixed fearfully onto the woman emerging from the mist, running toward him as if she were ready to throw herself on his hood in some overblown Mediterranean gesture. The driver quickly killed his dome light falling into villainous shadow, reversed his truck, swerved out of the driveway, and stepped on the gas with a youthful lack of compromise. She ran after it without concern or care. She could stand up to anyone. A lovesick thespian, her coward boyfriend, a fellow hick with a pump-action rifle.

"HE'S JUST TOYING with you," Masha was saying to her husband in the main house. They were in the bedroom, both of them naked, as they had recently stopped wearing clothes after Nat was tucked away with her photo of Jin and Llama Llama towel, their simple bedroom re-eroticized.

"But what if? What if!" the landowner shouted.

"Shhhh!" Masha said. From down the hallway they heard a loud Nat moan. (She was being dream-chased by a murderous hornet, and her father's voice sounded like the nearness of its buzz.)

"He's where I want him," Senderovsky continued.

"He's never where you want him. He's a wreck. He's dangerous. To himself and to others. He needs help."

"You can help him."

"I'm not sure I can."

"I could say something right now. I could talk about what you did."

"When things were different between us," Masha said, "when our marriage was in name only, I washed him in the shower and he came in my hand maybe two dozen times." Senderovsky was jealous at the extent of her honesty. How did one tell the truth with such ease? This is why they said, "Never marry a shrink."

"You don't have to live like this," she said, "all the lying and manipulating. We both know where it comes from. You were lied to since the day you were born. We'll make it work, I swear. I'll go back to private practice."

"Only if you want to," Senderovsky said, unable to acknowledge how much his wife would do for him. "Though it won't save the bungalow colony. We need a show on the air for that."

"I know how much you love this place," Masha said, "but it's only a placeholder for your memories. For a time when this was the only spot on earth where you had friends and were welcome and loved, and everyone spoke your language. Well, you have friends now, and you speak the language, and you don't have to pine for me anymore, you can have me every day and every night."

Senderovsky turned away from her and hid his face in his pillow. The father in him, the Boris, would not countenance tears. On second thought, they wouldn't come anyway, as if his ducts had been cauterized. He had never known what to do with the affections of others. When his mother would squeeze him as a child, her way of showing love, he would squeal "Mama, stop!" in delight, but his voice had long lost that register.

"*Dorogoi*," Masha said ("My dear"), "do it for yourself, if not for me and Nat. Save yourself from this endless heartache. It's okay to give up on a dream. The majority of dreams don't come true. Our whole country is learning as much."

"YOU HAVE TO fix it," Vinod was saying to Karen. They were lying, also naked, in the bedroom of her double-roomed family bungalow, a catbird screaming into their open window. They had turned off the air-conditioning and were now luxuriating in their common musk, a near century in the making.

"It hurts when you say that," Karen said. "Like everything I've done is monstrous. I gave the market what it wanted. Was it best practices all the way? Of course not. It never is. There were investors."

"Couldn't you have done something nice?" Vinod asked. "Something less coercive than Tröö Emotions?"

"They didn't want anything nice. We tried an algo for pet owners. People were already in love with their dogs. Like *in love*, in love."

"You have to fix it," Vinod repeated. "I know it hurts you to see him the way he is. And if you don't care about him, think about Dee and Ed. He'll never leave her alone. He's possessed."

"I'll never have another good idea in my life," Karen said.

"Why?"

"Because I never had a good idea to begin with."

"So why did you put everything you had into something you never believed in?"

"I don't know, *Vin*," she said loudly, turning away from him. "Not all of us are content with just being shat upon by society day in and day out."

He touched her shoulder and neck, noticed how she had folded her arms over her chest. His paucity of partners made him unsure of how fights were to be conducted between lovers. Like Senderovsky, he was ever the diplomat, but his meekness, or else his reserve ("our little *bhenchod* Brahmin," his father used to call him, even though they were of a merchant caste, even though he himself had so craved holiness), could seem affected and not helpful. *If I don't fight with her*, he thought, *I may miss a chance to make her less depressed.*

"It occurs to me," he began, "that all three of us—you, me, and Sasha—are products of our fathers' business failures."

"Honey, I have a shrink," she said. "Probably the best one in the city. You're practically all of my happiness right now, along with Nat. You don't have to do double duty here. Stick to your core competency, which is being Vinod."

"And I think you're trying to avenge your father's mistakes."

Karen moved back so that she was flush with him. "Put your arms around me," she said. He did. She had a small new pouch of a belly, which he loved atavistically, a sign that she was eating well, along with arms strengthened by swimming and hair as long as in her youth.

"He was such a loser," Karen said. "Such a handsome loser. They even had money back in Seoul, not a lot, but some, and he wasted it like he was Ed or something. He kept opening up stores where there was no need, where there was already a long-established competitor. Bayside, Douglaston, freaking Great Neck? What did he think, his smile was going to win him someone else's customers?" She sprang up, dark skin in the pale light. "Those handsome dads are the worst. They couldn't roll with it. You take the insults, you take the slurs. You make the money and you shut up. But not him. One strike against him and he'd curl up like a fucking pangolin. You know I'm more Korean than he is in some ways. He was the fucking dreamer, and then Evelyn took after him with her MFA. He didn't get it. What is business? It's daily hand-to-hand combat. Like, what does Sasha call it?"

"Stalingrad. But, honey, it can't be that all the time. We don't live in a war zone."

"We don't?"

"At some point the struggle ends. It can't be worth it."

"I can do anything in the world right now," she said. "We can travel to the moon. We can buy ourselves a senator in the South. We can live a thousand leagues under the sea. Anything is possible." She looked at him. "Now that I have you."

"And if everything is possible," he said, "then you have to help him. You have to act. It doesn't mean your product is a failure."

"My product is a failure and a half."

"You fix him and it's not."

"It'll look like a public apology."

"Imagine what that would mean, someone from your industry telling the world, 'We made a mistake. We hoped for the best, but it came out as usual.'"

Karen smiled, both dimples activated. "Listen to you talk," she said. "I've never heard you be so forceful." She kissed him, felt the furriness above his upper lip, stale moisture on his chin, an unbearable childhood cuddliness. He was thinking of it, too, the way they used to fall asleep on each other's shoulders in their childhood beds (fully clothed, of course), the TV still on. Their parents would see them and be shocked, Karen yelled at for the better part of a year. But eventually they made their peace. They had seen it on television, too. In this country, a boy and a girl well past puberty, just friends.

THE QUARANTINED ACTOR had been left huddled and yearning in the Petersburg Bungalow, Masha depositing meals in front of his door, her much-admired blueberry pancakes for breakfast, the leftovers of Ed's previous feast for lunch. He opened the window once and peeked out. "Mash," he said, "come in and talk to me. Just talk, nothing else."

She saw the pallor of his face through the stubble and the dregs of entitlement, and recoiled. A human being had been drained like some Mesopotamian marsh—and for what? "You're going to get better," she said. "Karen's going to sit down with you. Be strong, okay?"

"Won't you be my friend?" he said. "Won't you help me talk to her?" By which, she supposed, he meant Dee. She turned around and walked away briskly, her eyes on the second floor of her house, where her husband and daughter were playing a Russian card game called the Fool.

She felt it in her bones, the way the autumn would turn suddenly irrevocably cold, the way summer could be so quickly replaced by the unknowable. An American expression: "borrowed time." Followed by an image from her birthland: tanks in the streets moving in single file. She knew Senderovsky always topped off his gas tank for a run across the border, but the border was closed. Hunting season or no, the shots would continue to ring out over the distant hills, growing ever less distant. Back in her armoire-mirrored Rego Park apartment, Lara was laughing at her.

"WHAT DO I do?" the Actor asked, the words coming out mealy and indistinct. "How should I be?"

They were sitting on the living room couch in her bungalow. All the windows were open as a precaution against the virus. She showed him photographs, actual glossy printed photographs, of himself from various parts of his life, though quite a few were taken from his days in New Haven, those crisp, cosseted, promising but anxious "pre-" days, right before his big bang set in motion a whole other universe for him and his fans. "I don't understand," he said to Karen. "Shouldn't you be showing me pictures of Dee? Or maybe comparative shots with Elspeth? Other people I've fallen in love with?"

"No," she said. "Just you."

The photographs kept coming. He had no idea there were so many in the public domain. As he flipped through them, he thought of his mother. His beautiful mother, who either wouldn't let him out of her sight or couldn't stand the sight of him. They had identified the illness later on. He knew what it was, so it wasn't a big deal anymore, and he would not be defined by that. A Kodachrome of him in a bunny hat with a T-shirt bearing the name of a ski resort. A child with peanut butter on his nose (that couldn't be him, he was never so silly). Leaning out of the back seat of a car, head on his arms, moody. There was always a presence nearby, the whiff of her sickness, but so what? He willed himself to love the boy in the photos, but an ingredient was missing. Then again, if the ingredient had been there all along, would there have been the Actor?

"You're overthinking it," Karen said, although he hadn't said a word.

"I know," he said. "Overthinking is anathema to my work."

"The algorithm searches for a vulnerability in your eyes. In the creases of your cheek. In your gaze. In the tremble of your chin. The person you're looking at when the app is engaged is merely a substitution. We actually researched Method acting when we were putting the whole thing together. You're always substituting on the stage from your own experience. Finding the emotional trigger. Dee is a substitution. You're in love with an absence. When you look at the photo the absence is encoded in your own eyes. You're mistaking it for your love of her."

"I think I see it," he said. Karen noticed there was too much sweat on his forehead and not enough energy in the eyes below. His whole body was girding itself against some outcome.

"You can't just see it right away," she said. "It takes time. Live with it for a while."

"It's like the whole thing was a trap for me," he said. She recoiled from the quality of his breath. And from the fact that she was close enough to smell it. "Being good at what I do weaponized this against me," he said.

"I'm sorry," Karen said. "There are externalities to this technology."

"Which is to say you fucked up."

"Yes."

"On purpose."

Karen was silent. The Actor could no longer repress the cough that had been building since he first walked into the mauve room, seven Korean boys staring down at him from twice as many posters, and he raised his fist to his mouth. Karen moved away politely. He was also trying to repress the loose stool rumbling within him. For a second he thought he was back on a shoot in a foreign town, its tiny alleys thrumming with glazed pottery and fattened Europeans, where despite the ministrations of craft services he had eaten the wrong thing.

"I have to go," he said. "I have to get out of here."

He left the door open as he fled the bungalow, and Karen saw a doe, perfectly framed by the open portal, straining her neck to reach the tiny green fruit of an apple tree. The animal turned back to the commotion of the fleeing Actor, tensed her shoulders and haunches.

Karen regarded her with a half smile, the dream of connection, but she was already gone.

4

THEY LOOKED LIKE they were famous, all of them, even people Senderovsky had forgotten about, peripheral friends who spun off their own little groups, their own urbanized and suburbanized life streams. Whether the yellow time stamp at the southeast corner of the photograph read 1987, 1993, 2002, or any of the years in between, high school, college, the early years of his success, Senderovsky, Karen, and Vinod and the dozens if not hundreds of friends who once orbited them were brilliantly clothed, exquisitely framed by the camera lens (everyone wielding a disposable Fuji back then had been a budding fashion photographer), smiling, smirking, pointing with their lit cigarettes, sticking out their tongues, laughing at the native-born whites (who always seemed both timid and cocksure and trendily doomed), baggy jeaned, then tight jeaned, and garbed in *kawaii* panda hats from Japan, and posed in front of pay phones with a Coke can resting on top of the Bell Atlantic, and holding plates of what was then called ethnic food on their laps (food every bit as "ethnic" as they were), and being hairy and scary and cuddly and looking off in the distance peeved, and all those drunk faces and Asian flushes, and tidy rows of books surrounded by glasses with ashes in them, and showing off belly buttons and synthetic duds, setting up feuding cigarette packs on barroom tables, hugging their hairdresser on loan from Osaka, examining the tattoos of more adventurous folk, joining bands with either "Pale" or "Fire" in their names, reading *Geek Love* amid the paltry sands of Rockaway Beach, sitting legs crossed on the hood of a relation's dying Oldsmobile—and the care taken with every photo, because it would cost money to get the film developed, so that you couldn't just snap away, so that everyone did their best to come together, to form a tableau, to try to contain a world.

"I don't remember it like this at all!" Senderovsky said. "I just thought those were the puka-shell-and-Teva-sandal days. I thought we were all just trying to assimilate. But we were amazing! We looked amazing. Not just you, Karen, all of us. Jesus Christ, Vinod, you dressed in vintage Christian Dior."

Karen's assistant had sent up a half-dozen shoeboxes full of snaps, the better part of her predigital archive, and now the three of them were on the covered porch after dinner, orange candle glow bringing out the orange of the era, the orange of their polyester ski sweaters, the orange of Karen's 1999 hair. "It's so strange," Senderovsky continued loudly (he was drunk), "to think that I always wrote about us through this comical lens, but the reality on the ground was so different. We were happy children in a happy time. At least it was happy for us." (As soon as he said it, he wondered about the future that would dawn around his own daughter, what kind of early adulthood would be allowed her, if any.)

"I think there's a clear progression here," Vinod said, puffing on a joint. "After 1991, it's like all the work Karen's put into us is finally starting to pay off."

"Yeah, you didn't just come out looking so glamorous," Karen said. "Remember how much time I spent shopping with you geeks at Screaming Mimi's?"

"I remember spending a lot of money," Senderovsky said.

"And we had to buy you mussels and fries at Florent after," Vinod said, "as a 'finder's fee.'" He picked a photo, held it up for the wind to caress. His mood soured immediately.

"Is this the party Suj threw for Sasha when his first book came out?" he asked. "The one where Masha reappeared."

"And where you guys met Ed the first time," Karen said. "Remember you all thought he was such a pretentious asshole at first?"

"That was *also* the party when the deputy mayor or something was in our bathroom tooting coke," Senderovsky said. He always had to mention this (erroneous) detail as if it best captured the last truly wild moment of his past, the transition from party animal to married, respectable bourgeois.

The photograph in question showed Senderovsky standing next to a blasted, pockmarked Russian journalist at least two meters in height who was presenting him (for reasons now unremembered) with a plastic suit of armor, while the ever-hamming author—his book had just hours before received a thunderous review in the newspaper—held his arm around a thin, dolorous Indian woman in a tight T-shirt and baggy jeans, smiling with her mouth but not her eyes.

Vinod brought the photo closer. The three friends had always dated people from each other's homelands. Senderovsky spent three years with Suj, a kindly rich Sindhi girl, in the Fort Greene mansion she and Sasha had painstakingly gentrified and which her parents had bought her as an "investment." Vinod dated the difficult Korean academic. Even Karen's Leon Wiśniewski was Eastern European in family origin, if not quite Russian. And that very night Senderovsky would reconnect with the girl he'd been in love with since he was a child and, after much self-remorse and misdirection, leave the woman who threw him, as he would always acknowledge, "the best party of my life."

Vinod didn't know why the photos of this party hurt him so much, or why he was so bothered on Suj's behalf. He had not been the one ultimately rejected. The following photo was of the three friends lost amid the loud party that even the mansion's four stories could not contain. (Policemen were ultimately summoned and the inebriated non–deputy mayor had jumped out of a window.) Senderovsky was in the middle, trying to look cool, but his pinched red eyes telegraphing that this entire event, this new turn at stardom, was already way beyond his capacities; Vinod to his left, holding aloft the front page of the newspaper's book section, which featured Senderovsky posed in the most serious hand-on-chin Russian-novelist way possible (he looked like he was about to rescind serfdom with his next sentence); and to his left Karen, dimpled and glassy-eyed and possibly with a narcotic coating the bottom of one nostril, leaning into the fêted new author so sweetly, as if she had just met him for the first time and straightaway fallen in love, their bodies conjoined in one half of the photo, while in the other his and Vinod's torsos were farther apart, Senderovsky's arm swung around Vinod's neck as if he was draping it over an outsize armchair in a boutique hotel.

Vinod put the photo down. His friends were chattering away, reminiscing about Suj's best friend who had attended a liberal arts college in Ohio with her and whose nickname, perspicacious they had to admit, had been Gender, the subject she now taught at, of all places, New Haven.

Senderovsky was spinning a playlist called "Sahel Sounds" on the handsome red radio, but the Malian beats were not making Vinod feel any better. He wanted to ask himself why he was suddenly so down. He looked back and forth between his friends. Karen had been wearing a mask since her time with the Actor in their bungalow (she had also scrubbed every surface in their living room, even though this form of viral spread was no longer considered likely), and the blue gauze hid the pretty seagull of her lips.

Senderovsky, by contrast, was unmasked. And now Vinod felt a budding anger at his friend's naked face as the landowner recelebrated the greatest night of his existence, courtesy of a gullible desi girl, this just two years before he was to tell Vinod that his own novel was too "mired in history," too formal and distant and desperately unfunny.

"Formal and distant" was also how he had described Suj's behavior to them as he was seeking his friends' permission to untangle himself from the woman he had lived with and sponged off for several years and had at one point planned to marry. He had abandoned her just so that he could airlift Masha from the mountain airstrip of the distant past. Even then, Vinod remembered, he was urging med school Masha to pursue lucrative radiology instead of psychiatry.

"Look, Karen!" Vinod shouted. "Fireflies!" The meadow where he daily sat cross-legged with his reading material and contemplated unreality was now phosphorous with insects.

"You know, I have fond memories of fireflies, too," Senderovsky said. As Vinod expected, he began to speak of summers he had spent in Crimea.

Vinod snuggled up to Karen the way she had to Senderovsky in the triumphant photograph. "Give me a kiss," he said. "The fireflies are out. It's the snogging hour."

She pushed him away gently, trying not to breathe in his direction. "They'll still be here in a week," she said. To her eye, the nostalgia-invoking insects had a programmed quality. They were almost too perfectly randomized in their flashes, a hypnotic algorithm built to confuse the present with the past.

"You don't want to kiss me?" He spoke through the gravel of his accent, trying to sound romantic and *filmi*.

"I got to be careful," she said through her mask. She mentioned her deprogramming work with the Actor a few days ago. "He looked so sickly. I think he had the runs. Isn't that a symptom?"

"Okay, then don't kiss me," Vinod said.

"I got to look out for you," Karen said. She rubbed her left eye. She had been rubbing her eye for the past two days. It was as if a small insect had made a home beneath its lower eyelid and refused to be evicted.

"Why? I'm not an invalid."

"You guys," Senderovsky said. Ever since the Actor had returned, only to flee again, God knows where (he had left his Lancia behind), the atmosphere of the estate had changed. The goodwill and truces of the colonists were subject to inspection and revision. Maybe that's why they were out on the porch in the nighttime, trying to calm their passions.

When the lights were out and Karen had stilled the many devices around her, Vinod walked over to the couch in the living room where she had self-quarantined and draped his arms around her sleeping form. She snored mightily within his embrace, more than he remembered from their youthful sleepovers, but he found her sputtering mouth and kissed her. She slapped him away in her dream and, with a teenager's harrumph, turned to face the coarse hump of the couch. She rubbed her stricken eye against its fabric and moaned miserably. He bent down and took in the smell of her hair and her still-fluoride breath. His once-battered lungs filled with her and he went back to their bed slightly satiated, but lonely still.

What if there was more to Senderovsky's literary debutante party than he actually remembered? What if he was too old for his memory to cooperate with him, to understand what all those glossy photographs really meant? Surely, they weren't as simple as the camera-ready smiles posterity insisted were real. What if, over and over, he had been made a fool?

There was a piece of paper resting on her side of the bed, the excerpt of a lesson Karen had been teaching Nat, spelling out in Hangul and English the most important of Korean phrases: "My head hurts, eyes hurt, mouth hurts, legs hurt, there is too little, there is too much, I don't like it."

5

VINOD SAT IN the middle of his meadow on his Brazilian area rug
reading *A Hero of Our Time*. This particular edition of the
nineteenth-century Russian novel began with a mishmash of an in-
troduction by Senderovsky, mostly about how he wished for a literary
future without handsome heroes. Flocks of birds had taken up residence in the elms above the gentle reader and they would chatter
away for hours, but then suddenly stop as if someone had said something embarrassing.

Over the past week, Karen had developed—if that's the word—
pink eye, and now as a precaution, she lived on the couch away from
the other colonists, including her boyfriend. It drove Vinod mad. If
she was to isolate from him, then at least she should take the inner
chamber of the bungalow, and he could serve her faithfully with
food and drink and sleep on the couch himself. And, besides, as far
as the virus went, didn't pink eye affect mostly children? And besides,
she hadn't lost her sense of taste or smell like most affected people;
she could still appreciate the plates of Ed's cooking Masha dropped
off at the front door. And besides, she should stop scratching her
eye; he would keep replenishing her cold compresses if she only let
him. And besides, her assistant had already summoned for the steroid
drops with the aid of Masha's scrip.

Today the pink eye had worsened, and Karen had entered a state of
terror matched only by a sudden glue-like feeling of fatigue, as if she
couldn't separate her fingers from one another or separate her lower
and upper rows of teeth, much less reach up to poke out her eye.

(And that's what she urgently needed to do, to scoop out her very vision like what's-his-face, that motherfucking Greek king.) To hell with Vinod's "And besides." She had exposed herself to the Actor, who, dumb thoughtless idiot that he was, had brought his secret sharer into the colony. Why had she listened to Vinod and helped the Actor? Why had Senderovsky allowed him to return in the first place? Why hadn't Masha put an end to all this? Maybe she still hoarded feelings for him in the old-fashioned sequined purse she called her heart.

And, of course, the elemental part of all this: If it hadn't been for Karen's product, none of this would be happening. If only Vin would listen to her, if only he would go and live in the main house or take over the Big Island Bungalow now that Ed was cohabitating with Dee. If only she could give Nat another Korean lesson. The language needed constant reinforcement, and watching endless videos of Bomi the Spelling Octopus, who often made funny but instructive mistakes, wasn't going to do the trick. If her own mother had been stricter with her about that one damned thing, learning the mother tongue, she'd be a different, prouder person now. Maybe it would have all worked out.

Vinod heard a commotion above the meadow, one made by people, not birds. They all knew one another's voices by this point, and he could hear Dee and Ed quarreling in public, along with the panicked interjection of Senderovsky's anxious mezzo-soprano. What was happening? It was nowhere close to dinnertime. It must have been Karen then. She must have taken a turn for the worse. He should have stayed near her in the polluted front room of the bungalow, even if she shooed him away.

As he got up, his book fell out of his grasp. He reached over to pick it up, its garish onion-domed cover suspended in the grass, but came up with nothing. He reached for his area rug, but it was now too far away to reach. How could that be? It was right *there*. He lifted his arm after it, but came up with no more than a waving motion, as if the rug was driving off to carpet college and he, worried parent, was bidding it farewell.

The day felt impossibly long now as if it belonged inside an extra-terrestrial calendar. He must have been living inside a single day for weeks on end, as would a Venusian. He decided to breathe in the humid but wind-stroked summer air around him, but that very act, contract chest, pause, expand chest, now seemed to have too many steps to follow in short order.

Migraine colors flickered at the bottom of his vision. He knew what he had to do—trudge up from the meadow to their bungalow, but it now seemed like a half impossibility, as if he had to emigrate up the treacherous slope without the necessary papers. He took a few steps, then leaned into the ground before him with an outstretched palm for bracing. His calves felt hot, someone must have been strok-ing them with a warm hand, but when he turned around, his neck a painful vice, to look behind him, there was no one for companion-ship (even the sun was decked out in frilly clouds). Why must he climb this hill to the cluster of pastel bungalows, each showing him its backside? Why shouldn't he arrange a siesta upon the newly mowed velvet slope? What was the purpose of all this striving? Karen, he had to get to Karen. He continued to climb, keeping his hand out in front of him as a form of security in case he crumbled. By the time he reached the cedar steps of the covered porch, the first outpost of civilization, it took him a few seconds to figure out where he was exactly.

Once he opened the door to their bungalow, he thought he would fall into the grace of the shadow-laden air-conditioned room. But the air felt warm and sultry in all the wrong ways. His beloved was lying on the couch beneath a blanket, her golden shins and Japanese nov-elty socks sticking out below, a tiny compress on the left eye remind-ing him of the gold coins placed upon the eyes of the dead. "Karen!" he shouted. Only it wasn't a shout. It was a tiny squeal. She stirred miserably. Once again, as it had been for most of his life, they were together while being apart. But at least she was alive, still. He went into his room and fell on their bed. There was something he had to get out of the bottom of his luggage. That small stack of notarized papers along with a larger bundle of articles printed out in his Elmhurst studio during the earliest days of the virus. He needed only to find the will.

KAREN DISCOVERED THE paperwork three days later. He was lying flat on his stomach in their bedroom. She had her afflicted eye closed and was wearing gloves, a mask, and one of the plastic face shields her assistant had ordered for everyone in the colony on Masha's instructions. His suitcase was opened and looked ransacked, a torrent of black Jockey underwear and holey white socks, which she had been planning to replace when long-sock weather came around. "Vinod," she said. There was a murmur. She heard a long wheezing sound, the accordion trapped within. "Vinod!" she shouted, shaking his leg.

"Cover me," he said. His body shuddered lightly at regular intervals, mostly around his armpits and haunches, as if he were a cowering dog.

"Are you cold?" she said. "I'll get Masha to come and look at you. What is this?" She picked up the papers lying next to him.

"It's for you," he said, each word requiring a brief intermission. He now understood the term "to catch one's breath." He couldn't catch his. It kept running away from him. Now that he was marginally awake, he couldn't lie still. His muscles were flaring, his new muscles shaped by swim and sport. What a bloody waste, he could hear a Britishly affected uncle saying, despite his best efforts still unable to shake off the years of Gujarati and Bambaiyya Hindi. At the peak of the summer, with her in his arms, with Senderovsky admitting to his lie, he had bought the myth they were all selling him, of a healthy, successful, sexually active Vinod. Ha! All roads led to his shaking haunches, to the liquefied lungs.

She drew a blanket over him and tucked it over his shoulders and toes. At the top of the stack of papers, there was a printed form. VINOD S. MEHTA, she read. And then the jumble of numbers that constituted a low-rent Elmhurst address. And then capital letters: NEW YORK STATE DEPARTMENT OF HEALTH. Medical Orders of Life Sustaining Treatment (MOLST).

"Oh, fuck you," she said. "Fuck you, you fucking idiot." Inside the cocoon she had made for him, he kept drawing breath, his mouth opening for what looked like a dramatic inhale, but then coming up shortchanged, the hand of a child beggar in his original hometown pushed away from the windowsill of an ambassador at a stoplight. "I'm getting Masha now," she said, but he did not hear her.

HE WAS WALKING up the stairs, grasping the familiar curving teak balustrade. Right away he knew where he was and *when* he was, the massive rollicking front parlor and chef's kitchen crammed with hungry revelers below, heavy furniture all around but the immigrant's absence of national tchotchkes, the long bare walls miracle enough. He could hear Suj and Gender's liberal arts friends talking about food co-ops and continuous sexual discovery. He could hear his and Senderovsky's city-college friends, first-year law students at local midtier institutions, the three brothers that formed a Filipino indie band and then all went into advertising, a small herd of aspiring social workers and grade-school teachers, honking away in their outer-borough accents. "Vinod!" one of them said in passing, a blurry face, tendrils of dark hair, a gold chain from the unreconstructed parts of Queens, same intact accent as his own. "Where you going, *yaar*?"

"Help me," Vinod said. "The more steps I take up, the more . . ." The more steps were added in front of him, as if he was trying to climb up a downward-bound escalator.

"Let me get Suj," Gold Chain said. "Why don't you take a break in the meanwhile?"

"No!" Vinod said. "I have to keep climbing."

He kept climbing, the stairs multiplying before him. Others kept coming down the stairs, boisterous, shouting, seemingly happy people, their faces blurred in the hubbub, but he was the only one going up. Why couldn't he just turn around and go down with them to the raucous party below?

There was a hand on his elbow. It was Suj. She had the same grievous shadows beneath her eyes as he did, the shadows Karen tried to temper with her creams. "Let's sit down," she said to Vinod. He had forgotten her cut-glass accent. She had gone to Goldsmiths for a spell.

"I have to get upstairs," he said. "Could you do something about the staircase maybe? It's your house."

"Why?" she said. "What's upstairs?" She held his hand. Her fingers were long and thin. Her skin proved burning to the touch, like sandpaper left out on the desert floor, and he withdrew.

"Water," he said, weakly.

"What's upstairs, Vinod?" she repeated.

"Let's go up together and find out," he said. "We can form a team."

"Like an investigative team?" she said. "You're such a silly Billy." Her fine pink lips were cracked around the edges. "A silly billy goat. Don't look up." He did anyway. The ceiling was gone. Fast-moving city clouds passed without disturbance headed inland, hoping to make rain. He started shaking and she pressed him into her embrace. She smelled of alcohol and hummus. "Vinod," she said. "You should have gone to a better college. Why didn't you leave them behind?"

"Because I knew I'd catch up eventually," he said.

She was whispering into his ear now, warm alcoholic breath, soothing but strong. "You'll never catch up to those people," she said, the accent thicker now, motherly. "Not ever ever ever."

He was walking through the Meatpacking District, toward their apartment on Washington Street, a simmering five-story tenement. He was carrying something impossibly heavy and hot in his arms. He set it down. Examined it. Slats. Buttons. FRIEDRICH. "Sasha!" he shouted upstairs. "*Bhai!* I bought an air conditioner. Help me carry it up."

Sasha leaned out from their fifth-floor window, frizzy hair down to his shoulders, tortoiseshell glasses, pissy twenty-year-old look. "What do we need it for?" he shouted. "It's September."

"That's when you get the good deals. Help me! I'm dying here."

"I'm watching a Mets game."

"Since when?"

"I discovered sports yesterday. They're amazing. Oh, shit! You made me miss the touchdown. Stand there. I'll throw down the garbage from the fridge."

"No, I got to walk this up. Why won't you help me?"

"Take the elevator!"

"We don't have an elevator."

"Of course, we have an elevator. What's wrong with you?"

He dragged the air conditioner by the cord into the grimy vestibule. He felt like he was about to start having loose motions. He looked around the extinguished faux marble of the lobby. Fake gold chains, fake leather, fake marble. What a life he led. Everything was quiet except for the labored sound of his own breathing. He put his hand up to his mouth; there was no tube snaking out. The stairwell was to the left, but it was cordoned off with a sign that read STAIRS OUT, USE ELEVATOR.

And there was an elevator where none should have been, a thrumming little white box that made no sense in a five-floor walk-up of this vintage. He dragged the air conditioner inside by the cord and hit the floor with his elbow. "Hold the door!" a voice shouted. "Please, sir." Vinod stuck out his hand to keep the elevator from closing. The door sighed as it drew back to reveal a large winded man in a Mets T-shirt. He got in and looked at Vinod with kindly eyes, "Uncle" eyes, Vinod thought for some reason. He took up most of the elevator, but Vinod felt safe with him around. He did not want to be in the elevator alone, that prototypical city coffin. "What floor?" he asked.

The man smiled, his eyes on Vinod. "What floor, sir?" Vinod asked again. He liked that they were using "sir" with each other. Formality in an informal land. An old-fashioned civility. The man did not answer, but began to approach him, slowly, slowly, slowly, a tiny half step at a time like a shy goat, until Vinod could smell the dense complicated sweetness of his reek. "I have to get upstairs now," Vinod said. "I bought an air conditioner on sale." But soon he felt the man's stomach and breasts, each loose and inviting like pillows, leaning into him, pushing him against the wall, ever gently, but always insistently, as if he was trying to make an argument with his body. "Why?" Vinod asked. He heard the fullness of his accent. *Vai.* "Why are you doing that?" But the man kept pressing into him as the meager air pushed out of Vinod's lungs, and he kept staring at him and smiling the sad autumnal smile of his, his lips within kissing distance of Vinod's. He kept pressing into him, without desire but with his whole being, as if administering a vertical massage, and as much as Vinod tried to squirm out of the all-enveloping flattening mass, he could not. And as much as he wanted to protest, he could not. That was the most frightening thing of all: he could not speak. And he could not bring his hand up to his mouth to check for the tube. He realized, at the very last minute, that the elevator was moving downward, past the basement and into the core of the earth.

FOUR HANDS WERE directing him toward the bathroom. He was wearing a mask, but neither his lungi nor his Jockey underwear. He looked up. Karen and Masha had on their masks and face shields and in the dull red glow of the incandescent lightbulbs they resembled Martians. He shivered in fear, forgetting to be ashamed before Masha even as it swung like a metronome between his legs. "Did I have an accident?" he whispered.

"No, you're okay, honey," Karen said.

"Did you read the material I left?" he wheezed. "The MOLST and the articles? It's notarized."

"You shouldn't be talking," Masha said. "Concentrate on your breath."

"That party," Vinod said. "What happened at that party for Sasha? In Fort Greene?"

"I've arranged everything," Karen said. "We're going to get you well."

"No!" he tried to shout.

"Shhh." They lowered him onto the toilet.

"No, no, no, no, no." Every sound his body made was foreign, in need of translation.

ON THE COVERED porch, Masha and Senderovsky sat on one side of the dining table, Karen and her bandaged eye on the other, prosecutors facing the defendant. But, more accurately, Masha was the prosecutor, and Senderovsky should have been in the dock with Karen. Only her illness kept them on opposite sides of the table, although Karen claimed that with the steroid eye drops she was now on the mend, the rest of her symptoms abating. If only the same could be said of their friend.

Senderovsky, in his face mask, was but a pair of wet roving eyes, skirting the cedar of his porch, the couch where so many intimate candlelit postdinners had taken place with his best friends (just last week, just last week!), and the accursed community of fireflies beyond. Now both his wife and Karen wore face shields like two members of a welders' convention.

Eventually his gaze settled on the dark and empty Lullaby Cottage and he remembered the first conversation they had had upon his friend's arrival. Vinod had asked for his Teva-boxed novel, and Sasha had told him that he sounded valedictory. He wanted to shout to both women, "He came here to die!"

"Some friends," Masha was saying. "Some caretakers. You took every step imaginable toward getting him sick. You claim you three are the family you've never had, but you two are exactly like the families you come from."

Karen was unused to being attacked like this. She had an assistant to her assistant who was on the lookout for hurt in her online mentions. She had had her lifetime of being talked down to and called names and watching fingers of all colors pull ugly approximations of her beautiful eyes. But now she was being accused of—what? Murdering the man she loved? Murdering her best friend?

"Vinod told me I had to fix him!" Karen shouted, referring to the Actor. "He said it was my duty. I had to do it for Ed and Dee, too.

That's what he said, Masha, I swear to God. I had opened all the windows. We were mostly sitting apart on the couch."

"So after a lifetime of not listening to Vinod, of being the older sister, you chose this moment to honor his wishes. And you"—she turned to her husband—"allowed him back in. You really thought he would make a show with you? A show about an oligarch's son with a bad circumcision? Who on earth would watch that?"

"So we're the only ones to blame?" Karen said. "You could have stopped Sasha from letting him back in. It's your property, too."

This went on for a while, until snot bubbles began forming beneath Karen's face shield. Senderovsky could not understand his wife's anger at them. What had happened had happened. There was no pleading with memory for a do-over. They were living in exceptional times. It was Genesis in reverse, the species fading out one by one, the sky closing up above. And now someone had to pay. And now the goat would be sacrificed so that others could be cleansed. And now Vinod would pass from corporeal presence to the sad embellished memory of a historical time, to the ripple of a Fuji flash in Karen's photographic archive.

But Senderovsky would be fine with such a fate for himself. He did not explicitly want to die, but was ready to die. He was ready for the owner of the black pickup, that white-armed red-capped brute, to ascend the cedar stairs, to point the massive weapon at him and him alone, and to let loose the full vigor of his armament into the softness of his chest. Let his story culminate on this stupid fancy porch, to the Sahel Sounds on the red radio, to the cries of the mysterious yellow-shouldered bird. He killed his best friend, the newspaper's obituary might say in lieu of a rundown of his own run-down career. Sasha Senderovsky: a liar, a Teva-box thief, owner and proprietor of the Dacha of Doom.

Right before sitting down with his wife and friend, Sasha had seen the first rumors of the Actor's reappearance in and disappearance from his estate float through his social channels (had the state trooper squealed?), where he was personally tagged and all but accused of kidnapping and worse. He had parked his car sideways at the end of his driveway in a protective measure (as if the Actor's fans couldn't just drive around the gravel and proceed over the inviting grass) and had instructed the handyman to construct an ad hoc fence.

Face-shield Karen was now sifting through Vinod's documents with her white-gloved hands beneath the porch's yellow lights. "I'm having my lawyer look through all of this," she was saying. "But my guess is Vinod can do what he wants. Unless we declare him mentally incompetent or something." She looked at Masha.

"You're seriously asking me to do that?" Masha said. "Get your own damn psychiatrist."

"Okay, what about this," Karen said. "We allow the DNR to stand, but we convince him to rescind the do not intubate part."

"That's what he's afraid of," Senderovsky said. "The intubation." As a childhood asthmatic he could understand Vinod's fear of the ventilator. The idea of waking up and finding a tube in your throat, extending downward through your core, through the passages reserved for breath and food and drink and sound (as in "help me!"), of being at the mercy of a heaving machine, of the restraints around your hands—this medieval horror show conducted under the guise of an antiseptic hospital.

"He came here to die," Senderovsky finally said. "He told me as much when he came here. He figured his chances out. That's why he always had those papers with him."

"That was then," Masha said. "But his life his changed. He's in love now. He should be able to fight for—" Now she was falling into cliché. The idea of *fighting* an illness or *fighting* for love was just American militarism run amok. You could do a few things to better your chances against something like this virus, but if you were to die, you were to die. Maybe that was the gist of Vinod's stack of papers.

"I think he knows that after the early stages of love with me it's all going to go downhill," Karen said.

"That's just your depression talking," Masha said.

Karen shuffled through the papers again and read randomly from the portions Vinod had highlighted. " 'A forty-eight-year life span seems short, but only a century ago . . . If you look at the peer-reviewed extract labeled . . . Over eighty percent of intubated patients . . . For many of those who did survive, long-term effects included paranoia, "brain fog," . . . A living death.' "

"Those statistics are changing now," Masha said. "There are effective new treatments coming online, especially for people with compromised immune systems."

"Can you administer them as a doctor?" Karen said.

"I'm not a pulmonologist."

"Lots of doctors without relevant experience were pressed into service."

"Under the direction of those who know what they're doing. In a hospital setting. Someone should be taking oxygen levels constantly. There needs to be IV access. A pulse ox. A monitor. Steroids, if it comes to that."

"So," Karen said, "you think he should be in a hospital?"

"Jesus Christ, yes!" Masha shouted. "Seriously, what the fuck is wrong with you people?" Senderovsky coughed into his hand. "And you"—spoken to Karen—"shouldn't be around other people, even outdoors. I have a little child. Have you forgotten her? Aren't you worried for her?"

"He goes into a hospital, we'll never see him again," Senderovsky said.

"You don't know that," Masha said.

"What's the last thing he wrote," Senderovsky said to Karen. "Read it."

"We've all read it already," Masha said. "Stop being melodramatic."

Karen examined the Levin-Senderovskys with sadness. In the end, she thought, they'll make up, and they'll go to bed together, and they'll have each other. And I'll go back to how things were before I came down that driveway. Back to the loft on White Street and the morning and evening whir of solar blinds ascending and descending and the alabaster mirror in the foyer in which I can practice saying hello and goodbye.

" 'You're both people who relish control,' " Karen read from Vinod's final entreaty to her and Senderovsky, " 'so why take that very same control away from me? Why not give me a final dignity? I just don't want to die alone in the end. I just want to be with my friends.'"

"Well, we all die alone," Masha said. "It's tragic. The greatest tragedy of our lives, other than being born in the first place. By the way, how often did either of you see Vinod before all this happened? How often did you check in with him? Other than offering him money you knew he would never take. To make yourself feel better."

"What do you know?" Karen said to Masha. "You'll never experience anything like our friendship."

"And you'll never be a real mother," Masha said.

"Neither will you," Karen said.

Senderovsky reached over to comfort his wife. The unhappy voices echoed off his magnificent porch, the conversation never ending, like that of his parents, who could battle into the morning off a thimble of vodka and a few cups of tea. He was still thinking of his friend's death and his own. They were all supposed to be getting used to this, to the new science of it all, but this wanton destruction still did not make sense to him. He was a decent man, a convivial host, and a self-ordained ordoliberal. Four months ago, under the cover of spring, he had welcomed five guests of exceptional quality to his colony.

How did it get to this? How?

6

"GETTING MARRIED IS memorable time." A Russian-accented voice. "Extra memorable with Senderovsky Superior Wedding Album System." Vinod walked toward the voice in the dim haze of the airless warehouse, his Teva sandals slapping at the gray, dusty floors. "But first let me tell you about good screw! It is special re-inforced stainless-steel screw which postbinding allows the pages of your wedding album to lie flat. Hello? Meesees Fernandes? Hello?"

Mr. Senderovsky looked at the receiver in incomprehension, its twentieth-century dial tone issuing from it in one long flat line. Vinod realized that something was terribly wrong. He hadn't done his job properly. He brought his hand up to his mouth to check for the tube. "Fucking sheet," Mr. Senderovsky said, brushing back the last strand of hair over the olive pit of his head. "Sasha tell me this was good lead. Mother of college classmate remarrying oilman. Fernandes is not Spanish, but Filipino."

"I didn't do my job," Vinod said, voice shaking. "I didn't fix the label maker."

"Aw, fuck," Mr. Senderovsky said. "Aw, sheet. But what are you going to do? Slow summer anyway. No one get married. Too hot. Difficult economic climate because Clinton. Things fall apart, but what about center? Center does not hold. Kaput. Whole wedding album industry—" He made a fluttering motion with his hands to indicate its state. "But people like us, we are used to misfortune, *nu*, Vinod? What did we say when Indian engineers came to Leningrad: *Hindi, Russi, bhai, bhai*. Brother, brother. And so even in America we are all now *bhai*s. *Bhai*s in misfortune!"

"Mr. Senderovsky, can I make some cold calls? I've been working on my accent like you said."

"No, no, you are strong. You lift boxes."

"Let me try one call."

"No, no, your accent is too sick."

"Too thick?"

"Yes, what I say?"

"I thought you said—" They heard the doorbell and looked at each other.

"I did not make appointment," Mr. Senderovsky said, tugging at the pager chained to his Dockers. "Maybe idiot Sasha, marijuana user, forgot his key. Wait, did you make appointment?"

"How could I make it? You won't let me near the phone."

"So it is surprise customer!" Mr. Senderovsky scurried off toward the distant front door. "Hot sheet! *Village Voice* ad maybe worked."

Vinod looked at the old cream-colored public-school-teacher's desk from which his employer conducted his desperate business, and alongside it the little TV tray with a phone and folding chair where Sasha sat by his side for most of the summer like a minimum-wage lapdog, absorbing his father's politics and unhappiness. These small, cramped immigrant spaces were Vinod's favorites, whether his uncle's curried explosion of a "diner," where the native born and the just-washed-ashore could have spicy eggs for three dollars at a cramped counter bar; or his father's ever-failing computer store, where both of his brothers worked on their way up to Wall Street sales desks but where there was no space for Vinod, the Brahmin *bhenchod;* to this, the most outrageous of gambits, a wedding album business featuring Mr. Senderovsky's patented "special screw" technology, barely chugging away on the cusp of the Internet.

"Vinod," the Russian accent returned, "your girlfriend is here."

Girlfriend? Mr. Senderovsky was fond of jokes about Vinod's virginity. An entire summer at the office—sophomore year of college, was it?—had been spent arguing about whether oral sex constituted his entrance into manhood. Could he mean—?

Karen walked in wearing the same close-fitting bateau shirt she had worn at their first dacha dinner, only matched now with cutoffs that brought out the muscle of her thighs, the gloss of her knees.

She came up to Vinod. He could feel her closeness and the marimba of feelings that would chime within whenever she did so. He reached over to touch her semi-nude shoulder, like a bird softly tagging a nest mate with her wing. But something else happened now.

She took up both of his cheeks with burning hands and kissed him on the mouth, kissed him with all of her bottled-up youth and her still-innocent soul, and he felt her knee against his groin. Vinod couldn't stop kissing her, but he realized he was an employee of the mercurial Mr. Senderovsky and he had failed to fix the label maker. He pushed her away (had he really just done that?) and turned to his boss, who was shamelessly examining Karen's chest. "*Uka-uka,*" Mr. Senderovsky said to Karen. "We had official North Korean delegation visit institute in Leningrad once. Oh, such women in kimono come."

"*Hanbok,*" Karen corrected him.

"Sure, but I never try. Is probably tasty."

"Mr. Senderovsky, it's almost four-thirty," Karen said. "Is it okay if Vin knocks off for the day?"

Mr. Senderovsky sighed to indicate he was in favor of young love. "Go, go," he said. "I make reduction in pay."

"Tell Sasha we'll be at Florent," Karen said.

"Gay restaurant? Only if they don't convert you to their Greek ways." He laughed, gold-capped teeth at the edges of his Soviet mouth.

They were walking out on the cobblestone streets of the Meatpacking District, sloshing through the pools of blood and tallow that made the neighborhood what it once was, a glorious slice of Americana trapped between a doomed highway and a storied townhouse district. But now the blood coated his sandals and her Converse differently, because now they were *holding hands*. Vinod remembered how Ed's Japanese reality show revolved almost entirely on the moment two housemates reached over and clasped fingers over knuckles. If only her touch wasn't warm to the point of burning; if only the humid city air would let him breathe as he surveyed the signs around him:

FULLY COOKED CORNED BOTTOM ROUNDS
RABBITS 1.89 LB.
WHOLE LAMBS 99c LB.

"Listen," Karen said. "I lied about going to Florent. We'll meet Sasha there later. Let's go to your place and fuck."

Vinod could not say anything. His throat was dry and his feet covered in the splooge of other animals. His other life, his parallel life, had been good, no matter what anybody said. Forty-eight years in, he had seen Berlin and Bologna and Bombay and, at the last minute, his beloved with her pants off. But this life was almost too much. Just the thought of this tough stern woman in the flower of youth grinding into him on one of the twin Murphy beds that constituted over 70 percent of his and Senderovsky's apartment (there was also room for a hot pot, a torchère, a nine-inch television/VCR combo, and the mini-fridge in which they stored their garbage). They were approaching their ugly building. He was jangling his Mehta Computers Authorized Apple Dealers (they had not, in fact, been authorized) key chain. Vinod leaned over and whispered into her honey ear, "Karen. Listen. I had a thought. A couple of thoughts."

"You always do, babe. You could use a little mouthwash when we get upstairs."

"What if I had gone to New Haven? What if I had left you guys? Gotten my PhD? Published? Did a lot of national radio like Sasha? Developed a persona, funny or serious or somewhere in between."

"Shh," she said. "Don't talk about these things. You'll just tire your poor lungs out."

"I'm so excited, I can't breathe."

"I want you pretty badly, too," she said. But her eyes were sad and her dimples unfathomable.

"Suj said I could never catch up with you."

"Suj? Is that your slutty cousin from Connecticut?"

"Just another voice in my head."

"What do I always say?"

"I think too much. Born at the wrong time. I'll never catch up, will I?"

"You're about to put your hands on my breasts and we'll fuck so slow you'll forget how to talk."

"Oh my God," he said. Although did Karen ever really say things like that? Even to her tall H-1B visa Irishmen? The stuff about the mouthwash was spot-on, though. He fumbled with the outer door of the tenement, then made his way into the fake-marble lobby. The new elevator was waiting for him. He walked inside the stifling enclosure, horny and dazed. He turned around. She wasn't there. The elevator's lightbulb flickered and the temperature around him turned beige, dour, colonial. "Hold the door!" someone was shouting; it wasn't her. He knew who it was. What if he didn't hold the door? No, that would be impolite. He always had to hold the door; otherwise he wouldn't be Vinod Mehta. The large man in the Mets T-shirt slid in with his fawn-like brown eyes and his sensual mouth. It was pointless to retreat, but Vinod did so anyway. His assailant's sickly sweetness filled the elevator. It sighed and moved off its mooring. Once again, he had forgotten to check for the tube.

HE WAS CRAWLING up the stairs again, and with each step conquered, another would present itself. The noise from the party downstairs had stopped. There were no partygoers running down the stairs either. All he knew were the stairs in front of him and the task they entailed. There was a presence next to his own, and he could feel the thump of its palms against the stairs.

It was Masha. The Masha of 2001. The angular and bright-eyed pre-Senderovsky girl, a bob of auburn hair against a dark, near-Sephardic cast. She looked like the costar of a movie the Actor desperately wanted to be in, a movie the lesser blogs would term "difficult but illuminating."

"Vinod," she said, "I'm speaking in Russian."

It was true. While Vinod had never learned either of his best friends' languages, there was a Slavic mumble, unhappy at its core, issuing from beautiful young Masha's mouth. "I understand you!" Vinod said. "I've always understood you."

"Shh, not so loud," she continued, the sibilants spilling out of her.

"Everyone's telling me to shh," Vinod said. "But no one's helping me."

"How can we help you?"

"You're the doctor. What's your opinion?"

"I'm in my second year at med school."

"But you must have *some* opinion."

"Come with me to New Haven. Get your doctorate. Don't hang around with these clowns." The last word sounded like in English: *klow-ny.*

"But she loves me now. I made it."

"Wait until you get to the top of the stairs."

"What's at the top of the stairs?"

"Uka-uka."

"That's not a real word. You sound like Sasha's dad."

"Ouch." Pronounced: *aff-chhh.*

"Go down to the kitchen, Masha. He's waiting for you there. He's going to play it so cool, but the moment he sees you he'll have it all planned out. He always does. A man with a plan. A canal. Senderovsky. He'll leave her like the past three years never happened. He'll forget all the crying he did in her arms when his book was rejected nine times over."

"I've always felt bad about doing that to Suj," young Masha said. "My original sin."

"Wasn't your fault."

A deep sigh. Now her gray eyes looked faded, like the thrice-bought jeans they were reselling in her homeland at the time.

"A joke on top of a joke on top of a joke," she said.

"Your life?" he guessed.

"That's what I signed up for. At least there was money for a while. He was very seductive, at first. With me, with his audience. It didn't even seem like he was trying. You'd think, Wow, this guy knows what he's doing."

"When are the stairs going to run out, Masha? I just want to go upstairs. I just want to fall on a bed and plop down on the cold sheets."

"I know, honey," Masha said. She stopped crawling now. Her eyes filled with tears. "I wish you could," she said.

He stopped crawling and put an arm around her. "O, Mashen'ka," he said. *"Kak mne zhal' tebya."*

"Don't," she said, "Don't feel sorry for me." She pointed upward. Beneath her T-shirt, he spotted an untamed tuft of armpit hair. She was on her own wavelength back then, as free as any immigrant of their vintage could be. He followed her still-upturned finger with its implications of a biblical Renaissance painting, da Vinci's *St. John the Baptist* with his abundant smile.

"One more thing, honey." She gave him a folded piece of cloth with both of her hands. "It's not safe out there," she said. "You and Karen should wear a mask." She slipped the mask over his mouth and kissed him on the brow.

The stairs ran out, he had reached the top, and now he found himself beneath a pair of monstrously large feet clad in noncombat boots. Masha was gone. The party had resumed. People were running down the stairs again, screaming their pretty heads off. Standing above him was the pockmarked Russian journalist who was about to present Senderovsky with a plastic suit of armor as some kind of joke. The beetle-browed man looked down at Vinod in his face covering. "What eez zis?" he said. "Masked avenger?"

"Where do I go now?" Vinod asked.

The Russian pointed in the direction of Suj and Senderovsky's bedroom and spoke out of his third eye, his lips immobile.

"Hot sheet," he said. "Now *zis* you gotta see."

7

"So," she said. "Let's have the talk." They were lying in each other's arms, Dee still in her blue gauze mask, a single candle flickering against the walls, alternating between romantic and scary.

"Let me guess. You want me to have a career so that when you introduce me at parties you can say, 'My husband Edward works for an NGO.'"

"No, bobo," she said, taking off her mask, but letting it hang from one ear. "I'm never getting married. But don't you think it's time for us to leave? I mean the place is a shambles. It was fun when we all got together for dinner at the same table, but now that we're all quarantined? And why do you still have to cook for everyone like you're our chef or something?" She recalled the Actor calling Ed their master chef. "And it's definitely safer in the city. I mean three people have been infected already. Vinod's still contagious."

Ed slotted his head into the crook of her neck. He sighed. "I feel like we owe them something. Maybe not 'we.' *I* owe Vinod."

"On the Japanese show, as soon as two people couple up, they leave the house."

Ed picked up the snifter on his bedside table, one of his last bits of foppery, and took a drag of the eighteen year he had bought the other day to celebrate their three-week anniversary. He gave her a sip, too, eyeing the pale condensation she left on the glass.

"I hung out with Karen earlier," Dee said. "She gave us permission to leave. She said there wasn't much more we could do for him."

A pair of beams could be seen approaching through the window that faced the front lawn. They slowly grew in color, a dull white, then a tawny yellow, then a soupy orange, like the flash of a hydrogen bomb several Pacific atolls away. The sound of disturbed gravel that usually accompanied such high beams was missing; the intruder had bypassed the handyman's plywood fence and was now headed straight through the sea of grass. Dee jumped out of bed and moved the hams of her small pale posterior next to Ed's by the window. They stood there, naked, watching.

NAT'S HEARING WAS sensitive and she was a poor sleeper besides, a true Levin-Senderovsky. The strange whispery combination of truck tires floating over grass woke her up immediately and she scrambled to the window. Around the bungalow colony, motion sensors were throwing on the lights as the black pickup truck approached, a shadow among shadows.

The past two weeks had been difficult for Nat. It felt like Mommy was out to get her ever since Uncle Vin had gotten sick. Just the other day she had said to Nat: "You can knock it off right now with that tone, *or else!*" Mommy never said American things like that.

Nat had a recurring dream, which was perhaps too neatly explained by her own biography. She was born into a void, no parents were present at her birth, just a woman wearing a surgical mask beneath which was sheathed a long scary snout like a fox's, and then solitary Nat spent the entirety of her life (short as it was) journeying to find Mommy. On every continent, she would meet kids in their native garb who would make fun of her and tell her she was a weirdo for not having a mother or any true friends and that she should just go to her Quiet Mat and stay there. The dream always had a happy ending: Mommy was found, order restored, and a plate of glowing blini with marmalade served on their dining room table back in the city. But the next day the inexplicable would continue to fuel her nightmares, like when she overheard Mommy saying the other day to Karen-*emo:* "What if there's a putsch? What if the military takes over? What if we have to leave the country?" And Aunt Karen had said, "I have people who can get us out to Korea on a minute's notice. Don't worry. We'll be okay." Nat figured out the spelling of "putsch" and found out that it meant "a violent attempt to overthrow the government." So in addition to Uncle Vinod being sick and everyone eating Uncle Ed's dinners alone in their bungalows or on the porch with their heads in their hands, there was the possibility of *violent* and *overthrow*.

And now a dark truck was headed for the bungalows, running roughshod over the blue-green lawn, and Nat flung her window open and shouted, "Watch out, Steve! Steve! They're headed right for your winter palace!"

All of the colonists minus Vinod were outside now, their clothes hastily thrown on. Ed, armed with a heavy flashlight, had a vigilante air about him as did Senderovsky in his dressing gown, his fists tightened by atavistic memories of pogroms past.

THE ACTOR HAD moved into the international children's summer camp down the road, a camp he and Dee had once explored for weeks, finding new and inappropriate places for their lovemaking. This was the test. He had to live among the "happiest" memories of his life and then find a way to substitute for them. He had to take his sacred ground with Dee and trade it out for himself and his art. He had to embrace the absence that would always be at the center of his life, for he had already been claimed. Not by Dee, not by Elspeth, not by some lousy commercial algorithm. There was a stage here, by the side of the road, the stage they had used for their first tussle. Its wood was warped and it was covered in condoms and half-mauled Nerf footballs, but that made it even more important. It was not a stage, but a summons.

In the deepest of night he would forage. He would crawl up to the House on the Hill with his duffel bag, figuring out ways to avoid the automated lights by Dee and Ed's bungalows. In the kitchen, by the light of his torch, he would fill the bag with Ed's pork chops and sardines, his charcuterie and cornichons, until it was swimming in grease. The colonists were always coming in to help themselves to leftovers. A somnolent Masha once had to be avoided as she stood in the pantry eating the challah bread he was about to steal amid the

Saturday dusk. He curled up beneath the long country sink, listening to her mumble in her language.

Back at the camp, he would eat the cold excellent food with his fingers, then sleep contentedly through most of the hot late-summer days. He reclaimed all their lovemaking spaces. The overgrown tree house by the main road, the Japanese-style bell tower that would once ring in the meals for the international youth, the tennis court with its sad droopy net and burning tar, the spiderweb-coated Jack and Jill bathrooms that still stunk of humanity after all these years of disuse, the floor of the Music Cabin with its decals explaining how the tango was to be danced by aspiring Argentinians. He had stolen a pillow and a complicated-looking Soviet comforter from Masha's closet (the latter might well have been used in spaceflight) and turned them into an ad hoc sleeping bag, finding a new place to close his lids every night, a place to rebuild the world with an absence of her, an absence of everyone he no longer needed. Now he could go back to who he was. A summoned, serious man.

On the stage, in the dark of night, after some middle-aged local couple sliding up in a Korean sport utility vehicle had abused the stage with their pornographic sounds, leaving behind prophylactic evidence of their crime, after the commando-style foraging in Senderovsky's kitchen, but before the meal he served himself as a reward, he would go through his roles, from the high-school stage manager of *Our Town* to college Iago, to the all-too-redeemable skinhead of *München am Hudson* and the misunderstood Karen-grade evil genius of *Terabyte*, his last flop. He strode the stage, his voice booming, the coyotes up the hill duly reproached, until he found himself whispering instead of projecting, shuffling along instead of claiming the stage as possession. Everywhere he turned, the new absence greeted him, and when he looked down at his body, or caught his face in the mirrors of the Jack and Jill bathrooms, he saw the way his appearance had substituted for the work and therefore for the truth.

Was he good from the start, or was his rise a fluke? He needed imagination to take on the work he did, but had he overly relied on charisma and magnetism? And was it the magnetism that had won out in the end? He reprised his role in *Morning Glories,* when he had been just eighteen years old, dancing half naked in that stupid hat, clowning around. There was no imagination involved, just a need to captivate. He was no more than an expensive avatar. He was a way out. Senderovsky's daughter was maybe seven or eight. But all she cared about was that Korean boy band, because that's what it would take for her to escape her mother's reactionism. He didn't want to be an escape for others. He wanted to be supple. To move through this world like a nobody, like a woman in regional sales gliding through airport lounges in the previrus era, always moving, always herself. That's what acting was. You did not need to capture an audience, you needed to be captured yourself.

THE BLACK TRUCK appeared a week into his exile. It moored itself like a boat on the opposite side of the road, next to an Egyptian-style obelisk that listed some of the countries the former campers called home. The driver killed the engine, and the Actor silenced his *Hamlet* mid-Yorick while regarding the silent intruder. After he finished, after Hamlet was no more, the truck flashed its beams once, twice, then turned around and departed for the state road.

The truck came every night, always in the middle of a performance, always when he had discovered something true about the role he was playing. At first, the Actor resented this interruption, but then he learned to regard it as naturally as he did the soft palaver of grass in the nightly wind. Because this was an act of communication, there had to be an audience. And his audience was the owner of a sad ugly truck, a desperate soul who headed out each night in search of him. He—something about his vehicle spoke of a stunted masculinity— parked so far away that even with the windows rolled down he could not hear the Actor perform. He must have seen the Actor as no more than a small figure on a crumbling stage. And then he flashed his beams twice when the performance was over, not applause, merely an acknowledgment. Once, twice. Thank you, good night.

The Actor had started out with the moon waxing, providing enough natural light for him not to fall off the stage, but when the moon waned, the driver put on his lights, beamed them not directly at the Actor but across the broken tarmac of the country road. And the Actor was silently grateful. He thought he could see the occupant in the truck's cab now. Sometimes he appeared young and pock-marked, a high-school kid at best, and at other times bald and pinch faced and official, the local excavator or part-time town councilman. He was all of these things to the Actor, a projection, a substitution, and when the time came for the Actor to leave the summer camp, when Dee had been expunged and he reconstituted, he walked toward the high beams with his hands up in a formal surrender.

He mounted the cab and took a look at the body next to his. Just a body like his own, a florid respirating thing with its temporary leasehold on life. There were features to be sure, ginger muttonchops surrounded his simple cloth mask, what could have been a keloid scar peeked out long beneath one collar, but it was difficult to assign an age to the truck owner—forties? fifties?—who possessed a kind of indeterminate Danish blondness beneath a red cap that did not sig-nify politics, merely a stump-grinding service up by the state border. They did not say a word to each other. The driver pointed to his mask. "Oh, I think I've had it already," the Actor said. The driver remained silent and stared ahead, until the Actor slipped on his pais-ley mask, a gift from Dee. The engine started, firm, powerful, dutiful, an American valediction. They drove to the House on the Hill in si-lence, slid effortlessly across the grass of the front lawn. The Actor did not make eye contact as he climbed out of the cab. That would be offensive given their silence. But the driver turned on the dome light and finally spoke into the air before him, his voice a product of cigarettes, his body cradled around the wheel, pinched by rheuma-tism. "I didn't tape you that night with your friend," he said. "There's a guy across the river who does that."

"I'm glad it wasn't you," the Actor said.

The driver looked ahead with the low beams of his sleepless eyes. He spoke slowly, as if practicing a foreign language in front of the mirror, accents sometimes falling on the wrong word. "The early stuff, that's what I like the most," he said. "When you still wanted it. When you were young. The joy on your face back then. It was a blessing. You had been blessed. The universe celebrated the way you came together, your talent, your hunger, your smile. The way you let us know you were in pain. Honesty and grace. You can try to find something better beyond that, but you won't. When something extraordinary happens, you don't let go. Not for another person, not for the world. But that's what people do. They forget. They let go."

The Actor nodded. He saw the lights coming on in the main house and the bungalows. Before he slammed his door shut, he bowed shortly, stiffly, like they did on the Japanese reality show. Once, twice. Thank you, good night.

THE COLONISTS WERE witnessing two separate events. First, the re-arrival of the Actor after another long absence. He stood before them at the head of the drive, his beard floodlit to religious proportions, the bag from the California vineyard Ed despised static by his feet.

The other event consisted of the black pickup truck thundering through the grass to reconnect with the road beyond, its high beams already writing the next chapter of its odyssey. Nat's terrific eyesight could make out the single word SUPERDUTY stenciled across its rear.

"Put your mask over your nose!" Masha shouted to the Actor. "Don't come close!"

The Actor adjusted his mask, his eyes still skirting gravel. He looked out onto the audience and found Dee, who was dressed in a tiny satin blue slip Ed had bought her because it matched the color of her mask. Backlit by the halogen outdoor lights, her hair haloed, her body slight and trembling, she should have been unbearable for the Actor to see. But he merely smiled, the cover of near darkness preventing the colonists from enjoying his laugh lines, the handsome erosion of his face. "Dee, I feel nothing!" he shouted. "Dee, I've been working on myself."

Nat leaned out of her window to better hear the Actor's apologies. She wished to run down and throw herself into his arms.

"Who was in the black truck?" Senderovsky shouted. "Is that who's been watching us?"

"He's a good person," the Actor shouted back. "He helped me. He means no harm."

"How can we trust anything you say?" Ed shouted.

They all stood there, frozen, at an impasse. The Actor wanted to draw nearer. These were his friends, after all. They had spent most of quarantine together. "I came to make amends," he shouted. "To each of you." He did a head count. "Where's Vinod?"

The silence continued, the stillness, followed by the crunch of sneakers against gravel. Karen was running just as her trainer back west had taught her, crisp, elegant propulsions, her hands at her side, until she made a hook of the right one, which she would connect, full square, with the Actor's jaw.

He had been at the receiving end of mock punches behind the camera, and at first joyfully perceived it as such, a prank, an acting-out between pals, between equals, really, given Karen's lofty successes in the world. But suddenly his head was positioned at an unruly angle to his neck and to the rest of him, and his feet performed a quick tap dance up and down the driveway until they stopped, the known universe tilted, and his head joined his feet on the ground.

As he was recalibrating his consciousness, he heard the little girl running toward him, crying, and just feet away, her mother grabbing her, spinning her around, her shout deafening and rising above the confused susurrations of the small but rapt audience: "Natasha! NO!"

And he thought: I am still loved.

SEVERAL DAYS AFTER the Actor's second (and final) reappearance and his resequestration inside the Petersburg Bungalow, Karen was feeding Vinod gossip and dinner. Ed claimed he could not make a proper dal or anything Gujarati or southern Indian, but he did spice up a consistently brilliant vegetable biryani to Vinod's standards (he made it with both yogurt and milk in the Lucknow manner), and now his taste buds craved it for every meal, since he had, luckily, never fully lost his sense of taste or smell. What wouldn't he give for parathas and pickles, though. To Karen, his appetite signified he was "turning a corner," though he coughed with regularity and exhibited a smudged blue pallor like the electoral thumbprint used to prevent double voting in a poor country. He also had loose motions after every other meal and presented to her loving gaze a set of tired, drowned-looking eyes. Once, after he tried to wipe the toilet seat down after he had made a mess of it, he had fallen and banged his spine hard against the bathroom wall and had sat there stunned for most of the day. Since then, Masha and Karen kept him in bed, budding appetite notwithstanding, and Karen accompanied him on his bathroom runs.

"Dee told me she and Ed are having some really kinky sex," Karen gossiped. "Like cosplay or something. She wears a gauze mask while they're doing it."

"Oh."

"You and me will get back to it, too. Soon as you're well."

He smiled. "No masks," he said. "I want to see your darling face." She noticed the redness of his gums, and now his eyes looked too small for their sockets. It was hard to look at him and not try to embrace him these days. Harder still to imagine him as an adult moving through life under his own steam again. The boy she had chastised and mothered (or at least sistered) three decades ago had returned to her as such. Instead of applying eye cream, she now pasted his poor cracked lips with Vaseline. But he wasn't beaten down entirely; his gaze was still lightly male. Once she had come out of the bathroom naked and had sat down on the bed to slip on her underwear, and she noticed him looking at her body, examining the way it settled and creased. The folds above her hips, everyday, workaday, meant for a biological purpose she had never entertained, provided him with the pretext of trying to draw the next impossible breath. She got up, looking away shyly (for that was her secret, he now realized, that despite all her previous entanglements she was impossibly shy), put her hands at her sides, and drew her lips apart for him.

"SWEETIE," HE WHEEZED on another day. "I have these awful dreams. You wouldn't believe what happens. One after the other. I need something to take my mind off things. I can't concentrate on a book." What he left unsaid was that it was hard to read about people who were still in the bloom of life. "When I can't go back to sleep, I need something stupid."

"I got you, babe," Karen said.

That spring and summer it became impossible to glance out the window without entertaining questions of physics, of multiverses collapsing onto themselves, of time lines breaking off like Antarctic ice shelves. Was all this really happening: masks and tyrants, aerosol sprays and gun-toting clowns? Senderovsky and his family and guests had moated themselves into their biosphere for four safe months, until they were breached by the Actor's return, but others had developed different ways of coping. One such way was a return to the 1980s.

Karen found compilations of commercials from that era on her computer, and now the phlegmy cough emerging from the bungalow's inner bedroom was counterpointed by chirpy instrumentals, barking dogs demanding better pet food, and the blandishments of bubble gum and cars "made with pride" right here in the USA. Vinod had long found sleeping on his back or sides impossible, the accursed stickiness, the mucus, coursed through his chest and windpipe, but now he could doze off while sitting upright as the commercials prodded him into semi-oblivion instead of the pure slow annihilation of that elevator on Washington Street.

> Raise your hand, you know it, raise your hand, you got it, raise
>   your haaaaaand if you're Sure.
> Raise your hand, you feel dry now, raise your hand, you know
>   why now, raise your haaaaaand, if you're Sure.
> Confident, confident, dry and secure, raise your hand, raise
>   your hand
> If you're Sure.

He had sung these lyrics with Senderovsky during their high-school days ("confident, confident, dry and secure!"), as both of the immigrant boys had been accused by their elementary-school classmates of not smelling the way an American should. (Karen would always laugh at their particular Indo-Soviet predicament.) The commercial still mesmerized. Cowboys, policewomen, naval cadets, future supporters of the current president, all were raising their hands, showing off their deodorized armpits with confidence, all of them were "Sure" their scent was not just ambient but *gone,* devoid of all odor like a piece of plastic or else, at worst, tinged with a hint of processed sugar like a Quaker Oats chewy granola bar wrapper from the same period. And in the final shot, the Statue of Liberty herself was brandishing her barely clothed armpit for both the newcomer and the native-born to smell, for despite being born a Frenchwoman, she was an American now, dry and secure, confident beyond all reason.

"I think Jim's the most handsome guy in the world."
"Her smile just warms me inside."
"Her teeth, they're really beautiful."
"I love a bright, beautiful smile."
"I like fluoride. I like white teeth and freshness is a plus."
"Close-Up makes me feel all fresh especially if I'm going to be kissing Jim."
"Close-Up helps me get close to Lisa."

Lisa and Jim and their joint beautiful hair and their joint beautiful teeth were kissing now. They were kissing with all the concentration with which his mother chopped yam for winter *undhiyu* or with which his father tried to sell an Apple Lisa computer to an unsuspecting American. ("Not to rush you, sir, but I'm actually closing in ten minutes.") As they kiss, Vinod can sense his parents watching this commercial over his shoulder, scandalized, both of them thinking, *Are these two even married,* baka? And young Vinod thinks: Why does Jim need Close-Up to help him get close to Lisa? If he were Jim, he would be kissing Lisa's mouth even if her tongue was on fire (much like his has been for the past two weeks).

"It's not my fault, Mom. Sneakers just smell."
"Her mamma loves her. How does she know? 'Cause her Skippy tells her so." And now he feels it at the back of his throat, those tears

stoking the humidity that chokes him, tears for the missing American mama all three of them had never known, maybe a mama *no one* had ever known. He had been so affected by these commercials as a boy, staring at them openmouthed, heartsick, even while his brothers kept wrestling on the shag carpeting in front of their pleather frigate, calling each other "*chutiya* motherfucker" like the hybrid Queens children they were.

"Bain de Soleil for the San Tropez tan."

"President Reagan has decided to join hands across America this Sunday."

"Call 1-800-453-4000 to see if you qualify for food stamps. Mealtimes don't have to be tough times."

"Are you keeping up with the Commodore? 'Cause the Commodore is keeping up with you."

"Tonight at eleven, a big win for the homosexual community."

"My name is Tio Sancho, and I have made a taco shell that won't fall apart."

Tio Sancho was clearly not Indian, but, skin-wise, he was about as close to an Indian as it got on television. Now Vinod remembered trying to find his own face on his parents' RCA, some sense that he had a counterpart who ate Quaker Oats chewy granola, and whose mother made him disgusting dry Skippy sandwiches and kept a hawk-like eye over his single pair of Adidas and their gamy odor. Occasionally, Black people were allowed onto commercials, especially if it was for fast food or on a show with a large Black audience. And every once in a while, he would spot *her*. She was the lone East Asian girl, properly staid and sweet, always at the end of a medley of rambunctious white children, who feasted with uncommon grace on whatever junk was on offer. Maybe they let her drip some processed cheese out of the corner of her mouth, more out of being young than being mischievous.

Even then, even before he had met Karen, Vinod had kept an eye on those appearances, on those girls who were different, nonwhite, but unlike himself nonhated by the ad makers. And every time he saw a face like that he wondered what it would be like to be friends with that girl who surely had a dad who also hawked Texas Instruments computers and a mom who cooked food that would not go well with Hellmann's (okay, Korean potato salad with Kewpie mayonnaise excluded) and was too pungent to be brought to school in a *thali* or *dosirak* or even a *Fat Albert and the Cosby Kids* lunchbox. But now he wondered if the Asian girl at the end of the commercials was not there to sell the Hostess spurting pastry or whatnot, but rather to sell America. Like the Statue of Liberty showing off her armpit at the end of the Sure commercial, the girl spoke more to a Cold War ideal of America—look who we let in! Hardworking Asians! Whereas a Vinod-type presence in one of his white V-neck sweaters (all three brothers wore them on special occasions, cute as lambs) might have confused the audience. Why isn't that Brown guy selling us a taco shell that won't break?

As he thought about the Asian girl, Vinod succumbed to a great grave sorrow. He did not want to relive the past, nor to memorialize it, but with each wheezing breath he was drawing closer to the end, and the end meant never allowing himself to understand it. And that was the gift Senderovsky had given himself, the gift of sitting around on his ass figuring himself out. Didn't the Brahmin *bhenchod* deserve something similar?

But now he was back to self-pity, which was the one thing he wanted to avoid other than the *thwoosh-click, thwooosh-click* of the ventilator. Again, he whispered in his mind: I've seen Berlin and Bologna and Bombay, wondrous many-scented Bombay, and my beloved with her pants off.

Oh, mythical Karen of the CBS commercial break, with your Hostess mostess grin and your black silken bangs and your bridgeless button nose and your Technicolor dimples and Dolby laugh and your mother in the background, far behind the camera, watching her child star wearily as she thumbed through a copy of *Golf Digest*, must get home by six, *yobo* will be expecting dinner.

He opened his mouth but couldn't call out her name. She was the girl on the screen, cheese at the corners of her mouth, and all he could do was move his lips and hope she could hear him across time.

8

V INOD WAS SITTING on the covered porch, an oxygen cannula in his nose. Karen was next to him on the all-weather sofa, holding his hand or fiddling with the oxygen tank. A "stage" had been delineated by means of orange traffic cones on the natural terrace below, and to one side chairs were set up at a healthy distance from one another, filled with students from the local progressive college and some of the Actor's team from Los Angeles who had flown in on the fractal plane. Senderovsky's agent had an electronic cigarette dangling from her mouth and looked refreshed by the months of isolation in her Bel Air aerie. A camera crew was filming the proceedings and speakers were set up behind the audience so that the actors could be heard through their lavalier microphones.

The green lawn was littered with mousy rental cars and local hatchbacks, as well as one black pickup truck parked far by the road, its occupant leaning back in his seat with a pair of binoculars, his breathing hushed, his soul observant, ready to fall in love with the art.

Vinod took in the momentous scene in snippets, his eyes and brain and digestive system all failing to reach agreement on the import of the occasion. "You might have to take me to the bathroom," he whispered to Karen.

The Actor emerged to applause. He appeared restored to the magnificent ambivalence in which Vinod had first found him in the spring, pre–Tröö Emotions. He was dressed in long pants and a blousy shirt that brought to mind a Russian peasant on the steppes. "Tonight's presentation of Chekhov's *Uncle Vanya* is dedicated to Vinod Mehta," the Actor said, "who sits above us at his place of honor. Vinod, can you hear us okay?"

Karen leaned into him. "Can you hear okay? Is this okay? I know it's a surprise."

Vinod sighed into her ear and Karen shouted, "We're good!"

"I have lived with Vinod and his memorable friends for most of the quarantine period," the Actor said. "As some of you on social media may know, I've even fallen in love with one of them." There was laughter from the audience. "That . . . did not work out so great. But I'm okay now. We're good, as Karen just said. Oh, I should mention that Vinod is one of the finest people I've ever met. Decades ago, without asking for the rewards of authorship, he wrote an incredible novel about growing up as an Indian immigrant in America. I'm sure it'll be appearing soon at an independent bookstore near you."

"It's not about an Indian immigrant in America," Vinod whispered.

"With the exception of myself, tonight's presentation of Vinod's favorite play will be performed by amateur actors, my housemates, some local townspeople, and college students. The role of Alexander Serebrakoff, a retired professor, will be played by Ed Kim. The role of Helena, his twenty-seven-year-old wife, will be played by Dee Cameron . . ."

"This can't be happening," Vinod whispered as Karen adjusted the cannula in his nose. "Am I intubated? Am I dead?"

"They've been rehearsing for two weeks," she said. "It was his idea. He's so sorry he got you sick. If you feel tired, we can go home. They're making a movie out of it. Sasha says it'll help with the sale of your novel. You have to sign a release."

"The role of Ilya 'Waffles' Telegin, an impoverished landowner, will be played by Sasha Senderovsky. The role of Marina, an old nurse, will be played by Masha Levin-Senderovsky. Since we don't have a dedicated set, the stage directions will be read by Natasha Levin-Senderovsky. Finally, the role of Ivan Voitsky, better known as Uncle Vanya, will be played by myself. I have also directed this play. Now before we begin, let me quickly read out the names of the recent victims of police violence."

After he had read a dozen names separated by dramatic pauses,

Nat walked onto the stage in a sack-like kaftan Masha had sewed for her. Like all the actors, she did not face the cameras, but looked directly at Uncle Vinod. He smiled, absentmindedly, but with feeling, at the little child reading from the page the very words he had read in his meadow on his area rug not so long ago: "A country house on a terrace. In front of it a garden. In an avenue of trees, under an old poplar, stands a table set for tea, with a Samovar . . . It is three o'clock in the afternoon of a cloudy day."

The clouds would not cooperate with the stage directions. The sun blasted them with a merciless *razgar leta*. Despite their professionally applied makeup, the actors would soon sweat through their blowsy Cossack duds.

A stooped Masha walked on the stage in a gray wig. She sat down on a chair and began knitting an imaginary sweater. She began to speak in what sounded to Vinod like a fake Russian accent. Why would she do that if she spoke the actual language with near perfection? Vinod closed his eyes, and by the time they were open the Actor had materialized onstage in the form of Uncle Vanya; he had disheveled his hair and made a frump out of his shirt. This was supposed to be in line with the turmoil in Vanya's soul, but now Vinod felt bad for the Actor. He would always look too good for the parts he really wanted (no wonder he had played the actual cherry orchard in the Berlin version of the play), and the reviewers would punish him for his beauty. How desperately he wanted to transform into a huffing, clumsy thing like the car he drove, and how strikingly the visuals of his face played against him.

And now Senderovsky himself appeared in the role of Telegin, or Waffles, the impoverished landowner, his face covered with the pockmarks that gave him his name.

TELEGIN (Senderovsky)
My wife ran away with a love on the day of our wedding,
because my exterior was so unprepossessing.

It was the line Senderovsky was born to deliver, and yet it sounded rankly overdone, comedic, incapable of conveying the tragedy of

Waffles as interposed through the nontragedy of the modern failed landowner with his devoted wife and curious child and still-lingering reputation. The one thing that gave credence to his character was Senderovsky's persistent, unsilenced cough, the ill anxious child taking over the adult's nurtured body.

The play was fine. The Actor had worn the director's cap with aplomb and had coaxed a decent performance out of everyone. But Vinod grew drowsy and tried to tether his waning attention to the conversations between lovers and those who hoped for love. He was particularly drawn to Ed as the self-absorbed professor Serebrakoff and Dee as Helena, his young wife. Ed spoke with the formality he had bred in himself since birth, and she slipped, without caricature, into her innermost drawl. It was as if they were speaking two differing, warring, tongues.

HELENA (Dee)
You speak as if we were to blame for you being old.

SEREBRAKOFF (Ed)
I am more hateful to you than anyone.

(later)

HELENA
Wait, have patience; I shall be old myself in four or five years.

Vinod took note of the way Dee harnessed her inner smirk, the daily displeasure with herself. Later, the Actor threw himself at Dee, only to be rebuffed again and again (here the audience bestirred itself at the sight of the two famous social media lovers).

UNCLE VANYA (the Actor)
My past does not count because I frittered it away on trifles, and the present has so terribly miscarried! What shall I do with my life and my love? What is to become of them? This

wonderful feeling of mine will be wasted and lost as a ray of sunlight is lost that falls into a dark chasm, and my life will go with it.

HELENA (Dee)
I am as it were benumbed when you speak to me of your love, and I don't know how to answer you. Forgive me I have nothing to say to you. Good-night!

Vinod wished that Chekhov had given Dee more lines here, because her refusal of the Actor required so much more of her. But the Actor's pain was clear to see. As Zurich's *Neue Zürcher Zeitung* noted on the day the play was first streamed (please forgive the poor computer translation): "We see him broken into two; technology made of him her lover and then he worked hard on himself to make the love go away. But now once more he has subjected himself to the pangs of both love and rejection, and he must do so as a professional. It is not pleasant but edifying to watch this exquisite performer struggle and squirm. He is like the passenger of the last car to be backed up in the Gubrist Tunnel, his eyes dream of the light to come, but every moment he is standing still, unresolved."

And now despite his best efforts, Vinod drifted away, even as the camera set up on the porch recorded him, his eyelids drawing nearer one to the other, his head slumping toward Karen's mane, as she maneuvered his binoculars in front of him. But he did not lose consciousness entirely. An old fly basking in the sun set itself on his thigh. It didn't fly, it didn't buzz, it sat there contentedly, being alive in the presence of the universe. Vinod didn't want to get too Jain about it, but he refused to swat it, though it moved so slowly he surely could have robbed it of life. He enjoyed the old perhaps blind fly even as the second act concluded and the third had begun. He heard a generous warble and turned his head, slowly, painfully, to the side to witness a bird feathered with a soft white underbelly regard him with a shopkeeper's mien. A baby blue jay in flight bumped lightly against one of the screens, a slight loss of innocence. No play could compete with the sight of a long gray squirrel sitting on a high branch delivering an anxious monologue to no one in particular. The world was so full of pleasures it was impossible to think of the programmers in the interstellar Bangalore as anything but aesthetes. He wanted to get up, to walk over to the stage and hug the actors, thank them for the performance, and urge them to go to their lovers and their children, as applicable, and leave him be to the buzz of flies and the scrutiny of the avian world.

"Do you not want to look out of your binoculars, honey?" Karen asked.

"Just give me a second," he said. "I'm enjoying this." But he wasn't talking about the play. He coughed wetly for a minute or two, his body convulsing in the summer heat, but when he looked down the old gray fly remained on his trouser leg. It hung on to him with all of its sticky pads, even though it must have registered each cough as a major earthquake. How impoverished the world would be, he found himself thinking, if it contained no flies.

AFTERWARD, THE ACTOR visited Vinod on the porch, Masha and a camera crew wearing face shields and garbage bags in tow. He stood on one knee before Vinod as if proposing. He was about to deliver a speech, but the violence he had done to the elderly-looking man, who now appeared sunken chested and wheezing before him, the oxygen tank by his side and the cannula in his nose, struck him afresh in the familiar environment of the covered porch, the bourgeoisie pleasure dome of their elaborate meals. Drained by his performance (which he judged to have been deficient), he began the lines he had rehearsed: "Vinod, for what I've done to you—" But as soon as he hit the "you" part, the ridiculousness of his position hit him, and he barely had time to motion to the camera crew to turn off their feed, before he started to cry. This was not the weeping anyone had seen on the screen or in the West End, but a sputtering keening, broken into ugly half wails, that brought to mind religious women at a grave site upon the sudden, almost accidental realization that they would never be reunited with their loved one no matter what the holy books said, that now would begin their enhanced aloneness. The Actor had escaped from the clutches of Tröö Emotions, only to fall into this rank humanity. Finally, he had found what he was looking for.

The man in front of him was motionless, inured to his grief. He was looking down at his trouser leg. What was he staring at? Maybe he had suffered a stroke. "Is it true," the Actor said to Vinod, "that you were the one that had told Karen to fix me? That you were the one who made her do it?"

"Oh, shut up," Karen said. "Don't pass the blame."

"You shouldn't have come back," Vinod said. He continued to stare at the fly on his leg, wondering if it had died in the interim. He brought his hand to it, and nudged its surprisingly soft shape. The wings lifted. Vinod smiled. "You told me once you wanted to play haughty Serebrakoff," he said to the Actor. "But instead you played Vanya."

"I lost my sense of self-entitlement," the Actor said. "I felt I was ready for the challenge. I learned it by watching you. By understanding your humility. How was I?"

"You are Serebrakoff," Vinod said. "You are not ruined or helpless. You are good at what you do."

"But what do I do?"

"Maybe it's best that you don't find out," Vinod said.

The Actor looked up at him. Looked back to make sure the cameras were not filming. He got up, forgetting to wipe the nonexistent dust off his knee. "You should go," Karen said to him. "Leave here for good. Summer's almost over. Resort's closing down." And now the Actor wanted to slug her back, to deliver a backhand if not a left hook. Because it had all started with her, hadn't it? One tiny snap of a phone's camera lens. Instead he walked off the porch, the camera and microphone once again borne aloft and pointed in his direction.

On the cedar steps, he ran into Dee and Ed, still in their Russian garb, their arms linked. "Joel," Dee said to him. "Do you want to come down to the city?"

He looked at her, mystified, as if she had never spoken his given name aloud before. "Yeah," he said. "Sure. That would be great. My car broke down."

"You can catch a ride with us," Ed said. "We have space for you and maybe one piece of luggage."

"Okay," he said. He looked at the two lovers, examining them afresh, wondering, without malice, if they would survive as a couple in the difficult years to come, in the city, in their masks. "If you'll have me," he said.

"COULD YOU LEAVE, too?" Vinod said to Karen. "I want to speak to Masha."

Masha sat on the white rocking chair, adult sized but bought specifically to entertain Nat, its wild motions meant to make up for her lack of horsing-around siblings or friends. "How are you feeling?" Masha asked. "Was that too strenuous?"

"It was fine," Vinod said. "But it won't end well."

"I'm sorry I can't hear you," Masha said, adjusting her face shield and mask. She had taken off her gray wig, but still wore her kaftan, and her posture was bent as if she could not slough off her role as the old nurse.

"It won't end well for me," he said, louder now. Down on the front lawn, Senderovsky had taken on the role of traffic warden and was maneuvering a line of Subarus off the grass and onto the gravel driveway. The black pickup was long gone. "You have to stand up to them when the time comes," he said.

"What do you mean?" she said.

"Sasha and Karen."

"I can't stand up to them," she said. "When have I ever been able to stand up to them? And you have your MOLST."

"Karen will find a way. And Sasha will back her." He took a deep breath. "There was a man, they amputated both legs, his right arm, the finger of his left—"

"That won't happen to you. The odds of that—"

"He died anyway. Two months on the ventilator."

"Karen wants to fly in the best specialists."

"They'll have me in the hospital in no time."

"There are days when you show signs of improvement."

"It's not going anywhere. It's lingering." He took a deep breath, his intake meager. "My oxygen levels can plummet any second. My heart rhythms can go nuts."

"All good reasons to get the best care."

"Mashen'ka. Listen to me. You were in a dream of mine. You helped me up the stairs."

"You're getting overexcited. You need to go home and rest. This whole thing was ridiculous. I can't believe I was forced to act."

"You were good."

"I was not."

"Fine. But you're not an actor. You're Mashen'ka. You have to help me. You have to promise. Say it. 'I'll fight them.'"

"Vinod." His helplessness made her feel eleven again. Landing at the madhouse of an airport, her country's proud *bant* in her hair, the sleek luggage carts, the advertisements for products that could not have possibly existed, the lack of caps with socialist insignia above the mustaches of the immigration officers. She was so small again. As small as him. Vinod, the once adjunct professor and short-order cook. When you circled too close to the country's outcasts, they killed you. Just by association. This is what her old Soviet patients, the Laras, understood intrinsically: this country was a killing field. By associating with the killers, they hoped they would be spared. "I'll do my best," she said, wondering how she could keep that sentiment from just being words, "official phrases," as they called them in Russian. Also, it was what the housemates said to each other on the Japanese reality show. *I'll do my best.* As a worker, as a boyfriend, as an influencer. And then they failed anyway.

She and Karen walked him down the cedar steps and toward the bungalow, and he felt their warmth echoed in the warmth of the night. He thought of Uncle Vanya's words, "This wonderful feeling of mine will be wasted and lost as a ray of sunlight is lost that falls into a dark chasm," and thought: No, not for me. For me, it is not yet lost.

9

THE SPOTLIGHT FELL on Dee, the moderator, in her spaghetti-strap dress and high-cut bangs. Her smile was just a shrug with teeth but he would take it anyway. "I am pleased to welcome you to the Other Voices/Other Shores reading series," Dee said. "Tonight we have two of our nation's leading immigrant voices, Sasha Senderovsky, author of *Terrace House: The Dacha of Doom,* and the new-comer Vinod Mehta, with his debut, *Love Is Letting Go of Fear.* We'll start with a reading by Mr. Mehta."

The spotlight now fell on Vinod. He brought his hand up to his face to shield himself from the light. "Please," he said. "Can someone turn that down?" The light refused to dissipate. Vinod rose up, his body audibly creaking, some of the audience laughing. "I," he said. "I haven't prepared anything, I regret to say. I'm unprepared." There was more laughter from the quarter-full auditorium, the vicious city kind.

The spotlight suddenly shifted from him to Senderovsky, who gladly sprang up with a sheaf of papers. "Thank you, Vinod," Senderovsky said, pulling on his authorial turtleneck. "If no one minds, I will read from *Terrace House* extensively."

And as the Russian writer did so, as he entered the performative space from which he declaimed all his work (overblown accents, overdramatic comic pauses), Vinod sighed both in pain and relief. The spotlight had gone from him. He felt safe in its absence. And yet, there was also this fact: The spotlight had gone from him. *He felt its absence.*

"I'm sorry to stop you," Dee said to Senderovsky, "but we wanted to leave room for a conversation between the two of you."

"Oh," Senderovsky said. "May I at least finish reading act one? I'm not sure how much Vinod has to say." He sat down, dejected.

"Now, Vinod, you wrote this book in your late twenties," Dee said. "Why did it take you so long to get it published?"

"I can answer that!" Senderovsky interjected. "In Soviet times, some writers did not publish their books, rather they wrote *into their desks*, as we say in Russian. That is Vinod as well. He wrote into his desk."

"So he's a dissident?" Dee asked.

"Yes!" Senderovsky said. "He is a dissident from America's literary-entertainment complex. He is a dissident from the turbo capitalism that turns words into dollars."

"Can we maybe hear from Vinod himself?"

"Fine, fine," Senderovsky said. "He's a grown *bhenchod* now. He's even done *uka-uka* with our mutual friend." He visored his eyes with his hand against the spotlight and scanned the audience. "Is she here tonight?"

"Vinod," Dee said, "will you say something?"

The spotlight fell on him again. He saw his brothers in the front row, the two *crorepati*s in their finance vests, hairy knuckles, pointlessly elaborate wristwatches, the bright hum of their intelligent eyes that said all life was commerce and all commerce life. A stray thought embedded in his mind: Given the lay of the world, will they make it from London and San Francisco to my funeral?

May 21, 2017.

October 3, 2018.

The day his father and mother died, respectively.

And only four days after his mother died, Karen's had as well. An orphan and a near orphan, the two of them mostly on their own now. But would Senderovsky, for all his familial books and protestations, ever be anything other than his parents' son?

"Vinod," Dee prompted him with the Aryan blaze of her eyes.

Vinod turned to Senderovsky: "I saw your life and I didn't want that."

"Not want that?" Senderovsky said. "What was there not to want? I went from strength to strength for twenty years. I was unstoppable.

We're boys from Queens. We're supposed to just sit back and let the world decide for us?"

"Just the same, I did not want it."

"And look at you now," Senderovsky said.

"*Love Is Letting Go of Fear* is about your parents' courtship in India," Dee said to Vinod, "but it asks the same question Senderovsky's books ask of his parents. How did they turn out the way they did? How much was history and how much was them?"

Vinod now saw what was lying on the glass table in front of him, next to the pitcher of water and the vase of fake flowers. He opened the Teva box. Inside, he saw the manuscript. *Hotel Solitaire* by Vinod Mehta. He picked up the first handful of pages and got up, then walked over to the podium. "Wait a second, wait a second," Senderovsky said. "We're supposed to be in a conversation right now. He can't just start reading from his shoebox! Wait a second."

But Vinod began to read, and with each solemn word, with each descriptor of time and place, he felt his parents absence alongside him, the television set blaring in front of him with 1980s color, the pleather sticking to his shins, but the kitchen behind him empty of their tired voices, their anxiety humming like a cut nerve. It wasn't about history in the end, his novel, it was about them clinging to each other as the tidal wave of time rushed in and then slowly let out. It was about the elegant seething of the wave against the sand as it retreated back to where it came from.

"I'm sorry," Karen said to him from the chair Dee had just been occupying. She was dressed down in a sweatshirt that read MEDITATE and looked like she had just popped in off the street on the way to the laundromat. "I'm sorry to interrupt you, honey. But our time is up." She turned to the audience. "Won't you please give these two old friends a round of applause?"

The lights came on with a snap of an ugly circuit; they rose in heat and intensity until they crowded out everything before them, until everything was coated in 1980s nuclear movie light (*The Day After, Threads, Testament*). The light continued to envelop Vinod, and now he could hear something like rotor blades turning, churning, his papers flying off the table and into the audience. What was he to do?

What were his instructions? From first grade on, he had always had instructions. He couldn't just stand there and be enveloped in light. That's not why his parents brought him to this country, to be bathed in lumens. But then the audience and the stage and the light itself disappeared and Vinod was—

LYING IN BED next to her. The bed was soaked with their sweat and Karen was sponging a pearly burst of semen off her thigh with one of the threadbare towels Senderovsky's mother bought for him off a Ukrainian idling in a van. "Goddamn," Karen said. "You really should get an air conditioner."

He knew the reply to that. "Soon as they're on sale in September."

"I never know which one of you is cheaper: you or Sasha. Speaking of, I think he's waiting outside for us to finish. Like a dog."

Vinod cupped her breast, examined it in the gray city light of the 1990s. Yellow pollution, harbor skies, and, in his hand, those thin bright blue veins descending to the purple terminus of her softening nipple with its severe dimple-like indentation. "Wait," he breathed. "Just a little more time together."

"We don't want a pissy Russian on our hands. And it's not every day Florent sets up dinner on the pier for us."

"What? What's happening?" She was snapping on the neon T-shirt she got at the Stereolab concert, drawing her legs into one of his boxers and then a velvety miniskirt. Vinod got up. Out the window, the railway trestles of what would one day become a tourist park were rotting away like a distinctly American version of the Roman ruins, and the stench of blood and tallow from the meat-packers teased his nostrils. An Anglepoise lamp sat like a mantis on the desk he shared with Senderovsky, next to stacks of papers that were the respective manuscripts of their first (and in Vinod's case, last) books. The rectangular bulk of a Macintosh Colour Classic Pro originally intended for the Australasia market hummed industrially, its floppy-disk drive warbling dementedly to itself. Vinod remembered his father and Senderovsky's mother arguing over its price deep into the night—"Gujarati or Jew, who will win?" Vinod had whispered to his friend as they nervously drank beers in the back room, each hoping their parent would end on a gracious note, would give up the last fifty dollars that had formed a bloody wedge between them. Finally, at three in the morning, Mr. Mehta had reared up like a python and shouted at the Russian woman, "It's because of your son that Vinod is staying in the city! Such universities he was accepted to. And he throws it all away for a city college."

And Senderovsky's mother merely said, "*Tphoo*. Stop already being hysterical. It's not my son. He's in love with the Oriental girl."

Karen opened the front door—the only door—to reveal a pup-like, puka-shelled Senderovsky in wait for them. "How long does it take to orgasm?" he complained. "The whole building could hear you."

"Don't forget to take the garbage down from the fridge," Karen said.

Sasha sighed and opened up the fridge, where a Hefty bag full of Chinese takeout was crammed onto the single shelf, the outlines of cardboard boxes and metal handles perfectly visible from within its petroleum sheath.

They stepped into the asphalt heat and set off for the pier, passing the rows of Hasidic station wagons, their occupants being pleasured by transgender goddesses. "This is what real work is like," Vinod remembered Senderovsky once declaring from a window table at Florent, "blowing someone who thinks you shouldn't exist."

Vinod noticed that he and Karen now walked out in front, sweaty hand in sweaty hand, with Senderovsky following them, as if he was their child or their charge. Every few steps, Vinod would look back to see his friend, kicking his feet out in front of him in that strange way of walking he had, as if his feet were merely a projection, as if he wanted to kick them off like a pair of shoes. Vinod felt guilty about the loveless Senderovsky in this new formation, about the fact that in this version Karen wanted him and not some white boys in mesh shirts flirting with her after hours at the Cooler on Fourteenth. The fact that he and Senderovsky were both single for so long had been their tightest bond. He wondered how their friendship would survive in this universe.

They crossed the gritty unregulated highway with its overlarge American cars to get to the pier, which, downwind of a garbage plant, smelled like the city's glorious ass. Transgender kids, though they were called something else back then, congregated in shy self-conscious packs around the pier, and there were stray female college students reading *Geek Love*. "Look," Karen said. He saw now what awaited them at the pier's edge—a linen-covered table, before which stood three beautiful Florent waiters, dressed in pleated pants and skinny ties for the occasion. "Oh, my," Vinod said. "How did you make this happen?"

"You made it happen," Senderovsky said, glumly. "It was always you." A golden trail of cigarette butts and last night's condoms, some ringed with lipstick, marked the path to the table and the waiters. As soon as they were seated, the sun fell out of the sky to be replaced by instant night, the air around them sultry and dense with effluvia beyond identification, memories of beloved Bombay. The checkerboard of the partly lit twin towers glittered in the early dark like entry-level magic on a Texas Instruments computer.

The waiters were usually sassy and verbose, much like Florent Morellet himself, that debonair cross-dressing lunatic with his Bastille Day parades. One waiter—Miguel, was it?—always flirted with Vinod, gave him unasked-for but nervously appreciated back rubs, called him Short Circuit 2 affectionately (different times). But tonight the waiters were subdued and meek, like Eastern European proletariat. They lifted the silver lids off the assembled dishes in unison to reveal their usual fare: "Alex's mussels Provençale" with fries, "Evelyne's goat cheese salad," rillettes. Carafes of slightly chilled Beaujolais magically appeared. The kids at the mouth of the pier, playing "Groove Is in the Heart" off a cassette deck, eyed them like movie stars, blinding them with the flashes of their cameras. Karen and Senderovsky started eating maniacally, the fries quickly lost in the pools of aioli, the mussels being snapped back with oily fingers and sucked out with glee. When they would treat themselves to these meals, they would always think: *Goat cheese! Aioli! Shellfish! Rillettes! How fucking sophisticated are we? How far have we come from Queens?* But now all Vinod could think of was the smell of her sex on his fingers.

"Guys," Vinod said, "can we make a toast? Guys?"

But they paid him no attention, they slobbered up their mussels, coated slices of fresh hot baguette with crumbly goat cheese and silky rillettes, they drank down the carafes of out-of-season Beaujolais like water and demanded more from the waiters straightaway.

A garbage truck from the nearby depot headed farther downtown along the highway and, as it did so, the entire pier shook. Vinod felt a mussel stuck in his throat, only he hadn't eaten one. "Guys," he wheezed, "what about our toast? Won't you toast with me?" Karen reached into her vintage JAL flight bag and took out a stack of photographs in an envelope bearing the Kodachrome logo. "No! I don't want to look at photographs!" Vinod said. "We're having the best moment right here, right now. Why are you such ghouls for the past? Why?"

Silently, Karen passed him a photo just as another garbage truck rumbled down the highway, and now the pier was shaking in earnest, seagulls taking flight around them. The waiters bowed to them in farewell and began to make their way to the safety of the oil-slicked highway, orderly at first, then breaking into a run. But Senderovsky and Karen kept sitting there, looking at the photographs with one hand, cracking open the shells of their mussels with the other, like automatons.

"Guys, we have to get out of here," Vinod said. He looked down at the photograph. It was the one of the party at Suj's mansion. He, Senderovsky, and Karen were linked arm in arm, Vinod holding aloft the book review with his best friend's picture plastered over it. "This hasn't even happened yet!" Vinod shouted to his friends. "Karen, you can't have this photo yet. Karen, everything in due time, okay? Karen, I love you! Please, will you do something, please?" Now the pier moved from side to side in great rollicking heaves, and a storm of splinters rose up around them, even as his friends continued to sit there, plucking mussels from their shells and scanning the past.

Fine, Vinod thought. Fine, we'll all die together then. If this is how it ends, this is how it ends. The wooden slats separated beneath his feet, and he could see the dark river below bathed in a source of light he couldn't identify, too bright to be the moonlight, not dark enough to be eternity. The bottles of wine slid into the maelstrom, and then the table tipped over and disappeared. He tried to grab Karen's hand, but he kept missing it, coming up with nothing but photographs of the future, all those familiar faces, all those sinister young smiles.

There was a crack. Then: weightlessness. He never got to feel the river's embrace.

"SO YOU MUST be the famous Vinod." He was standing at the top of the stairs. All that climbing had finally paid off. He had been looking down the stairs surveying the scene in the parlor. Suj was introducing herself and Gender (sweatpants, sweatshirt, sweatband) to Masha, who was huddled with some of her studious-looking med-school friends. But where was Senderovsky? Vinod turned around. The young Ed smiled at him. "My name's Ed," he said. "I'm like a very, very distant cousin of Karen's visiting from Europa. Not the moon, obviously."

He motioned that they should journey into the room Suj had re-decorated to serve as Senderovsky's library. It was paneled a touch too walnut for its own good and contained many masculine books on its shelves. The municipal worker whom people were calling the dep-uty mayor was passed out on the floor, hugging one of the legs of the massive Chippendale desk (a true immigrant miscalculation) in the center of the room, while Evelyn, Karen's younger sister, was cutting lines of narcotic on the equally gargantuan coffee table.

"Where's Karen?" Vinod asked them.

Evelyn pulled a bra strap that had flirted out of her sundress and Ed formally fixed his ascot. "Who knows?" he said. "Free spirit, my cousin."

"Is she with one of those Irish boys?"

Evelyn looked up at him. She was prettier than her sister; her eyes always glowed with just the right distribution of anger and inno-cence. "I'm still alive, you know," she said. "Not that Karen would care. When I gained a little weight sophomore year she called me Pinot. As in full bodied."

"Of course she cares." Vinod got down on one knee and grabbed a dry little hand. "She loves you. She's been trying to find you. Your father is safe in Florida. And all siblings make fun of each other. I'm the youngest, too, and I was constantly humiliated. My brothers are both more successful than I am, too. They are *crorepati*s, meaning they are husbands to many crores. A crore is ten million rupees, or about a hundred forty thousand dollars."

Evelyn offered him a rolled-up dollar bill. "I don't do that," Vinod said. "I want to be in control."

"Big day for Senderovsky," Ed declared. "He gets his mug in the paper, he gets to meet Masha, he gets to meet me. But what are *you* going to do, Vinod?"

Vinod leaned against the desk, which contained several open-faced Evelyn Waugh novels, an academic work entitled *Spare the Child,* and the manuscript in progress of Senderovsky's second book, the one about the oligarch's son. "I don't know," he said. "I don't know what to do. Sasha's entering a new social class. I don't want to be just the friend who makes him feel better whenever he has a setback."

"Then tell him that," Evelyn said. "Stop being such a baby."

"I don't know where he is," Vinod said. "He's not downstairs. He's not reconnecting with Masha. That's what he should be doing."

"He's in the guest room," Ed said. "Waiting for you. You're the guest."

Evelyn did a loud snort of the powder on the table, akin to a nasal slurp of noodles. "Ahhh," she said, her face a full road map of dejection despite the pleasure surging through her twitching septum.

"This won't end," Ed said, "until you go to the guest room. And it is high time for this to end, no?"

The hallway was empty, although Vinod could hear someone crying in the bathroom, a young woman's powerful tears. He approached the guest room upon which a sign had been hastily affixed, KNOCK FIRST. He did not need to knock. The doorknob felt hot to the touch. It was dark inside, so dark. This was before smartphones lit up the night, before everything in our hands trilled and glowed. The guest room was empty except for the four-poster bed (more arriviste shenanigans). Outside, Vinod could hear a bus slowly and loudly

bend down to accommodate an old woman on her way down to Atlantic Avenue. Vinod knew that sound well, since he had crashed in
the guest room on countless occasions, even though he lived only ten
blocks away in a cheap studio. The floor beneath Vinod vibrated with
the sound of revelers. Gender must have put on the Spice Girls, always a teaching moment for her. He had no choice but to approach
the bed.

No choice but to notice the way Karen had—even in the supposed
throes of passion, even with all the drugs coursing through her
veins—folded her Throwing Muses T-shirt and Juicy Couture skirt as
if she were a maid at Senderovsky's Hotel of People's Friendship.

He remembered it now. The loud sounds his Russian friend made,
punctuated startled sounds (*Aaah! Naah!*) as if it were a century ago
and the czar's inspectors had burst into his *izba*. She bounced on him
lightly as if trying to knock a faulty knob into place. Her eyes were
closed and her progress slow, soundless, resigned to the hard work.
Vinod stood there, a ghost, and instead of rage he let the peaceful-
ness pour over him in sunshine waves. So what? People hurt one another, and no one hurt more than family. This was his real family. Not
an exaggeration. He had made it up the stairs; he had seen what he
had to see. He was now cleared for ascent someplace more beautiful.
He had finished the cycle, and now all he had was the breath that rose
within him, each inhalation clear, healthy, his own. And when he
opened his eyes, Karen stood before him, her silhouette blue and
otherworldly, sweat glistening in the triangle between her tummy
and breasts. "It's okay, honey," she said with her Dentyne breath.
"His pen is mightier than his sword." And when he said nothing, she
leaned in and kissed him on the cheeks, three times, Slavic-style. "I'm
sorry," she said, "but I'm doing everything I can to save you." He
looked down at the bed. His friend was gone. And although his hand
still felt the heat of her touch, she was gone, too.

HE WAS WALKING the downtown streets. The signs were familiar,
numbered streets, named avenues, but the houses were not. Sometimes he could spot the apartment buildings of yore, but most had

been replaced with country farmhouses, severe Federals, quaint eyebrow colonials, the occasional carpenter Gothic. Magnificent front lawns descended from these houses to the empty streets. This can't be, Vinod thought. How can the city support such low density? Who lives in these houses? A Dutch Colonial crafted entirely out of stucco to withstand the elements caught his eye. It looked like the main house on his best friend's estate, though without the great covered porch behind it. Could he trespass to its window to take a look?

Vinod walked along the grass in his *chappals* and no one stopped him. The air of the newly redesigned city was fresh and clean as if country storms had been hired nightly to reinvigorate it with sweetness. Vinod walked up to the house's modest portico. He peered into the window. The first thing he saw was his own reflection. He was young and handsome, his forehead painted with a tikka from the temple. Within the familiar living room, painted, bald, orange-clad sadhus had gathered around Masha's Steinway. They were reciting slokas in Sanskrit, using the closed piano lid to beat out a meter. Vinod stood rapt, his mouth dry. The holy men were lost to the *Mahabharata,* to the part where, if Vinod's memory served correctly, the snakes of the world were to be marked for sacrifice, though in the end, they continued to live among us—because such was the universe. The fact that he shared a particular branch of knowledge with these saffron ascetics touched Vinod. He wanted to join them now, to add his unsure voice to their surety (Raise your hand if you're Sure!). He wanted to learn a few of the eight-syllable verses and to be lost in their rhythm. At the same time, he worried their malodorous bodies would stain Masha's piano and make her think less of Indians. Just then, one of the congregants, it was impossible to tell his age beneath his coloring, regarded Vinod with cross-eyed intensity. He did not smile or nod, but his eyes said, *Come in.*

Vinod backed away. He turned around. Ahead of him, the great green lawn littered by fallen white tree branches and flanked by the familiar gravel driveway and beyond that the streets of the new rural city. From his position on the modest hill, he now saw windmills, the old Dutch kind, astride the few remaining apartment buildings. He was welcome to leave. But if he went out into this world, whom would he meet? Whom did he know, really, but the inhabitants of this house, the House on the Hill?

Vinod opened the front door and stepped inside. He was in the vestibule of his old apartment building on Washington Street. STAIRS OUT, USE ELEVATOR. Who awaited him on the fifth floor? Him? Her? Both of them in tandem, stuck in the summer sweat, with their love for him and their perfidy? The elevator doors opened. He stepped inside, smelled the cigarettes and the floral residue of women. The door began to close. "Hold the door!" he heard. "Please, sir!"

Only what if he didn't? Only what if he rode the elevator alone? Without the fat man? Without the air squeezed out of his lungs.

He would do it. He would let the door close.

"Entity responsible for this," Vinod whispered. "I hope and pray that you will allow me to reach the end point and exit from whatever you have created."

The door continued to close, but slowly, tempting him with his own kindness. "Please, sir, hold the door! Please! I have to—"

He kept his hand at his side. "Entity responsible for this," he began to chant like a sadhu, but in an entirely unholy language. "I hope and pray—"

"Sir, please. She's waiting for me. My wife is waiting for me. My family."

Entity responsible. His hand came up to stop the door. The door hit his hand against the rough steel frame of the elevator. There was a tremor of pain, unexpected. The door reared back and then smashed into his hand once more. Vinod cried out in pain. Oh, please, oh, please, oh, please. A final sloka rang in his ear now, all of the sadhus praying with him, their saffron voices gathering in pitch. Why? Why were there so many snakes in the world when they had been marked for annihilation? The elevator door cut into his hand, through the skin, down to the bone, past the bone, into nothingness. And he could not move away, and he could not save himself.

IO

KAREN AND SENDEROVSKY walked out of the hospital. Its portico resembled a busy provincial Hyatt, and the half circle of the driveway was lined with black Suburbans. People in purple scrubs moved around them with enviable purpose, lanyards clapping in the September breeze.

They passed by an ugly orange building labeled CITY MEDICAL EXAMINER'S OFFICE. Karen stopped by a garbage can to throw up. He moved aside the lapels of the blazer she wore over her gingham dress, the most formal outfit he had ever seen her wear, and did the same for her hair.

It had been a month since the metallic firefly roughly settled on the front lawn, beams blazing, rotors stirring up whirlpools of gravel, and the men with the stretcher approached Karen's bungalow where Vinod had been sedated, his MOLST ignored by his friends. And now it was over. They had not been allowed to see him in his final moments, but were instead given a sealed plastic bag containing his last effects: a T-shirt from the city college he and Sasha had attended, a checkered lungi, a cellphone brimming with desperate messages from relations across the globe, and a gold-plated Japanese watch. They were advised not to open the bag for seven days. Karen realized she had dressed up to collect a bag.

They continued to walk past the glassed-in medical pavilions, silently, their feet instructing them: downtown. They passed a cityscape of tall redbrick apartment buildings that resembled the ones they had grown up in across the river, then crossed a broad ugly street that

switched the scenery from projects and hospitals to an avenue of restaurants and bars. The outdoor tables of the Greek tavernas and ta-
querias were packed with college students and recent graduates
whooping it up among rows of ferns and plastic bunting. They found
a Filipino gastropub by a busy bike lane, charmed by a sign that addressed the riders zipping by: CAUTION FILIPINOS CROSSING.

It had been a week since the Levin-Senderovskys had returned to
the city so that Nat could prepare for the resumption of the Kindness
Academy. Senderovsky had been shocked by the row of Valentine's
Day cards lining the bookshelf in their small dark living room, the
last vestige of normalcy from February. "Do you want to be my Valentine?" one card addressed to Nat from her teacher asked. "You
otter."

"Are you hungry, honey?" Karen asked. "We haven't eaten since
last night."

The endearment touched Senderovsky. "I don't know why," he
said, "but I think just the sight of food will make me cry."

"Then we should order," she said. "Because we have to go on." A
bald harried waiter in the requisite square frames showed up, and
Karen ordered up and down the menu. Soon their table was crowded
with smoked fish pansit and chicken adobo in brown butter and crab-
fat fried rice and pork ribs soaked in banana-ketchup barbecue sauce.
They stared at the assembled dishes, at their steaming plenty, as if
they had just been insulted for their loss.

"You did everything you could," Senderovsky said. "We both did."

"If we're to remain friends," Karen said, "I don't want you to ever
talk about what I did ever again."

Senderovsky nodded. "How are we not going to be friends?" he
said. "What would be the point of anything?"

"Eat, eat," she said.

"Why you so fat?" he completed her mother's joke. They both
laughed. The laughter dispelled something. They began to eat in
earnest, the pork gently peeling from the ribs, crunch cigar-like
lumpia stuffed with Shanghai beef crackling between their teeth. "So
let's do it," Senderovsky said. "Let's sign the paperwork."

"Right now?"

"I don't want this day to end without something in my life moving forward. I want to be closer to you."

"I'll text my assistant."

"I'll text Masha."

"Can she bring Nat? She's out of school already, right?"

"You know who else we should text? Dee and Ed. Ed just bought a place like five blocks away."

"Just tell them we're not doing a memorial today. Not tonight, okay? We'll raise a glass to him and that's all. Promise me, Sash. And please tell Masha not to be harsh with me."

THE SUMMER HEAT had just been rescinded and now there were two beams of blue light arced over the downtown sky, that time of year. Masha spotted her husband and Karen up the avenue in their little Sukkoth-like enclosure. "Karen-*emo,* Karen-*emo!*" Nat was shouting. Bike riders whizzed by them, screaming into their ear bones about real estate deals and synthetic currencies. Karen ran toward Nat, nearly knocked down by a young woman in a wheelchair furiously making her way uptown, half of her determined face shrouded by a black mask. Karen lifted the child up effortlessly, despite the city weight she had already put on. That was the idea: that she would lift Nat up.

"We need to use everything to our advantage now," Masha had told her husband, one night after all their guests had left the House on the Hill, after Vinod had been airlifted out. She had given her thesis on the world Nat could expect growing up, one of corruption, falsity, and decline, even if the presidency changed hands. "I'm not saying we should share custody or anything. But let Karen be in her life."

Senderovsky had told her then of his plan to sell the estate to Karen for about double what it would be worth, but, as part of the agreement, they could continue to use it as their second home, though Karen might build another "main house," something piney and Californian, abutting theirs. Karen and Masha would co-parent, and Senderovsky, Masha thought, would provide a background conversational presence, a handyman of words. As soon as the papers were signed and the money for the house transferred, he would go back to writing novels, "more serious ones," he had promised himself.

Nat was now riding atop Karen's shoulders, shrieking rapturously at the change in altitude, and now Masha could hear Dee's chortle echoing along the avenue and see Ed's de-dandified form, just another happy oblivious stick-thin city dweller with his arm wrapped around his beautiful other, his mask cupping his chin.

"Karen-*emo*, why are you all dressed up?" Nat asked her.

"Should we tell her?" Karen whispered to Masha, who shook her head, "Not yet." But Nat had already started blathering happily about her day in school. Karen had hired a "push-in" counselor to help her make friends, even though this was against the Kindness Academy's policies (an unsolicited gift from Karen had just doubled their endowment), and now that BTS was becoming more mainstream, Nat had emerged as the keeper of all knowledge pertaining to the band.

"It turns out that Ada Morelo-Schwartz likes BTS, too," Nat shouted, "but she didn't even know that their name stood for *Bangtan Sonyeondan*, or Bulletproof Boy Scouts. How do you not know that?"

"Be gracious, *sladkaya*," Masha said. "Remember what Miss Franco said when it comes to making friends. Inside trade, outside trade."

"Keep listening," Karen seconded. "Keep exchanging information."

Dee and Ed had cornered Senderovsky and were asking him questions with the single-mindedness of new couples. Ed: "Did he suffer?" Dee: "Was he under the whole time?" "Will he be cremated?" But Senderovsky would just sigh, shrug, and peel the meat off his ribs. He had no answers. He told them they would be sent a link to a virtual memorial on Tuesday, midday, at a time convenient for a brother in San Francisco and another in London.

They sat there between the ferns and the busy bike lane, passing around plates of food, surrounded by faces that looked like their own. Masha had just noticed that since this morning her husband had stopped coughing. "I'm getting a really hygge feeling right now," Ed said.

"Please stop using that word," Dee said, her tone stern. "There's nothing hygge about what happened to us today." *Us,* Senderovsky thought. Even down in the city, they were still members of his bungalow colony. The summer of 2020, that year of imperfect vision, would hold them together forever. He reminded himself to call his agent concerning *Hotel Solitaire.* Vinod had not wanted his help in finding a publisher, but he would ignore his instructions once more.

Nat looked up the Danish term *hygge* on Karen's phone. "I know what 'coziness' means, but what's 'con-viv-i-a-lity'?"

They drank an alcoholic fresh melon drink sweetened further with pandan syrup and a margarita with calamansi honey. Karen's assistant dropped by, and she and Dee (whom she resembled down to the miniature hips and prominent coccyx) had gone to the same graduate writing program, although she had never enjoyed Senderovsky's drunken tutelage. The assistant had Karen, Masha, and her husband sign a stack of papers further fusing her boss with the Levin-Senderovskys. "I'm a notary public," she said, brightly, when Masha wondered whether a lawyer shouldn't be present.

And this is what they drank to: The future together. The survival, in perpetuity, of the House on the Hill, with room for all of them, and one day, Karen said, "maybe even for Nat's best friends or boyfriends or girlfriends."

The rain came suddenly out of the heavy skies. But the city dwellers, masked and unmasked, would not stand for this intrusion. All across the roofless Filipino neo-sukkah, umbrellas went up into the sky, defiantly, and the eating and drinking and laughter continued even as the world flooded around them.

When it ended, and the night began to shiver in earnest, and Nat's bedtime approached (a temper tantrum was just in the offing), the restaurant started blasting Sly's "Everyday People" as ambulance lights wailed uptown past the ferns and plastic bunting to the hospitals just ten blocks north, and a bout of reggae competed with the restaurant's speakers from the window of a parked old car across the street. ("How nineties!" Karen said.)

And although it was forbidden, they got up to dance with each other by the bike lane with its electrified deliverymen speeding at twenty miles an hour. "I am no better and neither are you / we are the same whatever we do," sang the welcoming Black voices on the stereo, and the dancers now believed that all of these statements were true, and that they would go on and meld even further with their countrymen and countrywomen (Ed had finally applied for citizenship at Dee's request), and they would be forgiven and accepted and sent out faces uncovered into the wider world, from Bogotá to Berlin to Bombay, where other people, equally happy, would dance with them, too.

Only Masha remained at the table, her hands over the notarized forms, protecting them from the rain's return, watching her daughter, who was unused to the sounds of late-sixties soul, dance spasmodically, trying to keep up with the grown-ups who were modeling happiness and impromptu pleasure with their own awkward gestures and composed smiles, facsimiles of what they had once been before all the knowing happened. There was too much honey in her margarita, so instead of finishing it she raised it to him and spoke his name aloud, which made just a slight disturbance in the September air around her, but which made the fact of his life true, as if the sound of his name contained everything about him. Counting six people, three of them her family, she motioned the waiter over, put on her mask, and asked for exactly half of the bill. A small apartment with low white ceilings awaited them, but it was entirely theirs, bought through their labors, paid off slowly in the American way. At long last, it was time to go home.

ACKNOWLEDGMENTS

I AM HAPPY to be reunited with my editor, David Ebershoff, who has guided me through many love stories super sad and true and has excised his share of big and little failures in my prose.

Random has been my House for five books now and I would like to thank the many people inside that tall, friendly tower who have read and promoted by work, starting with Andy Ward and Robin Desser, who both helped steer this boat when it was still taking on water. And huge thanks to Gina Centrello, Avideh Bashirrad, Maria Braeckel, Denise Cronin, Barbara Fillon, Ruth Liebmann, Leigh Marchant, Carrie Neill, Darryl Oliver, Paolo Pepe, and Melissa Sanford.

Denise Shannon has been my agent for over two decades and is always the first to read my work with a kind but critical eye. I thank her and the other helpful readers of this book: Doug Choi, Dr. Jonathan Gross, Paul La Farge, Krys Lee, Suketu Mehta, Sarah Stern, Ming Loong Teo, and Alex Turner-Polish. James Baluyut guided me through the making of Ed's *vitello tonnato,* which I highly recommend.

ABOUT THE AUTHOR

GARY SHTEYNGART was born in Leningrad in 1972 and came to the United States seven years later. His debut novel, *The Russian Debutante's Handbook*, won the Stephen Crane Award for First Fiction and the National Jewish Book Award for Fiction. His second novel, *Absurdistan*, was named one of the 10 Best Books of 2006 by *The New York Times Book Review*. His novel *Super Sad True Love Story* won the Bollinger Everyman Wodehouse Prize and became one of the most iconic novels of the decade. His memoir *Little Failure* was a National Book Critics Circle Award finalist and a *New York Times* bestseller. His most recent novel is *Our Country Friends*. His books regularly appear on best-of lists around the world and have been published in thirty countries.

Facebook.com/shteyngart
Twitter: @Shteyngart
Instagram: @shteyngart

To inquire about booking Gary Shteyngart for a speaking engagement, please contact the Penguin Random House Speakers Bureau at speakers@penguinrandomhouse.com.

*The following essay is exclusive content for this
Barnes & Noble edition.*

NO PLACE LIKE HOME

Gary Shteyngart

AT THE START of the pandemic, I found myself listless. I live
with my small family in a house very much like Sasha's in the
Mid-Hudson Valley of New York. But I have always been a writer
who enjoys the social life, indeed one who spends large chunks of his
existence on an airplane—in a very Ed Kim way—doing research for
novels in progress or giving readings and falling in love with the
Pittsburghs and Turins of the world. Now I was home. Nature became a constant companion; the hooting of the barred owl, the industrious doings of our property's bachelor groundhog (yes, he is
called Steve), all fascinated me as never before. I considered my options. Like most ex-Soviets, I could fall into an easy depression or a
prolonged bout of drinking, or a heady cocktail of the two. Or I
could try to make something out of the silence and the loneliness.
What could I make? Sentences. And paragraphs. Which led to chapters. And, eventually, yes, the book you hold in your hands. And
alongside Steve and the unnamed barred owl and the birches and
oaks of my property, the collected stories of Chekhov became a con-

stant companion. For what can be more Chekhovian than human beings plunked down among the rural vistas of an enormous country, trying to figure out where it all went wrong?

Like Sasha's, the best memories of my childhood relate to the Russian-speaking bungalow colonies that lie about forty miles to the west of my dacha. In those flimsy cabins I fell in love for the first time while marinating in the closeness of fellow immigrants trying to assimilate, but not wanting to let go of the thick explosive language of our birth or of the overcaring grandmothers pursuing us with bowls of kasha and sweet, sweet summer slices of watermelon.

And so, in my mind, I began to populate my property with an emergency set of guesthouses offering shelter from the storm at a time when the storm, both epidemiological and political, was raging all around us. During most summers I play the solicitous Sasha-like host to many of our friends, but because we have only one modest guesthouse, we usually see them one person (or one couple or one family) at a time. What if a whole horde of them—not that Karen or Ed or Dee or anyone else is a direct analog to any of my friends—descended on the property at once? What if fortysomething me could re-create my childhood bungalow experience, but with better meats and vegetables (and a lot less kasha)? And what if I could conjure up a funny self-involved semi-villain to keep Sasha and Masha and the rest of the gang constantly on their toes? Voilà, the Actor was born.

I began writing the novel in April 2020 and I doubt that I have ever experienced such joy in writing a book before. In some ways, amid the loneliness of the pandemic, the book and the characters became an imaginative lifeline. I dreamed of what it would be like if our covered porch brimmed with their dialogue, if the long walks I often took by my lonesome were joined by elegant Ed or defiant Dee or virtuous Vinod. As a lonely immigrant child I naturally made up my share of imaginary "cool American friends" (half of them were named Joe, for some reason), but now I pined for the sweet chatter of all my actual immigrant pals, the commonalities we shared in ending up in the unmagical borough of Queens beneath the clatter of the number 7 elevated line.

By the end of the summer, I had to undergo a corrective surgery that resulted in a cut nerve in a sensitive place, which led in turn to months of blinding pain and an inability to perform most basic tasks, save to lie in my bed and write. It was at this time that I wrote the final scenes with Vinod. They may lack the coherence and linearity of the rest of the book, but I wanted to write about pain and how the human body and hence the mind deal with the possibility of their own extinction in the most honest way possible, as I, too, lived a half-life of crazed dreams and reminiscences, the past and the present blending into one atop my sickbed.

The other pain I felt was psychic in nature, and extended to the character of Nat. I couldn't help but reward her with Karen's fortune at the end of the book, in addition to Masha's strong love and Sasha's more mercurial self-absorbed affections. But even with a leg up, and even though she is entirely a fictional character, I worry about Nat's capacity to feel too much as the world around her will lurch from crisis to crisis, from one self-inflicted calamity to another. That sense of care for one of my characters is new to me. (I've specialized in a world of antiheroes to date, morally dysfunctional hedge-fund managers and obese sons of Russian oligarchs, for example.) Perhaps it is because I now know what unbearable pain is like. Or perhaps it is because I am older and grayer and more in love with our fallen world than ever. And while I dream of taking an airplane to Turin, my heart remains at home, with Sasha, Masha, Natasha, and the rest of the gang. I hope you have enjoyed your time among them as well.

OUR COUNTRY FRIENDS
Barnes & Noble Discussion Guide

(CONTAINS SPOILERS)

1. The pandemic is the universal story of our times. Yet, if we are lucky, it's not the only story of our daily lives. How does Gary Shteyngart use the pandemic to tell his story?

2. The House on the Hill is both the novel's setting and one of its recurring themes and metaphors. What does Sasha and Masha's house, with its colony of bungalows, mean to the characters? What does it tell us about this story? What does home mean in this context?

3. All the characters come from someplace else. Discuss the characters' origins and journeys. Who are they? Who have they become? What are they trying to escape?

4. Try mapping the relationships in the novel, with one line representing the bond that forms (or breaks) between each pair of characters. What does this map show you that you didn't realize while reading the book? Which bonds are strongest or most tenuous?

5. Is Sasha the novel's protagonist? Why or why not? How does his personal history shape the novel's tone and point of view?

6. *Our Country Friends* is very much a book about adults—their desires and dreads, their fears and friendships, their love and longings—with one exception: Nat. Discuss Nat's place in the story and in the lives of these characters.

7. Everything changes with the arrival of the Actor. How do his fame and beauty disrupt the story? Whom does he remind you of?

8. What role does theater play in this story? Who is performing and why? Is *Our Country Friends* a comedy or a tragedy?

9. How do you interpret the dreams in Act Four? Are they "real"? Where else do dreams appear in the novel?

10. Some events change all of us. How has the pandemic changed these characters? How has it changed you and your relationships? If you were to isolate with a small group at a house on a hill, whom would you invite?